SHE'D LET THE LION STRAIGHT
INTO HER DEN

What was she thinking?

She could feel him behind her, almost like a physical caress. It was that ridiculously sexy brogue of his, she understood that. And the twinkle. Okay, and his mouth. Something about those hard lips, suddenly becoming very sensual and appealing when he smiled—which made no sense, set as they were in his otherwise rugged face. His jaw and cheekbones looked as if they'd been chiseled from a block of smooth granite. He had a beautifully shaped head, but with his hair clipped so very short, the whole aura should have been menacing rather than sexy.

So, why was she feeling all tingly, and warm, and, well . . . needy?

BOOK YOUR PLACE ON OUR WEBSITE AND MAKE THE READING CONNECTION!

We've created a customized website just for our very special readers, where you can get the inside scoop on everything that's going on with Zebra, Pinnacle and Kensington books.

When you come online, you'll have the exciting opportunity to:

- View covers of upcoming books
- Read sample chapters
- Learn about our future publishing schedule (listed by publication month *and author*)
- Find out when your favorite authors will be visiting a city near you
- Search for and order backlist books from our online catalog
- Check out author bios and background information
- Send e-mail to your favorite authors
- Meet the Kensington staff online
- Join us in weekly chats with authors, readers and other guests
- Get writing guidelines
- AND MUCH MORE!

**Visit our website at
http://www.kensingtonbooks.com**

The Naughty List

DONNA KAUFFMAN

CYNTHIA EDEN

SUSAN FOX

𝑘

KENSINGTON PUBLISHING CORP.
http://www.kensingtonbooks.com

KENSINGTON BOOKS are published by

Kensington Publishing Corp.
119 West 40th Street
New York, NY 10018

All Kensington titles, imprints, and distributed lines are available at
special quantity discounts for bulk purchases for sales promotion,
premiums, fund-raising, educational, or institutional use.

Special book excerpts or customized printings can also be created
to fit specific needs. For details, write or phone the office of the
Kensington Special Sales Manager: Attn.: Special Sales Department. Kensington Publishing Corp., 119 West 40th Street, New York,
NY 10018. Phone: 1-800-221-2647.

Kensington and the K logo Reg. U.S. Pat. & TM Off.

ISBN-13: 978-1-61773-113-6
ISBN-10: 1-61773-113-7

First Brava Books Trade Paperback Printing: October 2010
First Brava Books Mass-Market Paperback Printing: October 2011
First Kensington Books Mass-Market Paperback Printing: October
2013

10 9 8 7 6 5 4 3

Printed in the United States of America

Contents

The Naughty List

Naughty but Nice

DONNA KAUFFMAN

1

"Good Lord, more of the bloody damn things."

A cluster of the silver nuisances jingled and chimed cheerfully as Thomas Griffin Gallagher entered Cups & Cakes, the small bakery and coffee shop on the edge of the town square. He winced at the increased throb in his temples. The American celebration of Thanksgiving was still weeks away, but the town was already riddled with the festive touches of the pending Christmas season. In fact, everywhere he went in the rural little burg of Hamilton, he heard bells ringing. Each and every doorway or archway had one hanging somewhere; men in red suits standing over black kettles clutched at least one or two. Moments ago, when a trundling service truck with the damn things tied to the grille had come within an inch of running him down, they'd almost been the last thing he'd seen on this earth. Ringing and clanging, clanging and ringing.

It was enough to drive a bloke bloody, raving starkers.

The rich scent of coffee beans filled his senses, and the jangling bells went mercifully ignored as he shut the door behind him. He'd arrived in Virginia from Dublin two weeks ago, but the nagging headache wasn't due to prolonged jet lag. His arrival in the village proper that morning was the next critical step in his mission . . . and not likely to do anything to help the throbbing in his temples.

It was why he was in a cupcake shop—to gird himself with a bit of freshly ground armor. He took a moment to breathe in the most heavenly of scents and thought about that morning, almost one year ago, when he'd been informed by his Gallagher cousin, Sean, that the only Irish in him came from his mum, who'd been a Houlihan before marrying his father. Otherwise, he was a red-blooded American. It had explained many things, possibly among them the reason why he'd always preferred the rich, dark taste of coffee over tea. In fact, he could feel the pinch of the headache he'd woken up with already receding, just from the scent alone.

He walked up to the short tidy counter. Given the typical Yank's apparent addiction to the stuff, he was surprised that he'd yet to find anything comparable there. After mentioning as much to the owner of the rustic inn where he was staying, just on the outskirts of town, he'd been guided to this quaint little shop. Posh hotels were more typically his style those days, but the closest one to Hamilton was several hours away in Charlottesville. He supposed there were some who found the cozy, rural setting something of a respite from their usual hectic pace of life. Griffin, on the other hand, would have given anything for room service and a decent concierge.

However, if the coffee tasted half as good as it smelled, he'd have to thank Mrs. Crossley, the innkeeper, the next time they crossed paths. It hadn't been often of late, given the hours he'd been keeping since his arrival. One cup, then he'd brace himself for a day of trying to explain to the fine citizens of Hamilton how his ideas on globalizing the town's potential would revolutionize their little world. His plans were going to improve the quality of living for every man, woman, and horse presently living in Hamilton Township proper, as well as the surrounding county of Randolph. They would see improvement on every measureable scale. Who wouldn't want that?

At least, that's how he saw it. But he knew from personal experience with his family back home that not everyone understood or appreciated possibilities and potential. Especially those who had never had their fair share of it. He smiled again at the irony that this little village, thousands of miles away from his childhood home, was, in many ways, just as strangled by tradition and conservative thinking as West Cork.

He could only pray that, unlike those who had raised him, the fine folks of Hamilton—his blood family, as it were—would embrace his ideas, rather than turn a deaf ear before hearing him out. In order for them to fully realize the depth and breadth of his plans, he would need their cooperation.

But change was coming, regardless. Fearing his death was imminent, aged and frail Lionel Hamilton had signed off on Griff's every idea, knowing it would ensure the future for the empire that Lionel, along with his ancestors, had built.

Griff's train of thought was abruptly broken by a loud yelp coming from somewhere in the rear of the small shop, followed by a ringing crash of what sounded like metal on metal.

He gritted his teeth against the renewed ringing inside his own head, even as he called out in the ensuing silence. "Hullo? Are you in need of some assistance?"

What followed was a stream of very . . . colorful language that surprised a quick smile from him. He'd found Americans, at least the ones of his immediate acquaintance, to be a bit obsessed with political correctness, always worrying what others might think. So it was somewhat refreshing, to hear such an . . . uncensored reaction. He assumed the string of epithets wasn't a response to his query, but then he'd never met the proprietor.

He debated heading around the counter to see if she might need help, then checked the action. "No need to engage an angry female unless absolutely necessary," he murmured, tipping up onto his toes and looking behind the counter, on the off chance he might spy the pot of coffee. "Ah," he said, on seeing a double burner positioned beside an empty, tiered glass case.

He fished out his wallet and put a ten note on the counter, more than enough to cover the cost of a single cup, then ducked under the counter and scanned the surface for a stack of insulated cups. Oversized, sky blue mugs with the shop's white and pink cupcake logo printed on one side and the name on the other were lined up next to the machine. He didn't think she'd take too kindly to his leaving with one of those.

"Making an angry female even angrier . . . never a good thing." His mouth lifted again as a few more, rather unique invectives floated from the back of the shop. "Points for creativity, however."

He glanced at his watch, saw he still had some time, and took a moment to roll his neck, shake out his shoulders, and relax his jaw. He could feel the tension tightening him up, which was a fairly common state of late. But he'd never been so close to realizing his every dream. He fished out the small airline-sized tube of pain relievers he'd bought when he'd landed. Upon popping it open, he discovered there was only one tablet left. He shrugged and dry swallowed it.

He crouched down to look under the counter and had just opened a pair of cupboard doors when he felt a presence behind him.

"May I help you with something?"

Hmm. Angry female, immediately south of his wide-open back. He was fairly certain there were sharp knives within reach. Not the best strategy he'd ever employed.

Already damned, he reached inside the cupboard and slid a large insulated cup from the stack, snagging a plastic lid as well, before gently closing the doors and straightening up. "Just looking for a cup," he said as he turned, a careful smile on his face.

The smile froze as he got his first look at the cupcake baker.

He wasn't normally given to poetic thought, but there he stood, thinking her clear, almost luminescent skin made her wide, dark blue eyes look like twin pools of endlessly deep, midnight waters. It was surprisingly difficult to keep from looking away, every self-protective instinct he had being triggered by her steady hold on his gaze, which was rather odd. She was the village baker. Despite the tirade he'd just overheard, he doubted anyone who made baking cheerful little cakes her life's work would be a threat or obstacle to his mission. "I hope you don't mind," he said, lifting the cup so she could see what he'd been about. "You sounded a bit . . . occupied, back there."

"Yes, a little problem with a collapsed rolling rack."

His gaze, held captive as it was, used the time to quickly take in the rest of her. Thick, curling hair almost the same rich brown as the steaming hot brew he'd yet to sip had been pulled up in an untidy knot on the back of her head, exposing a slender length of neck and accentuating her delicate chin. All of which combined to showcase a pair of unpainted, full, dark pink lips that, even when not smiling, curved oh-so-naturally into the kind of perfect bow that all but begged a man to part them, taste them, bite them, and . . .

He looked away. Damn. He couldn't recall his body ever leaping to attention like that, after a single look. No

matter how direct. Especially when his attentions were
clearly not being encouraged in any way, if the firm set of
her delicate chin was any indication.

"Nothing too serious, I hope," he said, boldly turning
his back to her and helping himself to a cup of coffee.
After all, he'd paid for it. Not that she was aware of it as
yet. But he thought it better to risk her mild displeasure
until he could point that out . . . rather than engage more
of the fury he'd heard coming from the back of the shop
minutes ago—which he was fairly certain would be the
case if her sharp gaze took in the current state of the front
of his trousers.

"Nothing another five hours of baking time won't re-
solve," she said, a bit of weariness creeping into her tone.
From the corner of his eye, he caught her wiping her
hands on the flour covered front of her starched white
baker's jacket. "Please, allow me."

He quickly topped off the cup and snapped on the lid.
"Not to worry. I believe I've got it. I left a ten note on
your counter."

"I'm sorry," she said, sounding sincere. "It's been . . . a
morning. I'm generally not so—"

"It's fine," he said, intending to skirt past her and duck
back to the relative safety of the other side of the counter.
The tall, trousers-concealing counter. He just needed a
moment, preferably with her not in touching distance, so
he could button his coat and allow himself a bit of recov-
ery time. It seemed all he had to do was look at her for his
current state to remain . . . elevated.

Unfortunately for him, and the comfort level of his
trousers, she moved closer and reached past him. "The
sugar is here and I have fresh cream in the—"

"I take it black," he said abruptly, then they both turned
the same way, trapping her between the counter . . . and
him.

Her gaze homed in on his once again, but he was the one holding hers captive.

"Okay," she said, her voice no longer strident. In fact, the single word had been a wee bit . . . breathy.

"Indeed," he murmured, once again caught up in that mouth of hers. Those parted lips simply demanded a man pay them far more focused attention. *Step away, Gallagher*, he counseled himself. *Sip your coffee, gather your wits, and move on.*

"You're Irish," she blurted, somewhat abruptly.

He smiled. "All of my days."

The corners of her lovely lips tilted, but not quite into a responding smile. More the beginnings of a smirk. "You must be Thomas Gallagher."

"No' too many Irishmen in Hamilton?" he replied, not particularly surprised she'd heard of him. His arrival hadn't been kept a secret. Nor had the purpose of his visit— although it had been broadly misrepresented by some. Clearly she fell into the latter camp.

"Just one," she replied. "At the moment."

Interesting, he thought, given her reaction to finding out who he was, that she'd made no move to extract herself from their inappropriate, if accidental, entry into each other's personal space.

"That could change, you know," he said.

"So I hear," she replied.

He cocked his head, and drew on his considerable experience staring down the recalcitrant faces of the numerous corporate executives he'd faced over the past eight years as he dismantled their companies in order to rebuild them. It took a surprising bit of doing to pull off that stare with the beautiful baker. "What, exactly, do you hear?"

"Does it matter? After all, I'm just a cupcake baker."

That made him pause for a moment, but no, he hadn't uttered that very thought out loud earlier. His smile broadened. "And yet, a smart cookie."

She gave him a pitying look.

"Deserved that," he rejoined, with a quick, humble duck of the chin. His smile deepened when their eyes met again, but rather than be amused at his expense, her gaze remained steady and somewhat impenetrable. He returned the look. "Other than infiltrate the area behind your counter in search of what I was made to understand is the best coffee in Hamilton, have I done something in particular to make you cross?"

"Is it true you're planning on broadening the scope of industry here in Hamilton? And by broaden, I don't mean to the next county over. I understand you have aspirations to make us a global commodity of some sort. Is that an accurate assessment of your goals here?"

Ah. So, she wasn't a naïve optimist after all. He'd generally only heard such comments delivered in that flat, business-savvy tone from the highly placed corporate types he was used to dealing with. He tried to conceal his surprise. "You sound less than enthusiastic about the potential for community growth and strengthened economic stability," he replied directly, opting to treat her question in the serious manner he would have those of the executives. "Perhaps you should consider that your business in particular would be one almost guaranteed an enormous boost in revenue. And that's just for this location. There would be quid pro quo opportunities for you abroad, and you are poised to capitalize on a rather attractive niche market that would likely straddle both worlds."

"I'll take that as a yes, then?"

So serious for a cupcake baker. "Aye, I believe you could."

She deftly snagged the cup of coffee right out of his hand, then slipped out of the narrow space between him and the counter. "I'm sorry, Mr. Gallagher. No disrespect to your extended family here in the States, whom I adore, especially your . . . cousin? I suppose that's what Sean would be to you. I hope they will understand, though I don't much care if you do. You're not welcome in this establishment. I'd appreciate it if you'd leave now."

If he hadn't been so bereft at the sudden loss of his much-needed coffee—so close!—he might have been more amused by her combative attitude. He'd won over his share of hardened battle veterans and might have even enjoyed the challenge. At the moment, she was not his utmost concern. Not individually, anyway. He had a whole town of small business owners to win over. Better to absorb the loss of one to spare himself the time he needed to win over the many. "Hardly the spirit of the holiday season," he said, sending a longing look at the cup in her hand, steam wafting from the hole in the lid.

"Oh, I can be quite spirited, rest assured."

His gaze skipped right back to hers. *Oh, how well he could imagine that.* Far too clearly, in fact. And in great detail, if given the time. He held his long wool coat closed in front of him. "Surely you wouldn't be so heartless as to toss me out into the bitter cold without so much as a sip—"

She rolled her eyes. "For heaven's sake. Here." She shoved the coffee into his hands. "Stupid accent," she muttered under her breath.

"I beg your pardon?"

"No, I believe you begged for coffee—which you now have. So, if you would be so kind"—she gestured to the door—"I have cupcakes to remake."

"You have a weakness for accents, do you?" He grinned, then took a very quick sip when her scowl darkened.

"Mr. Gallagher—"

"Taking my leave, not to worry." He sketched a short bow, then as the flavor burst on his tongue, he lifted the cup toward her in a gesture of sincere reverence. "The innkeeper was right. Truly, a remarkable blend."

"Enjoy it," she said, the unspoken ending making it clear that it would be his only chance to do so.

"I plan to." He couldn't have said what made him do it, but rather then take his leave, he remained where he stood a moment longer, and quite deliberately allowed his gaze to roam down her chef's-coat-draped body, and back up again. Not that he could tell one whit what she was hiding behind the starched white linen, but his imagination filled in the blanks quite nicely. "Down to the last drop," he murmured, as he met her eyes once again.

It was simply payback for the abrupt eviction, and maybe a wee bit more for putting him so off balance. But his impulsive behavior backfired quite spectacularly when his caddish behavior didn't earn him the expected scowl and possible swift boot straight out the door, but rather a far more delicious bloom of hot pink spreading across her delicate cheekbones.

Bollocks. He'd have to take several turns around the town square in the frigid cold morning air if he hoped to have even the slightest chance of taking his coat off at any point during his upcoming council meeting. He could only pray the windy chill would do what his normally stalwart willpower had not.

"Good-bye, Mr. Gallagher."

"Have a good day, Miss . . . ?"

"Duncastle," she responded, polite to the end, despite her obvious dislike of him. When he didn't respond right away, she sighed, and added, "Melody Duncastle."

He nodded his appreciation, though he doubted she much cared. "Miss Melody Duncastle." Her full name suited her, he thought. From her milkmaid complexion to her courtesan mouth, which was where his gaze was lingering.

"I'd wish you the same, Mr. Gallagher, but we both know that wouldn't be sincere. Especially today."

He chuckled at that, appreciating her honesty. A shame it looked as if they were to be adversaries. He could have used someone like her on his side. If only he could stop thinking about what it would be like to have her on her back.

He quickly tipped an imaginary hat her way. "Top o' the mornin' to ye, then," he said, with a hearty, full-on brogue. "I'm sure we'll meet again."

"Of that you can be certain," he heard her mutter as he left the shop . . . whistling.

2

As the chiming bells on the door quieted, Melody wiped her damnably sweaty palms on her apron. "Wow," she murmured beneath her breath. "This is going to be a little harder than I thought." She relived the moment when he'd looked her up and down. And had to wipe her hands. Again. "Okay, much harder."

She'd heard a great deal about Mr. Thomas Griffin Gallagher, but none of the reports she'd gotten had described his lethal good looks. Nor had she gotten the impression of him as a charmer. Quite the opposite, actually. The words she'd heard associated with Griffin, as she'd heard he liked to be called, had been more along the lines of determined, detail-oriented, driven, and hard-nosed—which she'd translated into bullying asshole.

Of course, the only people she'd talked to who had actually met the man were other men.

There had been talk that he looked nothing like his American-born relatives. But she still hadn't been prepared for how startlingly different he did look. The whole town knew of his true heritage now that word had leaked out he wasn't actually blood kin to the Gallaghers at all, but rather the direct descendant of Lionel Hamilton's late wife, Trudy Hamilton, previously Trudy Haversham.

Hamilton Industries was the economic backbone that solely and uniquely supported the town's ongoing existence. Though neither Lionel nor his forebears had ever been perceived as warm, or even particularly likable types, there was no denying his stewardship of his family's many holdings had continued to make Hamilton a viable place to live and work. As such, there had been significant concern as Lionel's health had declined over the past several years. Trevor Hamilton, his great nephew and the only Hamilton heir, had made it clear he was not interested in taking on the family empire. What would happen to their town and their livelihoods as time marched on?

It had been during last year's holiday season that Holly Gallagher—then Holly Bennett—had taken over her mother's Christmas shop in neighboring Willow Creek, which was also where Sean Gallagher ran his popular family restaurant. The two of them, now married, had unearthed a diary written by a young, pregnant Trudy in one of the dusty antique desks buried in the shop's attic.

Apparently Trudy had been sent by her wealthy family in Richmond to a dotty old aunt in neighboring Willow Creek, to give birth to her out-of-wedlock baby in secret. The dotty aunt would see to the child's eventual adoption, but teenager Trudy and her newfound friend, Sean's own grandmother, had spirited the babe to the local parish, where he was placed with one of the many Gallagher families.

Melody hadn't heard the specifics on how or when Griffin's grandparents had returned to Ireland to raise the baby—who grew up to become Griffin's father—but she knew Griffin had been born and raised there, apparently never knowing of his real ancestry. Melody found that odd, given just how different he looked from the other Gallaghers. Surely there had been some speculation.

The joke around Randolph County was that there must be a Gallagher baby factory somewhere that popped them out on a conveyer belt, each meeting the same specific Gallagher baby criteria. The resemblance amongst them all, down to the last cousin—and there were endless numbers of them—was uncanny. Dark hair, flashing blue eyes, charming grin, above average height and build, all of which held true whether they were male or female.

While Griffin was certainly impressive enough in the latter two departments, he was neither dark-haired nor blue-eyed. In fact, it was his close-cropped sandy blond hair, slightly darker brows, and thickly lashed, pale-to-almost translucent green eyes that had caught her off guard when she'd come bustling out of the back.

He looked lean and rugged, even in a perfectly cut suit and overcoat that had likely set him back more than she cleared in a month. His face was hard and angular, giving him the almost brutish air of someone who could hold his own in a brawl. The slight bump on the bridge of his nose indicated he probably had. Then he'd smiled, and there had been a surprising twinkle in his eyes, an unexpected sensual curve to those chiseled, hard lips, all combining to transform him from street tough to fallen angel. One with a very tarnished halo, who would no doubt try to tempt her into any number of unwise adventures.

After losing an entire morning's work when her cooling racks had collapsed, she'd already been thrown for a loop, more concerned about replacing the crushed cupcakes for the Hamilton Senior Center centennial birthday celebration than rushing to see to the immediate needs of whoever was in the front of her shop.

To discover him behind the counter, and worse, finding herself hopelessly caught up in those ethereal eyes of his, and the naughty promises his smile was making . . . not to mention that absurdly sexy accent hanging in the air between them . . . well, it was no surprise she'd taken refuge in the anger and frustration she'd already built up toward him, even though their paths had never crossed. It seemed a lot safer than allowing herself to think, even for one tiny second, that she might be attracted to the man whose very presence in her little town was a threat to everything she held dear.

Ever since the discovery of the diary, the town of Hamilton couldn't stop buzzing about whether Lionel would recognize Trudy's descendant as a true heir to the massive Hamilton empire. Trevor had come back long enough to help Sean and Holly verify the story in the diary, eventually connecting Griffin with Lionel and reiterating his desire to live his life on his own terms. Last Melody had heard, he was doing quite well with that plan. He lived in North Carolina with his wife of several years, Emma. In fact, Trevor and Emma had just added to their menagerie of rescue animals with a bouncing baby boy.

Melody smiled at the thought as she brushed flour off the front of her jacket, thinking it nice that people followed their dreams and found happiness in their successes. She'd thought she'd done that very thing when she'd left Hamilton as a high-minded seventeen-year-old, intent on earning a law degree and living her life in the fast-paced, oh-so-current world of the nation's capital. By the time she'd entered law school, the grandmother who'd raised her was gone, and Hamilton was merely a fond memory of a childhood left behind for bigger and better things.

Melody snorted at that. Bigger maybe, but better, not so much. She'd lasted four years post graduation in the toxic hell that was life as a DC tax law litigator. Staring at her thirtieth birthday, worried about having the soul sucked directly out of her, she'd realized she needed a new dream.

She'd initially been lured back to Hamilton by her best childhood friend, Bernadette, the only one she'd remained in contact with over the years. Bernie had begged her to come and lend her tax and legal expertise in setting up Bernie's new bakery business. So Melody had taken her first vacation since . . . ever, deciding she could use the two weeks away from the merry-go-round her life had become to do some serious soul-searching and rethink her goals.

Instead, she'd found herself baking. A lot of baking, in fact. She hadn't reached any conclusions, but the baking had calmed her, centered her, given her something to do with her hands, and freed her mind from the endless loop it seemed to be on of late. When she returned to her life in DC, still unsettled and unhappy, she'd enrolled in a pastry chef course. Then another one. Followed by an entire semester, crammed in with her regular workload, at a local culinary school. She still hated her life as a tax attorney, but baking things helped level out the stress. In the absence of any other great life plan, it was better than nothing.

Then Bernadette had broken down and told Melody what had really led her to ditch her job as a senior advertising accountant with Hamilton Industries and follow her private dream to launch her own bakery . . . she had cancer. Starting a bakery was something she'd wanted to do before she died. With stage four Hodgkin's lymphoma, that eventuality was going to happen sooner than she'd thought.

Melody's path had become crystal clear then, all her priorities painfully and abruptly defined. Without a single pang of regret, at the age of thirty-one, she'd handed in her resignation, packed up her essentials, and walked away from the law degree she'd spent many years and a ton of money obtaining, along with a career that was the envy of many. Heading south to be with her friend for whatever time they had left, she'd learned how to run a bakery . . . and how to watch a best friend die. Ten months later, she was alone in Hamilton again . . . and the new owner of Cups & Cakes. Bernadette's dying wish became Melody's new lease on life.

A new life Melody had grabbed with everything she had. In the town she'd thought a part of her past, she'd found her future and more happiness and fulfillment than she'd ever thought possible.

"I'll be damned if some spooky-eyed Irish devil is going to screw things up now."

With that thought bolstering her, she squared her shoulders and headed back to the kitchen area to face the first disaster of the morning. She wasn't sure what she was going to do about the second one.

She'd had every intention of being at the town council meeting, along with a number of the town square business owners. The news of Lionel's bold new plans for the town—which had turned out to be Griffin's brainchild—had leaked out about a month ago and spread like wildfire. The speculation was that Lionel had known the truth about Trudy's bastard child all along, and had, in fact, gone to great lengths to keep it quiet. For decades. When he announced he was naming Griffin the heir who would be stepping forward to assist in guiding the future of Hamilton Industries, it had been the biggest scandal to hit the town in as long as anyone could remember.

Thomas Griffin Gallagher—and, rightfully, also a Haversham—was reputedly a mini-Lionel in his own right, already well on his way to establishing a burgeoning empire of his own in the U.K. His specialty, so the nosy hens of Hamilton had ferreted out almost before he'd set foot on American soil, was finding new ways to market and brand old concepts, old businesses, even entire old towns, and revitalize them into something prosperous, thriving. All for a percentage, of course.

He'd spun himself to be the pied piper of revitalization, a veritable Extreme Town Makeover magician. Until you dug a little deeper and discovered that not one of those little businesses, brands, or towns remotely resembled what it had been, once the reincarnation was complete. More prosperous? Sure. But lost in the reconstructed and homogenized shuffle was what had made the businesses, brands, and towns special in the first place. Melody understood in some of those cases, without change, there would have been no corporation, brand, or village left to save. It wasn't the case here. Hamilton wasn't failing.

There was a difference between saving a sinking ship . . . and changing things purely for greed and the desire of more-more-more.

Melody didn't care if Griffin took on the expansion of Hamilton Industries' global prospects, but as far as she was concerned, he could leave the town of Hamilton itself right the hell alone. "I just want the town I already have," Melody grumbled, as she started clearing the mess in the back room. She had enough cupcakes in reserve to cover the centennial birthday, but it would leave her shop empty of its namesake treats . . . and none of the reserve cupcakes had been decorated as yet.

After Melody had scraped the last of the dumped cupcakes and bigger cakes that had been on the bottom rack into the trash and shoved all the trays into the industrial-size sink, she got the mop to start on the floors. "Fondant on floors is so much fun to clean."

She blew her hair out of her face—again—indulged in another short swearing session as she looked at the green and pink slime coating her floors, then got over it and got down to work. As she started scrubbing she supposed she should be thankful the town meeting was keeping her shop thin of customers.

She needed to be at that town council meeting, to hear, firsthand from the man himself, exactly what the proposed changes were going to be for Hamilton, and to join ranks with the other shopkeepers to make sure their voices were heard, and heard loudly, in dissent.

It wasn't that she was opposed to finding ways to improve the financial bottom line of Hamilton. Lionel Hamilton and his predecessors had created the economic center that was still, literally, Hamilton town square. What had grown into Hamilton Hardware, Hamilton Automotive, Hamilton Gas, and even Hamilton Herefords over the past century had become Hamilton Industries, an ever-expanding conglomerate of business, both local and countywide, with Lionel's personal investments reaching across the country, and beyond, as far as the Pacific Rim.

Though its ever-growing business center was parked right outside the town limits, the town itself had never lost its old-time quaint charm. It was, to her mind, the absolute best of both worlds. Unique, diverse, yet traditional and close-knit.

Then Lionel had to go and introduce a land shark into their otherwise peaceful and nonthreatening waters. A man who was going to take their unique big-industry/ small-town dynamic and turn it into some kind of global, international theme park. She might make cupcakes for a living, but that didn't mean she wanted to live in a cookie-cutter world.

Muttering under her breath again as she got the last of the fondant off the floor, she emptied the rolling bucket and filled it with a disinfectant cleanser. "Lovely scent to greet my customers, first thing in the morning." She glanced up at the wall clock, then mentally juggled her commitments for the next forty-eight hours. The shop hadn't had a single customer this morning—if she didn't count the visit from the devil.

She glanced back at the clock again, then finished cleaning up, before scrubbing her own hands and finally taking off her chef's coat. She'd close the shop for three hours, hit the town meeting, then double back and reopen to catch the after-school/end-of-workday crowd. It wouldn't leave her any time to bake or decorate, but she could put in an all-nighter and get caught up. Eventually, things would even out. They always did.

3

Griffin stood to the side of the wide screen that filled most of the high school auditorium stage and narrated as pictures of his planned future for Hamilton scrolled across the screen. "By diversifying, and creating a unified theme for your village and the independent shops that line your charming town square, we can create a unique environment that will draw in not only your average American tourists, but travelers from far beyond your county lines, state lines, and even the shores of your country."

He was careful not to lay it on too thick, knowing better than most never to talk down to or underestimate an audience. The herd mentality was a good thing when it worked in his favor, but could quite easily shift against him. Then all his carefully laid plans would blow up in his face. "We don't want to change what makes your shops, your village, special. We want to focus on that, figure out what it is that makes the charming atmosphere you've created, then capitalize on it, smooth away the rough edges, and make what you've worked so hard to build a bright and shiny showpiece. You're sitting on a veritable gold mine here."

He scanned the audience, trying to gauge his relative success. Folks were nodding, sitting comfortably in their seats, seemingly willing to hear him out, even eager in some cases. More smiles than frowns, which was very good indeed, but he'd be happy with simply knowing their minds were open to change. He noted the door opening in the back of the auditorium, and stuttered over his next sentence as he spied the lovely cupcake baker slipping in and taking a seat on the aisle. He lost another critical moment wondering what she'd done to overcome her early morning crisis, or if she'd simply locked the door and decided to deal with it later.

The crowd began to murmur, and he quickly shifted his thoughts back to the far more important matter at hand. "This presentation is a preview of the more detailed information that will be coming your way at the official town hall meeting the end of this week. At that time we will encourage your questions and do our best to answer them, as well as allay any concerns you might have as to how these changes are going to affect you and your businesses personally." The crowd started to murmur in earnest, and he lifted a hand to stall what appeared to be the start of some questions and hand raising. "I don't wish to put any of you off, but I won't be taking questions this morning. I have brochures and printed information, detailing everything I've shown you and gone over this morning. My hope—our hope—is that you will take these materials, go over them, and think about everything you'd like to discuss, then send those questions and any concerns you have to the e-mail addresses provided. When we reconvene here at the end of the week, we can have a productive, comprehensive meeting that will launch us into the next phase of this exciting time of

growth and prosperity for you and your fellow business-
men and women."

He smiled broadly to the audience and clicked the
photo on the big screen back to the one of the huge
Hamilton Industries logo. "The information packets are
stacked on the tables outside the auditorium doors as you
exit. Thank you all for your patience, your participation,
and your enthusiasm in getting in on the ground floor of
what is going to be the most exciting thing to ever happen
in Hamilton village."

He listened to the applause, gauging whether it was
enthusiastic or merely polite, and was, overall, quite
happy with the tone of what he was hearing. But just as
people started to rise from their seats, a strident voice
rang out, freezing everyone for a moment, then returning
them to their seats.

"Mr. Gallagher, isn't it true that rather than capitalize
on the unique features of a town—I'm sorry, village—
you simply remodel it into your own vision of the place?
I realize that things are different in old-world countries
like England, Switzerland, and Italy, where I understand
you've had enormous success.

"But Hamilton is not some fourteenth-century village
in need of sprucing up, Mr. Gallagher. We don't need
people coming here looking for a theme park resort, five-
star hotels, and a championship golf course. We're already a
thriving community, happily capitalizing on the successes
of Hamilton Industries and our own individual business
acumen. If you're merely interested in making Hamilton
Industries more successful, thereby giving us greater
opportunities, then we'll all rejoice and give you our
undying support. More prosperity is never a bad thing.
However, it appears you're looking to fix a part of us that
isn't broken.

"I think I am speaking for the majority here when I say

we like who and what we are, and what we've become, through the hard work and sweat that comes with building our own business from the bottom up. In many cases, for multiple generations. Your own family can speak to that, Mr. Gallagher. Certainly that's something you can identify with, right? If you would focus all your growth potential energy, of which you seem to have an endless supply, on increasing the bottom line of Hamilton Industries, the rest of us will still stand to profit and prosper. But also keep what makes us unique. Otherwise, Mr. Gallagher, our 'village' doesn't need your help."

There was a moment of stunned silence, as the rest of the folks in the audience shifted their gazes between himself . . . and Melody Duncastle.

Of course it was her.

Griffin knew the next few seconds were critical in keeping the edge he'd worked so hard to gain. But before he could open his mouth to rejoin Miss Duncastle, and jovially charm the townspeople into continuing to give him their open-minded attention, someone put their hands together and began to clap. He couldn't make out who it was, but the sound came from the other side of the auditorium, drawing the gazes and glances of the audience as they, too, shifted to see. Then someone else started clapping, and another, and yet another.

The throbbing in Griffin's temples returned with a swift vengeance as he watched all of his carefully calculated work dissolve. The herd was turning against him. Or, at least, toward Melody Duncastle.

"Miss Duncastle," he said into his mouthpiece, loudly enough that for a moment, the clapping paused. He pounced on that single moment, knowing what came after would make his life easier . . . or a bloody living hell. "Miss Duncastle," he repeated, and the clapping stopped completely as everyone's attention shifted from her . . . back to him. *You've got the floor, Gallagher. Better use it wisely.*

"I'm sorry our initial meeting this morning didn't go well."
He paused to allow the murmuring to begin . . . and build.

"Mr. Gallagher, this has nothing to do—"

"Please, kindly allow me to respond to your statements
just now," he interrupted, careful to keep his smile wide
and his tone jovial. And if his accent deepened just a little
bit, well, they'd just think it was because he was feeling
the moment. "I've no desire—or I should say, we've no
desire to cloak or mute any of the wonderful qualities that
make Hamilton the special place it is to all of you. We're
aware and deeply respectful that this isn't simply where
you've started your businesses, but where you've chosen
to live your lives, raise your children. Hamilton Industries
has never done anything to thwart your growth potential,
quite the opposite.

"You've trusted us with your livelihoods, your families . . . you have no need to doubt that your trust is still
well-placed." He turned to the audience in general. "I
urge you all to read the information and to bring any and
all concerns and questions to our full town meeting. Not
only will there be Hamilton board members there but also
your very own town councilmen, whom you've put into
office. We'll all answer every question you have."

He saw Melody raise her hand, knew she was going to
take back the floor, so he preempted her next strike. "And
Miss Duncastle," he went on, turning on every bit of
charm he had. "I'd like a private meeting with you, directly, if possible. It's important to me, especially after
this morning, that you feel comfortable and confident
about the plans for Hamilton." He flashed a wider smile.
"I promise I'm no' the bad guy here, Melody."

The crowd's attention shifted from him to the baker.
There was a collective holding of breath. The use of her
first name had created an almost palpable intimacy, despite their location. The power was firmly back in his
hands.

As his gaze locked on hers, he knew he'd have felt a lot better about his chances if that same palpable intimacy hadn't affected him as much as it did the crowd. He'd have thought her outburst would have cured him of any kind of attraction toward her. But while his mind saw her as an adversary, and a more worthy opponent than he might have thought, his body had completely different ideas about the best way to handle Melody Duncastle. With the handling part playing a prominent role.

"Everyone, thank you for coming," he said, breaking the silence. "Miss Duncastle, we'll talk." And with that, he removed his mouthpiece and left the stage. Some might have viewed the move as a cowardly retreat. He viewed it as a preemptive strike. Concluding the meeting while he was still in control gave him time to regroup before they reconvened. Of course, he had no doubt at all that she'd be regrouping as well.

That thought shouldn't have made him grin.

But it did.

He was still smiling that evening when he approached the door to her shop just as she was flipping the sign to CLOSED. That hadn't happened by coincidence.

She paused in mid-flip, her distracted expression changing swiftly when she spied him. Her expression was smooth, polite even, but there was a distinct chill in her magnificent deep blue eyes.

He could live with that.

She pulled the door open, but blocked his entry with her body planted directly in the doorway. "I believe we discussed your patronage here."

"I'm merely here to set up a convenient time for us to meet."

"I don't believe I agreed to any such thing."

"Melody—"

"Miss Duncastle to you."

He chuckled at that, and could have sworn he saw the slightest lift at the corner of her mouth. So perhaps he had more of an opening than he'd thought. She'd given him his edge with her comment about his accent. He'd used it quite shamelessly at the meeting. Oddly, he found himself less willing to press the advantage. An illogical reaction, to be certain. He didn't need to impress her, just gain her trust. What better way than to turn on the charm?

"I was sincere in my offer, and my intent," he said truthfully.

"If your intent was to charm me into believing your snake-oil-salesman pitch earlier today, I'm afraid you'll be wasting your time."

All right. Perhaps not so much of an opening after all.

She smiled.

"Be open-minded enough to hear me out," he pressed. "You weren't there for the entire presentation."

"I'm pretty sure I got the bullet points."

Perhaps he should have gone with the brogue offense.

"I appreciate your stopping by, but, as you know, I'm a bit behind in production today and have a long night ahead of me."

"Perhaps I can be of some assistance—since my meeting was at least partly responsible for your work stoppage."

She lifted one perfectly arched brow. It didn't explain at all why his gaze dropped to her lips.

"What do you know about baking?"

"You forget, I grew up in a family-owned restaurant. Several of them, in fact."

"I was given to understand you were something of a renegade where your family business was concerned. You have nothing to do with those restaurants, am I correct? And haven't in some time."

He tilted his head, wondered just how severely he'd

underestimated her. "You've taken a personal interest in me."

"Don't flatter yourself."

"I don't believe I was. You've done your research."

"You also grew up in a small town. Village," she corrected, rather dryly. "So you must know there's no need to do much research, merely listen to the village grapevine."

"You've been riding me about the village thing. It's merely a cultural distinction. What is a town to you, a burg, is a village where I'm from."

She snorted. "Come now, Mr. Gallagher, you know quite well your use of that term was intended to make us feel oh-so-cozy."

"Griffin. I'm no' so averse to such familiarity." He rubbed his arms, though he honestly wasn't feeling the chill in the air one bit. "Perhaps we could continue this conversation inside?"

"I don't think that's such a good idea."

"Because?" He employed the twinkle, although, in his defense, he wasn't thinking tactically at that particular moment.

She rolled her eyes. "Because I don't need any distractions."

"Am I, then?"

"You know you are. You're a threat to everything I hold dear."

"Ah. I thought we were speaking personally."

"*We* weren't speaking at all. Now, if you don't mind—"

"Melody."

She paused.

"Let me in. Please. I'll trade work for talk. I'm a hard worker."

"Of that I have no doubt." She made him sweat another long moment, then finally, with great resignation, stepped back and opened the door wide enough for him to step inside. "You're not the type to give up, and I don't have time for this, so let's get it over with. But, fair warning, if I'm not getting my work done," she informed him as he took off his overcoat, "I'll be asking you to leave. And I won't take no for an answer."

"Aye. I'm well acquainted with your abilities in that area."

She nodded. "Good. Follow me."

He took a deep breath, savoring the scent of her coffee.

"Don't even think about asking," she said, walking straight to the back of the shop.

He smiled to himself . . . and followed her.

4

She'd let the lion straight into her den. What was she thinking?

She could feel him behind her, almost like a physical caress. It was that ridiculously sexy brogue of his, she understood that. And the twinkle. Okay, and his mouth. Something about those hard lips, suddenly becoming very sensual and appealing when he smiled—which made no sense, set as they were in his otherwise rugged face. His jaw and cheekbones looked as if they'd been chiseled from a block of smooth granite. He had a beautifully shaped head, but with his hair clipped so very short, the whole aura should have been menacing rather than sexy.

So, why was she feeling all tingly, and warm, and, well . . . needy?

"I've got one hundred cupcakes to decorate," she announced, as if by putting the workload out there, she'd create a wall of some kind. Whether it was a wall between her and Griffin, or her and her libido, she wasn't entirely sure. Nor did she care, as long as one of them worked. "I also have several other cakes to be baked and decorated, but I'll come down early to do the detailing on those."

"Come down?" Griffin glanced upward just as she turned back to look at him, then lowered his gaze to hers. "You live above your shop?"

It was a good thing she'd studied tax law. She'd have made a lousy defense attorney. "I do, Mr. Gallagher. Now—"

"Can we at the very least lower our shields enough to consider a first-name basis? I assure you, I won't mistake the familiarity with the idea that you've gone soft on me, or my plans."

She looked at him and desperately wished there were no soft parts in her. Starting with the ones that were eagerly responding to his every request. She scooped up two heavy oven mitts and thrust them at him. "You can be on oven duty," she said, in lieu of a response.

He didn't reach out for the mitts, but rather raised one eyebrow. On anyone else, the resulting expression would have looked malevolent at best. On him . . . well, let's just say her soft, tingly parts were getting a lot warmer.

"Griffin," she finally relented, rolling her eyes when he grinned and took the mitts from her.

"Wasn't so 'ard now, was it?" he asked, as he removed his coat.

"You're insufferable," she said, turning her back to him as she rolled the tall, aluminum racks toward the ovens in the back of the kitchen.

"Aye," he said, quite affably. "It's a large part of my charm."

Luckily he couldn't see her responding smile. Damn the man.

"And my success," he added, his voice coming from just behind her.

"I can understand the latter part." She carefully smoothed her expression before turning to face him. "The pans on the top three trays go in this one," she said, gesturing to the oven behind her. "The bottom two go in that one. Center the pans, front and rear, leaving several inches between them. They're already preset, just hit the timer button after you shut the door."

She was normally very compulsive about things like pan placement and rack spacing. Both were vital to a perfectly baked cake. At the moment, however, she couldn't afford to be picky. As it was, she was putting more pans in one oven than she'd like, but time was of the essence. She'd already set up the cupcakes that needed to be decorated on one of the worktables, so she headed over to it, leaving Griffin to do as directed. She would double back and check on them once she got the base frosting on the first tray.

"How long have you been a baker?" he asked, over the clatter of the pans sliding onto the oven racks. "Does it run in the family?"

"No," she said, knowing small talk probably wasn't a bad idea, but finding it a challenge. His presence was unnerving. Perhaps if she kept things casual and civil, she could gain a bit more knowledge about his plans for Hamilton. The more information she had, direct from the source, the better chance she'd have of getting her starry-eyed, fellow business owners to listen to her concerns.

She could hardly believe the pied-piper spell he'd cast over them. She'd known going in that the sentiment had not been running high in favor of the rumored new plans. So she'd been more than a little stunned to walk into the auditorium and feel a very distinct vibe of excitement, rather than frustration, or even outright anger.

She'd looked over the brochures she'd grabbed as she'd stomped out of the auditorium and quickly away from the inquiring eyes of her neighbors. Not that it had mattered. Every one of them had found one reason or another to drop by the shop later that afternoon. Some had been circumspect in expressing their curiosity about her apparent earlier run-in with Griffin. Others had been downright blatant. She shuddered to think what the rumor mill would be saying if they knew he was with her after shop hours. It led her to belatedly wonder if anyone had seen him enter as she was flipping the CLOSED sign.

Dammit.

"So, then"—came his voice from directly behind her left shoulder, giving her another little jolt—"what did get you into baking? I understand you've only been back in Hamilton for a few years."

She tried to turn around, then realized how small the space was between the worktable and . . . him. She seemed to be making a habit of that whenever he was around. Of course, like the gentleman he wasn't, he didn't shift to give her more space.

"I've been back almost four years now. I'm surprised, if you've been doing homework on me, that you don't already know why I came back."

"I know your best friend was quite ill."

"Yes. I came back to help with her business, and . . . be here for her."

There was such compassion in his eyes then, she almost couldn't believe it was the same grinning man of a moment ago, shamelessly using his charm and his accent to woo her good favor.

"God rest her soul," he added, with quiet sincerity. "I'm sorry for your loss, Melody. The world doesn't often see fit to populate our paths with those who become near and dear to us. It's a shame, indeed, to lose a single one of them."

He was standing so close, and sounded so damn . . . earnest. She wouldn't have thought he had it in him, but as close as she was standing to him, she was pretty sure she'd have been able to detect even the slightest hint of artifice. She wanted to ask who he'd lost, why his understanding was so keen. But the words wouldn't come. She didn't want to get to know him in that way. She didn't want to care about him.

"Th-thank you," she stammered, groping for the anchor her frustration and anger had provided her thus far with him . . . and coming up empty-handed.

"Was this her shop, then?"

"It was," she said, hearing the clipped tone in her voice. But at his continued look of sincere interest, she finally relented. "I'd helped her set it up a year or so before, and came back to help her run it when she became too weak to handle the workload."

"What was it you gave up to come back?"

"You mean, what did I do for a living before this? I thought you checked up on me."

"I asked after you with the innkeeper, the lovely Mrs. Crossley, but we were interrupted by new guests arriving before she got much further than telling me about your friend. I haven't had time to do more than that."

"Ah." She wasn't sure how she felt about his asking around town about her. "Well, I was born here, I left, I came back. Having been gone, I have a much greater appreciation for exactly what Hamilton has to offer. I'm afraid I don't see the tourist draw that you do. Nor do I think that's the right direction to push our town." One corner of her mouth kicked up. "Sorry, 'village.' "

To his credit, he smiled too. While her non-answer had diverted their conversation from the more serious direction it had been heading, it didn't do anything to create the distance she so badly wished to reestablish between them. Getting him out of her personal space would be a great place to start . . . she just didn't seem to be able to accomplish it.

"You'd like for your hometown to stay just as it is for the remaining years of your life. I can understand that, the sentimental attachment, the security that comes with the familiar, the trusted. But what you don't see is that if Hamilton doesn't reach forward, it will sink hopelessly into the past. And that won't allow you to thrive. Not as you could, if you'd be willing to embrace new ideas. I'm no' looking to destroy your home, Melody. I'm looking to expand on it, improve it, and with that, give you a greater opportunity for bigger successes."

"You seem to forget I did do my homework. I've seen the befores and afters of some of your handiwork."

He didn't seem remotely abashed by either her pronouncement or her clear lack of respect. He also seemed entirely too close to her. Still. She could see the tiny, darker flecks that tinted his almost translucent green eyes, could see that he had, indeed, broken his nose at some point. And there was a hairline scar that ran along the top of one eyebrow, and another still, high on his forehead, clearly indicating she hadn't been far off in her assessment of him as a competent, or at least willing, brawler.

"Some places required more work than others to shore up the foundations," he responded with the ease of someone who was quite used to defending his work.

It made her wonder how often he had to do that very thing. But rather than make her feel more confident in her arguments, she worried instead that she was going to be outmatched by someone who had fought and won the battle many, many times.

"In those cases," he went on, "the citizenry was happy to have their home restored in such a way as to guarantee its longevity well into the future. You were right about this not being an Old World town. But some of the ones you've researched were. There were few options for renewal without rebuilding, restructuring. It made sense to modernize, to give those villages every opportunity to become successful, thriving communities that could sustain themselves in the modern world, and into the future. Yes, old traditions may have to evolve into new ones. But age-old traditions, while cherished and fondly remembered, won't sustain a community alone. There has to be flexibility and room for reinterpretation, for building new traditions, new legacies. Isn't that the very core of your country's philosophy? If you didn't embrace growth, you'd all still be driving horses and buggies."

He made it sound so . . . necessary. So simple. But it wasn't.

He tilted his head, ever so slightly, and that mischievous twinkle seemed ready to surface in his eyes at any moment, in contradiction with the absolute seriousness of his tone and the set of his jaw. "If you'd spoken to any of the residents of those places, Melody, you'd have heard how happy and excited they are about their prospects for the future."

She sighed, and her shoulders slumped a little. He was good, she'd give him that. "Mr. Gallagher—Griffin—I—"

"Let me finish."

She nodded, so caught up in his eyes, the mellifluous sound of his voice, the vibrancy that radiated from him when he spoke about what he so clearly believed in, that she couldn't have looked away then if she'd wanted to. "Go on," she said, ceding him the floor, if not the victory.

The tension in his jaw relaxed just a bit, as did his tone, but the vibrancy was no less potent when he spoke. "I'm no' in the business of ruinin' lives," he said quietly. "I'm no' here to make your life, or any of those who live here, more challenging, or diminish, in any way, the things you love about Hamilton. I come from a place where traditions are important, too. I consider all of that when coming up with my plans."

She struggled to keep her head from becoming hopelessly fogged by him, to keep her thoughts clear, her arguments concise. "The pictures you have in the brochure make Hamilton look like some bright, shiny Future-World. You can't make a silk purse from a sow's ear. We're a dyed-in-the-wool, homespun-and-happy-for-it sow's ear. We don't want or need to be some kind of resort town getaway. Most of us are here because we like permanently being away."

"Melody—"

"My turn," she said, hoping he saw that she was just as earnest and sincere as he was. "We're happy you're here." At his arch look, she said, "We are, Griffin. Truly. We're happy that Lionel has someone he can trust to take over his business, so we can continue forward. With Trevor Hamilton bowing out, it's been a great concern, where the future would lead without a Hamilton heir at the helm. But if you'd just work on growing Hamilton Industries, the town will grow by default."

"But no' fast enough."

"What is the big rush? We're not unhappy with our slower way of life. We all know we're not going to get rich living and working here. We're not failing as a town, so—"

His previously open gaze grew shuttered. And a whole new kind of alarm sprang to life inside her.

Her heart squeezed hard inside her chest. "Is there something you're not telling me? Or all of us? Is something wrong at Hamilton Industries? Are we in some kind of trouble?"

"You're on the brink of achieving a success like you never dared hope for."

"That's not an answer."

"It's the answer I bring, Melody. It's an answer that will work."

She looked into his eyes and realized he was not going to give her anything more. She understood. His loyalties lay with Hamilton Industries. But that didn't mean she had to like it. "Perhaps you, and by extension, Lionel, should have more faith in the people who keep this town running. Why don't you focus on the people who run your company?"

"It's no' mine as yet."

"You know what I mean. Don't underestimate us, Griffin. You'll garner the kind of real loyalty and support you're trying to charm us into, if you tell us the truth. We don't scare off. And we don't give up."

"You've seen my list of successes, Melody, so I'm going to ask you, based on my track record, to trust that I know what I'm doing. I'm handling the situation the best way possible for everyone involved. Everyone."

She sighed a little at that and tried not to be frustrated. Before, she'd been prepared to dislike him and cast him as the bogeyman, come to ruin her bucolic little life. It was harder to do now that he'd allowed her to glimpse the real man behind the charming Irish accent and glossy PowerPoint presentation.

That man seemed sincere, smart, and very determined.

She broke their gaze, looked down, wanting, needing to regroup. And felt his knuckles beneath her chin, drawing her gaze back to his.

"I think you'll find that my way isn't a bad way."

She looked into his eyes, wanting to find what she needed, so she could get past the ball of fear in her gut. All she knew, in her gut and in her heart, was nothing was going to be the same again. She knew it, just as surely as she'd known moving back here to be with Bernie, to take on a whole new life challenge, was the absolute right thing to do. She prayed like hell this was going to work out half as well. "I hope, for all of our sakes, that you're right."

"I am," he said simply and without arrogance.

Standing, all but in his arms, their gazes locked, she felt connected in a way she hadn't ever been before, and certainly wouldn't have expected to be. She saw how easy it could be to trust him, to put her faith in him, let him lead the way, and believe everything would be okay. And she knew the townspeople would feel exactly the same way. Maybe her time in Washington had left her too cynical, too suspicious. But she strongly felt that she was right to protect what was hers, what she saw as the most valuable parts of the life that fulfilled and contented her. She hadn't thought she was alone in those feelings. She'd heard the same sentiment over and over, expressed by everyone in town. But she saw what had swayed them and understood the temptation. Lord knows she felt it. But that didn't mean she had to give in to it. Not when so much was at stake.

As she moved to break the moment completely, to shift away from him, do whatever she had to, kick him out if necessary, to regain her perspective—not to mention control over her own libido—he spoke.

"Do you know what I wish for, Melody?"

She smiled at him. She was finding it increasingly easy to do. *Danger, danger*, she thought. But she didn't step back. "That I'd stop being a thorn in your side?"

His lips curved, and somehow, that half grin was sexier than all the sparkling, charm-filled ones that had come before it. He had offered it naturally, rather than as a calculated play.

"That, too, of course. But I'm referring to a rather more . . . insistent, immediate wish." His gaze dropped to her mouth, then slowly returned to meet her eyes.

Her heart started an erratic tattoo inside her chest, and her skin had gone beyond warm and tingly to an almost steamy dampness that had nothing to do with the huge ovens cranking out heat. She should have stepped away when she had the chance. At the moment, she was rooted right to that spot.

"Which is?" The words came out as a damnably soft whisper.

The pupils in his clear green eyes expanded until they threatened to swallow up the rest. That darkness added an element that made him seem all the more dangerous.

"That I could court your favor quite personally, for reasons having nothing to do with business. And everything to do with kissing. Your lips tempt me. Mightily."

She swallowed reflexively against the sudden tightness in her throat. "How . . . direct."

"You wanted honesty."

"If only you could be so where it mattered," she said, her voice still not as strongly confident as she'd hoped.

"So tempting . . ."

"Honesty . . . or—"

"The natural color and shape of your lips is so striking. Your bottom lip fair begs a man to . . ." He trailed off, his gaze fixed on her mouth, then lifted back to her eyes. There was so much electricity, it was as if a live wire had brushed against all her nerve endings at once. She felt . . . carnally singed. And it was only an intent look. Were he to put his hands on her just then, she wasn't sure she wouldn't combust into a ball of flames.

"Griffin—"

"Miss Duncastle . . ."

She couldn't help it, she smiled.

He groaned, just a little, as her lips curved deeper. She should take some much-needed strength in the discovery that she held some sway over him, as he did with her. He with his accent and otherworldly eyes, and she, apparently, with her . . . lips.

Odd, but she'd always felt her strength was a keen mind. She should be insulted, perhaps, or at the very least feel condescended to, that his attraction was so seemingly superficial. Instead she felt rather primal and intensely female. And she wasn't at all upset about it.

His knuckles, still resting beneath her chin, uncurled, and his hand opened to slide up and cup the side of her face. For a man who purported to have made his fortune using his own keen mind, she was surprised to feel the calluses on his palm.

Although they perfectly fit the cunning, Irish devil who was tilting her jaw and lowering his mouth to claim hers.

5

Aye, Griff. What in heaven's name do ye think yer doin', lad?

No stern admonition or sudden return of sanity was going to save him from what he'd begun. If he were honest with himself, the desire for the kiss, for her, had been far more the drive behind seeing her again than anything having to do with his coming inheritance, Lionel, or Hamilton.

" 'Tis no' meant to persuade you," he murmured, a breath away from her lips. "I simply want to taste—" He paused for one brief moment, looked into her eyes, and liked to think it was his integrity finally showing up, needing to make certain she was a willing participant in the mutual exploration . . . but, in all honesty, unless she'd shoved him off, he'd have stolen a sip anyway. He'd just wanted to watch her while he did so.

In the end, he was rewarded in a way he couldn't have foreseen, and never would have expected.

"It won't," she whispered, those plum perfect lips brushing the barest hint across his. "Since we're being direct, I'll admit I'd like to know what you taste like, too."

The punch that breathy little admission delivered ignited the sparks already licking between them.

He took her mouth, and not in the gentle, seductive manner of a man who meant to stake his claim slowly, building trust and need at the same time. He took her mouth like a man half-starved for the taste of her, as if he'd been deprived of it for so long, he had no restraint, no civility left in him.

And, true to her claim, she responded with equal fervor.

Trays clanged, metal clashed, as he sank his hands into her hair and bent his head to hers, pushing her back against the worktable. He slid his tongue between those lips, then she did the same between his, both of them tasting, dueling, demanding. It was like plundering heaven. She tasted spicy, sweet, and dark, like something forbidden and exotic, known only to him, the lucky bastard who'd uncovered the buried treasure first.

Her fingertips flexed hard against his scalp as she held him where she wanted him, taking his tongue, taking him, then giving in return, taunting, teasing, until he wasn't sure whose gasps were whose, and whether the vibrating growls were coming from deep inside his chest or from the one plastered so tightly against it.

Some shred of sanity prevailed long enough for him to pull her up and off the worktable before they destroyed another entire night's work. He tugged her against him as he spun them around and pushed her up against a pair of oversized, stainless-steel doors.

The chill of the cooler doors made her gasp, but when he pulled her away, she grabbed the front of his shirt and yanked him right back close again. He was grinning when he took her face in his hands and claimed her mouth all over again.

She was tugging off his tie, and he was busily undoing the buttons on the front of her starched white baker's coat, when a shrill, insistent beeping sound went off, startling them into leaping away from each other—as if they'd been doing something wrong.

Only it hadn't felt at all wrong to him. Quite the opposite, in fact. Surprisingly so. "What is that?" he asked, a little dazed, breathing heavily.

"Cakes," she panted, pushing back the hair that had spilled down out of her bun. Silky, dark brown curls clung to her flushed cheeks. "Ovens."

"Don't," he said instinctively, when she started to gather the tumbled waves and knot them back up. He reached out, as if he had all the right in the world, and brushed aside a damp curl. The tips of his fingers caressed the smooth skin of her cheek. Her lips parted slightly, drawing him to trace his fingers across her bottom lip. He felt the slight tremble there, heard the catch in her throat. And his hunger for her surged right back, with a renewed vengeance.

He took a step toward her, crowding her back against the doors again. He watched her pupils expand, saw her throat work, knew that if he cupped her breasts, her nipples would be rock hard. The thought of peeling that starched linen from her body, and whatever else was beneath it, sent him from launch to orbit in a second.

"Th-the cakes," she stammered as he slid one hand behind her neck and tilted her mouth up to his again. She side-stepped, half stumbling out of his reach. "They'll burn." She scraped her hair back and, with less than steady hands, managed to get it into some semblance of a knot.

"Right," he said, letting his hand drop. He watched as she darted across the room, then leaned back against the closest worktable. He lowered his chin and closed his eyes with a deep sigh. "Well done, boy-o," he muttered. "Well done."

It was her sudden hiss that brought him fully alert again.

"What?" He was half across the room before she answered.

"Nothing," she said tightly, then quickly clattered the cake pans she was juggling onto the waiting cooling racks. She dropped the oven mitts and curled the fingers of one hand into a fist.

The cakes were a rich golden yellow, and their warm, sweet scent made his empty stomach growl. But he was more concerned with the color of her hand.

"Did you burn yourself?" He closed the distance between them. "Let me see, I can—"

She shooed him back as she shifted to the other oven in the smooth, almost graceful manner of someone who had danced between them many, many times. She handled the mitts better and was more purposeful, sliding out one tray at a time and placing them on a different cooling rack.

He didn't push her about the burn, he just got out of her way. "Do you ever tire of the scent?" he asked. "It's wonderful, and, along with your fresh roast, quite like paradise would smell, I imagine."

She didn't respond. He noted she didn't look at him, either. He should just let the moment go. Only he didn't want to. Hence his lame attempt at conversation. He thought her lack of response was because she was busy unloading her ovens, arranging cooling racks, and rearranging the hot racks inside the ovens. But once those tasks were complete and the beeping timer had ceased, she made herself enormously busy arranging the hot pans just so on the cooling racks, then going over to the refrigerated units and burying her head inside one, then another, rooting around . . . but coming out empty-handed.

"It's the one memory of my grandmother's place, of my childhood, that stays with me," he persisted. "The scents, I mean." Then he abruptly snapped his mouth shut. He didn't like her withdrawing, had wanted to keep her in the moment with him, but he had no earthly idea what had made him blurt out that little tidbit. He didn't mind sharing the personal stories of those he'd helped over the years. He considered those stories triumphs, business successes. He didn't share stories about himself. And definitely not about his childhood. Other than surviving it, there was nothing worth mentioning.

In fact, he should take the annoying intrusion of those blasted timers as the signal they surely were. A signal that it wasn't the time, nor the place, and she was most definitely not the woman to be distracting himself with. He had a very specific job to do. One that, if done properly, would become the single most important thing he'd done to date. Definitely the most meaningful. That opportunity was everything he'd dreamed his future could be. He'd tackled bigger jobs, even more prestigious ones, at least as far as the initial stages of the Hamilton project went. But it was very different from all the others. Because it was personal. It was his.

Where he could go with it, where he could take it, if he worked hard, and made the right decisions . . . went beyond his wildest dreams. And he'd allowed himself to dream pretty big. He'd had to. The last thing he needed at such a precipitous moment was a reminder of where he'd come from.

And yet . . . he'd been the one to bring it up. Even more startling to him was that he hadn't been lying. It was the best memory of an otherwise brutal childhood. The very best. He hadn't allowed himself to think about it in a very long time. Because it was hard, if not impossible, to think about one part . . . and not all the rest. A long time ago, he'd needed to use those memories, every vile one of them, to motivate himself when things were hard, or when he thought his wits weren't going to be enough to get him where he wanted to go.

They had to be enough—the only other things he had

were his fists. He knew, all too keenly, what it felt like to fight his battles with those. That sure as hell wasn't going to be his future.

"Look at me now, Da," he murmured beneath his breath. "Look at me now."

"What kind of restaurant did she run?"

He jerked his gaze up, and his mind away from that path. He shouldn't be here. He looked at her then, trying, struggling, to regain the perspective that was as natural to him as breathing. The perspective that steered him single-mindedly toward his goals. Being with her . . . wanting her as he did, was not the way to get there.

So, when he quite readily said, "Irish pub, actually," he knew with absolute certainty that somewhere between sipping her coffee and kissing her lips, he'd lost his mind.

"I know Sean's place over in Willow Creek is absolutely wonderful. Warm atmosphere, good hearty food, great music on the weekends. I've always felt a warm welcome there. Was your grandmother Gallagher's place like that? There's more than one Gallagher place in Ireland, I know. Sean talks about his extended family all the time," she added.

She was nervous, he realized. It was the only explanation for her sudden chattiness. *Welcome to the party, luv,* he thought, making no move to leave, as he bloody well knew he should.

"Aye, there are several. I grew up in West Cork." He'd started to say his branch of the family was from there, but skipped it. He was still unresolved about the information that had been kept from him all his life. A life that could have been improved far, far sooner had he known the truth. "Our pub was down by the waterfront, so it brought in an interesting . . . clientele."

She opened the cooler doors again, and came out with a large container. "Here," she said, handing it to him, then turning around to get another, and still another.

He put the first carton on a rolling tray beside the worktable. Apparently . . . he was staying.

"Sounds like an interesting childhood," she said. "Did you spend a lot of time in the pub? Or were you too busy going to school or"—she paused for a moment as she reached over the worktable, trying to set it back to rights, then glanced at him as she finished—"playing sports?"

He saw her gaze roam over his face. He knew exactly what she saw. And what she thought. Probably wasn't far off in her assessment. Most people assumed he'd earned his scars and odd bumps the hard way, by putting his fists up first, and thinking later. In actuality, he'd earned them a far, far harder way, but he never corrected the assumption.

"I worked in the pub my whole life, or as long as West Cork was my home, anyway. Everyone in the family did."

"Did you resent it?"

He caught her gaze then, and realized she wasn't asking idly, or making empty conversation. She was looking at him, and her expression was one of sincere curiosity.

"Because I think I would have," she went on, when he didn't immediately reply. "At least a little."

"I loved being in the pub," he said quite honestly. It was when he'd been the safest. For him that meant the happiest. "Not so much the bar itself, but the rest of it. Families came, no' just the men to play darts or lift an ale. Everyone we knew was there at one point or another over the course of the week."

Memories tugged at him, and he was quite surprised to realize that not all of them made him flinch and want to look away. It had been a very long time since he'd pulled them out and looked them over. Up until a year ago, he'd avoided thinking about the past. He'd gone home then, leaving Dublin for Cork for a brief spell, when he'd found out about Lionel Hamilton. About being a Haversham by blood.

And not a Gallagher.

"That sounds kind of nice, actually," she said.

"What did your parents do?" he asked, partly because he was curious, and partly because he needed to think a bit more about his past before he shared it with her.

"My father worked for Hamilton Industries as an account manager. My mother ran a daycare in our home. My grandmother—on my mom's side—helped out with that. My folks both died when I was three, so I don't have any real memories of them, other than the pictures and the endless stories my grandmother told me. She raised me after they were gone."

He set the last carton on the rolling tray, then walked over to her. "You've experienced a lot of loss in your life, Melody Duncastle." He laid his palm on her shoulder, turning her toward him. She didn't pull away. "I'm sorry for that."

"It was a very long time ago," she said, "but thank you."

"Your grandmother, she's gone as well now?"

She nodded. "Also a long time ago. Right before I started law—uh, college." She looked from his hand to his face. "You're very affected by that. By loss. You were before, when I spoke about Bernadette passing away."

She was right about that, he supposed, though he'd never thought about it. He'd had far too few people to care about in his life, and even fewer to care about him. He was sensitive to the bond of love, cherished it for the special and unique gift it was, and knew how critical the loss of it truly could be.

He had no earthly idea how he'd come to that moment, that conversation, that topic. But there he was. It was just as surprising as the fact that he was doing absolutely nothing to forward his personal agenda with her—getting her on his side of the Hamilton project.

He supposed exposing himself, talking about things

he'd rather leave unspoken, might have been seen as a tactical maneuver to gain her sympathy and her trust.

But even he wasn't cold enough, calculating enough, to mine his own past for gain. He'd go to many other lengths before trying that one. Hell, he might even accept defeat first.

"I know what it's like to have, and to have lost," he told her. "I've seen my share of it. Experienced it. It's never a good thing." It was the first lie he'd told her. Not all loss was for the worse. "Not for those left behind, anyway." That was a half truth, at best.

She stopped rolling out what looked like a slab of rose-colored modeling clay and turned to face him fully. Her gaze was direct, probing, and highly disconcerting. No one ever looked at him like that. "Is that why you do what you do? To help people gain rather than lose?"

It was a valid question. Stunning, because she very well might have a point. But he'd never put it together like that. Mostly because he didn't spend much time analyzing his past, or himself. "I have a knack for figuring out ways to make things, places, more attractive. When things are eye-catching, they attract attention. It's a simple law of nature. And it's . . . I don't know. I guess it always seemed quite obvious to me. How to improve things, how to make them more successful. But no one else seemed to see it. I could never figure out why."

"So it's like a puzzle to be solved for you."

"I suppose that's one way to look at it."

"Did you do that for your family? Help make the restaurant a success? Is that what launched you in that direction?"

He snorted before he could stop himself. "Hardly. Although it was certainly where I'd first noticed what could be done."

"So . . . why not help them?"

"For the very same reason you don't want my help," he said, with a dry smile. "They like things just as they are."

To her credit, she looked at least a little abashed, and nodded to concede the point. "But they are still doing well."

"On their own scale of measure, I suppose, aye."

"But not yours."

He didn't respond to that, simply held her gaze steadily. She knew the answer to her question.

"So, do you ever think their logic might apply here? That we're fine the way we are?"

"Cork, and my family's business there, or, more to the point, all of the family businesses, are doing fine without my help. Aye, that is the truth of it. I'd thought to take all of our independent restaurants and pubs and unify them."

"You mean, like making a chain out of them?"

"As you term it here, something like that, yes. The Gallaghers could have doubled their successes and provided more security for their countless offspring. Were any of them truly visionary, they could have taken it far, far beyond that."

"But they didn't want to. And, maybe more to the point, they didn't want you doing it for them."

"Correct on both scores." He purposely broke the intimate link their connected gazes seemed to have forged and turned his attention to the rolling cart. "Now, what can I do to help?" he asked, blatantly changing the subject.

"I'm sorry if my questions trespassed on territory you'd rather leave untouched."

" 'Tis all right. But perhaps we've wasted enough time and should be seein' to getting these wee cakes frosted. I used to be a fair hand in the kitchen when I was a boy, so if you give me a bit of direction, I imagine I can do a passable job."

She didn't respond right away, and he could feel her

gaze on him. It should have felt awkward or uncomfortable. But it was neither. He realized he felt comfortable with her in a way he'd never felt with anyone else. He wasn't entirely sure why. She was hardly nonthreatening, certainly not naïve. She was clever, smart, and very likely to poke and prod at things he'd rather she didn't. She would not be easily steered and definitely not readily controlled.

Yet, he'd never found himself so drawn to a woman, so swiftly and easily smitten. Maybe it was because of the challenge she presented. Not just from a business perspective, but also from the personal one. He never let anyone in. Not ever. No exceptions. Yet, he was falling all over himself to spill out each and every one of his deepest, darkest secrets. And he had more than the average share.

Perhaps it was because her interest was sincere; she truly wanted to understand him. He didn't feel judged when he offered up an answer. Instead, he simply felt more clearly understood. That was . . . well, quite an intoxicating thing. Something he hadn't realized he even wanted for himself. He'd never much cared what anyone thought of him, only of his ability to meet their business needs.

It led him to wonder what her needs were . . . and if there was any chance in hell he could be the one to meet them.

They'd been working practically side by side for several hours. She had a rolling rack full of cheerful, frosted cupcakes to show for their efforts, each decorated with a festive holiday touch. It was past midnight, and there was still an hour or two of work left, providing he stayed. Melody wondered why he had. But she hadn't asked. In fact, from the time he'd so abruptly changed the subject to the work at hand, that had been the only thing they'd talked about. Most of the time, they'd worked in total silence.

It should have been awkward. It had been a very . . . unusual evening between them. But it hadn't been awkward at all. Far from it. She wouldn't go so far as to say it had been comfortable; his nearness was far too disconcerting for that. But they'd found a good working rhythm almost effortlessly. He'd been right about having a natural sense for working with his hands, working with food.

She'd noticed that despite the strength in his big, scarred, callused hands, he could be quite gentle, precise even. As the night wore on, she'd given him more of the intricate work, short of the actual details he simply wouldn't know how to do without a great deal of practice. He'd turned out to be far more help than she'd expected him to be.

Still, as distractions went, he was a mammoth one. Not in terms of getting work done . . . but certainly in terms of his effect on her.

Griffin Gallagher wasn't someone who could traipse into, then back out of, her life without leaving an indelible mark. Even after one night spent together, she'd remember him in exquisite, unforgettable detail. Eyes like his could haunt, that accent would certainly resonate inside her thoughts and memories . . . and his kiss—she couldn't think about it if she had any hope of completing the highly stylized decorating she was attempting.

The man she'd begun to know, the few layers she'd peeled back, had been tantalizing to her. There was depth, and thoughtfulness, and a great sense of purpose. And a background he was clearly ill at ease talking about. There was a roughness and a refinement to him. She'd bet the former had come first, which meant he'd had to work hard to achieve the latter. He was complicated and complex, and he intrigued the hell out of her. The chemistry made him that much harder to ignore.

So, what should she do when the bubble burst, and they were forced to return to the real world, and the very real people in it? They were on opposing sides. Granted, she saw his side far more clearly . . . but the insight hadn't changed her opinion on his proposed changes to her home.

"Should I bring the larger cake over now?" he asked, as he gracefully took the tray of cupcakes she'd finished detailing and slid them onto the last storage rack. "Is the fondant soft enough for rolling?"

She smiled at that. "Listen to you, sounding like a pastry chef."

He shrugged, but smiled. "Not me. Growing up, I never fancied making desserts. Was always far more attracted to chopping things up, I suppose."

"Well, you'd have made a good baker. You've got the hands for it."

He laughed outright. The sound of it was rich, melodious, and surprisingly infectious, much like his voice. "These hams?" He held them up, the latex gloves he was wearing stretching tightly over his knuckles.

"You're surprisingly graceful with them," she said, her tone as dry as her smile. But she'd been sincere with the compliment. "If you ever decide to give up your burgeoning empire and the need to make the world over, I could use them here. A little bit of time and training, and I daresay you'd soon be challenging me as lead baker." She cocked her head. "Goodness knows what kind of innovative things your mind could come up with. We could put Cups & Cakes on the map."

She'd been teasing, but hadn't expected his expression to change like it did. She'd expected, maybe, some double entendre about her needing his hands, had—maybe—said something along those lines for that very reason. She just . . . was mixed up and turned on and tired out.

She wasn't prepared at all for the way his expression grew serious, or the way he took her shoulders in his big hands and turned her gently but firmly so he could trap her between him and the table.

She didn't reject the invasion of privacy. Hell, her body was all but throwing a welcome party. If she were being honest, she'd wanted his hands on her again since the damn oven beeper had gone off hours ago. But the look in his eyes wasn't sensual, or even predatory, though it felt like both to her. He was just . . . serious.

"You need to know something, Melody."

"What?" she said faintly. Her thoughts were all jumbled up with the riotous reactions his touch was setting off. She wished she could be more collected, more cool, but the simple truth was that despite the very civilized couple of hours they'd spent together, she was feeling anything but cool with him. No matter how well she got to know him, the civilized him, she'd bet there would always be that less-than-civilized element between them. Beneath all the refinement, he was still rough. In all the ways that appealed to every primal instinct she had. "Wh-what is it?"

"About the town, about . . ."

That jerked her thoughts back to some semblance of sanity. "Hamilton? What—what are you talking about?"

"You need to know, should know, but—dammit." He broke off, looked down, but didn't release her.

"Griffin?"

He lifted his gaze to hers. She'd never seen him so serious. She remembered his earlier comment after she'd asked him what the big rush was to change Hamilton into some resort town. The alarm she'd felt then was nothing compared to the sudden, sick squeeze that knotted her stomach.

"I know we've danced a lot around the idea of trust," she began, "but if you think this affects my life here, my future—"

"I don't think," he said quietly. "I know."

"So—"

"So, you're right. We've talked about trust. I need to know I have yours, Melody. To allow me to handle this my own way, on my timetable. I realize now"—he stopped, then started again before she could say anything—"we want to fix things, and we will. But explaining everything would cause panic, fear. This way—"

"Who is we?"

"Lionel."

"And you." She'd made it a statement.

He nodded. "Yes. He had things that needed working

out, solutions that he wasn't finding. Then I came along and—"

"Offered him those solutions."

"Basically, yes."

"Because Hamilton Industries is in trouble."

He simply held her gaze.

The knot of dread returned. "Does it have something to do with you being Trudy's grandson? There's been talk of Lionel using a chunk of the Haversham fortune to save Hamilton Industries. He came into all of Trudy's money eventually. Money that would have rightfully been—"

"That was a long time ago. And no, I'm not trying to swindle the old man out of his empire. I was happy building my own. I came here to understand where I came from."

To his credit, he didn't get angry or insulted at the question, but simply answered it directly. She liked that. He wasn't hotheaded or overly sensitive. She'd thought, given the scars, that he might be. She liked that he had himself under control. But just barely. Yes, she admitted, she liked that part, too.

"What has Lionel offered you?"

"That's just it, Melody. Everyone thinks I popped up out of nowhere, the lost grandson of an heiress, come to claim his fortune. And that Lionel is an old man with no heirs of his own, at least none who are willing to take on what he spent a lifetime sustaining and building. It's a huge burden, the one he was handed. Don't get me wrong, I know it was a challenge he relished. He's made life tough on Trevor for not being willing to take on what he sees as Trevor's rightful duties. Duties Trevor walked away from. The way Lionel sees it, Trevor essentially thumbed his nose not only at the family fortune but the family itself. Seems he wasn't too keen on playing Lionel's game."

"Are you?"

"I like knowing I've made a difference. And yes, I bloody well like to succeed. If success brings along creature comforts, I'm not going to play martyr or live like a monk. I worked hard for what I have. But 'tis no' the gain that motivates me, Melody."

"It does Lionel."

"Aye, it does seem so. He doesn't understand a man like Trevor."

"Do you? How well do you know him?"

"We've spent time together. I met with him before meeting Lionel. To answer your question, yes, I do. I respect his desire to live life on his own terms."

Melody's gaze sharpened then. "You're a lot alike, the two of you, aren't you? Only your terms are more in line with Lionel's than Trevor's."

He nodded, a glint of respect in his eyes. "'Tis true. Thank you for no' sayin' that as if it's something to be ashamed of."

"I haven't had any reason to think ill of you. I might not agree with your goals, because I don't see them as a good fit for Hamilton. But that doesn't mean I don't respect what you do, or have done."

"Fair enough. Thank you."

"You're welcome. So . . . back to Lionel. What was it like, meeting with him the first time? What is it he wanted from you? Or for you?"

"He wanted my help."

"He knew about you a year ago, so why wait until—"

"We've been working on this for a long time—it didn't just come together since I got here, Melody."

"I—I didn't really think about it that way. I guess"— she trailed off, laughed a little at herself—"I guess I didn't think about a lot of this. So, you're going to step in for him, then? When . . . you know, when the time comes? Is this all overwhelming for you?"

"I've had some time to come to terms with it. And"—

he paused, then went on—"finding out about my real heritage has forced me to go through a lot of things I thought I'd left behind for good. I thought, until tonight anyway, that it was best to leave them there."

"What changed your mind tonight?" she asked, truly surprised to hear him say that.

He peeled off his gloves and brushed her cheek with his fingertips. "Good memories. I'd somehow forgotten there were some of those, sprinkled in."

"I'm sorry I made you go back. I am," she went on, when he would have silenced her. "I didn't know. I mean, I suspected it wasn't good, your childhood, but then you said something about your grandmother's place and I guess I just wanted to understand you better. I thought if I got a sense of where you came from, I'd be able to figure out who you are now."

"Why does that matter?" He pressed a finger across her lips, and the touch made her shudder with renewed awareness. "Because it will help you figure out how to fight me?"

"Yes," she answered honestly. "At least, that would be the intellectual answer."

"There's a different one?"

"There's more to it than that—now. It matters, Griffin." She touched his face and was stunned by the way his eyes instantly darkened. His reaction to her gentle touch was . . . visceral. "I don't know why. We've only just met. But . . . it matters. That I know you. I didn't just *want* to know more. I needed to know. Not because I'm scared of losing the hometown I love to some re-imagined resort vision of yours. I'd have sworn to that before. But now . . ."

"Now?" he prodded.

"You're surprising me." She cupped his cheek, held his face, looked at him directly. "I don't know what this is, but it's not about Hamilton—the town or the company. And it's not about Lionel, or why you came here. Not this part. This part . . . is about me. I'm . . . you're—" She broke off.

"What are we, Melody?" he asked quietly.

"We're not like anything I've experienced. You're— different. From what I thought. From what I know. I'm drawn to you." She smiled a little. "And it's not just the accent, and not just because I wanted to taste you."

His fingers tightened on her, and she could feel him all but vibrating beneath her touch. Or maybe it was her. "You, the man . . . you intrigue the hell out of me. And . . . I want more. I want to know . . . everything. I wish to God you were here for any other reason, because I want what I want . . . and that includes keeping Hamilton the way it is."

"That's no' going to happen," he said gently. "No matter if the town as a whole rises up. We're going forward with the resort, the hotel, the golf courses, all of it." He braced her face. "We've no choice, Melody."

"Then why not tell me the whole of it?" she asked, just as fervently. "If I can't change it—"

"You can make it a lot harder than it has to be."

"So tell me why I shouldn't bother. Tell me, Griffin. I know your loyalty is to Lionel in this, but it's my home. I deserve to know. We all do."

He held her gaze for another interminable minute. "Lionel . . . has made some mistakes. Some bad ones. The decisions on how to fix it—they've been made, Melody. The money has been invested. We will go forward, and we must succeed. We'll need your help, the help of all of you, to make it the best success possible, and the swiftest, which is to everyone's advantage. But it will go forward regardless. Or you won't have a hometown." He pulled her in closer. "Without this change in direction, Hamilton Industries will collapse." He tugged her into his arms, and, stunned, she let him. "Lionel didn't offer me anything"—he whispered in her ear—"because he didn't have anything to offer. But if I save this . . . then what I save will be mine to build on." He kissed her temple, then nudged her until she looked at him again.

She knew her eyes were swimming with tears. Tears of loss, tears of shock, tears of grief.

"I take care of what's mine, Melody. I always have. And I always will."

7

He was going completely off the rails. Telling her things he'd agreed with Lionel not to speak of, ever, if possible. Griffin hadn't agreed with that decision, but he hadn't had the final say. Lionel understood his town, his company, his people, a hell of a lot better than Griffin did, so he hadn't fought him on it. But he knew secrecy had been the wrong way to go.

He wasn't sure he could trust Melody not to say anything, at least until he'd had time to talk to Lionel. He wanted to believe he could trust her. But she'd had a day to get to know him. And a lifetime to know her hometown. He knew who was going to win that showdown, every time.

"I need to talk to him—Lionel," Griffin said, "so if you could just give me that time before rounding up—"

"I'm not going to say anything."

He leaned back slightly, eyebrows raised. "I appreciate that. I don't know how long I'll need, but I'll tell you as soon—"

"No, I mean, I'm not going to say anything, ever."

He frowned. "Didn't you just get done telling me—

quite convincingly, I might add, that you'd fight me on this no matter what?"

"I did. And I'm glad you told me, glad you understood why it was so important to me. But you have a point, too, about not panicking anyone. That won't do you or them any good. Not if the company is in as bad shape as you say. If people panic and leave, look for work elsewhere, or start the great migration that has crushed so many of the small towns out this way, Hamilton won't be able to re-bound. As it stands, you have the support of the majority, at least if the gathering today was any indication. I meant what I said about trusting us, too, and I still believe every-one should know what's going on. You will need to tell them at some point, when the timing is best for both sides, but that will be your decision. Or Lionel's. Not mine."

He continued to study her. "You were all ready to take up the crusade earlier today, and now you're surrendering the field completely?"

"I didn't say I liked it," she said quietly and he saw the pain behind her seemingly casual declaration. "But I have no actual cause to fight for. You've made that abundantly clear. I'm not big on wasting my time. So . . . I'll have to . . . ac-cept that I can't change this. I don't know what your plan will end up meaning to me. What it will change for me. Knowing it's a fait accompli helps somewhat. I'm glad you told me. It gives me some time."

"Time?"

"To figure things out. Make choices."

"What choices?" he asked. "You realize, don't you, that the resort will almost certainly boost your particular niche business? With our plans for global partnerships, the world will be your oyster. You're only limited by how big you dream."

"Bigger isn't better for everyone, Griffin," she said gently. "I tried bigger. That's why I came back here. Well,

I came back for Bernie, but it's why I stayed. I was unhappy in Washington, unhappy in my career, unhappy with bigger, brighter, better."

"You were a lawyer there? In Washington."

She lifted a questioning brow.

"You stuttered earlier, over saying your grandmother passed away as you were heading to law school. What kind of law?"

"Taxes."

He groaned. "It's a wonder you didn't put a gun to your temple. My God."

"I was quite good at it," she said, without a shred of defensiveness—or any real emotion.

"But you hated it."

"With gun-to-the-temple passion," she said, then her lips finally smiled a little. A bit of life came back into those dark blue eyes, but not enough to hide the sadness that was still evident.

He felt badly for putting the sorrow there, but would have felt worse if he'd kept the truth from her any longer.

"The problem was," she went on, "I knew tax law wasn't for me, and I knew that I hated living in the city. I just . . . didn't know what else I wanted to be when I grew up. I thought I needed the stimulation of a bigger town, with more people, to push me intellectually. I didn't think I could find that kind of satisfaction in my hometown. I love everyone here dearly, but I thought my world needed to be bigger to truly fulfill what I saw as my potential."

"Sometimes, you do have to leave. You weren't wrong to try."

"No. No, I wasn't. You're right. I don't regret the choices I made. Or the education I worked so hard for. But while I was realizing those choices were sucking the soul out of me, Bernie was launching this business. I started to bake. And baking . . ." She let the sentence drift off on a sigh. A sigh so full it captivated him.

"Your eyes go all . . ." He lifted a shoulder when the words weren't there. It was an arresting sight, to be sure. "When you talk about what you do now, a look comes into your eyes. That's your soul, all aglow. But you know that."

She nodded, but looked surprised at his description. "You're very—"

"Observant," he finished for her, feeling somewhat exposed. She brought out things in him even he didn't know resided there. "It goes with my line of work."

"Thoughtful, was the word I was going to use. You put a lot of thought into what you do, what you say."

He had a laugh at that. "Most of the time, I'd say aye to that. But around you? Let's just say I haven't found it to be the case. Apparently I'll blurt out just about anything."

"I'll take that as a compliment."

He grinned. "If you say so. What is it about baking that soothes the savage tax attorney?"

"I'm not certain," she said, and that smile came across her face again. It truly did light her up from the inside. "I've given it a lot of thought, and I still haven't any idea. Except you used the right word: soothe. It's exactly that. I don't know that I needed soothing. I needed something I cared about more than taxes, maybe. But it wasn't like my life was horrible. Just not fulfilling. I only started baking to help Bernie. But it seemed to . . . I don't know, settle my mind, center me. Working with my hands, understanding the basic chemistry of cooking, and then applying imagination to that . . ." She shook her head, but the dreamy look was there again, and when she turned that smile on him, it was incandescent. "You'd think a tax lawyer wouldn't have a creative side." Her smile widened. "But, apparently, I do. And it has been an endlessly satisfying and gratifying experience, giving myself a chance to explore it."

It was at that precise moment, the very look on her

face, in her eyes, made an ache bloom inside his chest. For the first time in his adult life he let himself want something other than business success. He let himself want the one thing he'd very, very carefully made sure he'd never allowed himself to consider. He understood that the whole world did not operate the way his family had. Even in his own family, despite the passionate squabbling, he'd seen a lot of loving relationships. He just hadn't been part of one personally.

What he knew about love had a lot more to do with ducking punches and being constantly belittled for looking different, being different. He'd ducked, he'd hidden, he'd done whatever he could to avoid the kind of "love" his father had for him. His own grandmother had tried to protect him, but his father was her only child, and she doted on the drunken bastard. She'd done what she could for Griffin as her son's only son, scuttling him into her kitchen at the restaurant as often as she could, shielding him as best she could. But at the end of the night, she sent him home to sleep under the same roof as his father. There were only so many ways to disappear in a two-bedroom flat.

When Griffin had gotten older, he'd fought back. Against his father, against his cousins, against his schoolmates. Against everyone who belittled or made fun of him. Everyone except Grandmama. She'd at least tried to help him. She loved him, in her own way. It was as close to an honest love as he knew. But she also loved the violent bastard who had been his father. She hadn't wanted to involve anyone in what she viewed as a private family matter. She loved Griffin, but she hadn't made the torment stop. When he was finally old enough to make it on his own, at age sixteen, he'd left. He'd decided then perhaps love was an emotion best avoided altogether. At least where he was concerned.

He didn't doubt its existence. He'd even entered into

relationships, seeking companionship, if not much more. But he hadn't truly made himself available in any of them. He understood the self-fulfilling prophecy there. He hadn't been motivated or willing to reach beyond his past, beyond his choices, and change the pattern. He knew he was afraid of trying . . . and failing. He didn't want to know that about himself. So Thomas Griffin Gallagher had focused on the things he knew he could do.

The ache tightened further inside his chest as he watched Melody begin to work on her cake. His thoughts were inextricably twined, past and present. What he wanted, standing in front of him . . . and what he'd left behind. A year ago, he'd gotten life-altering news. About the diary. About his real heritage. All the pain, the hurt . . . and the rage, that he'd felt were so far behind him had come roaring back. All those years, his grandmother had listened to the mocking and the sneers. From inside the family and out. From his own father, who hadn't even been her natural-born son, but whom she'd loved, perhaps to an unhealthy degree for the fear of losing him.

They'd all taunted him mercilessly, about how he looked so different from the rest. And how ridiculous he was with all his fancy ideas of what they could make of themselves if they'd only listen to him. They'd thought he had no pride in his family, that his ideas were meant to denigrate their achievements. But they couldn't have been more wrong.

His grandmother had watched it all, and never told him. Never saved him by giving him the one thing he needed: a real family who understood and loved him for who he truly was.

Griffin had her diary, knew she'd been unable to conceive, and that having a child had been the cornerstone of her every desire. When she'd heard about the babe being given up, she and his grandfather had stepped forward, then fled back to Ireland, due to her irrational fear the Havershams would take the baby back. She'd never told a soul, claiming the baby as her natural-born son, for fear he'd be shunned by the family if they knew. Griffin's father had enough of the Gallagher look about him to get by, and no one had ever learned who his parents had truly been. But apparently Griffin had the look of Trudy's family, fairer of hair and lighter of eye. He'd borne the brunt of being the outcast, not only because of his different looks but because of his different demeanor and way of thinking. If he had only known . . . it would have explained so much. Saved him from so much.

But what was done was done. Whatever his last name was, or what blood coursed through his veins . . . didn't matter. He knew who he was and what he wanted. If Lionel Hamilton could get him one step closer to fulfilling his dreams, then he'd take that as the first stroke of honest-to-God luck he'd ever had, and build on it. It was the kind of foundation he understood. He knew how to grow that, nurture it.

Looking at Melody Duncastle he was filled with . . . want. Want of all those things he'd shut himself off from. Want of things that scared the ever-loving hell out of him. He looked at her, and he wanted what those dreamy, content, confident eyes could bring to his life. He wanted her to look at him and feel all those same things. He wanted her to look at him . . . and glow.

Bloody Christ, I never should have come in here this morning.

"I'm a very lucky woman," she said, as she continued the task at hand, bending down to begin a cluster of amazingly intricate roses. "To have literally stumbled into something that has been such a good fit for me. I do know that."

A lucky woman, he thought. No. Of the two of them, he

was the lucky one. To have met her, been beguiled by her, compelled to open up to her. In the span of a single day, she'd turned his head completely around, and his thoughts to things he'd never contemplated before. If that had been the first day, what would a lifetime of days with her be like?

Not that he'd ever know. He was no prize, that was for certain. She might have had the luck of the Irish in finding her true life's calling. But she'd never consider him a lucky catch.

What did he have to offer? Money? Yes, he had a pile of it, but she'd likely made plenty of that on her own as a lawyer. She'd walked away from that success to live over a shop where she put in far more hours than at any law firm, and all to live in a town that didn't even boast a single traffic light. Clearly, the one thing he had was the last thing that would impress her.

There was chemistry. Explosive levels of it. That, and not his fortune, could possibly get him laid—if he was very lucky—but nothing more.

"So, no . . . I don't want the big dream," she went on, turning the cake around, and starting another cluster at the top corner, oblivious to the blade she was sinking, so smoothly, deep into his chest. "I don't want to take my business global. I don't want"—she looked up from what she was doing, to him—"I'm sorry. I'm not meaning this as an insult, you understand that now, don't you? But I don't want what you're selling. I imagine most of the folks here will. But not me."

"So, what will you do?" he asked, trying not to care, to start building a wall of indifference, right then and there. She was no longer a thorn in his side. That's the only way he should be looking at her. She might be leaving Hamilton altogether from the sounds of things. He wouldn't have to risk bumping into the one thing he wanted that he couldn't have. He could focus, instead, on what he should be doing, which was launching the project. It was all good news.

So why did he feel as if the best thing that had ever happened to him was slipping through his fingers before he even had the chance to figure out how to hold on to it?

"I honestly don't know," she said. "It's a lot to think about. What about you?"

"Me?"

"You left Dublin to come here and take this challenge on. I know there is a lot of personal meaning in this for you, but, ultimately, is it just another job for you? I mean, are you uprooting your whole life in Ireland to come stake out a permanent home here? What about the business you left behind?"

"Who says I left it behind?"

"So you're . . . just temporarily here then?"

"I didn't say that. But with global marketing and technology, I don't have to be physically in Dublin to continue forward. In fact, I was rarely there."

"So you have jobs going on right now that you're overseeing?"

"I play a very specific role in setting up these kinds of paths for people to take."

"But you don't necessarily stay and watch them grow to fruition."

"That's not my job."

He watched her face, saw the edges of disappointment, and felt whatever wall he'd been building crumble to dust. He couldn't afford to allow hope to elbow its way in. She was pointing out the very reason why, even if he lost every bit of rational sense he'd ever had and decided to pursue her, it wouldn't have mattered anyway.

He didn't stay. It wasn't in his job description.

"What I do is see the path for others; I establish the

best way to get them there, set them up for success. Then I step back and let them walk that path to their own future." He lifted a shoulder. "I leave and go on to do it again for someone else."

"But this isn't a job you're doing for someone else. This time . . . I mean, isn't this going to be yours? Isn't the success of Hamilton Industries a personal success for you? One that doesn't end with the planning stages?"

"If you're asking me if I plan to stay here and run Lionel's empire, the answer is no. That was never the plan."

Her mouth dropped open, then snapped shut—pretty much describing what it felt like his heart had done in that same moment. Was it possible? Beyond all reason, she was acting like someone who was thinking the same kinds of things he was, about possibilities and taking chances. Why else would she be looking so disappointed in hearing that it couldn't possibly happen, even if she wanted it to?

Why in hell did that make him feel so bloody fantastic? It was anything but. They were lost to each other before they could even decide to begin.

It made no sense. She couldn't possibly truly want him. Griffin. More likely, she merely wanted to fan the sparks of the electricity crackling between them. He was merely mistaking that for the possibility of her wanting something more.

Maybe desire was all he was feeling, too. Perhaps they needed to give in to the heat. Take what was really being offered. It was the best way, maybe the only way, to distinguish what *was* from what *could never be*.

"So . . . you're not staying in Hamilton long term?"

He shook his head.

"Then . . . what is Lionel—I mean, who's going to run the company after—"

"The company—controlling interest in it, anyway—will go to me." He had less than no business telling her that. But what the hell. Nothing about that day or that night with her was following any predetermined path. So he chucked the path. It was all new territory, and he was following his gut—into the unknown.

What the hell was he thinking?

He suspected he knew what he was thinking *with*.

It brought him back to his earlier solution, a plan that would wind up with both of them naked. Afterward, he'd bet his future empire on the fact that it would all become perfectly clear to them both—it was about heat. Not about heart.

He had a hunger that he was damned well determined to feed. To hell with the rest. The rest would sort itself out.

It always did.

To that end, he started lugging the remaining cartons containing the quick-pour fondant back to the coolers and sealed the rolled fondant in their tubs.

"What are you doing?"

"Do those finished cupcakes need to get stored in something to stay fresh until morning?"

"Do—what? Yes, but—why are you putting those back?"

"Go ahead and put them where they need to be."

"I have to finish this cake."

"Is that one for delivery to someone tomorrow?"

"No, it's just for the front of—would you stop that?" She watched in disbelief as he rolled another cart to the cooler.

He paused long enough to look at her. For once, he let the walls drop completely away, let her see everything he was feeling, everything he was needing. "No," was all he said.

"Griffin—"

"We're going to stop playing baker for the time being."

"What are you talking about?"

He slid the last carton in the cooler, then strode across

the room, absolutely intent, knowing without a single doubt, exactly what he was going to do. His path, at least for the next few hours, was very, very clearly defined.

"The cakes can wait," he told her. Then he yanked her into his arms and slid the pins from her hair. "This, on the other hand, canno'."

He crushed his mouth to hers, and it only took the breadth of a single heartbeat for her to respond. She grabbed him right back . . . and took him on fully, willingly, and completely.

One of them growled. She didn't know which end was up, or down, and in that moment, didn't much care.

Far too many things had happened that day. The very last thing she needed to do was complicate an already seriously complicated situation by having anything more to do with him. Certainly that particular kind of anything.

Yet, it was the only thing she felt certain of. She wanted him. She might not be able to keep him, but with everything else she held dear up in the air . . . what she knew was that she wanted Griffin Gallagher. At that moment there wasn't anything she could do about her shop, her future, or the choices that were to be made.

But there was most definitely something she could do about Griffin Gallagher. And, more to the point, *with* Griffin Gallagher.

He wasn't the enemy any longer. He wasn't her savior,

either. She knew that. He was merely the harbinger of change. None of that mattered.

Melody couldn't have described in any accurate detail how it was they managed to store cupcakes and cakes and get up the back stairs to her place over the shop.

She fully acknowledged the pure insanity of the moment. And simply didn't care. Her whole life was on the brink of massive change. Again. Even if she decided to do nothing, her world was going to change. She had absolutely no idea what she was going to do, what she wanted to do.

And there was Griffin. The man who was both refined class and raw energy, who was presently all but carrying her up the stairs over his shoulder, caveman style.

She stopped thinking about tomorrow, and all the tomorrows after that, and grinned when he slid her down the front of his body in front of the door leading to her personal rooms. "I'll warn you," she said a bit breathlessly, "I keep my kitchens and store immaculate, but my personal space, not so much."

He was kissing the side of her neck, nibbling her earlobe, making her gasp. "I'm no' findin' the least bit of anything wrong with your personal space," he murmured as he continued his delicious journey along the sensitive skin beneath her ear, trailing kisses and nips down the side of her neck, pushing the heavy, starched collar of her chef's coat off her shoulders so he could continue his quest.

Melody fumbled with the door handle behind her. She always locked the door at the bottom of the stairs, so this one was usually left open. The door swung in rather abruptly beneath their weight, and the two of them stumbled inside.

Normally she'd have been a bit mortified for someone she was interested in to see her place in its current condition. But Griffin wasn't someone she would be seeing again, so what did it matter?

He certainly didn't seem to be noticing. "Bedroom?"

She grunted and nodded her head in the general direction, as he stripped off the light blue, long-sleeved Henley she wore under her white jacket. She was trying to do much the same with his pale green button-down shirt.

"Small space," he managed, as they tripped past the orange suede ottoman that sat in front of her stuffed, chenille-covered chair, then banged shins and calves on the small, wrought-iron base of her glass-top coffee table. They managed to squeeze by the couch without further damage, leaving clothing behind on the lush, floral-print arm at one end.

"I'm not up here much. I don't need much room," she panted.

Griffin lifted his head long enough to shoot her the most wicked grin. "Oh, but I do, luv." Then he pushed her backward through her bedroom door, and all the way to her brass four-poster.

"Stepping stool," she cautioned. The antique bed frame held her deep pillow-top mattress high up off the floor.

"Right," he said, then merely tossed her gently into the middle of it as if she was lighter than a feather.

She let out a surprised laugh, which ended on a indrawn breath of anticipation as Griffin stepped onto the stool, and loomed over her.

"You're a beautiful, beautiful woman, Melody Duncastle," he said, simply standing there, taking in his fill of her.

Rather than make her feel uncomfortable or self-conscious, his words had her all but quivering with the need for him to get off the damn stool and put his hands on her.

She was wearing nothing more than a bra, hot pink

drawstring surgical pants, which were her preference when putting in long hours in the kitchen, and whatever panties she'd pulled out of the drawer in the dark that morning. She didn't even bother to look down to find out. She didn't care.

He raked his gaze over her like a man starved for days who'd just been shown the buffet table. She was hoping he viewed it as an all-you-can-eat arrangement—she was feeling rather carnivorous herself.

"Are you going to stand there, or—"

"Or," he said quite definitively. Rather than jump her, which she'd have been quite happy with—and expected, given their rather animalistic approach to things so far— he knelt down on the edge of the bed, and gently, slowly, tugged her loose pink pants down her legs, pushing her knees up so he could slide her pants and ankle socks off completely. He tossed those over his shoulder, the twinkling glint in his clear eyes making her shiver, though she didn't feel the slightest bit of a chill. Quite the opposite. She felt like she was burning up from the inside out.

"Your turn," she said, her voice quavering with need.

He shook his head, and lifted her foot up so it rested on his shoulder. His dress shirt hung open, and the white T-shirt he wore underneath clung to a frame that belied his career as a businessman and looked far more like that of the street tough she'd earlier imagined him to be. Had it only been that morning?

Her mouth watered, imagining what the smooth, taut muscles of his chest and shoulders would feel like—taste like—once she got him naked.

But he had other ideas. He turned his head just enough to kiss the sensitive skin of her ankle. Then he gently bit her instep before moving his mouth back along her ankle and up over her calf. She was shuddering in pleasure, quivering with each, individual, hot kiss, her hips already quaking.

Her skin felt like a mass of live wire endings, feeling his every touch like a tingling series of shock waves, every one of which pulsated straight to her core. As he worked his way closer to the inside of her knee, he shifted his weight more onto the bed, sliding her other calf over his thigh, as he continued to kneel between her legs.

His gaze found hers as he began to slowly lick and kiss his way up the soft skin of her inner thigh. Her hands were splayed beside her head, her nipples two exquisitely sensitized nubs rubbing at the fabric of her bra as he made her back arch again and again with his devilish assault.

He pushed her back up the bed, so he could stretch more fully between her thighs. He slid one hand up over her stomach, cupping one breast, catching and rolling the nipple between two of his fingers.

"Griffin," she gasped, and would have arched violently against him, but the weight of his arm, and his shoulder pinning down her other thigh, kept her body right where he wanted it as he toyed with the elastic band of her panties.

"Are you ready for me, Melody?" he murmured against her thigh, not so much as taking a breath away from his steady decimation of her entire defense system.

"Do you . . . have . . . ?" She'd had some thought in her head about protection, but that concern slipped away like mist, replaced only with thoughts of how the tip of his tongue, sliding along under the edge of her panties, was so close . . . and yet, so damn far away from—"Oh!" she gasped, then another, longer, almost groaning "oh" followed as his tongue slowly, torturously, found its mark.

She didn't arch hard, but rolled her hips up to meet him, groaning deep inside her throat as the waves of pleasure washed over and through her, each one building to a higher and higher crescendo. He grunted his own encouragement, and continued making her move, dip, and sway beneath his oh-so-clever tongue. Then making her gasp and arch when he slid a finger into her, bearing her down onto the bed with the force of his flicking tongue, while he pushed.

She climbed up that last peak in a full rush, going straight over the edge, her body pulsing, almost convulsing under him. It didn't stop. And he didn't stop.

"Griffin, I can't—you have to—"

"Shh," he whispered, and his soft breath alone shot her straight up all over again. "Aye," he said, between kisses "but ye can."

He proved he was right. More than once.

Only when she was too limp to move, too satiated to do more than whimper when he finally slipped his finger out and moved his tongue away, did he slide off her panties, then move back off the bed himself.

She managed to roll her head to one side and watch him drop his own clothes to the floor. He was . . . magnificent. Modern-day gladiator was the description that came to mind. But then, she'd known he wouldn't be anything but magnificent. Not that it would have mattered at that point, but looking at him roused her again, when she thought she'd be spent for hours, if not days.

"Do ye have any"—he glanced at the nightstand.

"Mmm," she nodded, managing to make a vague motion with her hand, then watched with pure, unadulterated pleasure as he found a condom and rolled it on. She'd never thought the act a particularly sexy thing, but she'd had a very sudden change of heart.

When he climbed onto the bed, and over her, the look in his eyes made her feel purely female and utterly desirable. Her body was still humming with the delightful aftershocks of the very thorough attention he'd given to her.

As he moved over her, pulling one leg up and around him as he did, she arched to meet him, swamped with need all over again, before he'd so much as brushed against her.

"You are ready indeed for me," he said, grinning as he pushed against her, even as he slid his hands over hers, weaving their fingers together, and pinning her most deliciously against the bed.

"So what are you waiting for?" she taunted, her breath coming in short pants of anticipation, her hips quaking a little under him.

"What, indeed?" he said. Without needing so much as a guiding hand, he found her easily and slid into her fully with one, smooth stroke.

She moaned, he growled in appreciation, and they immediately began to move. It wasn't going to be some slow, carnal climb to mutual satisfaction. They'd exhausted any ability they had to do anything slowly with his intent, protracted seduction of her. She'd been compliant then, willing to let him set the pace, let him take his time. But she had little patience left. Even with the pulse-pounding ride he'd taken her on, he'd left her still quivering, still wanting. He was on top of her, inside her . . . and she was done following his lead.

As she'd anticipated from the first time he'd put his hands on her, their mating was raw, bordering on ferocious. As soon as she slid her hands from beneath his and took his face to yank his mouth to hers, he roared fully into her, losing any semblance of control.

Theirs was a needy, pounding mating. She gasped, he groaned, she screamed . . . and he came. It was glorious and intense and completely outside any realm of intimacy in which she'd ever indulged. In fact, no one had ever made her come alive like that. Certainly, no one had claimed her, ever.

But that was exactly how she felt, when he let himself rest his weight on top of her as he tried to find his breath. He started to move away moments later, but she slid her heels higher up his thighs and her arms around his neck. "I like this," she whispered.

"Mmm," was all he managed, but he stayed there a moment longer.

Would he simply roll off her now, she wondered? Get up, tell her it had been nice, and head out the door? Did he expect they'd do this again? How long would he be staying in town? Did she dare take up with him, knowing that one or both of them would be leaving Hamilton for good? Him for certain, which was all that mattered. She had no idea when he was planning on heading back to Ireland, but she knew enough to realize that she wasn't cut out for playing games.

He kissed the side of her neck, her cheek, the bridge of her nose, and then gently, her lips, before he moved off her.

She was surprised by the gentleness, and by her accompanying prick of tears. She squeezed her eyes shut briefly, willing them away, so she could be all casual and unconcerned when he made his excuses. Instead he surprised her further by rolling her to his side and tucking her body up against his. She glanced at him, but his eyes were closed. He was toying with the hair on the back of her neck, urging her cheek down on his chest.

She fit naturally—too naturally—against him. It felt good. *Okay, better than good, it felt bloody fantastic*, she thought, smiling privately. She didn't move away, or roll to the side of the bed and initiate his leaving. Although that would certainly have been the wisest thing to do. She'd worry later about the wisdom of drawing out the moment. She thought about the unexpected gentleness in him and snuggled closer, the motion purely instinctive.

For now, he was there, and he was hers.

W ell, that had been . . . something, hadn't it then?
He should be pulling on his trousers, making his
excuses. And getting right the bloody hell out of there.

Instead he was tugging her closer, molding her against
him, feeling his heart still racing beneath her soft cheek.
He couldn't seem to keep his fingers out of her hair, nor
could he stop wanting to tip her head back, lean down,
and kiss her some more.

Like a starving man, he was. A man whose appetite
had been well and surely slaked . . . though his body was
done for, the rest of him wanted what it wanted, which
was Melody Duncastle, plastered to his sweaty, happy
side. And what was the "rest of him" he referred to?
There was only one part he should be—could be—concerning himself with. And that part was temporarily out
of commission.

He stroked her hair, closed his eyes, and tried like hell
not to think about those other parts. He should be grinning like a loon, happy to have had a hearty round of it.
That was what he'd thought he wanted, was it not? Just
put out the fire, so the only thing left afterward were ashes.

Only that's no' how it felt.

He wanted her again. And very likely again after that. His body might not be up to the task, but that didn't slake the desire. The pure sexual craving.

Even as he thought it, he knew his feelings went far, far beyond that. He didn't only want to have her, watching her slowly come apart under his tongue, sinking into her, driving into her, rushing up and over her like a roaring train, and taking her with him. He wanted all of that, aye, indeed he did.

But he wanted far, far more. He wanted to know her. To know what made her laugh. To know what made her cry. To glory in the bliss she found in her work, and bask in that glow. She had the heart of an artist, which she was still discovering, and an intellectual's mind. She appealed to his earthy side, as well as to the part that yearned to share his professional successes with someone who could grasp the complexity of what he did. He had to be creative, too, only in an entirely different way. One he suspected she'd understand and appreciate.

He'd never once felt compelled to tell anyone about his past, nor to discuss what he did. He was generally too busy to think about the former, or to talk about the latter. He'd known her such a very, very short time . . . but there was something to her that had his full and complete attention. He'd no business wasting an evening, much less a whole night, with all the work he had in front of him. Yet, he wouldn't change the events of that day and night for the world.

That he'd put pleasure before work—hell, anything before work—was a miracle of noteworthy proportions.

One day. How could anyone feel so changed by a person they'd known for a single day? Her impact on him had been instant. It made no rational sense whatsoever, but there he was. And there she was. And he'd give almost anything not to have to leave.

Her. Hamilton. He resented anything that would deprive him of the time it would take to find out if their instant combustion could sustain itself. He'd never before cared enough to find out. In business he was always on the hunt, always the pursuer. But when it came to relationships, it had always been the other way around.

It occurred to him then the only other time he'd felt so certain of something was when he found a new project that would benefit from his attention. One he knew would be profitable for him and a remarkable new start for the people he wanted to help. He rarely, if ever, second-guessed his gut instinct on those occasions . . . and he was rarely, if ever, wrong.

Perhaps his certainty now wasn't such an odd, inexplicable thing after all. Maybe his gut just knew.

The problem was . . . what in the bloody hell could he do about it?

"You know, if you wind my hair any tighter around your finger, I'll have a perm," she said on a soft laugh, startling him from his thoughts.

She hadn't moved from where he'd cradled her, and she was presently tracing aimless patterns on his abdomen with her fingertips. It felt good.

He smiled as he untangled the lock of hair from his finger. "Sorry. What's a perm?"

She lifted her head then, and if he'd thought her eyes were deep blue pools he could drown in before, they were downright bottomless now. Suddenly drowning didn't seem like such a bad way to go.

"Seriously? Don't Irish women get their hair curled?"

"I wouldn't know, never really paid attention. If you mean those rollers they put in—"

She laughed. "Close enough."

He massaged her scalp a little, liking the feel of her hair sliding over his hands. "I didn't mean to tug it out."

"It felt good, actually, until right at the end." She

shifted a little, rolled into him so she could prop her chin and hands on his chest. "Why did you stay?"

"Stay . . . you mean now?" His heart sank, and it shouldn't have. Of course she wanted him out of there. She still had work to do, and he wouldn't be the least surprised if she headed straight back down the stairs to do it.

"No," she said, smiling up at him. She slipped her hand up and tracked her fingers over his cheek, along his jaw. "I like you right where you are."

Hearing that shouldn't have been the heady rush that it was. "I'm growing rather partial to the spot myself. So . . . what did you mean, then?"

"Tonight. In the kitchen with me. I know you said you wanted to talk to me, explain the situation, but you could have just laid it all out there in five, ten minutes. You certainly didn't have to put in the work you did."

"I believe you told me I had to work if I was to talk."

She grinned. "You bought that?"

He smiled, too, and tousled her hair. "I'll remember that for next time."

"So will I," she said dryly, then looked away.

"Hey," he said, when a few moments passed and she didn't look back at him. "I wanted to stay. It stopped being about talking up the project pretty much as soon as you let me in. In fact, if you want to know a secret, I'm no' too certain I ever much cared what we discussed. I just wanted to see you again."

She looked up again, clearly surprised. "Why?"

"Oh, I told myself it was the project, but once I was here, I knew it was more than that. You intrigued me, Melody. I wanted to know more." He tipped his chin up and kissed her forehead, effectively ending the line of questioning and, he hoped, his apparent inability to keep his trap shut. "Do you need to get the rest done tonight? Do you need more help?"

"No, that's not it. I can make do. Would you have stayed and helped if I did?"

If it would keep me around you awhile longer, I'd build kingdoms for you, he wanted to say. But, mercifully, he seemed to have at least some control over blurting out each and every one of his thoughts. "What, wasn't I doing a good enough job?" he teased. "By the last couple cupcakes, I wasn't even licking my fingers any longer."

She looked up more sharply at him, then knuckled him gently in the ribs. "Very funny. You Irishmen have a dry wit."

"And most of us a wet whistle. I'm sure there's some connection there somewhere."

"So, you enjoy a good ale, then?"

He shook his head. "Never touch the stuff."

"Really?" she asked.

He chuckled a bit dryly. "We're not all a bunch of loud, limerick-reciting sots, you know."

"I didn't mean that," she said.

He could see by the honest surprise on her face that she was telling the truth.

"It was simply because, growing up in a restaurant and pub, it would make sense if you had a—"

"Acquired a taste for a few nips now and again?" He shook his head, and tried to keep his tone smooth. She was poking in places she didn't know were tender. More than that, it annoyed him to no end to realize just how tender they still were. "Quite the opposite in my case. I don't touch any of the stuff."

She gave him a steadier look, and he realized she wasn't just talking off the top of her head. "I was going to say 'acquired a distinguished palate' but, either way, it's still a surprise to hear you don't drink at all. Not to be obvious, but is it because you saw too many folks who couldn't stop at those few nips?"

"Something like that." He felt even more the fool for letting her innocent questions make him feel so defensive. It had been a long while since he'd cared what anyone thought of him, or the family situation he'd come from. He would never have volunteered the information, but it was important to him that she knew who he was, though he couldn't have said why, since their time together would be limited. "My father, mostly."

She laid her hand over his heart, her expression instantly compassionate. "That's rough. I'm sorry. I can't pretend to know anything about it, but I'm sure I'm grossly understating when I say that couldn't have been a good situation for a child."

He could have pointed out any number of scars, some small, some more noticeable, like the ones through his eyebrow and along his hairline, that were part of what hadn't been a good situation. She wasn't pitying him, merely feeling bad that he'd had such a difficult time. There was a distinct difference. "No," he said. "It wasn't. I left when I was sixteen. My father died a few years after."

"You didn't go back?"

"No." He tipped her chin up, cupped her cheek, and smiled. It came easily, surprising him. "I didn't do too badly from that point on."

"They say what doesn't kill you makes you stronger, but I suspect a situation like yours might have gone the other way. It doesn't seem fair, for any kid to have to deal with that."

"I spent my fair share of time thinking about that, but it wasn't going to help matters."

"Your grandmother, the one whose restaurant you worked in, didn't she?"—Melody lifted her hand—"No, that's none of my business. I'll just say I'm glad you escaped, and that your path changed afterward. I'm guessing it didn't happen right away, though. How did you get from there to doing what you do now?"

"One thing about the Gallagher clan is we have a lot of cousins."

She laughed. "On both sides of the pond, yes. So, did another branch of the family take you in?"

"Not exactly, but they did help me find work." He'd never told his cousins in Dublin why he'd left Cork. Nor did he ask for help until he was old enough for them not to question his being on his own. The various branches of the family were close enough that they probably weren't all that surprised. "My Dublin cousins also had a restaurant. As did several other branches of my family. For a long time, I'd been trying to get my grandmother to see that if she could talk the other family restaurants into joining forces, they could all improve their individual places."

"You realized that? You were just a kid."

He lifted a shoulder. "I watched too much television in the pub growing up, maybe. A lot of news programs along with all the sports. Commerce intrigued me. Rebuilding, reimagining things to make them successful made sense to me. I don't know why I think like that, but I always have."

"They say inventors are born, not made. Maybe you're the same way."

"Maybe. But my grandmother and other family members wouldn't listen to me." It had been far more than merely tuning him out. They'd taunted him about his faery world ideas. His odd appearance, with his light eyes and hair, had engendered any number of faery jokes. He'd simply thought them idiots for not even giving his scheme a shot. "My cousins in Dublin weren't much more open to the idea."

"Really? I was thinking that was your first success story."

"I think of it as my biggest failure, actually. But you can't change what people don't want fixed."

"I asked before, but do you think maybe they feel as I do?"

"In some ways, yes. In most ways, they're simply too stubborn to hear they might not be doing something the best way possible."

"That trait runs in your family tree." She laughed. "I'm shocked."

He did have the good grace to smile, and, for the first time, soften his view regarding his family's choices . . . at least a little. "It was while working for my Dublin cousins that I made a few suggestions to another shopkeeper. He thought they sounded like a good idea and put them to use. I didn't make any money on that deal, but it gave me the confidence to flesh out my ideas. I started taking university courses while working, and that shopkeeper passed my name along, which led to a few small consulting jobs. And"—he shrugged—"it's hard to explain, but it became a business. Lots of stops and starts and going off in far too many wild directions, but that's what it took to figure out what would work. I was young, so it didn't matter if it wasn't good right from the start. I had the restaurant in Dublin as backup, always had a little cash in my pocket, and, eventually . . . well—"

"You had full pockets," she finished on a smile.

"Actually, for a very long time, I didn't. I put everything I made back into the business. Sent the rest to my grandmother."

"Was she doing okay?"

"She was fine. She had family to take care of her. But it was on me to do that, and I left."

"But—"

"I didn't say I regretted leaving. But it was still my place, my responsibility. I sent money, every month, until she passed."

"That was good of you."

"I wish I could say I did it for good, but it was part family responsibility, and part me wanting to show all my cousins back home what I'd made of myself. Not the most charitable of motives."

"I think you wouldn't be judged too harshly for that."

In point of fact, he simply didn't think about it. Not anymore.

"Have you ever gone back?"

"For her funeral," he said. "To finalize her property."

"Didn't the restaurant go to you?"

"No, it rightfully went to my uncle, who'd worked for her for years, and had taken over most of the day-to-day as she'd grown more infirm. It was his family's source of income, and they all worked there, too. It was the right thing. But she had personal things, and those I took care of."

One of those personal things had been her diary. He hadn't read it at the time, not caring to dredge up history that was already well and truly behind him. He wondered what he'd have done with the knowledge that he was half American by blood, if he'd known back then. He would have looked up the Havershams to be certain, and possibly traced their last living heir, the long deceased Trudy, to Lionel himself. But that was neither here nor there, now. Funny, but talking to Melody about it should have made it feel more immediate all over again. Instead, he felt more settled with his history than he ever had before.

"Do you keep in touch with them? Your uncle and his family?"

He shook his head. "I went back last year, after I heard from Trevor and Sean."

"About Trudy's diary."

He nodded.

"I can't even imagine what it would be like, to find out my family history isn't what I thought it was." Then her mouth formed a little *O* and she looked up at him again. "For you that had to be doubly brutal, coming from . . . a difficult past. Had you known . . . Do you resent not knowing? That your grandmother never told you?"

"She would never have betrayed the maternal bond with my father, not even for me. Protecting him was far too deeply ingrained by then. Besides, we were Gallaghers. And Gallaghers stuck together. To be fair, I'm sure she thought she was doing the right thing, keeping me in the fold, as it were."

"So, no one else knew?"

"Her husband, of course, but he died long before I came along. Everyone else thought my father was her natural-born son."

"But they all know now?"

He nodded.

"Do you feel . . . I don't know . . . vindicated in some way?"

"I thought I would. It did explain a lot. About why I look so different from all my cousins, and possibly even why my instincts follow industry rather than the traditional Gallagher love of cooking. Trudy's family were industrialists, too, like Lionel's. It's how they met and why they married."

"I know. It was a great love affair, not just a business merger. The stuff of legends in these parts."

"I know that, too. They were lucky."

She tilted her head, studied him with a half smile on lips he was suddenly dying to taste again.

"What?"

"You don't strike me as the sentimental type."

"I'm not. But I know what a bad union is like. If they could combine their family fortunes with a strong personal union, then more power to them."

"So, what did everyone think about your heritage when the truth came out?"

"I didn't ask, so I don't know." He didn't really care, either. "What I do know is that you are way too far away." He pulled her up on top of him. "Enough about me. I want to know all about you. Starting with this." He wove his hands through her hair, and drew her mouth down to his, effectively ending her line of questioning . . . for the rest of the night.

10

Melody wasn't sure who had been more surprised when Griffin was still there for breakfast that next morning and that he'd offered to make it himself. Best omelet and toast she'd ever had. More surprising was she'd enjoyed his presence, crowding her in the small galley kitchen, and delaying her second cup of coffee with an impromptu shower break. Both of them had had a very full day ahead of them . . . and yet, they'd lingered over that second cup.

She'd told him she'd brazen out his leaving the shop in broad daylight . . . well before Cups & Cakes opened for regular business. But he'd parked himself in her shop kitchen and worked from his BlackBerry while she finished the cake she'd left undone the night before, and got everything organized for the senior center birthday extravaganza. He'd left, all business-suit perfect, from the shop's front door—just another local businessman with a fresh cup of coffee to go—when she'd opened for business. Though Melody had found herself not caring so much if anyone realized he hadn't entered the store that morning . . . only exited it.

That had been six weeks ago.

And their one-night stand had extended to . . . she'd lost count.

Of course the whole town knew. There was a crispness to the air, and everywhere you looked, all the Christmas decorations were out in full force. That festive spirit seemed to amp up the pleasure everyone was taking in murmuring about their supposed romance. But Melody and Griffin kept up the open-for-business morning exit pretense nonetheless. The only difference was he carried his laptop so he could get more work done before the shop opened . . . and there was a second toothbrush in the china cup in her bathroom.

She liked that. She liked that a lot.

Too much, really.

It wasn't about the sex, although she was pretty sure there was a stupid, silly grin on her face at all times. Even that wasn't about the sex, either, if she were being honest.

The man spent all day in back-to-back meetings, had handled the town meeting with charming aplomb. At least, so she'd heard. Just to keep the chatter down, she hadn't attended. She already knew everything that was going to be said. No matter how long the day, he always made his way over to her shop at the end of it, some nights later than others. Most often he worked on an empty kitchen worktable in the back room while she kept up with the demand for Christmas-themed cupcakes. Or "the wee cakes," as he called them. Occasionally he helped. Occasionally she didn't need to work late.

Then they went upstairs and cooked together in her tiny strip of a kitchen, laughed and talked over food and a bottle of wine, often into the wee hours, before he took her to bed. Some nights there was no sleep.

She liked that a lot, too.

He was a part of her life, a part of her routine. She used to love the quiet of her work kitchen after hours, working alone, sometimes with a soundtrack, often humming her own tunes. Now she didn't want to think about the time when she'd be humming alone, to herself. What had felt peaceful and quiet, she knew would feel lonely and sad. She would miss him. Terribly. More than she thought she could stand.

When the town wasn't buzzing about the behind-doors romance going on between her and Griffin, people were buzzing about the coming changes to Hamilton. Everyone was excited. Melody wanted to be.

Nothing had been started yet, but she'd seen all the plans, down to the detailed blueprints and marketing brochures being used to woo overseas investors and companies that would almost act like exchange students. You build your shop here, we'll build ours there, and cross promote.

Griffin hadn't given up trying to talk her into at least thinking about it. He knew, better than she'd ever thought anyone could, how much the hands-on work meant to her. He knew she didn't want to be a bakery mogul. She wanted to be a baker. But as time marched on, his sales pitches to her had strengthened, not weakened.

She usually diverted him into telling her all about his business in Dublin, the other jobs he was working on, about his home there, the people who worked for him. Just as he saw the passion she had for designing cakes, she saw the true passion he had, not only for the people he helped through his visionary approach to rebuilding and revamping corporate entities but also for the people who had joined his team, shared his dream. They still took on the smaller accounts, and oftentimes, he told her, he took on jobs that his people didn't even know about. Not charging for those, just helping out because he could.

He was charming, successful, funny, and he made her feel like the only woman on earth every time he walked through the door. All he had to do was look at her, and she felt more alive than she could ever have believed possible. Baking was the only thing that had ever come close. She knew she was meant to do that.

So . . . it stood to reason that if she was meant to be a pastry chef, she was also meant to love Thomas Griffin Gallagher.

"What in the hell have you gone and done?" she said, as she bent over the second tier of what was going to double as both the anniversary and Christmas office party cake for Jim Traybill's real estate firm. Twenty-five years he'd run his brokerage. All from the same location.

Same godawful puke-green and gold leaf sign on the front above the door, too, she thought. Still with the missing *a* from Jim's last name, which had flaked off so long ago she couldn't remember ever having seen it.

She smiled, thinking about that. It would all change when they did the "unification" of the town square shops. Everyone would get new signs, new awnings, and, in some cases, newly updated storefronts—which they wouldn't be responsible for. It was all part of the renewal grants Griffin had secured with his investors. She'd seen the drawings for the proposed changes, which the shopowners consulted on. No one she knew had asked to change a thing from the originals, which were pretty charming, she had to admit. There was no denying their little burg would look sweet, all spiffed up, bright and shiny new.

But she was going to miss that puke-green sign.

She kept her opinion and her malaise about the coming end of the town she'd grown up in to herself. No point in being a buzzkill. But Griffin knew, and he drew her out, let her . . . whine. She smiled a little at that. She was such a whiner. Griffin indulged her, charmed her out of it most times, and bullied her out the rest. By bullied, she meant seduced. She'd tried telling him that distracting her wasn't going to make her forget. He generally didn't listen. And she generally let him distract her.

She'd also get over it. She had to. Because she was going to stay.

She'd given it a lot of thought, and had decided there was no point in leaving. She had no real desire to adopt some other small town that wasn't her own, just to say she was baking cupcakes in a rural setting. She had absolutely no intention to stop baking. So that left . . . assimilation.

"Like the Borg," she muttered.

"Bjorn?" came a sexy, accented voice from the kitchen doorway.

"No. Cylon."

He frowned. She laughed.

"Americans," he said.

"Which you partly are."

"Aye. Must explain why I can't stop hanging around you."

She looked up at him, and everything inside her warmed. "Must be."

"That, right there," he said, and slid his briefcase and gym bag onto the nearest empty workstation, before crossing to her.

She'd already put down her tools and turned to him, so he could sweep her up against him and kiss her senseless.

She liked that, too.

"That's why I keep coming back," he said, when he finally lifted his head. His eyes were glittering, and she wanted to have him right there on the worktable. And had. Actually.

"Why?" she asked.

"Because when you see me, you get that same look in your eye."

"Same look as what?"

"As when you talk about your cakes."

She laughed, but could feel her cheeks heat up. "You like it that you excite me as much as a cupcake?"

"Aye," he said, folding her more tightly into his arms. "It's what I knew I wanted most, that first night here, in your kitchen."

"What are you talking about?" He teased her, endlessly, about pretty much everything and anything. But he'd never once said anything like that before.

"When you talked about your passion for baking, you looked . . . luminescent. It was the first time I'd ever let myself really want something else."

"Something . . . else?" She thought he was teasing her still, but though his eyes sparkled and his brogue grew thicker she'd never seen him so intent. So . . . serious?

"Something that had nothing to do with my business. Something . . . just for myself."

"What was it?"

"For you to look at me with that same passion."

She looked down, feeling overwhelmed and more than a little exposed. They'd talked, laughed, prodded, cajoled. But one thing they hadn't done was talk about their feelings . . . or their future. Because they couldn't have the latter, there was no point in discussing—exposing—the former.

Apparently that was going to change. And she wasn't sure she was ready. Because a talk about their feelings would lead to a talk about the end.

"Griffin," she said, lifting her chin. "I'm not—"

"Hey now," he said quietly, dipping in for a kiss. "I lost my sparkle. What did I say?"

"We don't . . . we don't talk like this."

He cupped her face. "Maybe we should."

A hot stab of fear pierced her heart. No. She simply wasn't going to. She felt like a child, thinking if she just closed her eyes, she could will time to go backward instead of forward, and she could stay where she was, in the perfect place, with this perfect man, forever.

"Melody."

But, of course, that wasn't going to happen. It hadn't worked when Bernie had been drifting in and out of consciousness her last few days, and it wasn't going to work now.

She lifted her gaze to his. "You're leaving, aren't you?"

His mouth tightened, just a little, at the corners. She already knew him well enough to know what that meant. The regret she saw in his eyes chipped at what little control she had left. She'd tried her hardest not to think about the day he would leave, but when she had, she'd tried to believe she'd somehow be strong. Insouciant, even. Able to celebrate her fortune in having had him in her life for the time they'd been together.

All true. But she hadn't envisioned curling into a sobbing mess while being confronted with the finality of it.

"Melody, I—"

"I guess I didn't think it would happen so soon. You're right, maybe we should have talked more about what was coming." Almost by silent agreement, they'd never discussed at what point he wouldn't be needed in Hamilton any longer. She just thought it would be a point far away. "We haven't even started with the first phase yet."

"It's no' that. I'd hoped to stay longer."

"Is something wrong? Back in Dublin?"

"Not wrong, just . . . complicated. All business matters, no worries, no' anything personal. But . . . I'm needed there."

"For how long?"

He simply looked at her, his eyes growing increasingly more miserable.

"You're not coming back?" She barely choked out the words. "But—" She cut herself off. But what? What had she expected? She'd known this. It was her own fault they hadn't prepared themselves better for it. She could have asked, could have made it a part of their ongoing discussion.

But she'd been too busy enjoying her little dreamworld. It had been enough harsh reality dealing with the fact that her town was going to morph into a miniature Disney World before her very eyes. She'd told herself she deserved to have some fun while she could.

Stupid, stupid plan.

"Melody," Griffin repeated, taking her face in his hands. "You'll recall I didn't come in here unhappy."

"You're much better than me at putting on your happy face. We both know that."

"It wasn't a put-on face. I was a man with a plan when I walked in here. It was your very happy face lighting up when I walked in that removed any doubt I might have had about my plan."

"Plan?"

"I don't want to leave you. That smile, the way you instantly light up for me, I don't want to get to the end of my day and not have that waiting. My days have always been planned around work, as were more of my nights than not. What brought me joy was success in business. Now, I get to experience that through the day, with the knowledge that when that day's work is done, I'll double that joy by coming home and sharing it with you."

He'd said "coming home," she noted in some distant part of her brain that wasn't buzzing loudly with panic. She tried desperately to quiet it so she could hear what he was saying to her. Had he realized what he'd said? Did he know the rush of pleasure that sentiment brought to her?

"I'm not sure how I ever thought my life was full. I decided, long ago, that relationships weren't something I was made for. I never wanted them." He pulled her closer. "But I believe I was made for you. And I want this. I want you."

"Griffin," she whispered, looking into eyes glowing with what he'd claimed he'd seen in her own. If she hadn't been so worried, so confused, and trying so hard to stave off the crushing avalanche of grief she knew was coming her way, she'd have felt the warmth of it all the way to her toes. "You're . . . leaving. I don't understand."

"Why do you think I've been trying to talk you into expanding your shop globally?"

"I don't want to run an empire. That's your job. I want to bake."

"I know. I'm hardheaded, and also so out-of-my-head besotted with you, that I clearly haven't been thinking straight. But I do listen. I do."

He'd said besotted—which was a lot like love. And exactly how she felt about him. Only she'd never told him. Because they didn't talk about that. Should she tell him now? Would it make a difference?

All she knew was that she felt better. Knowing. So she had to think he would, too.

"I know what you mean," she said, surprising him. "About not thinking clearly. I'm having a hard time, right now, thinking at all, because I can't even stand the idea of not seeing you. Ever. I'm . . ." She faltered, not because she was scared to say it, but because she was scared to feel it. But silence wasn't going to make the feelings go away. "Griffin, if anyone had told me, that morning when I found you behind the counter, that you'd consume my every waking thought, and every single one of my nights, I'd have called them crazy and offered them a cookie. But you're right. It took one day." She smiled. "Besotted. I rather like that word."

She hadn't realized how much fear he was feeling, too, until she saw the nerves twitch as he tried to smile, but failed to sustain it.

"What?" she asked. "Tell me."

"I was listening to you, Melody. All those nights that we talked. I've watched you work, often when you had no idea I was watching you." His smile grew then. "I'm not always glued to my BlackBerry, you know."

"Yes, you are," she said, and they both laughed.

"There are moments, here and there," he said, the lingering smile moving to a grin, and that light returning full force to his eyes. "I know this is what you're meant to do. I know the joy it brings you. I've watched you handle your books like the overly educated shopkeeper you are, but I know you aren't motivated by increasing your bottom line, or investing for future growth potential."

"If I was, I'd have already done that."

"I know. So I'm not asking you to think about going global with Cups & Cakes. I'm just going to ask you to consider relocating the one shop you have from this village . . . to a different one."

"What do you—"

"My village, Melody. I want you to come to Dublin. We'll find the perfect spot."

Her head was spinning . . . but not in panic. It was with . . . excitement. She had decided against leaving Hamilton because she'd had noplace else to go that mattered to her. But Griffin mattered. Wherever he was would matter to her, too. Could she adopt a whole village? "Would the Dubliners accept me?"

"I fell in love with you in a single day. I'm sure you'll work your magic on them, too. One cupcake at a time, if necessary."

"Sugar shock them into it, you mean," she said dryly. Her mind was still on the "I fell in love with you" part, and she basked in the heady glow of the words for a bit, even as her mind was already racing ahead, to all the possibilities. It was scary, and not a little exhilarating. The thing that made her mind up was that even though it was terrifying to contemplate uprooting not only herself but her entire livelihood, she had absolutely no doubts about being with Griffin.

"Wait. Can I do that?" she asked. "Open a shop in Ireland? Aren't there laws?"

"You can work for a period of time on a visa." He shifted back long enough to slide his hand in the pocket of his overcoat. "But you could stay forever, as my wife." He pulled out a small ring box.

She gasped. Okay, now she was truly hallucinating. She'd gone from dreamworld, to crazy town. In her wildest dreams . . .

"I'd thought to ask you come the new year. Time for new beginnings and all that. Or, if I couldn't wait, which I'm pretty sure would have been the case," he said, grinning when she smiled, "I'd have had Saint Nicholas pay us a short visit next week on Christmas. But the time came upon me sooner than I'd planned . . . and I don't want to go back without you."

"I don't want you to, either."

"Is that . . . does that mean . . . will you?"

It turned out he was quite adorable when he was flustered. She'd never once seen him lose his composure. Unless he was on top of her, making her come as he thundered through his own release. But that was different. His hopeful look claimed her heart just as fully as he'd claimed the rest of her. "It does," she said, her smile trembling as the full force of the moment came over her.

"You'll have time to know for certain," he said in a short rush. "We'll apply for the visa and you can take that time to find the right place, and find out if you can stand having me in your—"

So very adorably uncertain. "Griffin, I'm saying yes." She pulled his mouth to hers and kissed him. Fiercely. Possessively. And reveled in it. When they finally came up for air, she remembered . . . about the ring box. "Can I see it?"

"Oh! Oh, right. Of course. This is brilliant!" He all but jumped and did a fist pump. She might have joined him. "Here." He opened the box, working to get the hinge to spring free.

"When did you get—oh, Griffin, it's stunning. That setting."

"It was me mum's engagement ring. Passed on to me."

"You just . . . carry it around with you?" she asked, stumbling, saying anything that came into her head, until she could pinch herself and make herself believe this was really happening. She couldn't take her eyes off it. It wasn't big and ostentatious, which suited her just fine. "It's so charming, and so beautifully set." She finally lifted her gaze to his. "I'd be honored, but . . . are you sure, Griffin?"

"I had it sent to me three weeks ago."

"Three weeks—really?"

"Remember the night you had to do all the cupcakes over for the Brunelli shower because—"

"She found out it was a boy after not wanting to know, and announced it the day before the surprise shower, and her mother-in-law simply wouldn't hear of having gender-neutral colors. Even on the cupcakes. Oh, I remember." Melody smiled. "You stayed up half the night helping me. I was afraid you'd finally give up and walk away after that. I was not exactly a cheerful camper. But then, I'd had other plans for the night."

He wiggled his eyebrows. "I know. You came upstairs and I saw all the trouble you'd gone to—"

"Well, we'd missed all of Thanksgiving together with everything else we were obligated to do and I just wanted something that made me feel like I had . . ." She drifted off then. She hadn't told him her motivation behind cook-

ing him a turkey and some of the other traditional dishes
she'd always had growing up. She'd had to cater the civic
center event that day, and Griffin had used the empty offices at Hamilton to run daylong conference calls back
home so he could catch up on his work, uninterrupted.
She'd never really felt she lacked family on that holiday
as she'd usually been working the community affair and
enjoyed the festive event just as much as a family dinner.
Or so she'd told herself.

But she'd missed being with Griffin that day, and
watching the other families enjoy each other's company . . .
had made her wistful. So she'd picked the next time they
both had time free, which had been a few days later, and
decided to cook him a big meal. He didn't have to know it
was her Thanksgiving. But she did.

And then . . . the great cupcake do-over had happened.

"You wanted to create a moment, a memory, that made
you feel like part of something more than just yourself.
Or even a member of the community. You wanted us to
have that meal, together. And I wanted that, too. You have
no idea how badly."

She knew now, about his background. All of it. For
him to want anything that resembled a family gathering . . .
"Griffin, if I'd known, I'd have told Mrs. Brunelli to take
her gender-neutral colors and—"

"I sent for the ring the next day. I didn't know when I
was going to ask for your hand, Melody, but I knew then
it was just a matter of making sure you wanted it, too."

"We've never said . . ."

He grinned. "I took a chance."

She grinned. "It's about to pay off. Can I . . . ?" She
nodded toward the box in his hand.

"Let me." He slid the ring from the aging, crushed vel-
vet cushion, then set it aside to take her right hand.

"It might not—it fits," she said in wonder, as he slid it
on her ring finger.

"I might have borrowed one of your rings, just for a day."

She looked up from the joyful, charming antique ring adorning her finger to look at Griffin. "So, you're telling me that Mr. Henneman knows." He was the only jeweler in Hamilton.

"Melody . . . everybody knows."

She started to ask how, then laughed at herself. She'd been so intent on keeping her little fantasy bubble intact, she'd tuned out all the chatter and gossip about what anyone thought of her and Griffin. "So . . . what's the word?" she asked, admiring her ring as she slipped her hands up his shoulders and around his neck. "Should I have been placing bets down at Hannigans?"

He shook his head. "The odds suck."

She felt a little deflated at that. "Really?"

"Unless you were going to bet against us. Everyone thinks you'll say yes."

"Oh!" She grinned then. "Well, turns out they were right."

He lifted her up into his arms and spun her around. "How much work is left on the Traybill cake?"

"I finished just as you came in." She leaned down and kissed him.

"Perfect."

He scooped her up in his arms, which elicited a little squeal of surprise. She liked the caveman thing, too, as it turned out.

He leaned over just enough so she could reach the worktable. "Grab that red one. The chocolate one, too," he said, meaning her pastry bags.

"Why?" she asked, even as she leaned down and snagged them both.

"I thought we could start planning the wedding cake design a little early." He turned and headed up the back stairs. He bumped them through the door and didn't stop until she was in the middle of her bed.

She hadn't had the chance to make it since they'd left it earlier that morning. The linens were in a heap, and the pillows were still arranged in the way he'd moved them under her stomach so he could—

"Oh!"

He'd slipped her surgical pants down and had started to create his own version of a rose . . . on her inner thigh.

"Damn," he said. "That didn't come out right." He leaned down and caught her eye as he licked it off. "Let me try again."

"It's dark in here, you can barely see. You don't know how to do roses yet."

"I know." He grinned. "Lucky you." He slid her panties off, and started another one. Right in the middle of— "Damn," he said, seconds later.

Her hips rose to meet his tongue. "Lucky me, indeed," she gasped. She reached for him, but he was intent on having his way with her . . . with his usual maddening, perfectly torturous, slowly wrenching thoroughness, until she was quivering, shaking, and clutching at him. "Come here," she managed, grasping his arms as he settled between her thighs.

"Oh, I'm coming, luv," he said, treating her to a cheeky wink.

Then he slid inside her, but rather than slip his arm beneath her back, and move immediately into the primal rhythm they both so easily gave themselves over to, he stayed, buried deeply, and slipped her hand from his neck, turning it palm up, where he pressed a gentle, beautifully sweet kiss in the center of it, then curled it closed, so the diamonds on her ring finger twinkled in the moonlight.

"Ye have me heart, Melody mine. Ye've made me the happiest man on earth, agreeing to come back with me, to my home. I'll do everything in my power to make sure ye never regret it."

"I know I won't," she said, caressing the side of his

face, as she lifted her hips and he slid more deeply inside her. He already knew her body so well, so instinctively, she was swiftly climbing to another peak. She moved her hips beneath him, also knowing his body so well that she knew just how to take him with her.

They kept their rhythm slow, their gazes locked, and each stroke was like a promise. As she felt him gather, he lowered his mouth to hers, to claim her in the same instant that she would claim him. She whispered against his lips, "I know I won't, because we're already home, Griffin. That's always going to be wherever we are together."

"Then welcome home, luv," he said, grinning as he took her mouth . . . and the rest of her heart. "Welcome home."

Epilogue

It wasn't how he'd have wanted the reunion, but Griffin had been happy that Sean and his very pregnant wife, Holly, along with Trevor and Emma and their trio of rapidly growing boys, had been able to attend Lionel's memorial service. The tribute to Lionel and the Hamilton empire had paid due respect to all he had done during his lifetime and his tenure as reigning keeper of the Hamilton legacy.

"Who'd have imagined the auld codger would last another four years?" Sean said, as they settled themselves at one of the far tables in the grand resort dining hall.

The elaborate and elegantly styled room was packed with large round, white linen-draped tables, all filled with people who'd come from the world over to pay their respects. While the mood graveside had been somber, and the attendance much more intimate, the atmosphere was decidedly more social at the resort.

"The reins are finally passed," Trevor added, lifting his glass toward Griffin. "Cheers to you, cousin."

Everyone laughed at that. Griffin had come there feeling disconnected from most of the family roots he'd left behind, only to find brand-new connections on American soil that had opened his mind, and his heart, to reestablishing old connections when he'd returned home.

But no connection was so wonderful as the one he'd found in his marriage.

"I just can't believe how much Hamilton truly changed," Melody said as she settled in next to him. "I know I saw all the plans ahead of time, but this . . ." She gestured to the room they were in, but he knew she was picturing everything beyond it. She hadn't stopped gaping at the town since they'd flown in several days ago. "I can't believe the difference, and in just a few years. I would never know this was my old hometown."

She said it easily enough, even laughed, but Griffin knew how hard it had been for her to drive the streets and no longer be able to see it as the place where she'd grown up. There was still work to be done, but it was, by far, one of Griffin's crowning achievements. But he appreciated and understood the grief she was feeling.

"I know," Emma said, taking her place next to Trevor after seeing their children safely to the sitters' suite. "I don't recognize it either. Hard to believe I used to work here." She looked at Sean. "Have you noticed an increase in business in Willow Creek? I'd have to think this development has created a bit of a boom for you."

"More than a bit," Sean said, "that's for certain."

"His cousin Mick is thinking of opening another restaurant here in Hamilton, at the resort," Holly added. "Something maybe less traditional, with a more sophisticated menu."

Sean laughed. "I'm the one with the culinary pedigree, and Mick ends up running the gourmet branch of the growing Gallagher legacy."

Holly nudged him. "You could have done that if you wanted to."

"And give up Willow Creek? Not on your life." He placed his hand over his wife's stomach. "Or this one."

The women made *aw* sounds and took turns placing their hands on Holly's stomach. It wasn't the first time since marrying Melody that Griffin had thought about the eventuality of their own family, but Holly's pregnancy brought it home to him in a far more visceral way. It surprised him just how much he wanted a child.

It was a testimony to just how changed a man he was, that the idea excited him almost as much as it terrified him. He thought that a perfectly normal reaction.

"So, will you have to stay long during the transition?" Trevor asked Griffin.

He shook his head. "We've had plenty of time to plan this all out. The COO has already been the de facto head here for the last three years. Nothing will change much, in house. Melody and I are only here for the services, and to sign a few papers."

Melody smiled. "I'm glad you ended up with the mountain retreat," she told Emma and Trevor. "That's where you two first met, right?"

They glanced at each other, smiled, and nodded. "Yes. I'm not sure what we're going to do with it," Emma said, "but we won't do anything right away."

"She has a certain room she's dying to get into," Trevor said, then regaled them with the story of Lionel's secret room, which they'd found by accident during their time at the retreat, but had decided not to intrude upon.

"It's where he kept all of the documentation about Trudy's past, and the agreements between them concerning her fortune, right?" Holly asked.

It was Melody who answered. "Yes. So many secrets. Hard to believe Trudy agreed never to search for her son."

"We don't know that they didn't," Trevor said. "But no contact was made"—he looked to Griffin—"which was a shame."

Griffin shrugged and slipped his arm around Melody's shoulders. "I've become a firm believer that all things happen for reasons grander than we might know at the time. In the end, everyone got what they wanted most, am I right?"

Smiling and nodding, they all lifted their glasses, though Emma and Holly reached for water glasses, rather than the champagne that had been poured for each table before they'd arrived. It took a moment for Griffin to realize that Melody had reached for water as well.

Using his own water glass, he'd started to propose a toast, but turned to look at her instead, his glass shaking a bit in his hand. "Too early for a bit of the bubbly, luv?" he managed, not sounding remotely as casual as he'd hoped.

"Oh, no," she assured him.

Those lovely midnight blue eyes of hers still took on that special glow he'd come to cherish over the past four years. There seemed to be an additional something special about them.

"About, oh, six weeks too late, actually," she finished.

Emma and Holly squealed. Sean and Trevor shared a quick grin with each other, then looked at Griffin, on hold for any cue from him before congratulating him, manly comrades-in-arms first, dads-to-be second.

"You're . . . ?"

She sipped her water, trying to look oh-so-innocent. "I didn't tell you before we left, because you'd have never let me get on the plane."

"You can fly up until your third—" Emma started to say.

"Tell that to Captain Worrywort here," Melody said.

"I am no' a worrywort, or any kind of wort," Griffin said, clearly affronted, feeling more than a little poleaxed.

"You almost came unhinged when you found me up on that scaffolding outside the shop last summer."

"You could have fallen to your death."

"I was ten feet off the ground."

Everyone laughed, and he had the good grace to look a little abashed. Though he'd have made the same choice again. A lot of things in his life had taken on far less importance over the past few years. Melody's importance to him had only grown. And now she was carrying . . .

"Griffin," Melody said, sounding a bit alarmed.

"Just give me a minute, luv," he said, then bagged trying to look as if he had any control at all and dabbed the corners of his eyes on his sleeve. "Come here." He pulled his squealing wife into his lap, and everyone raised a glass. "To getting everything we ever wanted in this life." He looked at his wife, who'd never glowed so beautifully. "And then some."

All I Want for Christmas

CYNTHIA EDEN

1

The strains of Elvis's "Blue Christmas" drifted in the air as Christie Tate tried really, *really* hard to disappear inside the women's restroom.

"Did you hear?" The more-than-slightly catty female voice asked from a few feet away.

Christie hunched her shoulders and stared at her heels.

"Charles Crenshaw is already seeing Vicki from accounting. I mean . . . what's it been? A week? Two? He and Christie were—"

"I think he was seeing Vicki on the side," another female voice chimed in, oozing sympathy.

Fake sympathy.

Christie glanced at the gleaming black door, aware of the heat building in her cheeks. Was this what she'd become? A thirty-year-old woman hiding in a bathroom stall?

She knew those voices. Marsha Chad, a marketing assistant, was the one with the fake sympathy. And the other one—

"I heard Charles thought Christie was just . . . boring,"

said Lydia Clyde. "I mean the woman's a genius, but when it comes to men and sex, she's—"

Enough. Christie's spine shot up at the same instant her hand slammed into the bathroom door. The door flew forward and she caught the sound of two feminine gasps.

Her eyes narrowed as she took in the two women. "Lydia. Marsha." So what if her cheeks were flaming? She wasn't going to hide in the bathroom another second.

Not thirteen anymore. Not the nerdy girl.

"Christie." Lydia's blue eyes bulged. "I didn't realize you were—"

Christie jerked the faucet on and washed her hands. "For the record"—she lifted her head and met her own gaze in the mirror. *Backbone, girl, backbone.* How many times had she heard her mother say that over the years? *Don't ever let them see you break*—"sex with me is never boring."

She saw their jaws drop. *Good. Great.* She kept her chin up, kept her back straight, and with really fast steps, she was able to escape that hellhole.

And trade it for another one.

Christie burst from the women's restroom and walked straight into the full-on madness that was the Tate Toy Company's annual Christmas party. Bright lights. Elaborate bows. Mechanical toys—trains and soldiers—that marched across the floor. Christmas trees. So many giant, colorful Christmas trees. Normally, she would have loved the sight, but right then, she just wanted to escape.

She sucked in a sharp breath and tasted pine. Christie glanced to her left and found her ex, Charles, arguing with Vicki under a giant piece of mistletoe. The pretty redhead's hair tumbled down her back as she shook her head at Charles, then she jabbed a finger into his chest. Trouble in paradise?

I think he was seeing Vicki on the side.

Jerk.

A waiter sidled by her. Christie grabbed a glass of champagne and drained it in one gulp. Elvis kept singing.

Can't get much bluer than this, buddy.

She marched forward, putting more distance between her and Charles. *Can't attack.* Because that wouldn't be classy. A lady couldn't go up and jump on her ex's back as she started to pound the crap out of him. A good girl wouldn't do that. She'd been raised to be a *good girl.* Good girls became ladies, right?

But she was damn tired of being good. Damn tired of being gossiped about. Damn tired of it all.

Even tired of Elvis. And she loved the King.

Christie marched through the crowd, stopping only to pick up a few more glasses of champagne. Oh, but that bubbly went down nice and fast. Some folks tried to talk to her, but if they didn't have a tray of champagne flutes near them, she kept going.

Kept going until . . .

Until she reached the giant black chair that waited in the middle of the room. Santa's chair.

Presents wrapped in red and green paper surrounded the massive chair. Small surprise gifts for all the staff at Tate Toys. Santa would be coming soon. He'd be there to hear all their Christmas wishes. There to make those wishes come true.

Christie's fingers tightened on the champagne flute.

Then she caught a glimpse of Santa, and she spilled the rest of her champagne over the front of her red reindeer shirt.

Wow.

Santa was a stud.

She swallowed as she got a good look at the jolly old elf. Santa stood just inside the doorway of Tate Toys, a thick sack flung over his left shoulder—and what a nice shoulder it was. Actually, Santa had *two* nice shoulders. Nice, wide, broad shoulders that more than filled the red coat he wore.

Her gaze tracked slowly down his body. No shaking like a bowl-full-of-jelly there. Oh, no, that man—*Santa*—was built. Tall, strong. His muscled thighs stretched the red pants and his powerful legs disappeared into a pair of knee-high black boots.

Santa stalked toward her. A fluffy white and fake beard covered his face. A bright red hat hid his hair. All she could see were sparkling green eyes and high, tanned cheekbones.

"Have you been a good girl?" His voice was a dark, deep rumble of sound.

Christie licked her lips. "I—"

"Of course, she has," a voice behind her said with a laugh. Her brother. Jeez, had Daniel caught her ogling Santa? "You know Christie's always the good one," he said.

At his words, her blood seemed to ice. Right, the good one. That was her. Growing up, she'd been the one closeted away with books while Daniel had been out chasing girls and getting chased by the law.

More laughter floated in the air, and she realized they'd caught the attention of other staff members. Everyone seemed to be watching her. Watching and staring.

Good girl. Good *boring* girl.

That's me.

Her stare flew back to Santa. His head cocked toward her. He seemed to be . . . waiting. For her?

"Everyone gets a present this year!" Daniel's shout boomed behind her. "We'll start our line, and hey, Christie can be Santa's first victim!"

Victim? Since when did Santa have victims? But everyone was lining up, pushing forward, and they were obviously eager for their gifts.

What? Had Daniel put Christmas bonuses in that sack? Knowing him, probably.

Santa set down his bag. Then he rolled his shoulders. Those big, wonderful shoulders, but wait—that roll, that was familiar to her. Those green eyes had been familiar, too.

Her heart suddenly beat a little faster.

"Go on, Christie," Daniel urged as he gave her a nudge. "Someone has to get the game started," he whispered the last part in her ear. "You do it, they'll all do it."

She didn't care what everyone else did.

"Why don't you go and break Santa in, Christie?" Daniel said, raising his voice a bit. "Come on, just go tell the man what you want for Christmas."

Santa had taken his seat on the giant chair/throne. He tilted his head back and stared at her. Then he patted his lap and crooked his finger. At her.

More laughter.

The champagne seemed to burn in her belly. From the corner of her eye, she caught sight of Charles heading toward the end of the growing line. He was minus his new girlfriend.

"Uh, Christie?" Daniel's voice was whisper soft again. "Everyone's waiting."

Let 'em wait. The words were on the tip of her tongue. But a good girl wouldn't say that, right?

Santa patted his muscular leg again. "Come tell me what you want." His deep voice carried so easily.

Christie shoved her empty flute at Daniel. "Get rid of this, will you?" She sucked in more pine-tasting air and got ready to tell Santa *exactly* what she wanted.

Her steps were slow but certain as she approached the Santa Stud and his throne. His eyes were on her, so watchful.

Do it. The whisper came from deep inside. A challenge, a dare. It came from the wilder Christie, the side she always kept so carefully controlled.

Do it.

What did she have to lose?

She stopped in front of him, and the long edge of her skirt teased his boots. "Um, hi." Right. That sounded confident and sexy.

Santa caught her fingers with his gloved hand and *pulled.* Christie found herself on Santa's lap. A lap that was even harder and stronger up close. Her left hand flew out and pressed against his stomach as she struggled to balance herself.

Definitely not jelly in there. Though she hadn't felt them often in her life, a woman knew rock-hard abs when they pressed against her, even if those abs were hidden by a slightly rough red coat.

"Hello, there." His breath blew against her hair. "No need to be afraid of old Santa."

Obviously, he didn't know her that well. If he did, he would've known that she was afraid of *everything*.

She glanced back up at his eyes. Very faint laugh lines graced the edges of his green eyes. No old St. Nick. A Santa in his prime.

A Santa with a toes-curling sexy voice.

He released her hand and began to search through his bag of presents. She kept straddling his leg. Not so graceful.

"I'm sure I have something in here for a good girl like you."

She saw red—and not just from his suit. Christie broke as her wild side surged free. She grabbed his hand.

Santa froze. His gaze caught hers once more.

Her heartbeat shook her whole body as she told him, "You don't have what I want in there." She pitched her voice low, not wanting anyone to overhear. "Trust me on this. What I need isn't in that bag."

Those gorgeous eyes narrowed a bit. "What is it that you want for Christmas, pretty lady?"

She leaned in even closer, trying hard to balance on his legs. Santa sucked in a sharp breath, and she was about fifty percent sure she hadn't kneed him in the groin. "I want . . ."

His head inched toward hers.

The white of his beard tickled her cheek. Christie inched up, heading for his ear. This was a request she needed to whisper.

What am I doing? What?!

Her gaze darted around the room. Daniel was talking to one of the managers, totally oblivious to her. From the end of the line, Charles stared at her with a furrow between his pale brows. Marsha and Lydia were in the corner, whispering. Probably talking about her.

Boring . . . I think he was seeing Vicki while they were together.

Her back teeth clenched. *So tired of playing this game. For once, once . . . I just want to take what I need.*

"I can keep a secret," Santa told her, his voice strangely quiet, carrying only to her ears. She turned back to him, forgetting the others as he said, "Tell me what you want."

Right then, there was one thing she wanted, and those gleaming eyes seemed to promise it to her. Christie wet her lips, leaned in even closer to St. Nick, and let her wild side free as she quietly confessed, "Santa, I want a *really* good time." *Sex with me is never boring.* If only.

He stiffened beneath her, his whole body hardening.

"Know where I can find that?" she asked, her voice husky as she pulled back.

His eyes seemed to burn her. "Oh, I think I—"

"Come on, Christie!" Daniel called out. "Stop hogging Santa! We've got a line here."

124   *Cynthia Eden*

She eased off Santa's lap. He grabbed her wrist and held tight.

"I know," Santa finished, that deep voice sending a tremble right through her.

Oh, she just bet he did. Christie tugged her hand free and hurried back as the champagne-induced courage began to desert her.

"Wait, Christie!" Daniel said. "You didn't get your present! You can't—"

"Maybe I'll get it later." She brushed by him as her heart raced too fast. *What did I just do?*

"Don't worry. She'll definitely get her present later."

Oh, hell. *His* voice. She'd propositioned Santa Stud . . . and the guy had accepted her offer.

Jonas Kirk watched Christie Tate's sweet ass as she all but ran away from him. Her words echoed in his ears.

Santa, I want a really good time. Holy shit. Had the woman wanted to give him a heart attack? Or just a serious hard-on?

"Dude . . . *the presents*," Daniel growled the words.

Jonas realized he was straining to see Christie's ass. Couldn't really help that. The woman had a first-class ass. Put that with her come-and-get-me, blue bedroom eyes and the mouth made for sin . . . and you had a woman who'd been tempting him for almost fifteen years.

And she'd just asked me for sex.

Screw the presents. Jonas waved his hands toward the bag. "Christmas bonuses are inside . . . come and get 'em!"

Daniel's eyes—several shades lighter than Christie's—bulged. "What are you doing?"

The crowd swarmed.

Jonas yanked off his beard. "Spreading Christmas cheer." He shoved through the group. Sure, he'd promised his buddy that he'd pop in and play Santa, and Jonas didn't really mind the gig. It was a nice break from his usual routine of catching criminals but—

He knew Christie, and he knew when the woman was about to run. After all, she'd spent most of her life running from him.

Because she knows how much I want her?

He'd always tried so hard to hold the hunger in check when he was around her. Sweet Christie Tate. The girl-genius who'd been dropped in his college class even though she was only sixteen. The girl with the slow, innocent smile. The girl who *always* smelled like strawberries. The girl who'd become a woman he craved. A woman who'd been hands-off for so long.

A woman he wasn't about to let vanish.

He rounded the corner and caught a glimpse of her hair, long and black, right before the elevator door closed.

Shit.

Jonas shoved open the stairwell door and rushed down the stairs. If he was lucky, he'd catch her in the lobby.

A few moments later, his palm shoved into the exit door. He ran into the lobby, aware of the guard jumping to his feet with wide eyes.

"It's okay, Jamie." The cop worked after hours at the toy company, getting a little extra cash for the holidays. Several of the cops in the area pulled guard duty at the toy shop. "I'm just trying to catch—"

The elevator dinged, a soft peal of sound, and then the doors slid open.

Christie glanced up, and her eyes widened when she saw him. "J-Jonas?"

He lunged through the doors and caught her elbows. He pulled her close. *What?* Why was she so tense? Was she regretting her confession now that she saw the man who'd been beneath the beard?

Can't back out. Won't let her.

His lips crushed down on hers. Jonas caught her gasp with his mouth, took in that soft rush of breath, and then his tongue pushed into her mouth.

Champagne and strawberries. Figured she'd taste that damn good. A growl built in his throat. *Addictive.* Yeah, he'd always known one taste would probably push him over the edge. Good to know he'd been right.

Her hands rose to his shoulders. Small, delicate hands. *She* was small and delicate. A dancer's body on a woman who always swore she didn't have an ounce of grace.

He expected those hands to push against him. To shove him back. Instead, her fingers curled over him, and Christie urged closer. She rose onto her toes, stretching her body against his, and she opened her mouth wider.

Sweet hell.

Her tongue touched his. His entire body went on high-freaking-alert. They stumbled back a few steps. His hands—then her shoulders—hit the rear wall of the elevator.

The things she could do with that tongue . . .

Ding.

Jonas wrenched his head up. What was he—

Christie's mouth pressed against his throat. Her tongue tasted his skin, and the edge of her teeth bit lightly into his flesh.

The damn Santa pants were *too* tight over a certain eager portion of his anatomy, a portion that couldn't wait to be a whole lot closer to her.

His hands slid under the back of her shirt and touched warm, soft skin. So smooth. Better than silk. His fingers rose, curling, easing forward and caressing her stomach. Then his hands rose up and trailed over her rib cage, and, oh, yeah, that was the edge of her bra. Close now, so—

Ding.

The damn elevator doors. Jonas threw a fast glance

over his shoulder. The doors opened. Jamie frowned at him, two guys in suits stared with wide eyes, and a woman in red smiled.

Wrong place.

He forced his hands to slide from under Christie's shirt. Jonas forced himself to let her go and to step back.

Jonas took a deep breath. He still tasted champagne and strawberries. "Christie—"

She blinked at him and shook her head. Her lips were red and glistening. *From my mouth.* Right, like he hadn't pictured that scene before. Except, they hadn't been in an elevator and they hadn't—

"Jonas! The kids are upstairs! Santa needs to give them their gifts!"

—been surrounded by strangers and her brother. Because Daniel was closing in on them now, his turtleneck looking a little too tight around his bobbing Adam's apple.

Daniel skidded to a stop and threw his hand up, barely stopping the elevator doors from closing once more. "What are you doing? I need you! The employees always get to bring their kids in for the presents." Daniel tossed him the Santa beard. "Christie, this is your favorite part!"

Because Christie designed most of the toys made by the company, she was usually front and center on the toy distribution.

"Uh, Daniel," she mumbled, "I think I'm going to—"

Daniel jumped in the elevator. "Catch the next one!" he tossed to the folks in the lobby. He punched the button for the third floor. "I had to chase you both down three flights of stairs." The doors slid closed. *"Three flights.* Let's just get back up there and make this a merry damn night, okay?"

Jonas glanced at Christie. Her heart-shaped face seemed pale. Her eyes were on the mark she'd left on his neck.

A smile curved his lips. After a moment, her gaze met his. He lifted his hand and touched the mark.

The music kicked in then, the notes filling the elevator as Elvis began to sing.

Maybe she hadn't been a good girl after all. It definitely looked like Christie Tate had a naughty side.

One that enjoyed a good ride in an elevator.

2

She'd asked Jonas Kirk to sleep with her. No, she'd asked Jonas Kirk—badass police detective—to give her a really good time.

Christie was 150 percent certain the man could deliver on that good time.

She watched him from the corner of her eye. He didn't look all tough and macho right then. Well, okay, he *kinda* did if you looked past the red suit and beard. He was *ho-hoing* it up with the kids, handing out the presents that she'd organized days before.

"What was happening in that elevator?" her brother asked, and she jumped. Daniel had a tendency to sneak up on people way too much.

She forced a smile. "We were talking."

"Right. 'Cause when you talk, you make out."

Oh, crap.

"I know the breakup with Charles was hard on you."

"Daniel, I—"

"I should have fired the guy, holidays or no damn holidays."

She turned her head a bit, sizing up her brother. At just

over six feet, he had a lean, wiry build. His face was open, warm, handsome. "You would never fire someone at Christmas." Even he had limits.

"He hurt you." His jaw flexed. "We don't need him. I can fire him right—"

"I don't need you to fight my battles." Her gaze tracked back to Jonas. He was taller than her brother by a couple inches, and his shoulders were wider. His skin was darker. His eyes . . . She straightened her shoulders. "Charles doesn't bother me. I've moved on."

A low whistle was her answer. "I hope you're not moving where I *think* you're moving."

She should look away from Jonas. Yes, she should. But he bent to reach into the sack again—*nice butt.*

"You know Jonas isn't the committing kind."

Her gaze snapped to Daniel.

His brows, a lighter shade than hers, rose. "Yeah, sis, I saw the hickey you left on his neck."

Why couldn't the floor just open up and swallow her?

"You *know* him, Chris. You know Jonas never stays with one woman too long."

She'd gotten that warning before. She met her brother's gaze. Heard Jonas's voice rumble. Goose bumps rose on her arms. "I don't want forever." She'd tried to find forever before, only to get disappointed.

Daniel blinked. "Chris . . ."

"I'm a big girl. Trust me, I know exactly what I want." *Not what, who.* Jonas. "Stop worrying about me."

"He's my best friend! I don't want my sister and my—"

She patted his shoulder. "Stop worrying. And um, maybe lower your voice." She jerked her thumb over her shoulder. The kids were watching them now. "We've got an audience."

His teeth clicked together as he snapped his jaw closed. Turning on his heel, he marched toward the giant Christmas tree.

Christie knew her cheeks were burning again, but she made herself look at their audience. An audience that included an avid Santa hunk. When she met his stare, she swore she could feel his touch. His hands—big, strong, callused—sliding under her shirt. Edging up her stomach. Getting closer, so close to her breasts.

Oh, yes, she knew what she wanted. The question was . . . would she really be brave enough to take it? To take him?

She slipped away from the crowd when someone called her brother's name. Her elbow bumped into a wall, and the pain barely registered.

Sex with Jonas. Sure, she'd fantasized about just that thing, a time or twenty.

But the real thing? Her throat dried up. Oh, jeez. It would be . . .

He glanced up at her, and his green eyes seemed to burn right through her.

Incredible.

Because he was a man who *knew* how to give a woman a good time she'd never forget.

An hour later, Jonas had emptied his second sack. All the presents were gone. The kids had vanished. The staff left at Tate Toys could only be described as skeletal. As he watched, a few more folks trailed for the elevators.

Another holiday party down.

But his job wasn't finished. Not yet. Santa still had one wish to grant. Hmm. Where was his lady? His gaze swept the room. The last time he'd seen her, she'd been trapped against that back wall.

The spot was empty now. The tree lights twinkled, throwing a mix of colors on the wall. No Christie.

He tossed his hat and the beard down next to the bag. Had she left? Turned tail and run?

If she had, he knew where she lived. Not like he couldn't find her.

Just in case she hadn't fled the building, Jonas stalked down the hallway leading to the "lab"—Christie's domain. Her office was on the right side of the hallway and her playroom, a giant workroom/lab, was on the left.

He went to the right. Didn't bother knocking. The door was open, so he walked right in and found Christie hunched over her desk.

She looked up at him, her eyes widening. "What are you—"

He caught the doorknob and closed the door with a slow, deliberate move. *The woman needs to learn not to tease.*

Christie shot to her feet, and the chair rolled behind her with a groan of its wheels. "You were with the kids, you were—"

"Kids are gone." He stalked toward her. *I want a really good time.* She'd known she was talking to him. She had to know. Right? "Pretty much everyone is gone but you and me."

That pink tongue swiped over her lips, and he almost growled. *Still playing with fire.* Did she know how badly they could both be burned? Time to teach the woman not to play with a hungry man.

He put his hands on her desk and leaned across the heavy wood. "That good time you wanted . . ."

Her eyes were locked on his.

"You want it here? Now?" How far would she go? He'd caught the whispers while he was handing out the toys. Seemed Christie and her boyfriend, a dumbass named Charles, had split. A chatty chick named Lydia thought Christie was looking for some revenge sex.

He didn't enjoy being a stand-in.

"Here?" Her voice was a squeak. Her gaze shot to the closed door, then back to him. "But you—"

"I never took you for a tease." His hands curled, forming fists on the wood.

"I'm not!" Instead of jerking back, she leaned forward and put her face temptingly close.

"Then let's see about that good time." He caught her arms, pulled her even closer, and took her mouth. Because no way, no way would she still taste like—

Champagne and strawberries. Woman and lust. Everything *he* wanted for the holidays.

Oh, hell, trouble.

Christie's hands dug into his shoulders, and she yanked him closer. Her mouth opened wider, and her tongue slipped right past his lips.

Not teasing.

Revenge sex.

She moaned into his mouth. Two more seconds, and he'd be over that damn desk.

But Christie pulled back. Spots of color stained her cheeks. Her breath came hard and fast.

"Change your mind?" he growled as he forced his body to back away. Either back away or lunge forward. And cops weren't supposed to lunge at women. Well, not at *innocent* women.

"No." Her fingers touched her lips. A quick, light touch. Then she skirted around the edge of the desk and came to him.

Came to him.

"I just wanted to get closer." She was real close right then. In front of him. Caged between his body and the thick desk. "This is better." She rose onto her toes again, reaching for him.

Jonas caught her wrists and didn't let her touch. Not yet. "You really think you know what you're doing?"

She flinched.

What the hell?

Her pointed chin came up fast. "Despite what you may

have heard out there, yes, I've got a pretty good idea what I'm doing." She tried to tug her hands free.

He didn't let her. "Did you know who I was?" If she said yes, that would be good enough. So what if she just wanted a quick screw to punish an ex for walking? He'd take the pleasure, but she damn well needed to know who was giving her the orgasm that would come.

"What are you—"

"Did you know I was the guy playing Santa?" He'd been called in at the last minute. Daniel had originally hired another—

She laughed. Not the normal response women gave him. "Of course, I knew it was you."

"How?"

Her voice softened as she said, "No one else has eyes like yours." Her lips curved in a half smile, revealing the faintest hint of the dimple in her right cheek. "Do you really think I would have just crawled onto any Santa's lap?"

She'd better not plan to be crawling on any other laps. He moved fast, and in a blink, Christie was sitting on the edge of her desk, he was between her spread thighs, and her mouth was open and ready beneath his.

Her scent surrounded him, light and feminine. Beneath the soft material of her sweater, he could feel her breasts pushing at him. Her nipples were tight, hard, and he was dying to know—would they taste like strawberries, too?

Christie's hands shoved under his coat, and her palms touched his back. Her touch seemed red hot, scorching his flesh.

He bit her lower lip, that full lower lip that had distracted him more times than he could count. Christie Tate. The woman who'd taught him long ago that smart was so damn sexy.

The woman who'd barely seemed to know he existed, until tonight.

Good time, here we come.

He pulled back just enough to grab the bottom of her sweater, then he yanked it up and over her head. Rudolph landed in the corner and—*hell.*

A black lace bra cupped her breasts. Black lace surrounding pale skin. His fingers slipped beneath the thin straps, easing the bra off her shoulders. She watched him with those bedroom eyes. Watched and waited and *shit, but she had beautiful breasts.*

Small, but perfectly round. The nipples were dark pink, so ready for his mouth. He leaned forward and let his breath blow against her nipple.

Her palms slammed down on the desk and she arched her back. "Now who's the tease?"

The woman had bite. He hadn't expected that from Christie. Hadn't expected *a lot* from her. His mouth was less than an inch from her breast. *Taste her. Taste her.* He swallowed. "How much . . . ah . . . champagne have you had tonight?" The words emerged as more growl than anything else.

But Christie must have understood because she said, "I'm not drunk, Jonas. I know exactly what I'm doing." She paused—then said, "Do you?"

Oh, hell, no, the woman had just taunted him. "I manage." In three minutes, he'd *manage* to make her come. That would be just the start of the fun he had planned.

His mouth closed over her left nipple. Her sigh filled his ears, and *oh, yeah, better than strawberries.*

Her hips arched against him as he licked and sucked, learning her flesh. *Christie fucking Tate!* Too smart, too rich, too sexy as she moaned beneath him.

Her brother had never needed to tell him to keep his hands off. He'd known she was off-limits to him for years.

Still knew it, but . . . *screw it.*

His hands grabbed the flowing material of her skirt and yanked it up.

Hands most definitely on.

"Jonas!"

His hand was on her thigh. Soft, supple skin. So close to touching her sex. All he had to do was slide his fingers under the elastic of her panties. Would her panties be black, too? A scrap of lace to match the bra?

His gaze met hers. Passion had darkened the blue of her eyes, but wait . . . was that fear? Was she afraid of him? Sure he'd pulled some dangerous undercover cases when he'd been busting ass in the Narcotics Division of the Charlotte PD. But he hadn't even gone close to Christie then. He'd made a point to stay away from temptation. He'd transferred out of that department now, and . . . the woman had to know he wouldn't hurt her, right?

He pressed a light kiss to her lips. "Trust me."

A small furrow appeared between her brows. "That's . . . not easy for me."

He knew *that* about her, too.

Her gaze dropped to his hand.

His fingers began to slide up her thigh, pushing the skirt with the slow movement. "Tell me to stop," he told her. One word, and he'd back off.

One word.

Christie didn't speak.

He saw the black edge of her panties. His cock jerked; the thing was so eager for her that he ached. His hand looked too big next to her flesh. Too rough.

But he wasn't backing off. Not unless she gave the word. His index finger eased under the edge of her underwear and touched warm, wet woman.

Fuck.

Christie wanted him as much as he wanted her. His hand caught the lace, pulling too hard, and it snapped.

The lace fell between them. "Spread your legs wider."
His gravel-rough command.

She was still looking at his hand when she moved to obey.

A light covering of midnight black hair. Pink flesh. His hands, touching her, sliding between the folds, finding the center of her need.

Her breath came faster, harder, when he stroked her. Her hips arched up when he pushed his index finger knuckle-deep inside her.

Watching. Watching.

Where the hell was the mistletoe when he wanted it? He knew just where he wanted to kiss. Just exactly where—

The door flew open, banging against the wall, and Jonas whirled around with his fists up.

"Hey, look, Christie, we really need to—" a tall, blond dumbass of a guy began.

"Get the hell out." Jonas kept his voice lethally soft. He also kept his body in front of Christie's.

The blond dumbass staggered to a stop. "What? Who are you—*Santa*?"

A choking sound came from behind Jonas.

Dumbass stepped forward even as his face flushed a dark red. "You're making out with the guy in the Santa suit, Christie?" Shock had his voice rising.

"Doing a bit more than that," Jonas told him, lifting a brow.

The guy looked like a fish—a blond, dumbass fish—as he tried to suck in air. "You . . . can't . . . Christie and I are—"

"We're not anything anymore, Charles," Christie said, her voice too calm and far too cool for a woman who'd been burning hot in Jonas's hands ten seconds ago. He glanced back at her. Her sweater was gone, but her skirt was in place. He shrugged out of his coat and wrapped her up, fast, before Charles could see—

Charles. Revenge sex. Shit.

This was the ex? *This guy?* Jonas straightened his shoulders. "You're interrupting." He hadn't even gotten his three minutes.

But old Charles must have gotten some kind of second wind. Suddenly he came barreling forward, and Charles launched his fist right at Jonas.

Christie screamed. Jonas twisted to the side, did a fast dive, and caught the dumbass with a quick maneuver that took Blondie down, face-first, onto the desk.

Jonas held Charles's hands pinned at the base of his back. The idiot kept bucking and swearing and promising to rip Jonas's head off. Right. Like that was going to happen. "Charles, this is not your Christmas." A deliberate pause. "Dumbass, you just assaulted a police officer."

3

Charles froze. The guy had finally realized he was screwed to hell and back.

"Jonas." Christie's breathy voice was like a stroke right over his cock.

He looked up at her, grinding his back teeth. She looked mussed and sexy, and he'd been close to paradise. Until the dumbass had interrupted.

"There's been a mistake," Dumbass said.

Jonas kept his eyes on Christie. She bit her lower lip, and her gaze darted between him and Blondie.

"Charles . . ." Her breath expelled on a rush and Jonas's brows snapped together. He didn't like the look she was shooting Dumbass. "You shouldn't be here."

Damn right he shouldn't. Jonas tightened his hold around the guy's wrists.

"D-didn't know he was a cop!" The ex gasped out.

"Right. 'Cause it's fine to assault people, as long as they aren't cops," Jonas snapped. Idiot. "Let's see if a night at the station can—"

"Jonas!" Okay, now she was back to calling his name.

Well, not so much calling it as nearly shrieking it in horror. "You're taking him in?"

His jaw ached, and Jonas realized he was still gritting his teeth. "Does it matter to you?" But the real question was . . . *did the ex matter?* Dumbass was still pinned. Christie pulled Jonas's coat closer to her and stared back at him.

"Christ, this is a *mistake!*" Dumbass wailed. "I saw you with Christie and I just—"

"We're over, Charles," she said, her voice cold. *Not seeming to care so much.* "Who I'm with, who you're with—doesn't matter. That's what *over* means."

Okay, that was good enough for Jonas, and because he was suddenly feeling so generous, he eased his grip and let Dumbass flop over.

The guy stared up at him with wide gray eyes. Jonas glared down at him. "This is your warning, asshole. You ever come at me again, you're in jail."

The gray eyes darted to Christie.

Jonas stepped closer to her. "You heard the lady. *Over.* So unless you have Tate Company business with her, stay the hell away." He put his arm over her shoulders and pulled her close. Territorial? Yeah, that was him.

But he finally had a chance with Christie, and no dumbass was going to ruin that for him.

The blond swallowed and tried to straighten up. "I . . . Christie—"

"Go, Charles. I think you're drunk. Y-you need to catch a cab and sleep this night off."

Another bob of his Adam's apple, and Dumbass finally staggered out.

The anger that fired Jonas's blood didn't cool as the door closed with a soft snick. "Is that what you wanted?" he demanded.

Revenge sex. If Lydia had been right, Christie had just

scored a major hit. Gotten her jealous ex to take a swing at the new man.

But she shook her head and, for an instant, sadness slipped over her face. "No, I-I almost had what I wanted but . . . maybe it's just not in the cards, huh?"

She shrugged out of his jacket and handed it back to him. Silently, she found her sweater and dressed. A light red stained her cheeks. *Embarrassed?*

Hell, he *had* been moving fast with her. But wasn't fast what she'd wanted?

In seconds, her clothes were positioned perfectly, but her hair was a bit wild, and her lips were still red and swollen.

Then she leaned up and pressed that sweet mouth against his. A kiss too light, too fleeting. Her breath whispered against him. "Good night, Jonas." Her hand hovered over her stomach as she pulled away, and yeah, that was definitely fear in her eyes.

But what was she afraid of?

He watched her walk out of the office, her steps sure. He bent down and picked up the scrap of lace that had fallen on the floor.

He could give Christie everything she wanted, if she'd just trust him. The problem was . . . he didn't know if Christie was afraid of him or herself.

His fingers tightened around her panties. He didn't know, but he'd damn well find out.

He hurried out of her office, narrowly avoiding a collision in the hallway with a redhead in a dark green dress. "Have you—have you seen Charles Crenshaw?" she asked quietly. "I think"—she took a deep breath—"I think he came here looking for Christie."

"They're both gone," he told her and saw her eyes widen. *Oh, wait, shit, could this be Vicki?* Lydia had been talking about the redhead, too. Lydia had liked to talk about everyone. "They didn't leave together."

"Oh." Relief flashed across her face.

Right. Whatever. She could deal with Dumbass. Charles wasn't a priority for him anymore.

Only Christie mattered.

The snow had just started to fall when Christie heard the knock at her door. She'd been staring out the back window, thinking about—*who else?*—Jonas and what an idiot she'd been.

Running away.

Nice. Smooth.

Seemed like she'd spent years running from him. No, not from him. From herself.

The knock came again, harder. She frowned. Okay, usually the delivery driver just knocked once and left her package on the doorstep. She hurried to the foyer and peeked out the peephole.

Not the delivery driver.

Jonas stood on the other side of the door. Her hand slapped against the wood. *Oh, damn.*

Her fingers were shaking a bit as she fumbled with the lock and the doorknob. *Don't screw this up again. Try to be cool. Confident. Act like you're a woman who's had lots of sex. Lots of great sex on desks and hell, everywhere!*

He'd almost made her come on top of a desk. Her knees jiggled a little as she yanked open the door. "Jonas!" Her smile felt huge on her face.

He stared at her a moment, then blinked and shook his head.

Her smile dimmed a bit. Why was he looking at her like that? Snowflakes had fallen onto his battered black leather jacket, a jacket that made his golden skin look darker, his black windblown hair sexier.

Sexy. That was the word that always sprang to mind when she thought of Jonas. Jonas with the bright eyes and slightly crooked nose—courtesy of a bar fight he'd broken up when he'd been a rookie cop.

His lips—the top a little thin, the bottom perfectly biteable—curved a bit.

She cleared her throat. "What are you . . . um, doing here?" The words were a little too high. Not the confident air she'd been going for.

His black brows rose. "Mind if I come in?" A puff of white appeared before his mouth. "Damn cold out here."

Oh, yes, right. She opened the door wider. Jonas stomped his boots on her mat, then crossed the threshold, immediately making her feel that her doorway was too small. He was too big. He was—

He had a package in his hands. A small red box with a dark green bow. "I brought you something."

He'd never given her a present before. Not once, and sometimes, it felt like she'd known him forever.

Known him, wanted him, had too much champagne and finally asked for her secret desire.

She pushed the door closed behind them. Her eyes were on the present. It looked small and innocent in his big, gloved hands. Of course, there was nothing innocent about him. She knew that.

"Don't worry," he told her, flashing a smile that revealed his perfect white teeth. "It's not going to bite you."

But I will. The words seemed to hang in the air as she stared at him. Christie gulped and stepped forward to take the present. "It's . . . uh . . . not Christmas yet." Not for another week. They'd had the party at Tate Toys last night because it had been Friday night. The perfect opportunity for a party because not many folks had to get up early the next day.

"Anything wrong with an early present between

friends?" His gloved fingers brushed hers as she took the gift. A lick of heat seemed to shoot right through her body.

She was holding the present too tightly. "Is that what we are? Friends?" She tasted the word. Jonas had been on the cusp of her life for so long. When she'd transferred to Duke University, he and Daniel had already been room-mates. Jonas had treated her like a kid sister, too. She'd been crazy about him. One look in those green eyes . . .

She shook the present. Didn't hear anything.

Jonas shrugged out of his coat and hung it on the rack. His gloves hit the table. "We could be friends." His head cocked to the right as he studied her. "We could be more."

Lovers.

"Don't crush the box," he murmured and she realized her hold had turned into a death grip.

Her breath expelled slowly and her fingers relaxed a bit. Jonas turned away and headed into her den. He whis-tled lightly. "That's some tree."

A bit of the tension eased from her body and her smile came back. "Thanks. Daniel helped me get it inside." The tree brushed her sixteen-foot ceiling. "It took me two days to decorate it but—"

"But you love Christmas, so you had one hell of a time, right?" His eyes were on her, seeming to see so much.

"Right." Softly spoken.

"You're the one who decorates Tate Toys every year, aren't you?"

How did he—

"Daniel's told me how much you love this time of year." His gaze darted to her jingle bell sweater. "And it's kinda . . . easy to see."

She lifted the present. "I-I'll just . . . put this under the tr—tree." Dammit, she hated her nervous stutter. Just when she thought she'd had the thing under control, Jonas stared at her and—wham, it was back. She sucked in a breath and tried again, "I-I'll just put this under the tree with the—"

"I'd rather you opened it now."

Why did his voice sound like sex? Well, not *like* sex, but that rumble made her think of sex. Of sheets and darkness, of a strong body surrounding hers and of a growl telling her to—

"Actually, before you open it, we need to talk." He stalked toward her. The fire crackled behind him and sent a blaze of warmth into the room. "Over the years, we haven't done much *talking*, have we?"

She shook her head, aware that her heartbeat had kicked way up.

"I've done a lot of watching you." His gaze was on her. His hand lifted and brushed a lock of hair back from her cheek. "Sure as hell a lot of fantasizing."

What?

"But not a whole lot of actual talking."

She might have swallowed her tongue. Christie tried to clear her throat, then said, "You never . . . seemed much interested in talking." After he'd graduated, he'd joined the force. He'd fast-tracked to the narcotics division then—

"When I was undercover"—he shook his head—"you didn't want to be around me."

"That's not true! I—"

"I spent my days with criminals. I lived their lives." His hand dropped. "I didn't *want* you to know the things I did. Didn't want any part of that world to touch you."

He'd cared? Her stomach tightened. "I . . . didn't realize you'd even—" *Noticed me.* Okay, she couldn't say that. She had her pride. But the years had trickled away, and he'd spared her the briefest of greetings when their paths had crossed. She hadn't thought he'd noticed her as a woman, and she certainly hadn't realized the guy was interested.

Until last night.

"Always the princess," he murmured, and his gaze raking around her house, "safe in the castle."

She stiffened. Yes, the Tate family had money. A lot of it. But she wasn't some spoiled debutante who didn't know the meaning of work, and she wasn't some weak-willed woman who'd break at the first sign of a bleak reality. "I don't live in a castle. I live in the real world. I work every day. I earn my own money, I—"

He kissed her. A light, sensual brush of his lips that halted her words and stirred the need that had built within her.

"I know what you do," he muttered, pulling back from her. "I know so much more than you think."

Her brows lifted even as she licked her lips. *Trying to taste him.* She had it bad. A crush that should have ended years ago, but now—

I know he wants me. There was no holding back for her.

"It's not about revenge, is it?"

He'd lost her. Totally. "Uh, Jonas—"

"I heard one of your coworkers last night. The folks who saw us in the elevator spread word pretty fast about what we were doing."

Making out in that tight elevator. His body pressed to hers. His tongue in her mouth.

More, please. "Ah, how does that mean I want revenge against you?"

"Not me, baby. Your ex. The dumbass who came barreling into your office like he had some kind of right to be there, with you."

A surprised laugh broke from her lips. "Charles? You think I want revenge on Charles?" She shook her head but never eased her hold on the package. "My brother owns the business, remember? If I wanted revenge, the guy would be out looking for a new job."

His gaze measured her. "But you don't work that way."

No. "You heard what I told him. Charles and I are over." She forced a shrug. "End of story." The minute Jonas's lips had brushed hers, she'd barely even been able to remember Charles's touch.

"Good to hear." His gaze dropped to the box. "Got a deal to offer you."

A deal?

"You told me what you wanted last night."

Ah, yes. Champagne and false Christmas courage. A dangerous mix. "I told you but, um, you were the one who followed me." She had to point that out. It wasn't like she'd forced him to do anything. "You came after me, you kissed *me*."

"And I plan to do a hell of a lot more than kiss you." His voice roughened.

Christie rocked forward a bit.

His eyes narrowed. "You want your good time? Well, baby, I can promise you the best sex you've ever had."

She locked her knees. "Awful s-sure of yourself." Since she'd had three lovers who'd delivered only average sex, and one other guy who'd been *really* disappointing, odds were high that Jonas could make good on his promise. Not that she'd tell him and his ego that.

"I'm sure of you," he said. "When I touched you . . ."

Her nipples tightened.

"You went up in flames. Since I'm going to do a lot more touching, I know just how hot your body is going to burn for mine." His green eyes glittered. "I can give you what you want for Christmas. Exactly what you want."

She knew he could. "Great sex, no strings," she whispered. *Not boring, not with him.*

The faint lines around his eyes tightened.

She'd heard her brother talk often about Jonas and his women over the years. Jonas and his flavor of the week. Daniel had been right when he warned her last night. Jonas wasn't a commitment kind of guy. "Not forever." The words slipped out.

He gave a hard nod. "Just sex."

Her chin lifted even as her heart slammed into her chest. She'd been brave last night. She could pull on the mask again. "The best we've *both* ever had." No stutter.

His breath came harder. "Open the box."

Her fingers jerked at the bow. Ripped away the paper. She fumbled with the box top, opened it, and found—

A small scrap of lace. She lifted it up, and the dark red lace dangled from her fingertips. *Panties.* He'd given her panties. Really sexy, really hot panties that wouldn't cover *anything*.

A wild girl would love this gift. She'd laugh, wear those and nothing else for her lover. A wild girl would do just that.

What about a good girl pretending to be wild?

She dropped the box, but kept the lace in her hand.

His eyes were on her face. He seemed even . . . bigger now. Or maybe her room was getting smaller. "I tore your panties last night."

Oh, God. Heat rose in her cheeks. Yes, he'd torn them, and she'd *left them* in her office. Smooth.

"Figured the least I could do was give you a new pair." His hand lifted and tangled with hers. "A pair for you to wear just for me."

Jonas Kirk was standing in front of her, promising her great sex, and giving her sexy underwear. This scene was really similar to a dream she'd had last week.

His head tilted toward her. "You up for this?" he dared her.

What? Did he think she was all talk? That she'd turn

away when things got too hot? Hadn't he realized she was desperate for the heat?

"Stay here," she told him, her voice too husky. She eased around him. Christie forced herself to walk, nice and slow, and added a little roll to her hips as she left him. *Watch me, watch me.*

At her bedroom door, Christie glanced back just in time to catch his gaze on her ass. More confident, she threw him a smile.

Then she closed the door and shut him out, right before her knees buckled.

4

Jonas sucked in a deep gulp of air. The fresh scent of pine filled his nostrils even as the taste of Christie stayed on his tongue.

He rolled his shoulders and paced toward the glittering tree. Okay, so he hadn't fucked things up too badly. She was still interested in him. Well, maybe not *him*, but in having *sex* with him. No-strings, no-promises sex.

He'd sure had plenty of that in his life.

The door creaked open behind him. He swung around and took a hard punch to the gut—or at least, it sure as shit felt like he did.

Christie stood in the doorway, her long black hair loose around her face, her deep blue bedroom eyes tempting him . . . and she was naked.

His cock shoved against the front of his jeans, and he lunged toward her.

"The panties fit," she told him, her cheeks a little red, and he managed to jerk his gaze off her breasts—freaking beautiful breasts with tight pink nipples—and he saw that she was wearing the scrap of lace.

Not naked. Still so sexy he hurt.

The lace rode low on her round, perfect hips. Hips that he'd grab and hold tight while he drove into her. Hips that—

"Jonas, is everything—"

"Perfect. Everything is fucking perfect." He took two steps and stood before her. Stood and just stared. *Damn.* Her skin was so smooth. Pale and perfect and he had to touch her. His hands lifted and skimmed down her shoulders. She shivered.

She wants me, just as much as I want her.

"The bedroom—it's behind me and—"

He shook his head, caught her hand and pulled her with him. Back across the room. Back toward the glittering Christmas tree. A thick rug was spread between the tree and the fireplace. *Perfect.*

"Are you going to—to take off your clothes? Y-you should—"

He gently pushed her down onto the rug. "Not yet."

Her breath blew out in a rush. He lowered onto his knees. Stared more and realized he had to touch. Not just with his hands. With his mouth.

He knew just where he wanted to start.

"Jonas, are you—"

Her words ended in a gasp when he licked her breast. She arched up toward him. *Just as responsive as last night.* So, no, he hadn't been imaging things. Hadn't made it better in his memory. One touch—*fire.*

He spread his lips wider and took her breast deeper into his mouth. Tasted. Sucked.

Jonas heard the rasp of her breath. Her hands rose and locked around his shoulders. The faint edge of her nails bit through his shirt.

"Easy," he whispered as he lifted his head.

But his "good" girl shook her head. "I don't want easy. I want you." Her hand went to the buckle of his belt. "And I want you now, Jonas."

She unhooked the buckle, went for the snap and the zipper—

He backed away from her. "Not yet." He wasn't going to let the first time be too fast or too hard. He'd promised her the best sex she'd ever had, and he was damn well going to deliver on that promise.

"Spread your legs," he ordered, his voice dropping to a growl.

Her legs shifted on the rug, then parted.

The zipper was probably making a permanent imprint on his dick.

He positioned his body between her legs, letting his jeans brush her flesh, and giving him a perfect view of her body.

She stared at him, eyes wide, lips parted, pink tongue darting just behind her teeth. *Waiting.*

He stretched over her and took her mouth. Jonas kissed her long and deep and let his tongue take and claim. He took her mouth the way he'd be taking her body.

Mine.

He'd make sure she didn't forget him, not any time soon. Not ever.

Jonas licked his way down her neck. When he came to the spot just under her left ear, her hips rocked up against him. He stilled. Then licked her again.

Another fast rock.

So his lady had a sweet spot. He bet she had more, and he was ready to find them all. But first . . .

His fingers eased under the lace. *Sweetest spot of all.* He found her already wet, the flesh plump and eager. A moan trembled in her throat.

He bit lightly on her neck, and when her hips arched, he let his index finger dip inside her.

She shuddered beneath him. *Fuck yes.*

But . . . not yet. He pulled his hand away from her and

kissed his way down her body. Jonas took his time with her breasts, licking and sucking those dark tips. He loved the feel of her nipples on his tongue. The taste—still strawberries—still driving him crazy.

Her thighs lifted and squeezed him. "I can't—*more!*"

He'd give her more. He'd give her everything she could handle and everything she couldn't.

The curve of her stomach tempted his mouth. When his lips pressed just under her belly button, she gasped his name. Another spot. A weakness for her, a temptation for him. He bit her, then sucked the flesh. Jonas marked the area, and she trembled beneath him, as her hands rose to clutch his shoulders.

His head lowered more. He licked down her abdomen and let his breath blow against that lace.

"J-Jonas . . ." Sweat beaded his brow as he looked up at her. Lust and need burned in her eyes. "Jonas, I want you to—"

Taste me.

The words hung in the air between them. But she bit her lips and her gaze dropped.

He blew against the lace once more. Her hips lifted helplessly. "You want me to touch you again?"

A jerky nod.

His fingers caressed her through the lace. He traced lightly over her sex, feeling the material dampen. Christie was ready for him, and he was insane for her.

He lowered his mouth to that lace. Jonas kissed her through the fabric and felt her body go bow tight. It wouldn't take much to push her into a climax. Not much at all.

His fingers pulled on the lace. His control slipped away, breaking from him as her scent teased him and—

And the lace ripped.

"Buy you more," he promised as he tossed the scraps aside. He put his mouth right on her and tasted her flesh like he'd wanted. When his tongue pressed against the center of her need, Christie came, shuddering beneath him as she whispered his name on a long, hard sigh.

But he didn't stop. Wasn't close to stopping. He tasted and he took and when she came against his mouth a second time, he felt the trembles of her orgasm.

He pushed away from her. The drum of his heartbeat filled his ears. It took two seconds to ditch his jeans. Two more to slide on his condom and then he was plunging into her. Driving as deep as he could go. The ripples of her release teased his cock, and he drove into her, faster, harder.

His hands caught hers. Their fingers threaded together. Their eyes locked.

Thrust.

So blue. So dark. Her eyes held his. Wild with lust.

The tree lights glittered down on them. Shining.

Thrust.

Her legs were around his hips, holding so tight. Her ankles pressed against him, and she met him, thrust for thrust. He drove into her, deeper, harder.

"Jonas!"

He climaxed with her—and it was fucking incredible.

Eventually, they made it to her bed. Had sex again. Slow and tender this time. Christie was pretty sure there wasn't an inch of her body that Jonas hadn't kissed.

She felt so *good*. No, better than good. Better than she'd ever felt.

"You sure know how to deliver on a promise," she murmured as her hand trailed down the muscular expanse of his chest.

His eyes opened, and he turned his head toward her.

"That was definitely the best sex I've had," she told him.

His lips parted, but she leaned forward, fast, and kissed him. *Don't tell me any lies. Don't tell me I'm the best. Don't.*

Jonas wasn't like her. Sheltered didn't enter his vocabulary. She knew the guy had been with more sexual partners than she had. She didn't want to hear lies from him, not now, not ever.

"Another rule for us," she whispered as she pulled back and smiled at him. Christie smiled so he wouldn't see that it mattered to her. "No lies, okay?" She'd had plenty of those from her other lovers.

From Benjamin, her first lover. He'd sworn he loved her, but really just loved her family's money. Yes, she'd found out about that. Thanks to Jonas. When Ben had started talking about an engagement, Daniel had used Jonas to dig up background information on the guy. It hadn't taken long before they found out about Ben's debts. When her dad had offered Ben ten grand to walk . . . the guy had run.

And now the dust was still settling from Charles. Another lover who'd lied. Another mistake.

"I've never lied to you." Jonas's deep voice rumbled beside her.

No, he hadn't.

"Then let's not start." Her hand stilled on his chest. "I don't want you to promise me forever." Ben had done that. Forever had lasted two months. "I don't want you to tell me I'm the love of your life." Ronnie had done that. He'd told her she was great. Wonderful. They'd had sex— the sex that had just been . . . bad. The great love affair had ended fast. "I don't want to hear all the pretty lies that men can use."

His hand caught hers. "Didn't realize you were so cynical, Christie."

She laughed at that. "I didn't realize I was, either."

He brought her hand to his lips. "Then let's go ahead and clear the air."

Her brows rose.

"I'm not sleeping with you because I want a slice of that Tate money." He bit the pad of her palm. "Yeah, I remember that dick Ben. He thought he'd hit pay dirt when he found you in college."

Had she really been so naive? No. But it hadn't been college, she'd been in grad school then. "I never agreed to marry him." She hadn't loved him. Even then, she'd—

"I didn't want him using you. I know it pissed you off the way that scene went down." Another bite, then a lick of his tongue. "Daniel and I wanted you safe."

"And here I didn't think you'd ever cared." She tried to sound flippant.

His hold tightened on her hand. "There's a lot you don't know." His breath feathered over her hand. "When I'm with you, I'm with you. There's no one else for me." He paused. "Or for you. I'm not the sharing kind."

"Neither am I." But how long would they have together? Just how long would her wish last?

"This holiday is mine," he told her, and he leaned forward, catching the back of her head. "You made your wish, and this year, you'll get it—me—as many times as you can handle."

His lips were so close to hers. "I-I think I can handle quite a lot." Everything.

This holiday. She'd take him, she'd take the pleasure he gave, and when the new year came . . . well, she'd deal with that then.

Now, she'd deal with the big, bad, sexy detective in her bed. Christie parted her lips and kissed her Santa Claus.

* * *

The beeping woke her hours later. A long, steady pulse of sound. She threw out her hand, reaching for her alarm clock, and her hand hit warm, male flesh.

"It's mine," a deep voice growled.

Her eyes flew open and she saw a dark shadow pull away from her and rise from the bed.

Wh—Jonas. Sex. Pleasure.

She blinked a few times, fast. Those first few moments after waking were always a little fuzzy for her.

But—*what* was his? What was—

"North and Byron. Right. I'll be there in fifteen minutes." His voice didn't sound so sleepy. He seemed completely awake. Aware. Distant. She squinted as she tried to force her eyes to adjust to the darkness. Jonas was on a phone. That's what the buzzing had been—his phone ringing.

She sat up in bed and pulled the covers to her chest. A glance at the alarm clock told her it was only a little past four a.m.

Callused fingertips brushed her cheek. "I have to go."

She jerked a bit, surprised to find him so close.

His hand dropped.

She reached out at once, fumbling in the darkness. "What's happened?"

"Baby, you don't want to know."

She found his hand and held tight. "I told you. I'm *not* some princess in a castle. I can handle your life."

He exhaled, the sound a rough sigh that drifted to her. "A man shot his wife and turned the gun on himself. They need me at the scene ASAP." He pulled away from her and she missed him instantly. "You know I transferred to homicide."

No more undercover missions for him. Daniel had told her that. But . . . still blood and death.

Clothes rustled. He was dressing. He'd be leaving

soon. She jumped from the bed and rammed her thigh into the nightstand that she'd *known* was there. "Wait!" She scrambled, dragging the sheet with her and caught him at the bedroom door.

"I have to go, it's my job. You know—"

"Come back when your work's done." The words slipped out. She didn't want him going back home alone after this case. His voice had been too cold when he told her about the crime. Too emotionless. It wasn't a crime that didn't matter to him. No, this one would matter too much.

Jonas kept saying he knew more about her than she realized. She knew a heck of a lot more about him, too. Far more than he suspected.

She flipped on the lights and saw his face. The tight lines, the hard mask. "Come back to me when your work's done," she said again. "I'll be here. I don't care what time it is." *Come back to me.*

"I have to secure the scene, talk to witnesses. I have to—"

"I don't care how long it takes. I'll be here."

He kissed her then. Too fast, too hard, and she knew he had to go. Christie followed him to the garage door. He'd pulled his car inside earlier.

She watched him leave. When the garage door opened, she saw that it had started to snow again. Soft, drifting snowflakes floated in the air.

She pulled the sheet tighter around her body and felt the chill seep into her bones.

A man shot his wife and turned the gun on himself. A horrible crime. So terrible. So brutal.

And . . . it was Jonas's worst nightmare. She knew it. After he'd dug into Benjamin's past, she'd wanted a little vengeance. So she'd dug into Jonas's life. She'd found out his life wasn't nearly as perfect as she'd thought.

Not even close.

When Jonas had been sixteen, he'd come home to find his mother's dead body. She'd been killed by a man she knew and loved—Jonas's father.

"Come back to me," Christie whispered, but Jonas was already gone.

He didn't come back. Christie stared at the clock on her bedside once more. Ten p.m. There'd been no call, though she really hadn't expected that. No call . . . and no sign of Jonas as the hours had slipped by.

She should go to bed. Okay, she was *in* bed, but she should go to sleep. Stop thinking about him. Stop worrying.

But she'd seen a picture of him years before when she'd done her vengeance digging. A grainy photo of him at his parents' funeral.

He'd been alone then.

She shoved back the covers. She'd be damned if she left him alone now. She wouldn't—

Something thudded against her front door. Her heart raced even as she jumped to her feet. Thudded? No, wait that was knocking—*pounding*—at her door.

Christie ran down the hallway. She almost fell when her socks slid across the foyer floor. But she made it to the door and pressed her eye to the peephole. The porch light fell across Jonas's stark face.

She wrenched open the door as fast as she could.

No present waited in his hands this time. No smile lit his face. He stared at her with glittering eyes. The snow had turned into icy rain, pelting down behind him. She grabbed his hand. "Come in, Jonas! Hurry!"

He let her pull him across the threshold. "It's late. I shouldn't be here."

"This is *exactly* where you should be." She shoved off his coat. He'd changed shirts, jeans.

His gaze dropped. "I stopped at my place, I should have"—his hands flexed, balling into fists—"should have just stayed there. You don't need to—"

"I need you." More than she'd realized. So much more. His hands caught hers and held too tight.

"Jonas." Her chest hurt. "It's okay, I know—"

He kissed her. Not the sexy, hungry kisses he'd given her before. The kisses that teased and tormented and made her want more. Things were different. He was different.

The kiss was rough, demanding. His tongue drove into her mouth even as he lifted her into his arms. The bite of his fingers stung her arms, but she didn't stop him. She wrapped her arms around him and held on as tight as she could, her grip as fierce as his.

They made it to the bedroom. He tossed her on the bed and stripped while watching her with his too-bright stare.

She didn't wait for him to touch her. Christie yanked off her T-shirt and shimmied out of her shorts and panties.

He grabbed her ankle, pulling her to the edge of the bed.

"Can't wait this time." There was a dangerous edge to the words. Tension held his body tight. A muscle flexed in his jaw. *"Can't wait."*

She parted her thighs wider for him. "I don't want you to wait." She'd told him before that slow and easy wasn't what she needed from him. "I just want you."

"Careful what you wish for," he muttered. He had a condom on already. She hadn't even seen him pull out the packet.

He plunged into her, slamming balls-deep in a thrust that stole her breath. She'd said she could handle it, handle him, but she hadn't realized . . .

Her hands pushed against his shoulders.

Jonas froze. His gaze held hers. Rage boiled in his stare. Lust.

Fear?

"Christie . . ."

She rolled her hips beneath him as she tried to find a better position. Then his hand was stroking her, pressing in just the right spot. His mouth went to her neck, and when his tongue licked her beneath her ear, a moan slipped past her lips and the tension eased away from her body.

This was Jonas. She could trust him. He'd keep her safe. Give her pleasure, always.

He withdrew. Thrust deep again. Still hard, still wild, but she was ready for him. Her hands held tight to his shoulders. The bed shook beneath them. The headboard banged into the wall.

More. Harder. Deeper.

His teeth pressed lightly against her throat. His hands caught her legs, and he lifted them high, even as he drove into her. Again and again.

The orgasm hit her, sweeping over her on a fierce wave of pleasure that had her tensing and digging her fingers into his flesh. His head shot up and he stared down at her with eyes that blazed too bright.

Too much lust. Too much need.

"Christie . . ." He took her mouth. Kissed her as he came.

She held him as close as she could and felt the frantic, thudding beat of her heart.

Her heart . . . or his?

In the aftermath, they didn't speak. He pulled away from her, when she wanted to hold him close. But they were just about sex, right? Not emotions. Just sex.

So why was she blinking back tears when he withdrew from her? Why was she swiping those teardrops away as fast as she could while he was in the bathroom?

She pressed her damp hand against the bed, trying to wipe away the evidence, and she hurriedly slipped under the covers. The sex had been intense. Almost too intense. The climax had hit her when she hadn't expected that much pleasure. It had dug through her, hollowing out her body until she felt like only a thin shell remained.

The lights clicked off, and the room plunged into darkness. She was grateful for the darkness then. It was so easy to hide in the shadows.

Was that why Jonas had turned off the lights?

The bed dipped when he climbed in beside her. She wanted to roll toward him, but—yes, dammit—fear held her back.

He reached for her instead, smoothing his fingers down her arm. "Did I hurt you?"

What? "No, of course not!"

"I was rough, I shouldn't have—"

She rolled toward Jonas and grabbed him. "You didn't break me. You didn't even bruise me." But she might have bruised him. There at the end, she'd held on as tightly as she could.

His hand broke from hers, and his fingers traced her cheek. Her breath caught. *No, don't let him feel—*

"Were you crying?" His voice was gruff. "Jesus, Christie, I *did* hurt you!"

"Has anything ever felt so good," she asked him slowly, "that it made you cry?" The pleasure had been that intense. So intense she hadn't wanted it to end. She'd just wanted more.

"There haven't been a lot of good things in my life lately," he told her. His lips pressed against her cheeks as he kissed away the tear tracks. "Not until now," he murmured, and her breath caught.

No, no, he couldn't mean what she thought. *Just sex.* "I was worried about you." It seemed safe to make the confession in the dark.

Silence. Tension hummed in the air. "No need, baby. It's my job. I take down killers every day."

But not killers that hit so close to home. Suddenly, she wanted to break through his shell and force him to open up to her. "I know what happened."

"Yeah"—he slid away from her—"an asshole high on drugs shot his wife and then turned the gun on himself when the cops showed up. A wasted—"

"I don't mean today." Her tongue felt too thick in her mouth, and her heart still beat too fast. "I mean . . . b-before . . . with y-your parents." Of course, the stutter would be back. No way to hide her nerves.

The silence was painful. Then he rolled away, fast, and light exploded in the room when he hit the lamp.

He stared down at her, naked, eyes narrowed. "What the hell are you talking about?"

Good thing she'd already pulled up the sheet. "I-I know what happened to your family." *And how hard today must have been. So hard that when you came back—*

"How?" he bit out.

Ah, now this part was dicey. "Jonas—"

"Did you call Daniel when I left? Did he tell you that shit about—"

"I've never talked to Daniel about this." She took a breath, a deep one. *No stutter.*

"Then how did you find out? Who've you been talking to?"

She tucked the covers around her legs. "I found out over ten years ago. Right after you discovered that Ben was a gold digger." Her shoulders lifted and fell in a shrug that was anything but careless. "You tore into my life, so—"

"So you thought it was only fair to tear into mine." He spun away and yanked on his jeans. "Dammit, I did that to protect you! Your father and brother asked for my help! I'd just started working as a cop, we were all worried—"

"I know." But back then, she'd only been angry. Hurt.

Humiliated. The family had bought off her lover. They hadn't tried to talk to her, they'd just tried to run her life.

Not anymore.

"How?"

She blinked. "It wasn't hard, Jonas." Everything was public record. "I knew you'd been born in Athens, Georgia. I just searched through some of the newspapers online and tried to find a reference to you."

"Because you wanted some payback?"

Because she'd wanted to know him. "I saw a clipping about their deaths. A picture of you at the funeral."

He stopped pacing near the foot of her bed. "All this time, you've known?"

She gave a quick nod.

"Why didn't you say something?"

I didn't know what to say. Sorry just didn't seem to cover the situation. "Why didn't you?" she asked instead, her voice soft.

The laugh that came from him held no humor. "We already covered that you and I didn't *talk* much." He strode closer to her. "You knew and you still came to me?"

She didn't understand.

His hand lifted, as if he were going to touch her cheek. But his fingers fisted and fell away. "I knew I shouldn't have touched you."

Now that was bull. "You're the man who *should* have touched me." *Long ago.* It was late and the words were weak, but she continued, "I-I'm sorry about your parents. That must have been terrible for you. I can't even imagine what it must have been like—"

His head snapped up. He stared at her with glittering eyes and a clenched jaw. The angry mask was back in full effect.

Her chin notched up, too. She clutched the sheet, tucked it under her arms, climbed out of the bed, and grabbed him. "I *know* I don't understand how it felt, okay?

But I am sorry you had to go through that. No one should ever see—"

"The bloody bodies of their parents?" His lips twisted. "I see bodies every day. It's my job."

"That wasn't your job."

"*That's* why I do my job. *That's* why I became a cop."

Yes, she'd thought as much. The newspaper report had said . . .

"He was on drugs, Christie. My old man was so strung out he barely recognized his own family. My mom had kicked him out. She was trying to get a better life for us."

A life that ended too soon. That fist was back, squeezing her heart too tightly. She didn't let Jonas go. Christie kept her hands on him, her eyes on his.

"He broke in. By the looks of the place, I know he came looking for money. He trashed everything. My mom—she must have been trying to stop him when he—he—" His lips snapped closed. But she knew what came next.

Sixteen. He'd been through so much, so young.

"The cops told me it looked like he tried to help her. He even managed to make a 9-1-1 call. Hell, maybe the asshole finally realized what the hell he'd done. He called the ambulance for her, and then he killed himself. One shotgun blast to the head."

But Jonas had arrived before the ambulance. He'd been the one to find the bodies.

She wrapped her arms around his neck and let the sheet drop. She held him as tight as she could. Her lips pressed against his neck.

"You should be telling me to get the hell out now." His arms weren't around her. His body was held stiffly, too tense and hard. "My dad was an addict who killed my mom. You know what kind of bloodline I've got, you don't need to be—"

"Shut up, Jonas." Now he was pissing her off. "You're

not your dad." She lifted her head. "You're a good man, a good cop. You just got a real crap hand dealt to you."

His eyes widened a bit.

"Now get back in bed," she ordered him, hoping her voice sounded tough and strong. Hoping he didn't notice that her hands were shaking a bit. The new Christie she was trying to be—the wild girl who went after what she wanted—well, she wouldn't let her man walk away. Not after the hell he'd had today. She wouldn't wilt under that hot green stare. Wouldn't flinch from the pain in his past. No, the new Christie would be tougher than that.

Jonas slowly climbed back into bed with her. Her breath eased out when his head touched the pillow. *Good.*

She hit the lights and plunged them back into darkness because she could only keep the veil of that new Christie up for so long.

Jonas's arms came around her, pulling her against his body. A warm, strong body. A strong lover. One who was hers, for a brief time.

No commitments. It was just supposed to be about sex, right? And just sex meant no emotions.

So why the hell was she blinking away tears again and hoping that none of the drops fell onto his arms?

The cops told me it looked like he tried to help her.

The new Christie might be bluffing her way through the game, but underneath that fake cover, she was the same woman. A woman who cared too much. A woman who had one very big weakness.

A weakness who was holding her in his arms, close to his heart.

5

He was in trouble. Jonas stared at the small green box in his hand and wondered how the hell something as simple as no-strings sex could become so complicated.

Ah, but then, the answer was simple. Christie was involved—and the woman tended to complicate everything.

"Hey, man, you shouldn't have!" A pale hand snatched the present out of Jonas's grasp. He shot to attention—too late—and saw his partner, Scotty McKenzie, clutching the present. "I didn't get nothin' for you!" Scotty declared, his voice too loud.

Jonas shook his head. "Trust me, man, that's not your size."

Scotty blinked, then laughed, a deep, rumbling laugh that sounded like a train engine. "Then I'm guessing it belongs to the lady you were so hot to see last night. The one who had you smelling like a damn strawberry patch when you came to the crime scene."

Yeah, her smell had been on him, and he'd liked it. It had helped to combat the stench of death all over the place.

"Didn't even know you had a lady." Scotty threw his

body in the wobbly desk chair. "I mean, not one that you
stayed with longer than a weekend." He tossed the box
back to Jonas.

Jonas caught it in one hand. He'd already stayed the
weekend with Christie. And, at first, he'd done just what he
promised. *One hell of a good time.*

The last thing he'd expected was to get a call about a
scene like that, with *her* there.

He put the box on the desk top and ran a hand over his
eyes. When he'd gone back to her place, his control had
been shot. Rage had ridden him, the fury that he'd held
close for so many years.

He'd been desperate to get back to Christie. He'd
known she'd help him banish the past and forget the blood.
He'd also known he was walking a real thin line, but he'd
gone back anyway.

Call him a damn moth to the flame.

He'd been on her too fast, too hard. The sex had been
rough and wild. But she'd opened her body to him. Held
tight. Changed the fury to passion.

Good time? No, that didn't even come close to describing last night.

Then she'd blown his world apart with her little confession. All these years she'd known.

"Hey, man!" Scotty rolled his chair forward. "You with
me?"

Jonas blinked.

"What?" Scotty's lips lifted in his usual crooked grin.
"You realizing you already spent too much time with this
one? Gotta be careful, she'll think you're attached."

His gaze darted to the box.

"Tell you what"—the chair wheels squeaked as Scotty
rolled closer—"I'll do you a favor since it's the holidays.
You don't want to leave some poor woman on her own
during the holidays." He threw his arms out wide. "Since

I'm a generous, bighearted kind of guy, I'll take her off your hands."

"The hell you will." The words came out bullet fast.

Scotty blinked. His smile kicked up even more and he said, "Ah, like that, huh?"

Shit, no. "She and I have a deal." Not just a weekend. "The holidays are mine." After that, reality could come back.

In reality, he and Christie weren't—

Scotty whistled. "Oh, you've got it bad."

Maybe.

"Jonas?"

He whirled at the sound of that husky voice. A voice he'd never in a million freaking years expected to hear in the bullpen.

But, there she was. Christie stood just inside the door-way, right under the gold garland Scotty had stapled up yesterday. Her black hair hung loose around her face, her eyes were on him, wide, blue, and welcoming, and her lips were lifted in a warm smile.

"Oh, man," Scotty whispered, "I could *so* make her holiday."

"Mine," Jonas snapped. "Don't even think it." He strode across the bullpen, aware that the other detectives had noticed her, too.

Christie wasn't wearing a Christmas sweater today. She was in all black—black turtleneck, black pants, and long, sleek leather coat. The woman looked so sexy he was suddenly hungry for a bite . . . of her.

She hurried forward. "Oh, good, I was hoping I'd catch you!"

He caught her. Jonas snagged her hand and pulled her close. He leaned in and kissed her, fast and hard. *Back off, Scotty.* And all the other hungry jerks who were close by should get the message, too.

A wolf whistle split the air.

He expected Christie to break away at the sound, but her hands just lifted and wrapped around his shoulders, and she pulled him closer.

He let the kiss linger, enjoying her taste. After a few moments, when he finally pulled back, her eyes seemed to shine even more.

"I was . . . um . . ."—her gaze darted around them—"this is the first time I've been in a police station."

He could believe it. Not like the Tates were hauled in a lot for questioning.

Her eyes narrowed and she nodded. "I like the garland."

She would. If it was a Christmas decoration, she'd love it. He noticed the necklace then. A thin gold chain circled her neck, a chain attached to a tiny Christmas tree.

He dropped his hands and stepped back. "Um, Christie?"

Her eyes were still on the garland. Scotty had wound it all the way across the room.

Jonas's breath eased out as he stared at her.

"Hey, man!" Scotty's hand slapped down on his shoulder. "Introduce me!"

Christie's gaze flew back. She smiled a sweet, shy smile, directed at Scotty.

Jonas growled, then cleared his throat and managed to say, "Scott McKenzie, this is Christie Tate."

"I'm his partner." Scotty offered his hand. A hand Christie foolishly took. The guy brought her palm up for a lip-smacking kiss.

She laughed, a quick but lush sound. "Nice to meet you."

She probably meant it, but only because she didn't know Scotty well yet.

Scotty frowned at her. "Tate . . . where do I know that name?"

"You've probably met my brother. Jonas and Daniel are old—"

Scotty snapped his fingers. "Tate Toys!"

She nodded. "Yes, I work—"

"My nephew loves the Ricky Rocketshooter Robot!" Christie beamed.

"The first time I saw that thing fly across the room"— he shook his head, laughing—"I wanted one, too."

"I can get you one," she offered.

"Nah . . . those things sold out weeks ago."

"I've got connections." She bit her lip. "Actually, I made Ricky, and right now, I'm working on Rover, his sidekick. It'll be a dog who can fly. He'll be remote controlled, too, and he'll interface with Ricky—"

"You're bullshitting me," Scotty said, inching closer to Christie. "How the hell would you even go about making something like that?"

"Well, I studied engineering and robotics so—"

Jonas stepped in front of his partner before the guy could swallow Christie because Scotty was all but salivating over her. "Back off, *partner.* The lady and I need to talk."

Scotty's eyes squinted. "Lucky SOB." He stretched and peered at Christie over Jonas's shoulder. "Nice to meet you, ma'am. If you get bored with old Jonas here, you can—"

Jonas put his hand on Scotty's chest and shoved. "Why don't you get started on the Harris paperwork?"

With a smirk, Scotty sauntered away. Jonas turned back to Christie. "Sorry about that."

She blinked. "About what?"

About the dick who was drooling on you.

He caught her hand and pulled her into the nearest empty interrogation room. At least they'd have some privacy there. He shut the door with a soft click. "About last night," he began. Oh, shit, there was no easy way to do this. Come to think of it, he'd never had to do this with his other lovers. "I'm sorry."

A little furrow appeared between her brows. "For what?"

"For jumping on you like I was damn well starving."

Her smile flashed again, and he saw her dimple wink. "But I liked that."

The thudding of his heartbeat filled his ears. They were alone. The door was closed. He could put her up on the table . . .

"I liked everything we've done"—she lifted her hand and trailed her fingertips down his chest—"and everything we're going to do."

This was the shy girl who'd barely looked his way over the years?

Then he noticed the pulse pounding too quickly at the base of her throat. He caught the slight tremble in her fingertips. From lust? Oh, yeah, sure, one very swollen part of his anatomy hoped so . . .

But her eyes had already fallen away from his, and she was easing away, a little too fast.

Fear? Christie should know she had nothing to fear from him, and she didn't need to prove a damn thing to him.

But he had a lot to prove to her.

"You were right," he told her, "the case last night got to me. Made me remember . . " *Mom!* Her body. The blood. The scream that had burst from his throat. He sucked in a deep breath. "I wasn't in a good place when I came to you."

"I wanted you to come back to me." Her eyes met his and held. "I'm glad you did."

A man could really only take so much. He caught her chin, tilted her head back, and let his lips whisper over hers. If those cops weren't out there, each one of them no doubt straining to hear what was being said, he'd devour her.

Tonight. The holidays weren't over. Not yet. He still had time with her. Time to make her want and need just as badly as he did.

"I'll come to your place after my shift tonight," he said against her lips. He loved that fireplace she had. Loved the feel of the flames behind him and her soft body beneath his.

Her hand pushed against his chest. "I . . . ah, that's why I'm here."

He couldn't help the tension that tightened his shoulders.

"Actually"—she took a deep breath, one that made her breasts rise nicely—"I'm here because I was Christmas shopping in the area, and I realized I wanted to see you."

No lies. The tension slipped away.

"I could have called." She gave a little shrug. "But I— I just came to see you. I hope . . . I hope that was okay."

The uncertainty was plain, not hidden behind a too-bright smile, but obvious in the small, sexy stutter that had slipped free. He liked the confidence, but he liked the vulnerability more. When it came to her, was there a damn thing he didn't like?

Trouble.

"I'm having dinner at my parents' tonight. A family Christmas get-together." The words came out in a rush. "You're welcome to come with me."

To the Tate house? He'd been there with Daniel before, but never for the big holiday party. He'd avoided the annual family party like it was the plague. To him, it was.

Christie's gaze searched his. "Not part of the agreement, is it?"

Just sex.

Not families. Not dates to celebrate.

"Forget it." She gave a laugh. One far too strained and

fake for Christie. "It was just an idea. You don't have to come." She raised onto her toes and kissed his jaw. "We can meet tomorrow. We still have plenty of time."

But time could pass too quickly. Life could. "I'll be there."

Her breath blew against his neck as she looked up at him. "You will?"

He managed a jerky nod. *What am I doing?* "We'll probably give your dad and brother a heart attack, but what the hell?"

Her laugh was real this time. "Right, what the hell?"

"I'll meet you there," he offered, thinking fast. "My shift ends at eight. I'll come by then." *I'll drink enough to make it through the glares Daniel will give me.* Glares and maybe a punch. Or two. Because he knew how his buddy would react.

"Then we can go back to my place." Her voice became huskier. "Or yours."

He thought about his place for two seconds. "Yours." He smiled. "I like the way your skin looks when the tree lights shine on you." On her breasts, on the curve of her stomach. On that pink flesh between her thighs. Oh, yeah, he liked that.

A rap shook the door. "Captain wants us!" Scotty called, his voice way too happy for that announcement. No one was ever happy to talk to the captain.

Jonas pressed a quick kiss to her lips. "I'll see you tonight." He opened the door and found Scotty standing too close.

Scotty grinned. "See you soon, Christie."

Christie murmured something nice and polite back to him. Jonas turned his head and caught sight of his desk, and the package still on top of it.

He hurried forward and scooped it up. When he turned back around, Christie was already under the garland, heading for the exit. "Christie!"

She glanced back. Same welcoming smile. Same bright eyes.

And the same punch hit him in the gut. Dammit. He hurried forward and offered her the gift.

As soon as she saw the package, her skin flushed. "Jonas?"

"I was gonna give it to you tonight."

"Ain't that sweet!" a detective's voice rang out. Bronte, a guy he would pound later.

Her hands tightened around the box. "Thank you." She lifted the box to her ear and gave it a quick little shake.

He kissed her, fast but deep. "You can thank me after the party." She could do anything she wanted tonight.

He sure planned to do just that.

Christie waited until she was back in her car and then she ripped open the package. When the green silk panties tumbled out—thong underwear—she wasn't surprised.

She was turned on.

She knew just what she'd be wearing tonight for her cop.

Maybe she'd let him rip this pair off, too.

"So you're going to meet the family, huh?" Scotty asked as they grabbed their coats at eight and got ready to head out the door.

Another day from hell. Holidays could bring out the best in people, but they could bring out the worst, too. He and Scotty had spent hours at another crime scene. A robbery gone bad. The shop owner hadn't been the one to wind up in the body bag, though. The robber must not have expected the guy in his eighties to fight back.

He had.

Jonas yanked on his gloves. "I already know the family." Too well, so he knew what kind of welcome he'd get when he showed up with Christie.

Because they also know me too well. Well enough to understand that he shouldn't be with Christie. He'd always known it, too.

"Take my advice with this one," Scotty said, his grin sliding away. "Don't screw up."

Jonas raised a brow.

"Seriously. This one isn't like the others."

Christie wasn't like anyone else.

"We're both gettin' too old to spend our holidays alone." Scotty looked out the front doors of the station. "There's got to be more than crime scenes waiting on us. If you're smart, you'll take that 'more' that's standing so close to you." He inclined his head. " 'Night, partner."

A cold blast of air swept inside when Scotty left.

Jonas lifted his collar and got ready to follow his partner.

"Yo, Kirk!"

His hand hesitated in front of the doors. He glanced to the left and saw the desk sergeant waving him over. He and Carl had known each other for years.

"Hey, aren't you friends with Daniel Tate?"

A fast nod.

"My boy Jamie is working as a security guard there."

"I saw him the other night." Jonas turned away from the door. There was something in Carl's voice. "There a problem?"

"I know it's not your beat, but, since you know the family and all"—Carl leaned over the desk—"Jamie called about an hour ago. Said there was some trouble in one of the offices."

"What kind of trouble?" Jonas's phone vibrated in his pocket. "Hold on, Carl." He stepped to the side as he put the phone to his ear. "Kirk."

"Jonas! Shit, man, I need you." Daniel's voice was way more tense than normal—and normal usually *was* tense for Daniel. "Can you come down to the company? Someone . . . someone broke into Christie's office and trashed the place."

What? Fuck. "I'm on my way." He spun around.

"Wait!" Carl called out. "Don't you want to know—"

"On it, Carl, thanks." The cold air hit him in the face as he raced for his vehicle. *Christie's office.* What the hell? As far as he knew, there had never been any trouble at Tate Toys.

So why was it starting now? And why was some asshole targeting Christie?

Uniforms were on the scene when Jonas arrived at Tate Toys. A cop he recognized, Officer Larry Piner, stood just outside Christie's office doorway, questioning Daniel and jotting down fast notes.

Daniel caught sight of him. "Jonas! Man, thanks for coming so fast." Daniel ran a hand through his hair and gestured to Christie's office. "Can you believe this shit?"

Jonas's gaze raked the room. Piner's partner was inside, carefully navigating through the wreckage. Papers and files littered the floor. The computer screen was busted into about a hundred pieces. The desk was overturned. The lamp smashed.

"You sure there was no one working here today?" Officer Piner asked.

"I'm sure." Daniel's hand dropped. "Everyone on this floor is off the rest of the week for the holidays. Hell, everyone but the folks in distribution are off, and they're all down at the warehouse. We've only got a skeletal security staff in this building. No one else should be here."

Just Christie's office. Someone was sending her a message. One Jonas damn well didn't like. "What about cameras?" he asked as anger built in his gut. "You got 'em turned on, right?"

Daniel nodded his head in agreement. "We've got them downstairs at the entrance, but that's where a guard is posted. If anyone came in, he would have seen 'em."

Not if he'd been in the john. "Get the tapes," Jonas ordered, walking slowly into the room. "Have you called Christie?"

Silence.

He tossed a glance back over his shoulder. "You've called her, right?"

"No." Daniel's lips pressed together. "It's so close to Christmas, and I mean, *look at this place.* I don't want her coming in here and seeing this crap!" His hair stood up, probably from running his fingers through it too many times. "Christie can't handle this stress right now, not on top of that whole mess with Charles. Hell, I just want you to find out who did this, and I want that asshole arrested!"

Jonas glanced toward the filing cabinet. Every folder had been yanked free and the contents scattered. The drawers hung open, deep and empty. He pulled out his phone.

"Are you calling in a crime scene team?" Daniel asked, and there was excitement in his voice. "Good plan, man, let's *CSI* this asshole."

Jonas just shook his head. A ring filled his ears. One. Two.

"Hello." Her voice was soft and husky.

He took a breath. "Christie, it's Jonas."

"What are you doing?" Her brother's desperate yell grated in his ears.

Jonas ignored him. "I'm not gonna be able to make that dinner tonight." No, he'd be working this case until he figured out what the hell was going on. "There's been a break-in."

"But"—hesitation, confusion—"you work homicide."

This case was different. *Personal.* "The break-in was at Tate Toys. It's your office, Christie."

"What?"

"I'm down here now with the investigating cops. I want you to come by. You'll know if anything is missing." He exhaled. "You can come in tomorrow and make a listing then, if you want. You don't need to cut out on your parents—"

There was a rumble of voices in the background. Christie spoke to someone else, then she told him, "No, I'm on my way. Mom and Dad will hold dinner a bit. Don't worry, they've got plenty of guests here to keep things going."

"Be careful, baby." He ended the call and held the phone a moment, his gaze sweeping the office once more.

Someone tapped him on the shoulder. He turned around. Daniel glared at him. "You called her—"

"She had a right to know. She's not some fragile doll that's gonna break with a little stress." He'd been wrong about her, and Daniel was too. *All those years . . . she'd known.* Hell, no, Christie wasn't going to break. She'd been right when she told him she didn't live in a castle.

Sure, she'd been sheltered. The family had cosseted her in college. He'd helped by digging into old Benjamin's background. But Christie didn't need them to run interference anymore. She was a grown woman. Strong, smart, sexy.

"No." Daniel's eyes narrowed and his gaze seemed to shoot blue fire as he snarled, *"You called my sister 'baby.' "*

Oh, shit.

"You're sleeping with Christie?" A man's voice shouldn't get that high.

Jonas got ready for the punch he knew was coming. Daniel had a real killer right hook.

Christie hadn't dressed for the office. She'd dressed for him. Bought the new emerald green dress to match the panties. Maybe that was overkill, but she'd been feeling sexy at the time. Good thing she'd brought her coat with her. Otherwise she'd be flashing a lot of skin as she rushed down the hallway.

Christie skidded to a halt on her two-inch heels, a very precarious halt, and she eyed the mess that was her office. *"Sonofabitch."*

Daniel was there at once, reaching for her, his eyes worried, his face tense. "It's okay, Christie, I know this is *upsetting*—"

"Yes, it's upsetting." Major understatement. "Some jerk ruined my office!" And her files. Oh, jeez, it would take forever to get those organized again. So many hours lost.

"Don't worry about this tonight." Daniel caught her hands and held them tight. "Just go back to our parents, relax, and—"

"Trust me, Dan, I'm really not in the mood to relax."

She was so mad her skin felt like it was burning. She craned her neck. "Where's Jonas?"

A muscle flexed in Daniel's jaw. "Jonas works the stiffs. We don't need him on a vandalism case. And it's just vandalism. I don't think anything was taken from your office."

Not taken. Just destroyed. "*I* need him."

"I was hoping you'd say that," Jonas muttered from behind her.

Daniel swore.

She whirled around and found Jonas sauntering back from her lab area. As he came closer, she noticed the redness on his jaw. "Jonas?" She hurried back into the hallway, nearly toppling only once in her shoes. "What happened?"

"Must be something about your office," he told her, his lip curling a bit. "Makes folks want to assault cops."

Her fingers skimmed his jaw. "What?" His words sank in and her eyes widened. "Charles? Did he come back? Did he do this?" He'd actually hit Jonas? Had he been the one to trash her office, too?

"Nah, not him, not this time."

"It was me." Daniel's arm brushed hers as he came to her side. "I punched the asshole." He glared at Jonas. "And he didn't punch back."

Jonas inclined his head. "Didn't arrest you either. Guess it's your lucky night."

Daniel rocked forward. "You're screwing my sister!"

Oh. Ouch. Christie slammed her hand on his chest. "No." She kept her voice quiet and cool. A real effort, but the new and improved Christie could manage that effort. "Your sister is screwing *him*." She didn't even stutter when she tossed that out.

Daniel's eyes bulged.

"And if you try to take a swing at him again . . ." Because that really pissed her off. She wasn't sixteen. She didn't need him fighting her battles anymore. Fighting her battles or her lovers. Hadn't she told him that enough times? "If you swing at him again, I'll punch you." Her right hook was even better than his.

Daniel blinked. "Christie?" He asked like he wasn't sure he was talking to his sister.

She kept her hand on his chest.

"I told you she could handle a little stress." This came from Jonas.

More than a little. She'd been handling stress all her life. Try being thirteen in a room full of eighteen-year-olds—stress much?

Daniel's gaze bored into her. "Christie, you know what he's like."

"He's your best friend. He's had your back for years. Yes, I know." She bit out the words. "He's strong and loyal and—"

"Not when it comes to women." Daniel caught her hand and tried to tug her away from Jonas. She wasn't in the mood to be tugged. "When it comes to women, he's just like *me.*"

She shook her head. "You're—"

"No commitment, Christie."

Jonas rolled his shoulders.

"When's the last time I brought someone home for you to meet?" Daniel pushed.

Never.

"Sex is great. Sex is fucking fantastic." Daniel huffed out a breath. "But I'm not looking for forever right now."

Neither is Jonas. The words hung unspoken in the air.

She took a moment to make sure her voice wouldn't waver. "I'm not a kid who needs looking after anymore." She licked her lips and did the hair-toss she'd seen other women do, the move that made them look like they were confident and in charge. "I'm a woman who knows what she wants."

"Damn right." Jonas sounded pleased, almost proud.

She ignored him. "I don't want forever."

Daniel's eyes slit so much he seemed to squint.

"Men aren't the only ones who just want—what did you call it? Fucking fantastic sex."

Daniel's jaw dropped.

"Jonas and I understand each other. What's happening is between us, not you." Christie glanced at Jonas. His eyes were on her, and his expression—well, crap, what was wrong with him? He was glaring at her.

Glaring when she was trying to stop him from getting into another fight with her brother.

"Uh, Ms. Tate?" the uniformed officer called out tentatively.

She'd forgotten about the other cops. Oh, fabulous. Had they heard everything? How fast would this little conversation get repeated at the station? No wonder Jonas looked pissed.

She cleared her throat and looked at the cop.

"Since you're here, ma'am, we need you to do a sweep and determine if anything was taken."

"Right." She sucked in what should have been a cleansing breath. It wasn't. Christie stepped back and pointed at both Jonas and Daniel. "You two going to behave?"

Glares were her response.

"Fine." She shifted her focus to Jonas. "Feel free to arrest him if he swings again, or if you want to punch back, we both know he's got a glass jaw." With that, she left them, aware that her strong front was about to shatter.

Her knees shook as she headed back toward her office. The damn heels twisted beneath her and she almost went down hard. Only a quick grab of the wall saved her, the wall and—

Jonas's hand, catching her under her elbow.

"Sexy as hell, baby," he breathed the words in her ear

and she realized her coat had come open to reveal the green dress. His gaze dipped to her cleavage. "Sexy as hell," he whispered again, "but those shoes could be lethal."

He bent and ran his hand over her calf. A soft, sensual caress that had her breath catching.

He eased off her high heel. The left shoe, then the right.

Her stocking-clad feet touched the soft carpet.

"Watch your step," he told her, and for an instant, she couldn't move because the warning in those words was too heavy. The man wasn't just talking about walking. So about what? Them? The attack in her office? She forced her shoulders to straighten and she pushed away from him. She grabbed the heels, clutching them too tightly, and even though she was tempted, Christie didn't look back.

"I don't know what kind of game Christie thinks she's playing." Daniel spoke only after Christie disappeared with Officer Piner. "But she's not up to handling you."

Jonas realized he was still staring after her. "Sometimes, I don't think you know her well at all." He slanted Daniel a measuring glance. Dangerous territory. He could well lose his friend over this.

She's worth it.

"You *don't* know her," Daniel snapped right back.

Yeah, he did. "I know she's stronger than everyone gives her credit for." Stronger than he'd given her credit for in the beginning. That woman wouldn't break when reality shoved its ugly face before her. No, she wasn't going to break—period.

"So what? You think that makes it okay for you to screw around with her?" Real fury vibrated in Daniel's voice. *"She's my sister! And you're not—"*

Jonas spun around. "Save it, Daniel." *And you're not*

good enough for her. Yeah, he got that picture. "This isn't about you." Just her.

But Daniel blazed on. "You're not the kind of guy who's going to settle down. Hell, until six months ago, you were a different man with every case you took! Christie isn't like you—she *wants* stability. She wants a family. She wants forever."

But she'd only asked him for a few nights. She'd told him she *didn't* want forever.

Or she just didn't want it with him.

"I told her to be careful with you." Daniel crossed his arms over his chest. "I warned her, but she didn't listen."

"I'm not gonna hurt her."

Daniel just stared back at him. Then he exhaled. "You've known her all these years. So long. Why now? Why'd you finally make a move now?"

Because you're right—until six months ago, I was a different man almost every damn day. I was drowning in the crime and the hate and realized I had to get out. And when I got out . . . there was Christie. As perfect and tempting as she'd always been and this time . . . "Because she wanted me."

"Plenty of women will screw you, you don't have to—"

"She *wanted* me," he said again. "She knew me, and she still wanted me." Dark shadows on his soul and all. "With Christie, I wasn't gonna be fool enough to turn away from her. Not even for the sake of our friendship. So just deal with it, asshole."

Daniel blinked at him. "Wait, man, are you sayin'—"

"I'm saying it's none of your business, and I'm saying the last thing you want to do"—he let the steel ripple beneath his words because he was tired of explaining himself and tired of playing the nice guy—"is get between me and Christie."

Because nothing would keep him from her, and friendship could only stretch so far.

Silence.

"I don't *think* anything is missing." Christie sounded uncertain as she appeared once more in the hallway, with the cops at her sides. "The files"—she shrugged her shoulders—"will take me hours to sort through, so I can't say for certain. But . . . I didn't really have anything of value. The computer is still there—smashed—but there. The fax machine, the printer, all my photos—everything *seems* to be still inside."

Officer Piner—Larry—had his notebook out. "If something wasn't taken, then it seems like this was a personal attack against you."

Jonas forgot about Daniel and hurried to her side.

"Does anyone have a grudge against you, Ms. Tate?" Larry asked.

Her brows rose.

"Did you fight with anyone recently?" Larry's partner asked. He was a young guy with blond hair and ruddy cheeks.

Christie's gaze darted to Jonas. "There was an . . . incident the other night. Right after the office Christmas party."

Daniel pushed closer. "What kind of incident?"

Her hand rose and caught the edge of her Christmas tree necklace. She pulled on the bottom of the tree, stretching the thin gold chain. Her gaze went back to Larry. "A situation with my ex became a bit heated."

"What?" Daniel demanded. "Was Charles causing trouble? I knew I should have fired—"

"Does this Charles have a last name?" Larry interrupted.

"Charles Crenshaw." She dropped the necklace. It fell back into the lush cradle of her breasts. "But he wouldn't do this. He's an accountant, for goodness sake. He wouldn't—"

"Take a swing at a cop because he was jealous that you

were with another man?" Jonas offered quietly. "I think you're underestimating the accountant."

Her lips thinned.

"I think so, too," Larry murmured. "And I think we're gonna be wanting to have a talk with Mr. Crenshaw." He glanced at Daniel. "Is there any way he could have gained access to this building without being on the security camera downstairs?"

Before Christie had arrived, Larry had gone with Jonas to view those tapes. And they hadn't seen anyone. Only Jamie, the security guard. No one else had entered the building or left. Not until Daniel came by a little after seven.

Daniel frowned. "The cameras rotate. I guess . . . if you knew the timing, you *might* be able to avoid 'em, but there's still Jamie."

"Who didn't see anyone." Larry shut his notebook.

"Maybe we're looking at the time all wrong on this," Jonas said quietly. They'd only gone back over the day's footage. "Maybe the attack didn't happen today. Maybe it happened after the party."

When everyone was leaving. Too much activity. Too many people.

Sure, the computer would have made noise when it was smashed, but he'd seen for himself just how deserted this area of the building had been that night. All of the action had been in the common areas. No one would've even heard the crash.

And there'd only been a few people left hanging around after Santa had finished all his deliveries.

He slanted a hard glance at Daniel. "Why'd you come to her office?"

"I wanted a printout on the projected development of Rover."

Right. Rover the Robot.

"I thought I'd show the info to Dad tonight. Figured he'd get a kick out of it. He loves Christie's designs."

Jonas nodded. "So if you hadn't come by, no one would have even noticed the destruction until after Christmas." What a hell of a present for Christie to return to. Maybe that was what the asshole wanted.

"I'll be needing Mr. Crenshaw's address," Larry said quietly.

"And I'll be coming with you to talk with the jerk." Jonas shook his head. "I knew I should have let that dumbass spend a night in jail."

Christie shook her head. "Look, Charles might have been angry, but he wouldn't do this. He backed off, remember? He knows things are over between us. Hell, he's already seeing someone else. Vicki Jasper. They'll probably get married one day and have little accounting babies." She sucked in a deep breath. "He's *not* the kind of guy who would destroy my office."

"Then who would?" Jonas asked, stepping close, catching her scent and wanting to touch her so badly that he ached. "Who else would do this? Who else would want to hurt you?"

If she'd give him a name, he'd get busy tearing the bastard apart.

Her gaze held his. "No one. I can't think . . . *no one.*"

But someone was out there. Someone who had a grudge against her. Someone who was going to pay.

And Charles Crenshaw was at the top of his list.

Jonas didn't go back to her parents' house with her. Her parents saved dinner for her and Daniel, had kept their guests waiting so they could all eat together.

Her father was furious about her office, and he kept tossing out threats left and right. Her mother seemed worried, her voice quiet and concerned as she asked questions.

And Daniel—well, he still seemed pissed.

There was an extra seat at the table. An obviously empty seat. She'd asked her mother to make room for Jonas, and Clara had. Room that wasn't needed.

"Christie, dear, what happened to your friend?" her mom finally asked in her soft, southern drawl, just as they were beginning the second course. Maybe her mom was trying to take the focus off the vandalism. Maybe she was simply curious. Clara was known for her curiosity— ahem, nosiness—as much as for the slew of beauty pageant wins she'd racked up as a younger woman.

Christie's hold on her knife tightened. "Jonas is working on the investigation about the incident tonight." *Incident* sounded nice and vague. She really didn't want her aunts, uncles, and assorted cousins knowing that her office had been trashed, quite possibly by an ex-lover.

"Jonas?" her mother repeated and a smile stretched her lips. "Oh, well, he'll get to the bottom of this and—"

"No, Mom." A long sigh came from Daniel. "What Christie means is that Jonas can't be *here* because he's working the case."

"Such a shame," her mother said, still obviously missing the point. "I invite him every year and he never—"

"Jonas was my date," Christie interrupted, figuring it would be best to just break in with the news.

"Your date?" her mother repeated. Then her smile widened and her blue eyes gleamed. "Oh, finally, you're picking an interesting man!"

Yes, she was. Her gaze shifted to her father. She knew he'd heard everything.

He stared back at her. "You know what you're doing?"

She nodded.

He picked up his fork. "I always rather liked Jonas."

What?

Her father aimed his fork at Daniel. "You like him, too, so don't be glaring at me, boy."

"He's *dating* Christie."

Her father glanced her way once more. "Then that makes him one lucky man."

Christie swallowed. "Thanks, Dad."

"I learned my lesson with you years ago, sweetheart." A grin edged his mouth. "You weren't ever really interested in that Benjamin, were you?"

She shook her head.

"Sometimes love can make a man do crazy things." He dove into his plate, came back up, and said, "But my girl is damn smart, and if she's chosen to be with Jonas, then that's fine by me."

Daniel hung his head. "He *is* a lucky bastard."

She thought about Jonas's past. No, he wasn't lucky. She was the one who'd had all the luck.

Daniel happened to look at her then. His eyes narrowed on her face. "Christie?"

People talked around them. Her mother turned away, chatting with a cousin. Daniel scooted toward her. "You . . . know, don't you?" he asked.

She still hadn't managed to take a bite of food. She let her fork drop. "Know what?" Jonas's secrets were his. Not her place to tell them.

"I'll be damned." Daniel's eyes swept her face. "He told you."

No, I already knew.

"As far as I know, he's never told anyone but me," he said.

Her temper began to boil. It had really been one hell of a night. The break-in. The fight between Jonas and Daniel. Finding out her ex might be gunning for her. "He told you because he trusts you, Daniel. You're friends, remember? Even if you're acting like a jerk, he still sees you as his friend."

His gaze held hers. "I'm sorry," he said softly, slowly.

"Don't tell me," she muttered. "Tell *him.*"

The doorbell rang then. A long, echoing peal of sound, and Christie couldn't help it—her heart started to race.

Then a few moments later, Jonas walked into the room, and her heart nearly jumped out of her chest. His hair was swept back, and the leather coat stretched across his shoulders. He stopped when he saw the packed table. The spread of food. All those relatives.

She stood up, shoving her chair back. "Jonas!" She couldn't stop the wide smile that lifted her lips.

He smiled back at her. A hesitant curl of his mouth that made the man look even sexier.

Daniel rose, too. "Come on over here, man," he called over the din of voices. "We've got you a seat waiting." Daniel's hand squeezed Christie's shoulder.

Her brother really could be a good man. He just sold himself short too much.

Jonas came around the table, his steps a bit slow. The bulge of his weapon was gone. He'd been armed when he met her at Tate Toys. He'd been a cop then. Now, he was coming to dinner just as a man. *Her date.* Christie took his hand and pulled him down beside her.

Just sex? Who was she kidding?

"Glad to see you, Jonas," her mother told him, flashing her dimpled smile.

"Son, we've got plenty to eat," her dad said, waving his hand over the table.

Jonas blinked and shot her a questioning glance.

She caught his hand beneath the table. "It's Christmas," she told him. "And you've been welcome here with my family for years." But finally, *finally,* he'd come to celebrate with them.

His fingers tightened around hers.

She had to swallow the lump that rose in her throat. Daniel leaned forward and said bluntly, "Sorry for being a dick."

To which her mother immediately shouted, "Oh, Lord, language! Don't let Grandma Addie hear that kind of talk!"

"Too late!" came Addie's ninety-three-year-old cackle, because she loved that kind of talk. Her husband of seventy years had been a sailor.

When Daniel winced, Jonas laughed. His head tilted back, and a deep rumble of laughter shook his chest.

Christie stared at him, speechless, lost. So lost—in him.

Right then, she knew exactly what she wanted for the holidays. Not just sex. Not fleeting pleasure. *Him.*

Too bad she couldn't have what she wanted.

Jonas followed her home. Kept her taillights in sight at all times. Kept her in his mind.

They hadn't been able to find the ex. Jonas had gone with the cops to Charles Crenshaw's house, but he hadn't been there. According to a neighbor, Crenshaw left town yesterday. An annual trip back to see his parents at Christmas.

So the guy *could* have trashed the office Friday night, then—calm as you please—driven to Cincinnati to see his family.

But Jonas didn't like the whole damn situation, and until he got a better handle on just what the hell was happening, he planned to stay close to Christie. Not that staying close was any kind of hardship.

She pulled into her driveway and the garage door began to open. He followed her, aware that the routine seemed way too comfortable and easy. *Like I'm coming home.*

Bullshit, of course. Her place wasn't his home. Not even close. His home was the barren apartment over on Bentley. The place that hadn't even sported a Christmas tree until noon. He'd picked the thing up during lunch. He'd been worried Christie would come to his place and, well, hell, the woman loved Christmas. He'd needed the tree for her.

He climbed out of his car and slammed the door. Christie waited for him by the doorway, a warm smile on her lips. The same smile she'd given him at her parents' place, the smile that made him feel like he'd taken a punch in the gut.

For that sweet curve of her lips, he'd gladly take a hit.

He hurried to her, aware of the grind of the garage door as it lurched back down. His gloved fingers slid down her cheek. Her dress was driving him crazy.

Christie laughed lightly and turned away. She unlocked the door and walked inside—

Then she froze. The lights in the den and kitchen blazed cheerfully, but Christie wasn't moving.

"Christie?"

"I turned that light off when I left." Her hand pointed to the kitchen.

Shit. He shoved her behind him. "Get in your car. Pull out onto the street. Lock the doors and stay there." He took a step forward.

Christie grabbed his hand. "What are you doing?"

He had his phone out. "Calling for backup." And checking the place out. He threw her a hard stare. "Go, Christie. Now." He didn't want her around any danger.

Her delicate jaw tightened. "Be careful, Jonas."

"Always, baby."

She slipped outside, and he got ready to hunt.

7

Her house hadn't been trashed. As far as she'd been able to tell in those brief moments before she fled, nothing had been taken, just like nothing had been taken from her office. But Christie *knew* someone had been inside her place. She always turned the kitchen light off when she left. Always.

Someone had been there and turned it back on.

She could tell by the way the uniforms on the scene were eyeing her that they didn't necessarily believe her story.

When Jonas came back to her side, she straightened away from her car, hugging the coat tightly to her. "Do you think it's Charles? Is he really trying to—"

"Charles is in Cincinnati."

"Since when?"

"Nine a.m. I got a trooper who owes me a favor up there to check in on your ex. I didn't think you wanted me to mention it at the party with all those people there, but"—Jonas shook his head—"Crenshaw's not our guy."

Someone else out there wanted to scare her? Why?

"I want you to come home with me tonight," Jonas told her. "Let the uniforms keep searching here."

"Do you think they'll find anything?" *Someone had broken into my house.* The goose bumps on her arms weren't just from the cold. Fear had lodged inside her.

His lips thinned. "Doubt it."

"Someone *was* here, Jonas." She wasn't crazy. She *was* more than a little obsessive compulsive, and she always turned out that kitchen light when she left.

"I believe you, that's why I want you with me. Until I find out what's happening here, I want to make absolutely certain you're safe."

She could be safe at her parents'. At Daniel's. If she went with Jonas, she'd be getting a lot more than just safety.

That was exactly what she wanted. "Okay, but can I get some clothes first?"

His gaze raked her, hot in the cold air. "I'll take care of that for you."

She licked wind-dry lips. "What's happening, Jonas?" She didn't mean between them. The situation between them was way out of control. "Why is someone doing this to me?"

He opened the car door and ushered her inside. "I'm gonna find out, baby."

"This isn't your case." No dead bodies—*thank God*—no need for him to be here. "Daniel might have called you in before, but you don't have to work this."

"You're involved." His eyes glittered. "That means I'm involved, and I'm not backing off until I find out what's happening."

Her hands tightened around the steering wheel. "I didn't mean for any of this to happen." Things had spiraled out of control. "It's all gotten so complicated," she whispered and caught the narrowing of his eyes.

"Baby, sex is complicated."

With him, it was. Complicated and hot and wild and what she needed right then to banish the cold that snaked through her. *In my house.* Why?

"Keep the vehicle running and stay warm. Harris over there"—he nodded to a cop standing near a patrol car—"will keep an eye on you until I get back."

She grabbed his hand. "You really think I need someone to watch me every minute?"

His stare bored into her. "*I* need him there." The faint lines around his eyes seemed deeper. "It takes someone damn ballsy to walk right into your house. Whoever this dick is, he's not getting close to you again."

This wasn't the way her Christmas should have turned out. When she'd made her wish, she'd just wanted—

He kissed her. She expected a hard, fierce kiss. Instead, it was the gentlest whisper of lips. "I'm the only one getting close to you."

Then he was gone.

And she wanted him back. Close again. As close as she could get him.

She'd never been to his apartment before. Christie wasn't sure what she'd expected, but the relaxed feel of the place suited Jonas.

She liked the overstuffed couch—the couch that faced the flat-screen TV. The overflowing bookshelf wasn't a surprise. She'd known Jonas loved to read.

But she didn't expect the tree.

A small Christmas tree, wilting a bit, stood in the corner of his den. Some gold garland—like the garland she'd seen at the station—had been tossed around the tree. No presents were under the tree. No tree skirt. No, um, water that she could tell. It wasn't an artificial tree, so it *really* needed some water.

Jonas came up behind her. "It's a piece of shit, isn't it?"

Despite the tension that had been riding her, Christie found herself laughing. "No, I think it's gorgeous." She'd always been a Charlie Brown tree fan. "But, Jonas," she turned in his arms, "you might want to consider watering it. If you want the tree to live until Christmas."

His cheeks stained a bit. "Figured I forgot something." He shook his head. "I knew if I didn't get a tree, you'd—"

Whoa. Wait a minute. "When did you get the tree?"

"Today." He bent his head and his lips pressed against her neck.

Her weak spot. She held onto his shoulders, aware that her knees trembled. "Wh-why?"

"Because"—his breath blew over her flesh—"you love Christmas."

Well, yes. Didn't everyone?

He caught her hands and pulled back. "There wasn't much for me to celebrate in the years after my parents died."

No, there probably hadn't been.

"I bounced around in foster care until I hit eighteen. And then . . . hell, your brother invited me home every holiday, but I didn't go with him."

"Why not?"

"Because seeing other families hurt too much." He dropped her hands and glanced toward the tree. "There were only a few trees left on the lot. It really didn't look that bad earlier."

Seeing other families hurt too much. "I-it just needs some water. The tree's gorgeous."

She saw his mouth tighten. "It's not like yours."

"That's because I spent *two days* decorating mine, and I forced Daniel to help me." *Next year you can help.* She bit the words back. There wouldn't be a next year. The wish she'd made had time limits.

She wrapped her arms around his waist.

"When I worked undercover, I didn't have days off for the holidays. I didn't *want* my Christmas to be free."

But this year was different. "Jonas, why'd you transfer out?"

Silence. Then, "Because I realized there were things I *did* want. Things I wanted more than the job."

What do you want? The question trembled on her lips. The bolder, braver Christie would ask. But that woman wasn't there at the moment. Too much had happened tonight. Doubts surrounded her. Fears.

"I hope you get everything you want," she said instead and meant it. Jonas deserved to be happy.

"So do I," he muttered and his mouth took hers. The kiss was harder, deeper. "Because I'm damn well realizing how much I need you."

Wait—what had he said? "Jonas—"

His tongue thrust into her mouth. His hands pushed the coat off her shoulders, and it hit the floor.

"Did you wear this to drive me crazy?" The words were growled against her lips.

She managed a nod.

"It worked."

He lifted her up, carried her, and placed her on the table near the wall. "I wanted you from the second I saw you tonight. You were nervous, scared, and I wanted to keep you safe—*and I just wanted you.*" His hand pushed under her skirt. "Oh, hell, *garters?*"

They'd been so sexy in the store, and she'd never worn them before. They'd looked great on the mannequin. Sexy and fun.

"We're not making it to the bedroom, not for the first time." His blazing eyes held hers. "I'm fucking starving for you."

When had a man ever told her that? When had a man ever looked at her with such need?

No other man. Just Jonas.

"I don't need the bedroom." She let her hands trail down his chest. Thanks to the table, she was at the perfect height to touch and tease. And, really, it was her turn to play. She caught the buckle of his belt and unhooked the leather. He'd already ditched his jacket and gloves. Time for the rest to go.

He sucked in a sharp breath when she unsnapped the pants and eased down the zipper.

"Wait."

He was telling her to stop? Her jaw almost dropped.

But he yanked a condom out of his wallet and slapped the foil packet on the table. Ah, that was her man. Always prepared.

She reached for his cock. Already up, thick, bobbing toward her. She hadn't gotten the chance to touch that flesh before. Hadn't been able to explore him as he'd learned her.

Now she did. She squeezed his length, stroked from root to tip and enjoyed the way he hissed out her name. He was warm, strong, and she knew he'd feel so good inside.

"Told you"—he caught her wrist. Held tight—*"Can't wait."*

Ah, but she was having so much fun. "You haven't seen my underwear yet." She kissed the hard line of his jaw even as her hands pumped his cock. "Do you think I'm wearing your gift?"

She felt the shudder that worked through him, then he was shoving up her dress, hiking it all the way to her waist. Revealing the silk of her emerald panties.

His hands climbed up, the callused fingertips sliding under the garters, caressing her skin. Goose bumps rose on her flesh. *"Jonas!"*

His finger edged under the panties. Found her core.

"Wet and tight." He grabbed the condom with his left

hand, then used his teeth to rip open the packet. "So fucking good."

She put the condom on him. Rolled it down his length and enjoyed the way his flesh jerked toward her.

He positioned his cock against her. Christie's hands flew out and pressed behind her, slapping down against the wood as she fought to brace herself when he pushed deep, so deep inside.

Better than good.

Her breath panted out.

He started to thrust. Fast. Faster. The table shook beneath them. Trembled. No, was that her? The table? Oh, crap, they were going to break—

Jonas pulled her up against him, lifting her off the table. Christie wrapped her legs around him and held on for the roughest ride of her life.

His mouth was on hers. His cock in her. She squirmed against Jonas, taking him even deeper. He held her tight with a steely grip at her waist. He took a few rough steps to the right, and her back rammed into the wall.

They didn't stop. Couldn't.

Deeper. Harder. Faster.

The pleasure hit her, sweeping through her body as her sex clenched around him, and Jonas was right there with her. His cock jerked inside her as he came, and his mouth tore from hers. Their eyes met, held, and she watched the green seem to go blind with pleasure. Pleasure that vibrated through her body.

When she could breathe, when the drumming of her heart wasn't the only sound she heard anymore, Christie realized she was still up against the wall, pinned by her cop. Held so tight. Over his shoulder, she could see the tree. Slumping a little more now, but . . . *for me.*

She smiled and pressed a kiss to his shoulder.

Jonas eased back and stared down at her. Not glazed

with lust and pleasure anymore, his gaze saw *her*. Maybe too much of her.

She tried to put on her confident front. "I don't think you ripped the panties that time."

One black brow rose. "Yeah, baby, I did."

Oh. She wanted to smile. After everything that had happened, he still made her feel happy. "Guess that means you owe me another present."

His hands tightened around her hips. He stepped away from the wall, but still held her close. The man was strong. His muscles rippled beneath her touch as he carried her down the hallway.

"Guess it means I do."

They turned and entered his bedroom. Big bed. Dark blue comforter. Lots of room to stretch and play.

He lowered her onto the bed. Her fingers caught his jaw, felt the rasp of the stubble there. "Make me forget again," she whispered, knowing she was revealing a weakness, but with him, she didn't care. "The only thing I want to think about tonight is you."

What would happen when the holiday ended? Would he go back to his cases? She'd go back to—what? Not another lover. Not after him. Who'd compare?

Not another accountant. Not another guy who fumbled in the dark.

She only wanted him.

"Baby, for tonight, I'm all yours."

That was the problem. She didn't just want tonight. So how did she go about asking Santa for forever?

Especially when forever was against the rules.

"I heard about the trouble your lady had at Tate Toys," Scotty said when he saw Jonas at the station the next day. "Hell of a time for something like that to happen."

It sure was. Jonas yanked out his chair. He didn't want to be in the precinct today. He wanted to be with Christie. She'd headed back to Tate to rifle through the mess in her office with Daniel. He'd asked her if she was okay . . .

And that chin had jumped two inches into the air. *I can handle this.*

Sure she could, but he still wanted to be there with her. "Looks like someone was in her house last night, too."

"What?" A line furrowed Scotty's brow. "A vandal at work and a visitor at home? Man, that's not good."

"Tell me something I don't know." *That's why I should be with her.*

"Any leads?"

"Only one that was a dead end." But Crenshaw *could* have been the one to trash her office. He'd been in the area that night. Hell, Crenshaw and that redhead had been the only two he'd seen in that wing.

But even if Crenshaw had trashed her office on Friday, there was no way the guy could have pulled that break-in at her house. Not unless the accountant was freaking Superman.

"She seems like a real classy lady, despite the fact that she's taken up with you." Scotty crossed his arms over his chest. "You need any help on this, you let me know."

"Thanks, I will." He had to give a report to the captain, but after that, he was free and clear for the afternoon. He planned to spend that time focusing on Christie and the jerk who was screwing with her.

"I didn't realize she was the one to create Ricky Rocket-shooter." Scotty sounded impressed. "That thing's sold out of all the stores this year. Bet that next robot—what'd she call it—Rover? Bet he's gonna make a killing for Tate Toys, too."

Jonas paused. "Just how successful is Ricky?" There were no small kids in his world, so it wasn't like he spent a lot of time studying toy trends.

"I read an article the other day that said Ricky's number three on the list of top ten toys for the year."

Number three equaled a crap load of profits for Tate Toys, and with Rover waiting in the wings . . .

Money. Greed. Always perfect motivators for crimes. "Sonofabitch." He grabbed his file. "Call Tate. Make sure a security guard is on the floor with Daniel and Christie at all times." He'd tell the captain he had to go, the briefing could wait.

"All right, man, but wait—what are you thinking? You know who trashed her place?"

"I know that at this time of the year, people get desperate." He shook his head. "And money can make folks crazy." Folks you'd never suspect could cross the line if they thought the payoff was strong enough.

With Tate, the payoff seemed to be *too* tempting.

Her house key was missing. Christie flipped through the keys on the key ring once more. She always kept backup keys in her filing cabinet. Last night, she'd checked through them fast, and it had seemed like they were all there. No, *six* keys had been there. But two of the keys were wrong. Just extra keys that she'd never seen before. Substitute keys someone had placed on the ring.

Her house key and her lab key were missing.

Her gaze darted around the office. She'd spent an hour with Daniel, organizing all those files. No data seemed to be missing. Just her keys. Keys that had been carefully substituted so she wouldn't even realize they'd been taken.

"I know how he got into my house," she said, and Daniel's head whipped toward her. She held up the keys. "My backup is gone."

His eyes narrowed.

"And what else is gone?" Jonas asked, appearing in the doorway.

Daniel and the security guard, Sam, both turned to face him.

Her heart gave a little kick when she saw him. Hell, what else was new?

He filled the doorway, looking tall, strong, and dangerous. He had his badge clipped to his belt, and she could see the bulge of his weapon.

"I thought you were working at the station." Not that she wasn't glad to see him.

"I told the captain something important had come up." His gaze dropped to the ring. "The lab key isn't on there, is it?"

Her fingers curled around the ring. "No."

"This"—he waved his hand to the room—"is all flash. A distraction. *You* aren't the target."

"Then why'd the jerk go to her place last night?" Daniel wanted to know.

"Because he's looking for something." Jonas eased out of her office and glanced down the hallway. "Something that would either be in the lab or in Christie's house."

Her breath rushed out.

"If I'm right," Jonas said, "this isn't personal, it's—"

"Business." Daniel shot to his feet. "Sonofabitch. *The lab.* Someone's trying to steal our models!"

Jonas gave a grim nod. "You been working on any designs at home?"

"I-I took a prototype home for a few days."

"Let me guess." Jonas rolled his shoulders and the butt of the weapon peeked at her. "Rover, right?"

"Yes." The robot hadn't been working just right, and she'd wanted a chance to tinker with him over the holidays.

"Where's he now?"

"I brought him back last night. He was in my car and

when you called about the break-in, I brought him back"—she pointed behind him—"and Daniel put him in the lab."

Jonas turned his attention to Daniel. "Anyone else here today?"

"Ah . . . just Vicki from accounting. There was some kind of glitch with the payroll checks. She came in to—"

"All about the money," Jonas muttered. "I'm gonna need to get in that lab, *now*."

Daniel shoved his hand into his jacket pocket. "I've got a key." He was already heading for the door, nearly racing with the security guard.

Christie was right on their heels.

They marched down the hallway, the faint melody of Christmas music filling the air as it drifted through the speakers.

"Let me go in first," Jonas murmured. "Then, Christie, I want you to do a sweep and see if all the Rover material is still there."

He reached for the door, but didn't have to use the key. The lab was unlocked.

Well, hell.

He swung open the door.

The Rover prototype was still there—clutched in Vicki Jasper's hands.

"Vicki?" Daniel called out, shock and anger mixing in his voice.

Vicki spun toward them, her dark red hair swirling over her shoulders. A wide, laughing smile spread her lips. "You caught me, Dan!" She gave a light, twinkling laugh as she sat Rover back down. "I just had to sneak in and get a peek at old Rover." She dusted off her hands. "I was taking a break, stretching my legs a bit, and I—"

"How'd you get inside, Vicki?" Christie asked her, aware that Jonas and Sam had both tensed at the sight of the other woman.

Vicki blinked her warm brown eyes. "The door was open. I walked in." A shrug. "Why? Is-is there a problem?" Another laugh eased past her lips, but this one sounded a bit nervous. "You left the door open. I just walked in to look around."

"We didn't leave the door open," Christie said with certainty. "We haven't been in here today."

"The room was locked tight last night," Jonas added, his voice cold and clipped. "I checked before I left."

Vicki's gaze flashed from Christie to Jonas. "Okay, um, I'm sorry I came in here." She began to edge away from the table. "Numbers can get a little boring sometimes. You know what I mean, Dan. You're a numbers guy, too. I wanted a little break." Her smile flashed again. "A chance to see how the other half lived."

Christie stared at her and felt sad. "You shouldn't be here, Vicki."

"No," Daniel said, the word heavy. "You shouldn't."

"What? You're going to fire me for walking in the playroom?" Vicki's eyes hardened a bit. "Come on, what's this really about? Is it about me and Charles? Christie, we didn't mean for anything to happen, okay? We never meant to hurt you. We didn't plan it, we—"

"I don't care about you and Charles." But, wait . . . when had Vicki first hooked up with Charles?

Right after I announced plans for Rover at the company meeting in November.

"You're lying," Vicki snapped. "I know you're angry, but let's all calm down, okay?"

"We are calm, ma'am," Jonas said, stepping closer to Vicki. "Now I'm gonna need you to do me a favor."

Vicki's gaze jumped to him. She must have seen the badge, because her eyes widened. Or maybe she'd seen the butt of his weapon.

"I need you to empty your pockets, real nice and real slow," Jonas ordered her.

"What? I don't have to—"

"Vicki." Daniel's voice snapped like a whip. *"What's in your pocket?"*

And she crumpled. Her lips trembled and teardrops slid down her cheeks even as she shoved her right hand into her pocket—and the hand came back up, holding two keys.

Christie was too far away to tell for certain, but her gut knew those were her keys. "Why?"

But it was Daniel who answered. "Because if there's one thing Vicki knows well, it's money. You ran the numbers for the project. You knew what we had coming, didn't you?"

Jonas took the keys from Vicki. She wasn't looking at any of them, just the floor.

"Probably planning to sell the prototype to a competitor." Daniel yanked a hand through his hair. "Vicki, this goes without saying but . . . *your ass*—"

"Is fired," Christie finished because even her Christmas goodwill had its limits. Vicki had passed those holiday limits. Actually, she'd blown right through them.

"Hot damn." Scotty held up his Ricky the Rocket-shooter Robot, and a wide grin lit his face. "You know you've just become the most popular guy at the station, right?"

Jonas let his brows climb. "I didn't do anything."

"No, but your girlfriend sent every cop in the precinct a Ricky the Rocketshooter Robot." He whistled. "If you make a cop's kid happy, you make a cop *very* happy."

"She and Daniel appreciate the PD's help." Help in nabbing Vicki before she'd walked out of the company with a prototype apparently worth more than a few years of his salary. "They wanted to do something to say thanks."

The captain came up and slapped Jonas on the back. "My son's been begging for this all year. You know how hard it's been to find one of these little bastards?"

Not so hard for Christie and the folks in distribution at Tate. "If your son likes that," he said, "tell him Rover's coming next year."

"Thanks to you, he is."

Christie.

He spun around. She was there, just a few feet away.

Wearing her long, loose cashmere coat and staring at him with that soft smile on her face.

He hurried toward her, aware of the cops milling around, those calling out "Thanks" and "Merry Christmas." The gifts had sure put them all in good moods.

"What are you doing here?" He took her hand and enjoyed the silken feel of her skin.

"I wanted to come by and make sure the robots were delivered safely." Her gaze swept the room. "If anyone was left out, let me know. Tate Toys can make sure everyone is taken care of." Her gaze returned to him. Warmed. *"Everyone."*

Oh, she'd already taken care of him.

"Jonas . . . can we talk a moment?"

His heart rate kicked up. "Sure." He tugged her toward the back of the station. He couldn't use the interrogation room again. A suspect was inside. All the interrogation rooms were full. It was one of those days.

He tucked her into the far corner and braced his hand near her head, leaning in and effectively closing her off from the others. "Is something wrong?" Warmth was in her eyes, but she was biting her lower lip and her gaze kept darting away from him.

"You've helped me a lot in the l-last few days. Standing by me when the break-in happened at Tate, giving me a place to stay—"

"Baby, having you in my bed was no hardship."

She blushed, just a bit.

"Then handling Vicki and the fallout. I know you didn't need to be on the case and—"

He bent and pressed a kiss to her lips. "How many times do I have to tell you? You were involved, so that meant I was, too."

Her eyes searched his. What was she looking for? What did she want to see? If he didn't know, how could he give it to her?

"I broke the rules," she whispered.

He frowned down at her.

Her hand came up and pressed against his chest. "It wasn't supposed to happen." Was that anger in her voice? Or fear? Either way, the woman had him worried.

"What rules are you talking about?"

She swallowed. "Just sex. Not forever."

Those rules.

"I asked you not to lie to me, but I came here tonight because I need to tell you . . . I'm the one who's been lying."

What?

"From the beginning, I-I've been lying, Jonas."

The din around him seemed too loud. Too many phones were ringing, too many voices buzzing. Scotty had started a round of "Jingle Bells," and too many tone-deaf cops had joined in for the song. "Run that by me again."

Her body trembled against his. "I've been lying to you from the beginning."

She looked so beautiful it hurt him to stare at her, and the twist in his gut told him he shouldn't ask but, "What did you lie about?" *Wanting me?* No, hell, *no.* The lust between them had been real. The pleasure too good to be faked.

"I want more."

He shook his head. Dammit, he couldn't hear her. He grabbed her hand and hauled her behind him. He shoved open the precinct door, and they rushed outside. The lightest flakes of snow had started to fall. "Tell me again," he demanded, the fury and fear in his blood too hot for him to feel the cold. "Tell me what you want." *Was she cutting him loose now?* Right before Christmas?

It was the last damn thing he'd expected. He thought of the present he'd bought for her earlier. Tucked nice and safe in his desk drawer. Hell, no, this couldn't be happening. "My time's not up yet."

"I-I know."

"What do you want?"

"You." The snowflakes caught in her hair. She drove her hands into the pockets of her coat and rocked back. "I didn't just want a good time that night. Didn't just want any man. I wanted *you*."

He stared at her.

"I've wanted you for years." Her lips lifted in a smile, but her dimple didn't flash. "Guess that night . . . guess I finally got brave enough to go after what I wanted." Her shoulders slumped a bit. "But deep down, I'm *not* brave. I'm scared, I'm nervous, and right n-now, staring at you"—her laugh was a little desperate—"I feel like I'm making the worst mistake of my life. I probably should just keep my mouth shut and enjoy the time we have left, but—*I made the wrong wish.*"

He stilled. "What wish did you want to make?"

She looked up at the sky, at the falling snowflakes. They kissed her lashes and whispered over her face. "I don't want you just for the holidays."

His hands curled into fists.

"I've watched you over the years. I've seen the women come and go, and I *know* you're not the kind of man to commit."

Why the hell did everyone keep saying that? *Because that's the way I used to be.* Not anymore. Not with her.

"But that's the kind of woman *I* am. I might have pretended I wasn't—I might have said I just wanted the pleasure, too . . . but with you, *I want more.*" Her chin was up. "I'm not going to lie anymore. Not to you, not to myself. *I want more.*"

"More?"

"Not just the sex. Don't get me wrong." Her words tumbled out. "The sex is incredible."

A uniform stumbled past, eyes wide. Jonas growled at him.

"But I like just lying in bed with you. I like being there for you when you come back from a hard case. I like it when you're with me and my family." Her breath blew out on a white cloud. "Jonas, I just like it when you're with me."

The cold still hadn't touched him. Couldn't, not the way his blood pumped so fast and hot. "Christie . . ."

She straightened her shoulders. "I had to tell you how I felt, Jonas. I'm going to start doing that, you know. Telling people what I really feel and think. Life's too short to waste, isn't it? If you don't take chances, then you can't—"

He pressed his lips against hers and tasted the snow and the strawberries that he'd always crave. "When you're nervous," he whispered, "you talk fast. Did you know that?"

Her eyes widened a bit.

"You don't need to be nervous around me. Haven't you realized that yet?"

"No, you're wrong. You're the one who makes me the most nervous." Her eyes never wavered as she told him, softly, "Because you matter to me."

His heart jerked hard in his chest. "Not just sex, huh?"

Her head shook. "It never was. Not for me. I shouldn't have let you think—"

"It wasn't for me, either, baby."

And just like that, Jonas found out how to make Christie Tate speechless. She stared at him a few seconds, her mouth hanging open a bit. "Wh-what?" That stutter squeezed his heart.

"The first time I saw you, you were wearing a pair of glasses with black rims. You had on jeans that were two big, sexy black boots, and a blue shirt that made your eyes even darker."

"Th-that was years ago. I don't even . . . how do you remember that?"

"Because, baby, I remember everything about you." Always had. "I knew the minute I saw you that you were too good for me." His smile flashed. A real smile. One he didn't have to fake. With her, he never faked. He just . . . was. "You were too damn young for me, then. Too young and too good, and I tried to stay the hell away from you."

The snow fell harder.

"I knew I was going into undercover work. I knew what it would do to me." He still didn't want her to know the places he'd been. The things he'd seen. Christie—she was the light he'd held close all those years, and she didn't even realize it. "But I had to take those jobs." Would she understand the driving need that had haunted him for so long?

Blood. Death.

"I know you did," she said, her voice a bit sad. "But Jonas . . . you didn't have to do that alone."

His hands squeezed her shoulders. The woman would break him one day, if he wasn't careful. But with her, he'd always tried so hard to be careful. "Do you know why I left Narcotics?"

She shook her head and the snowflakes drifted through her dark hair.

"I wanted something more." If he was going to tell her, he'd do it right. "No, screw that. I wanted someone. I wanted you."

"Jonas—"

"You never dated anyone seriously. I thought—fuck, I don't know what I thought." *That you felt the connection, too. That we would be together one day. That there was plenty of time.* Then he'd seen her with another man one day when he'd gone to Tate to meet Daniel for lunch, and he'd realized time had run out. If he didn't move, he'd lose her. "Do you know why I was playing that Santa gig? When I'd barely celebrated Christmas before?"

"I thought you were a replacement—"

"Because you were going to be there. You weren't the only one who wanted something special for Christmas this year. I did, too, baby. I wanted you. I wasn't going to sit on the sidelines anymore. Wasn't going to let life pass me by while I—" *Tried to slay demons who were long dead.* "While I just watched you go."

She blinked, once, twice, and then her dimple flashed. "Jonas . . . did you know? When you're nervous, you talk fast." She rose onto her toes and looped her arms around his neck. "I'm not going anywhere."

He pulled her closer. As close as he could get her. "Neither am I."

Her lips trembled—not with sadness. They trembled and stretched into that slow, sexy grin that had stolen his heart years ago. "New rules?"

"Damn straight."

"Sex."

"Lots of it."

"The *best* sex."

"With you that's what I always have." Not just sex, so much more. He'd known that from the first touch.

"Strings?" she asked softly.

"Enough to tie you up." *Forever.*

She laughed at that and he kissed her the way he needed to kiss her. Long and deep and hard.

He'd finally gotten just what he wanted for Christmas. *Christie in his arms.*

Just what he wanted—and everything he needed.

Christmas Eve. This year, Jonas wasn't spending it undercover with a bunch of asshole criminals he hated. He wasn't at the station, manning the phones.

He was in bed with Christie. His body relaxed, sated from the sex. *The best.* Hell, yeah, and he'd be ready for another round soon. They had too many years to make up for, and he was too hungry.

His hand slowly trailed up the smooth curve of Christie's back. She stretched into his touch, then turned her head and he leaned forward to kiss her.

"One more rule," he told her, whispering the words against her mouth.

Her brows came together. "What do you mean?"

"Come with me." He slid from the bed and quickly pulled on a loose pair of sweatpants. Christie followed, snagging the silk robe he'd bought for her.

When they went into his den, the little tree was glowing. Christie's touch. They'd decorated it together last night. Decorated. Drank wine. Laughed. Made love while the snow fell.

Presents were under the tree. Some for her family. Some that Christie had brought over for *him.* Even one for Scotty.

And a special one for her.

He pulled her down in front of the tree. Jonas reached for the small red box with the bright green bow.

Christie laughed. "Ah . . . want to start a tradition, huh?"

He turned back and caught the sexy gleam in her eyes.

"I'm all for that," she murmured, "and by last count, you *do* owe me another pair."

She took the box from him, and, as was her way, she lifted it up to her ear. Her grin kicked up as she shook the box.

Then faded. "Wait . . . that doesn't sound like—"

"Open it," he told her, his voice rougher than he'd intended, but he knew that this moment might just be the most important of his life.

She stared at the box, then ripped the bow off and tore into the package.

When she opened the ring box, he held his breath.

"Jonas?" She looked up at him, her eyes so wide.

"I don't want to have any more Christmases without you." He pulled the ring from the box and offered it to her. "I told you there was one more rule. This time, I want forever."

"If that's what you want"—she lifted her hand—"that's what you're getting."

He slid the ring onto her finger.

"You've been very good this year," she whispered, rising to nip his ear.

Not good enough for her. But he'd try to be. For the rest of his life, he'd try to make everything good enough for her.

She eased back and stared into his eyes. "I love you, Jonas Kirk."

"And I love you, Christie Tate."

"Merry Christmas."

His lips brushed hers. "Merry Christmas." His arms pulled her close. The woman he'd watched for so long. The woman he'd needed.

The woman who'd given him a *really* good time that he'd never forget, and the woman who'd just promised him forever.

Now, he had everything he wanted, right there, in his arms.

Merry Christmas, baby.

Tattoos and Mistletoe

SUSAN FOX

AUTHOR'S NOTE

I'm delighted to be part of Brava's 2010 Christmas anthology. Thanks so much to my wonderful editor, Audrey LaFehr, for extending the invitation. Thanks also to editorial assistant extraordinaire Martin Biro, for always making the process run smoothly.

I'm also deeply grateful to my critique group (Michelle Hancock, Betty Allan, and Nazima Ali), the Novelistas (Delilah Marvelle, Lacy Danes, and Christina Crooks), Loreth Anne White and Susan McFee Anderson, and last, but definitely not least, my terrific agent, Emily Sylvan Kim of Prospect Agency.

And of course, thanks to my readers, and especially the ones who take the time to drop me a note. It always brightens my day to hear from you.

Readers can e-mail me at susan@susanlyons.ca, write c/o PO Box 73523, Downtown Postal Outlet, 1014 Robson Street, Vancouver, BC, Canada V6E 4L9, or contact me through my website at www.susanlyons.ca (where Susan Fox shares a den with her alter ego, Susan Lyons). You'll find excerpts of Susan Fox and Susan Lyons books at my website, as well as behind-the-scenes notes, discussion guides, a monthly contest, recipes, e-newsletter signup, and other goodies.

1

Ten years ago, Charlie Coltrane left Whistler, British Columbia, taking only her ratty old backpack and the certainty that she'd never return.

And now, here she was, back in the damned place, riding in a cab from the bus station to the B&B she'd inherited. From beyond the grave, Aunt Patty had, for whatever bizarre reason, found the sole motivation to make Charlie return to the place where she'd grown up. The place that, like Patty, had treated her like shit from the day she was born.

Well, screw Whistler. She wasn't the same loser kid with a bad rap, she was a Toronto businesswoman. In a few days she'd have her aunt's B&B tidied up and on the market, and she could blow the town once and for all. With the sale proceeds, she'd open her own tattoo parlor in Toronto and achieve her dearest dream: to be her own boss, making a living from her art.

Shading her eyes against crisp winter sunlight, she noted lots of new buildings, but the town still had the flavor of a Pacific Northwest version of a Swiss village. The color palette hadn't changed either. Under a frosting of snow and a hodgepodge of tacky Christmas decorations, the forest and earth tones were harmonious, but boring.

In her day, she'd spiced things up, roaming Whistler at night and painting graffiti art on the post office, liquor store, and some upscale shops. That Halloween mural she'd done on the wall of the police station, with the skulls and zombies, had been totally inspired.

Those blandly painted buildings still made her fingers itch. She grinned. Now, that would be a way of letting Whistler know Charlie Coltrane was back in town.

The grin faded. Nope. As a kid, she'd had to live here and had learned to put on a tough-girl shell, to pretend to the town—and to herself—that she didn't care what anyone thought. Now, she'd rather fly under the radar.

Yes, she'd changed. The old Charlie had been fuel for the gossip mill: graffiti, cutting class, suspensions, driving without a license, being thrown in juvie.

People had assumed the kid of two loser drunks had to be a loser, too. That gave Charlie two choices: let them know she gave a fuck, or tell them to fuck off. She'd had enough pride that the first choice wasn't an option.

Suspensions were preferable. Even a night in juvie. *Yeah, thanks for that, Aunt Patty. For not coming to claim me when Mom and Dad were too shit-faced to do it.* The driving without a license had been to take her dad to emergency. And yeah, she'd cut class, missed exams. Who cared about school when her parents fought all night and she couldn't study, much less sleep?

"White Gold." The taxi driver announced the subdivision.

She leaned closer to the window. More Christmas glitter assaulted her eyes: sparkling lights twining through trees, fake icicles hanging from eaves, gross rubber snowmen.

He turned onto Nancy Greene Drive. "What's the address?"

"It's the Mountain View B&B."

She grimaced at the decorations, reminders that Christmas was two weeks off. The worst time of year. A stream of bad Whistler memories filled her mind, and she squeezed her eyes shut. But how not to remember? Especially the afternoon she'd come home to find that her parents and her home had gone up in flames. If she'd been there, not sketching in the woods . . . But she couldn't remake the past.

"Here we are." The driver stopped the cab and glanced over his shoulder. "You know this place shut down after the owner died?"

"I know." Charlie had to stay at the Mountain View. It was a term of her aunt's will. "It's okay." Even if it hurt to be back, she'd keep her goal firmly in mind.

When she paid him, he said, "You're the niece? The one who used to live here, who inherited?" His eyes were bright with curiosity.

What rumors had he heard? It seemed that at its core Whistler was still a small, gossipy town, underneath the gloss of tourists and seasonal workers. "I am."

Before he could say anything else, she slid out of the cab, tugging her bag behind her. She hoisted it on her back and stared at the B&B. The basic structure, a homey wooden chalet, was appealing, but the paint was faded, and a couple of shutters hung crookedly. Surprising. Her aunt, a pretentious snob, used to keep the place in tip-top shape.

Charlie stared at the front walk. Roughly shoveled, it had been immaculate the day she'd left town.

When her parents died, Patty, who'd shunned the family, had been forced to take her niece in. After the funeral, she told Charlie, "I'll do my duty and let you live with us until you finish grade twelve. But there will be rules. You will *not* embarrass me."

Yeah, right. "You don't want me," Charlie'd said, "and I don't fucking want to be here."

Her aunt had ordered her not to swear, but hadn't denied the truth of her words.

In that moment, Charlie's last hope had died. Why should Patty want her, love her, when her own parents hadn't? Five minutes later, she'd been out the door with everything she owned—the art supplies she'd been carrying the day of the fire—in that crappy old pack she'd got from the community services thrift shop.

Memories sucked.

She took a deep breath. Then, as the scent filled her nostrils, another. Mmm. Pine and snow. She'd forgotten the smell, so fresh and pure. It made her think of days spent hiking in the wilderness and sketching deer, snowshoe hares, the pattern of ice on a semifrozen river. The few happy times she'd enjoyed here.

As she strode resolutely up the walk, she noted the two trucks in the driveway: a battered old one and a newer 4x4 with BANFIELD RENOVATIONS on the side. Good, the work was under way.

The lawyer, Jeff Mattingly, had said her aunt had been giving the place a face-lift, but the renos had been put on hold when she died. It was a condition of the will that in order to inherit, Charlie had to live at the B&B and ensure the job was completed.

She stood outside the closed door. Should she knock? The screech of a saw suggested no one was likely to hear. Mattingly had couriered keys to her, along with the legal papers she'd needed to sign, so she dug them out, unlocked the door, and stepped inside.

"Holy shit!" Whole walls were missing, and a ceiling. This wasn't renovation, it was demolition.

Stunned, she set down her pack, stripped off her heavy jacket, and shook back her long, near-black hair. More comfortable now, in jeans, a turquoise tank, and a zip-

pered top in a rich plum shade, she made for the source of
the noise. Competing with the saw was a radio playing
the Black Eyed Peas. Loud. She liked the Black Eyed
Peas. The saw, not so much.

A muscular guy around her age, clad in jeans, a faded
gray tee, and a tool belt, stepped through a doorway.

"What the hell is going on?" she demanded.

Surprise crossed his face, and what a face it was: broad
planes, strong angles, and sexy stubble all dusted with
gold—or, more likely, sawdust. The same dust that clung
to coal-black hair tousled by the goggles he'd shoved atop
his head.

A white smile flashed. "You're Charlie Coltrane. Jeff
Mattingly said you'd be arriving."

The saw stopped, and a short, wiry guy, several years
younger, hurried through the door behind him. "Hey, LJ,
d'you want me to— Oh, sorry, boss, didn't mean to inter-
rupt." His curious gaze scanned Charlie. "Bet you're Ms.
Coltrane. My mom had you in her math class at Whistler
Secondary. Ms. Anderson?"

She winced. "Not my biggest fan." Not that she'd had
fans in Whistler.

He grinned. "Heard about the graffiti on the gym wall.
Sweet!"

Her lips quirked. "I thought so." She'd done carica-
tures of the teachers, including his mom. And received
her second—no, third—suspension.

"Joey," LJ said, "what did you want?"

"Oh yeah, right."

The two men launched into a carpentry discussion that
made no sense to Charlie, and she leaned back against a
huge freestanding stone fireplace. Despite her angst over
why these guys were destroying a perfectly good B&B,
she could take a moment to enjoy the view.

Namely, LJ. Hunky guys in tool belts were a rarity to
her, but she could get addicted. The old tee and jeans

showcased rippling muscles, and when he gestured to Joey, his movements were strong and confident.

He was noticing her, too, casting appreciative glances that heated her skin. She unzipped her top, leaving it open to reveal her tank and the snout of her dragon tattoo.

When the men finished talking, Joey left, and LJ came over. "Sorry. He's an apprentice, and scared to do anything without asking directions—which is mostly a good thing." He grinned, lips full and sexy, blue-gray eyes glinting out of that gold-dusted face.

A shiver darted across her skin. There was something familiar about those eyes.

Only ten minutes ago she'd had a flood of Christmas flashbacks, including the high school dance. Her townie date had turned out to be a jerk, then attacked her in his car. Then that science-geek kid rescued her, only to reject and humiliate her.

What had that kid's name been? Something appropriate like Chester. Hadn't his eyes been rather like LJ's, behind thick lenses? She found herself asking, "Do you have a brother?"

The saw started up again, a room or two away.

Raising his voice, he said, "No, a kid sister. Why?"

She shook her head. Loads of guys had blue-gray eyes. She had to stop letting bad memories distract her. "So, LJ, what's going on? Mr. Mattingly said the place was getting a face-lift. I expected cleanup and basic repairs, but you're knocking out walls."

He took a step closer, eyes crinkling appealingly. "Patty said the older a woman gets, the more heavy lifting is required."

Reluctantly, she grinned. When it came to heavy lifting, he was one man you'd want around. She could smell the fresh, woodsy scent of sawdust, and her fingers itched to brush it off his strong cheekbones, to let her fingers drift over his warm skin.

"She signed off on the plans in October," he said. "She paid for the work and we got under way, then she died. Just got started again after Mattingly said you'd given the okay."

Maybe her aunt had decided on major renos just to keep LJ around. The idea was tempting. Or would be, if it was anywhere other than Whistler. Even tool-belt guy couldn't make the town appealing.

She planted her hands on her hips. "I didn't okay all this."

His gaze followed her hands and lingered on the curve of her hips.

Trying to ignore the sexual awareness that prickled her skin, she said, "Rework the plans to do just the essentials, and be finished in a week. You can pay back the balance."

He raised his gaze to linger on her chest—on her dragon's snout, hissing fire across her cleavage. That had been her first tattoo, the dragon that protected her heart. Too bad he couldn't keep her nipples from tightening.

LJ focused on her face. "I've already paid for a lot of the supplies."

Frustrated and confused, she shook her head. "Why didn't she do this for the Olympics?"

"I told her she should. But since her husband died seven, eight years ago and she moved into the suite up-stairs, she only did minimal maintenance. Said she didn't like change."

Charlie gestured around. "This is a lot of change."

"Yeah. It was like she had a new lease on life."

"I wonder why?" To Charlie's astonishment, after more than nine years with no communication between her and her aunt, Patty had tracked her down and phoned in the summer. In her brusque way, she'd told Charlie it was time to come back to Whistler. Charlie'd given a bitter laugh, said, "When Blackcomb Glacier melts," and hung up.

"She said the past can chain you until you figure out

how to free yourself." The saw had stopped, and LJ's words fell into the silence.

Charlie mulled that over. Obviously, Patty hadn't meant guilt over the way she'd treated Charlie or she'd have apologized. Phoned back. "Talking about her husband's death? Maybe the renos were her way of moving on."

"I guess." He frowned. "She was wearing herself out, though. Or maybe she was sick and didn't realize it."

They exchanged glances. Patty had died suddenly, in her sleep, of heart failure.

"Sorry," he said. "Should have said I'm sorry for your loss."

She shook her head. "Maybe I should mourn her, but I barely knew her." That was Patty's fault, not hers. Screw him if he was going to judge her for that.

2

L J—Lester Jacoby—saw the defiant tilt to her jaw. It was one thing about her that hadn't changed. Charlie Coltrane didn't apologize to anyone for anything.

"Makes sense to me," he said. Patty had been a bitch to Charlie and her parents. Married to an older guy, a successful businessman, she'd been a social climber. She ran the B&B and played gracious hostess, but avoided the messy reality of her sister's family.

Despite the hostess thing, Patty'd struck him as a private woman, one with a deep core of sadness, maybe regret. Over the years he'd worked for her, whenever he mentioned Charlie, she'd shut him down. More chains, he figured, and her will was an attempt to right past wrongs.

"Well, Aunt Patty's gone, and now this project is mine." Charlie pushed off the fireplace and wandered across the room.

Ever since he'd heard Charlie was coming back, he'd been antsy with curiosity. Now, he couldn't take his eyes off her. She didn't recognize him—well, maybe his eyes—and he wasn't about to remind her of the geeky kid he'd been, but he'd have known her anywhere.

She was still the sexiest female he'd ever seen.

The saw was silent, and a Carrie Underwood song accompanied Charlie as she strolled around, frowning and shaking her head. He should've brought out a copy of the plans and explained things, but instead he leaned against the fireplace, cocked a hip, and watched.

He'd first noticed Charlie the day he started grade ten. A scrawny math and science geek whose mother chose his clothes, skipping a grade hadn't helped his confidence. Then he'd seen one familiar thing: his old backpack, which his mom had donated to charity. The girl who wore it slung off one shoulder was in his grade, and she was the most fascinating human being—outside Dana Scully on *The X-Files* and Samantha Carter on *Stargate SG-1*—he'd ever seen.

She'd had that badass attitude, which was pretty hot, but so was the softer, vulnerable side, the side she hid from the world. He only saw it because, let's face it, he'd pretty much stalked her.

As she gazed out a window into the front yard, he remembered how she'd looked: short hair streaked with fluorescent colors, Goth makeup, outrageous clothes in weird colors and styles. In grade twelve, the tattooed outline of a dragon had appeared on her shoulder, draping over her chest and down her upper arm.

Now, her style was natural: glossy, near-black sheets of hair rippling past her shoulders, olive-toned skin, dark lashes and brows accenting hazel eyes. No jewelry but for a few hoops and studs in her ears. She still loved color, though. The figure-hugging top was purple and the tank bright turquoise. The tattoo had been completed, the bold dragon sexy against the soft upper curve of her breast.

Then, she'd been skinny, like she didn't get enough to eat. Now, she was slim, but definitely curvy. A beautiful, sexy woman who moved with lithe grace around the opened-up rooms.

Ten years, and his body's response was still almost impossible to control. He felt like an insecure teen again. The geek who was the butt of jokes, not the object of any girl's interest.

He remembered driving Charlie home after that dickhead attacked her. Though he'd been only sixteen, not licensed to drive alone at night, he'd taken the family car while his dad was inside chaperoning the dance. She'd given him a thank-you kiss and it had been the sweetest moment of his life. Then she'd shocked the hell out of him by offering him a blow job. He'd shocked the hell out of himself by saying no. She'd been hurting, putting on that badass act to hide her vulnerability. He couldn't take advantage. It wasn't as if she'd actually *seen* him. Wanted him.

Things had changed, he reminded himself. He'd filled out, had laser eye surgery. Women found him attractive, and Charlie'd been checking him out.

Hell, if she made that same offer again—he wouldn't say no. His cock throbbed, imagining the sweet, wet inside of her mouth. His gaze followed her as she walked across the room, and he imagined stripping off those vivid clothes and kissing every inch of her soft flesh.

In truth, he was still kind of a geek—how many men read science texts as a hobby and attended sci-fi cons?—but when it came to physical stuff, he was confident. He could build a solid, beautiful house and he could bring a woman sexual ecstasy.

Charlie settled against the fireplace beside him, and sighed. "This is overwhelming."

"We'll talk about it tomorrow. Why don't you get unpacked and settled?"

"I guess," she said unenthusiastically. "The will says I have to live here."

He moved over to stand in front of her, and she tilted her head up, nostrils widening as if she was inhaling. He mustn't smell too sweaty, because a smile touched the corners of her mouth.

He inhaled, too. Her spicy, exotic scent mixed just right with the odor of sawdust, intoxicating him. "Your aunt's suite is on the third floor. It has a great view of the mountains."

After the cleaning service sent by the lawyer had finished, LJ'd taken a look at the bland rooms. Remembering how Charlie had loved vibrant colors, he'd added bright sheets and towels. Now he imagined Charlie, fresh from the shower, wrapped in that big red towel, and his groin tightened. Slowly, seductively, he added, "And a big, comfy bed."

Sexual awareness flared golden in her hazel eyes. "*Comfy* though it may be," she drawled, "I don't intend to be here long. I want you to finish up as quickly as possible."

"Do you?" The lawyer'd said she was in a rush to sell, but LJ wanted enough time to get to know her. He'd done his fair share of dating, but no girl had ever sparked his libido or fascinated him the way Charlie had. "I thought women appreciated a man who knew how to take his time and do things . . . thoroughly." At the thought of long, slow, very thorough lovemaking with her, his mouth went dry.

Her lips twitched. "Sometimes a girl's more interested in results."

"Satisfaction guaranteed," he said softly.

She tossed her head and tilted it back against the fireplace, gazing up at him. The gesture sent her dark hair rippling back so he glimpsed another tattoo starting behind her ear, then losing itself in the cascading hair.

Catching him looking, she raised both hands to scoop up her hair and lift it out of the way, then turned so he could see a chain of stylized feathers and flowers decorating her nape and upper back. Unconventional and striking, as he'd have expected. She'd been a skilled artist, even when she painted sides of buildings.

"Nice tat." It emphasized the delicate shell of her ear, the slender line of her neck, the soft down along her hairline. He wanted to trace it with his tongue.

His cock was uncomfortably hard, pressing against his fly.

"Thanks." She let her hair fall in a shining wave. "I designed it."

He'd figured.

"I'm a tattoo artist," she said, challenge glinting in her eyes.

"Seriously?" Over the years, he'd guessed everything from biker chick to running an art gallery. "Cool."

"I think so." Challenge turned to teasing. "Let me guess, Mr. Tool-belt Guy. You don't have a single tattoo."

He rested his hand on the wall above her head, caging her in on one side. The gesture brought his body within inches of hers. "Want to look for yourself?"

"That just might be the best offer I've had all day."

"Just might be? I'm insulted."

"The guy beside me on the plane did suggest I tattoo his willy, as he phrased it."

LJ winced.

She chuckled. "Wimp."

He managed not to wince again. The old insult stung, but he knew she was only teasing. "I can think of better things you could do with my—" He broke off. Yeah, he wanted sex with Charlie, but he also wanted to get to know her. "Have dinner with me."

"Um . . ." Her brows pulled together slightly. "If there's a double entendre in that, I'm missing it. Or did you mean, have *you* for dinner?"

He suppressed a moan. "Thought it might be nice to get to know each other over dinner. Whistler has some great restaurants."

The light left her eyes. "I don't think so."

What had he said wrong? "You've had a long day and must be tired, but you need food. We'll go wherever you want. Splitz has great burgers, The Bearfoot Bistro's one of my favorites, and you still can't beat the old RimRock Café. Feel like seafood by the fire?"

She turned her head and, without touching him, slipped out from between him and the wall and stepped away. "No, thanks. How about you revisit the reno plans tonight? I want to be out of here in a week."

"A week? Impossible."

She walked over to collect her backpack and jacket, then turned and stared at him. "Make it possible." For the first time he saw a resemblance to her aunt. Not in her features, but in the sense of sadness, perhaps regret.

When she headed for the stairs, he gaped after her, too stunned to grab her bag or even point her toward the elevator.

She'd been into him. He knew it. And then she'd blown him off, just as if he was the old nerdy Lester. What the hell was that all about?

Charlie dragged the heavy backpack upstairs. The staircase ended on the second floor, but LJ'd said Aunt Patty's suite was on the third, so she walked down the hall. Passing a dozen open doors, she noticed signs of wear and tear. But it would be a quick fix. Slap on paint and buy bright bedspreads. See if there was decent hardwood under the worn carpet.

At the end of the hall she found an elevator and a door that led to another set of stairs. She took the elevator up and entered a clean, comfortable apartment: living room, bedroom, and bath; no kitchen; way too much chintz. It was depressingly bland, but in good condition.

The living room looked out onto the street. The bedroom, at the back, had the promised mountain view—spectacular, as a gentle sunset stroked ten shades of peachy-pink across the white-capped peaks.

LJ had lied about the bed. It wasn't all that big, only a double, but she could imagine getting cozy with him in it. Atop the chintz bedspread lay a stack of sheets and pillowcases and another of fluffy towels. She smiled at the unexpected touch of marigold-yellow linens, a scarlet bath towel, an aubergine hand towel, and a teal facecloth. Not her aunt's. Who had put them there? Who on earth—except her—would enjoy such a mishmash of vibrant color?

She hefted her backpack onto a chair, then sank down on the side of the bed. Some things had been worse than she'd expected. The scale of the renovations. The small-town rumor mill. God, even that apprentice had heard stories about her.

And the memories, triggered by the Christmas decorations and by LJ's eyes.

Some things weren't so bad at all. Damn, the contractor was hot. She didn't meet many tool-belt guys in The Barbed Rose, the ritzy tattoo parlor on Yonge Street where she worked. LJ was so . . . earthy and masculine.

There were definite possibilities there. A little hot sex to fill the empty evenings until the renos were done? That's where they'd been heading when he spoiled things by asking her to dinner.

No way was she going out, where she might run into someone like Joey's mom. The Ms. Andersons wouldn't care about the changes she'd made in ten years; they'd just see the piece-of-trash bad girl.

Sounds carried from downstairs. The radio, the intermittent whine of the saw, an occasional male shout. LJ, the apprentice Joey, and someone else. The noise was companionable.

Charlie unzipped her pack. Shoving aside the few

clothes she'd brought, she took out a sketchpad and sets of water-soluble oil pastels, water-soluble crayons, and watercolor pencils. Drawing was as essential as food. In fact, as a teen, any money she'd earned had gone to art supplies, not to stock the bare shelves in her parents' kitchen.

She set up at a small desk by the bedroom window. The light wasn't the brightest, but it didn't matter. She drew the way she breathed: by instinct, not deliberation.

When sounds faded away downstairs, she put aside the sketch she'd been working on—gold dust on sculpted male cheekbones, steady blue-gray eyes framed by dark lashes—and walked across to the living room of her aunt's suite. Both trucks were gone. Now that night had come, the Christmas lights up and down the street were even more sparkly.

Directly across, in a town house, golden light glowed from uncurtained windows. Downstairs, a tree glittered in silver and gold. Upstairs in the kitchen, a man poured wine and a woman stirred something in a big pot. Charlie hated Christmas trees and wasn't the domestic sort, so why did she feel a twinge of yearning? Maybe because the scene was the polar opposite of the way she'd grown up.

Hungry, she found a phone book and ordered a Greek pizza. In the morning she'd head into Whistler Village before most people were up and about, buy enough groceries to last a week, then hibernate until the renos were finished.

Hibernating would be a lot more fun with the sexy tool-belt guy to heat up the nights. When she wasn't travel weary and in Whistler shock, she'd see if he still looked as appealing. If so, she'd flirt him out of thinking about food, and straight into her bed.

3

The next morning, LJ yawned as he drove to the B&B. He'd spent a mostly sleepless night, thinking about Charlie. Sexy, intriguing, baffling Charlie. Yesterday she'd triggered his old insecurity. But whatever'd made her pull back, he was determined to overcome it.

At the coffee shop, he duplicated his order for a cranberry bran muffin and strong coffee. With any luck, she wasn't into vanilla soy designer drinks.

As planned, he arrived at the Mountain View before his crew. Joey was a good kid but hadn't mastered the use of an alarm clock. Will, a few years older than LJ, drove from Creekside with his wife, a pretty redhead who worked in a clothing shop and dreamed of being a designer.

Banfield Renovations was LJ's company. Over the years he'd bought out his uncle, who'd taken early retirement.

Hoping Charlie was up, he unlocked the front door and went through to the kitchen. When he saw her at the kitchen table, wearing a long-sleeved tee the shade of a ripe peach, her shiny hair pulled into a messy ponytail, he

felt a rush of that old, overwhelming feeling of pure fasci-
nation.

Before he could find his tongue, she gestured toward
the open pizza box in front of her. "There's no microwave,
and the stove's in the middle of the floor. I can't heat this
up."

Her disgruntled expression freed his tongue and made
him grin. "Morning, Sunshine."

Humor kinked her lips. "Easy for you to say. You've
had breakfast." She yawned. "I'd kill for coffee."

Remembering their easy banter the day before, he said,
"What else would you do for it?"

Another twitch of her lips. "Can't even think about
that until I get some caffeine in me."

"In that case"—he put the muffin bag on the table,
along with a lidded takeout cup and his own insulated
mug which he'd had filled to the top—"here." He shoved
over the cup, then opened the bag. "Brought sugar and
milk."

She shook her head. "Black's great. This is nice of you."
She took a cautious sip.

He sat across from her and reached into the bag. "I can
be nice, Charlie." He held up a muffin temptingly.

"Oh, yum." She grabbed it. "*Really* nice of you."

Relieved she'd gotten over whatever had been bugging
her yesterday, he gave her his best suggestive grin. "I can
be *really* nice."

"I just bet you can." Grinning, she tore off a chunk of
muffin. "I bet there's a string of women who'd attest to
that."

There had been, when women first started noticing
him. He'd had a lot of geek years to make up for. "I don't
kiss and tell." But casual sex wasn't all it was cracked up
to be, and the couple of serious relationships had run their
course. Truth was, no one had ever compared to the
image of Charlie he'd carried around in his head.

"Aha. A love 'em and leave 'em guy." She put the bite into her mouth.

"Nope. Haven't loved one yet. Closest I got was a year-long relationship, but we both knew something was missing. And no, I don't lead them on." He'd never take advantage of a woman.

She studied him like a cat sizing up a bowl of cream. "I bet some of them get their hopes up."

"Can't stop a person from hoping." Just like he'd once hoped Charlie Coltrane would see beyond his geekiness.

She nodded. "Yes, a person's responsible for their own feelings." A pale ray of morning sun slanted through the window and she tipped her head into it, smiling. She had a beautiful face, so much prettier without the weird makeup she used to wear, and a long, elegant neck. "And right now, I'm feeling good," she said. "Caffeine, food, sunshine." One lid lowered in a slow wink. "Scenery's not all that bad either, Tool-belt Guy."

"Same goes, Tattooed Lady." Hard to sound cool when his sixteen-year-old self was doing cartwheels inside his grown-up body—a body that was responding to the early morning freshness of her unmadeup face and tousled hair, not to mention the slender, curvy figure showcased by that T-shirt.

Trying to find something clever and sexy to say next, he didn't know whether to be sorry or relieved when the front door opened and Will and Joey trooped in.

After he introduced Will everyone sat around the table and he filled Charlie in on the general plan: open up the rooms on the first floor, turning small ones into larger, more dramatic ones, then move on to totally renovate the second floor.

"Uh-uh." She held up a hand in a STOP signal. "Forget renovating the second floor. Let's rip up the carpets, since you say there's good hardwood underneath. Other than that, fresh paint, new bedspreads, curtains, and linens, and that'll be enough."

"Patty wanted—"

"Do I look like Patty?"

The three men chuckled, and she grinned back. "I'll start the painting myself."

"Murals?" Joey asked excitedly.

"Yeah, that'd do wonders for the sale price," she said wryly. "Better stick with neutral."

"Patty had taupe in mind." LJ waited in anticipation.

She didn't disappoint him. Screwing up her face, she said, "Bleck. That's not neutral, it's hideous. We want light and warm. Pale golden yellow."

"Come with me and pick out the color." He wanted to get her alone again.

She shook her head. "I need to buy groceries. A tool-belt guy ought to be capable of finding paint the color of butter."

"Okay. But it's not in the deal that you have to help with the renos." He liked that she was taking an interest, though. Maybe she'd come to care for the place and want to stay.

She thrust to her feet. "Anything to get the job done faster."

Or maybe she wouldn't.

Four hours later, LJ headed upstairs to the second floor. Who'd have ever thought he'd see the onetime graffiti muralist rolling creamy yellow paint onto the walls? She was up on a ladder in the middle of the hall, her back to him, humming along to the music drifting up from downstairs. He took a moment to enjoy the view.

Curvy butt in snug-fitting jeans, hair pulled up in a sloppy pile, arms and shoulders bare because she'd stripped down to a red tank top that looked vivid against the pale yellow wall.

"Charlie?"

She broke off humming and swung around on the ladder, smiling. "Uh-huh?"

"We're breaking for lunch. Gonna have something delivered." She'd stocked the fridge and cupboards with enough supplies to last a week, but he hoped to tempt her into eating with them. "Join us?"

As she carefully placed the roller in the paint tray, he stepped closer, studying the dragon. It was fully revealed but for a red strap that lay like a collar across its neck. The body curved around her shoulder, the tail wrapped her upper arm almost to her elbow, and the head came down over her collarbone. The mouth was open, breathing flames across her chest and into her cleavage.

Lucky dragon, hugging her body like that. "Cool tattoo." The work was intricate, dramatic, beautiful.

"Thanks." She gazed steadily down at him from the third step of the ladder. "He guards my heart."

Was that a warning? Why did her heart need guarding? "And the one on your neck?"

"It's a memorial to my best friends. Ginger was the warmest, most wonderful human being I've ever met, and her husband Jake came second. He did my dragon, got me started tattooing. The feathers are for him, he was Cree, and the flowers are for her because she loved them."

"They're . . . gone now?"

Still holding his gaze, she nodded. "An accident on an icy road."

"I'm sorry."

"Me, too." Her hand stroked down the back of her neck. "This way, they're always with me."

"That's nice."

They were both quiet a moment, the only sound a rock

tune from downstairs, but it wasn't an uncomfortable silence. He liked the new Charlie. The old one would've come up with a flip comment rather than reveal something personal.

"Any more tattoos?" he asked.

Her eyes warmed, sparking with sexy mischief. "Wouldn't you like to know?"

The idea was tantalizing. "No question. Want to share?" She wouldn't have anything as conventional as a butterfly at the small of her back, but just thinking about the small of her back made him horny.

"I'm afraid I don't know you that well," she teased back.

"That could be remedied." He opened his mouth to ask her out for dinner again.

A voice called out from downstairs, competing with the music. "LJ? Chinese or Thai?"

LJ raised his eyebrows at Charlie. "Your choice."

"Either's good."

"Thai," he called downstairs. "Order enough for Charlie, too."

"Thanks for the invitation," she said. Then, with a grin, "But you'd better stop goofing off. You're on a tight timeline."

He headed back downstairs, feeling only a little guilty that he'd misled her when they'd discussed the renos earlier. He'd let her believe the work could be completed in a week, when really it'd be closer to two.

He wanted two weeks. Enough time for them to get to know each other. For him to find out if Charlie was just a teen crush or the woman his heart had been waiting for.

An hour or so later, Charlie sighed contentedly as she took her last bite of chicken in yellow curry sauce. Not only was the food great but she liked the three guys.

Hanging out with them was fun, like being at The Barbed Rose except without the sniping that made her long to set up her own business and hire her own, more compatible colleagues.

It was the best social time she'd ever had in Whistler.

It didn't hurt that LJ sat across from her at the kitchen table, sending her flirtatious glances when Will and Joey were concentrating on their food. He'd pulled a flannel shirt over his white tee, and its blue plaid pattern made his eyes even more vivid.

He shoved the container of stir-fried beef with basil toward her.

She shook her head. "I'm full. Great food. But you should have let me pay my share."

"Nah, I've got it." He winked. "Won't complain if you make lunch for us one day."

"I'm no fancy chef, but I make a mean roast-beef sandwich, and I can open a can of soup with the best of them. Of course, if you actually want *hot* soup, someone's going to have to reconnect the stove."

"We'll find a corner where it's out of the way," Will assured her. "Whatever you need, just let us know." In his early thirties, he had a strong build, but his wire-rimmed glasses and neat mustache and beard looked more professorial than blue collar.

"Thanks."

Joey, wiry and redheaded, polished off the basil beef. "You're really a tattoo artist? Like, seriously?"

"Seriously."

"I thought they dressed all in black, and their arms were covered in ink."

She grinned. "I didn't say I was your *typical* tattoo artist. I love doing tats, but I love drawing, painting, and graphic design, too. As for being covered in tattoos, that's not my style. For me, each is a serious decision with personal significance." She glanced at LJ. She was used to

people asking about her tattoos, and liked the way he'd re-
acted. Interested, but not prying.

"I've been thinking about getting one," Joey said.
"Maybe you could do it."

"A tattoo's serious business," Will said. "You have it
for life."

"That's right." She always made sure her clients knew
what they were doing. Studying Joey's face, she said,
"What do you have in mind?"

"I've always had a thing for eagles. They're so, you
know, wild and free and strong. I've seen some flash in
two or three tattoo parlors, but it didn't feel right."

"Flash?" Will asked.

"Designs," she told him. "You find them in albums and
on walls in tattoo parlors." She turned back to Joey. "I
don't work from flash. I develop an original Coltrane for
each client." People said she had a magical ability to create the right tattoo. All she did was ask questions, listen,
and use a bit of intuition.

"Would you do one for me?"

"We'll talk some more."

"It's time you guys got back to work," LJ said. "I'm
heading out, back in half an hour."

"The dog?" Will asked.

"Yeah. He's too old to be left alone all day."

"You have a dog?" Charlie asked.

"Long story. He's my sister's, but she's in Vancouver
working on her law degree, and our parents are on a
cruise. So, I have dog duty. Poor guy, he's not used to
being alone."

Charlie loved animals. They didn't label and judge the
way people did. "Bring him here."

* * *

Twenty minutes later, LJ let Romeo, Emily's twelve-year-old beagle, out of the truck. Might Charlie remember him?

As a pup, Romeo'd been an escape artist. One summer morning when he was less than a year old, he'd gotten out of the yard. That afternoon, the vet phoned. The pup had been torn up by a bear. Charlie had found him in the woods, bleeding and unable to walk. She bound up his wounds and took him to the clinic.

Lester knew it wasn't the first time she'd rescued an animal. He'd followed Charlie more than once. Enough to know she'd preferred the outdoors to home, had roamed around with a sketchpad in her backpack, and had a soft spot for animals.

He leaned down to stroke the beagle, rubbing his hand over the parallel scars that marred his glossy coat. "You're about to see an old friend, boy." He opened the front door of the B&B, and the dog darted in. Romeo might be twelve, but he was active, healthy, always curious. He ran around sniffing, then headed to the kitchen. LJ followed, smiling as Will and Joey stopped work to pat Romeo.

The dog's tail wagged happily, then he paused, scenting the air. He put his nose to the ground and headed out of the kitchen and over to the stairs. Up he went, LJ behind him, to the second floor. Spying Charlie on her ladder in the middle of the hall, Romeo let out an excited bark and ran over.

Smiling, she set the paint-loaded roller down in the tray and climbed down the ladder. "Well now, who's this?" She squatted as Romeo leaped up to bathe her face in doggy kisses. Laughing, she caught his face between her hands and held him a few inches away. "Okay, boy, I like you too, but we've only just met."

"His name's Romeo," LJ said.

"You certainly live up to your name, don't you, lover boy?" She stroked the dog's silky ears, ran a hand down his back, then stopped. Bending closer, she studied the scars. "Oh, my." She plunked down on her butt on the drop cloth. "I think I know you."

"He sure knows you. Guess you never forget the person who saved your life."

She stared up at him. "Your sister's dog? Then you"— she frowned in puzzlement.

When Emily, twelve at the time, had wanted to thank Charlie, their parents had said no, she was a bad kid from a bad family. Though his folks cared too much about appearances and had some stupid, old-fashioned views, he'd heard enough about Charlie's parents to not take his sister to their place. On Sundays Charlie helped out old Mr. DiGiannantonio, so that's where he took Emily. Their parents found out, and he and his sister were grounded for a week.

"I brought her over to Mr. D's to thank you." When Emily'd been gushing out her thanks, Lester had stood aside. Charlie had barely glanced at him. He wasn't even sure if, on the night of the dance a year and a half later, she'd realized he was the same guy.

"You're . . . No, you can't be. You have the same eyes, but you're LJ. He was, uh, Chester?"

She'd noticed his eyes. Then and now. "Lester. Lester Jacoby. Never did like Lester, so now I'm LJ."

Charlie was still shaking her head slowly, in denial. Her cheeks paled and she pressed her hands to them. "The Christmas dance . . ."

So she *had* known he was the same guy. "Yeah, that was me, too."

"Oh, my God." Eyes huge with shock, she thrust herself clumsily to her feet. Without another word, she rushed away.

Well, shit.

The dog sat on his haunches and let out a sorrowful whine.

"Yeah, tell me about it." LJ rested his hand on Romeo's head and tugged gently on a silky ear. "So, what do we do now?"

Another low whine.

"I have to talk to her. And you're coming with me. She likes you better than me."

4

When a knock sounded on Charlie's closed bedroom door, she kept staring up at the ceiling from her position on the bed. LJ was Lester? The geeky genius hadn't gone on to some brilliant career in science or math, but had turned into the hot tool-belt guy?

Tool-belt Guy was the boy who'd saved her from rape, then thought he was too damned good to have her mouth on his cock?

Another knock.

What's more, *LJ* hadn't bothered to tell her he was Lester. "Go away," she yelled.

"Not gonna happen." The door opened.

"Get out." She glared at him, pissed off and mortified.

The dog scrambled across the room and leaped onto the bed, where he again lavished her with kisses. She sat up and caught his head between her hands, evading his tongue.

LJ dragged the desk chair over to the bed and straddled it backward, his arms resting on the back. "That was a bad night. I'm sorry if seeing me reminds you of it."

"Bad?" she snapped. Then she sighed. He had, after all, saved her from Drew. She shoved a pillow behind her back and Romeo curled up in her lap. "It could have been worse. Would have been, if he'd caught me."

"That guy was a dickhead."

"Understatement." Drew was a wealthy townie who came up to snowboard on weekends. She'd fallen for him and invited him to the dance, planning to flaunt him and show the other kids she wasn't such a loser.

Yeah, she'd known he liked to party, and yeah, he'd been pressing her for sex, but she'd figured he was just being a guy. If he cared for her, he'd understand that her virginity mattered to her. That she wasn't going to be like her mom, going with whatever guy caught her fancy, ending up pregnant by some stupid drunk.

But he hadn't cared. He'd proved it that night, treating her like shit in front of her classmates. "I was an idiot to invite him." She drew comfort from the dog's soft fur under her hand.

"You didn't know he'd try to rape you."

She huffed out a breath. "He'd probably heard my rep. Every guy at school thought I was a slut. Except for—"

"The guys who spread that rumor," he interrupted.

Her eyes widened. "How did you know that?"

When LJ just shrugged, she shook her head in puzzlement, then went on. "When he dragged me out to his SUV, I said I never wanted to see him again. And he said"—she took a breath—"He said I was a cheap cunt who was only good for one thing, and I'd better fucking well give it to him. He grabbed me—" She broke off, shuddering as she remembered Drew ripping her dress, wrenching off her panties.

"You fought back and got away."

She'd run, flimsy dress flapping around her, high-heeled sandals soaked with frozen slush. She'd heard

Drew come after her until a male voice screamed, "No!" and Drew yelled, "Fuck you!" She'd stopped and peered over her shoulder.

Lester, that scrawny kid, had thrown himself in Drew's path and was punching him. "Run, Charlie!" he'd hollered.

She gazed at LJ. "I got away because you stopped him."

When she'd left the lighted parking area, she'd hid behind a tree, wracked with shivers, and looked back again. "He beat you up, and I didn't help you."

He leaned forward over the back of the chair, blue-gray eyes intent. "The girl isn't supposed to protect the boy. And you came back."

"After he was gone." Tears frozen on her cheeks, she'd stumbled back. Lester'd had a bloody nose and a split lip—and a big smile. By some miracle, his glasses weren't broken, and he said he'd drive her home. He'd wrapped her in a blanket from the trunk of his car and she'd felt protected, almost as if someone actually cared for her.

Her tears had thawed, begun to run again. Self-pity wasn't her style, but that night she'd cried—until Lester awkwardly offered sympathy. Then she'd recovered her pride, her tough-girl shell.

When he'd stopped in front of her place, she made a flip comment about thanking her knight in shining glasses, and leaned over to plant a quick kiss on his cheek.

At that moment, he turned his head. Their lips touched, then locked together with a strange combination of tenderness and hunger. Tears had filled her eyes again. No way would she let them fall. She pulled away, reached for his fly, said cockily, "How about I give you a real thankyou?"

He'd been hard beneath that fly, hot against her hand as

she'd unzipped him. His cock filled her hand. Less than half an hour earlier, a boy had tried to rape her. But she was in control, proving something to herself, and to Lester—that Charlie Coltrane wasn't vulnerable.

When she'd bent her head, he thrust her away. "No! No, Charlie."

Rejecting her. As the pain rushed back, her stomach clenched. She huddled against the head of the bed, holding Romeo close in her arms, and glared at LJ. "Oh yeah, it was one hell of a night. Ending with you blowing me off." Her wording struck her and she gave a bitter laugh. "Rather than letting *me* blow *you* off. Like your fucking swollen cock was too damned good for my slutty little mouth."

Shocked, LJ stared at the beautiful woman curled up tight against the headboard, hugging Romeo and glaring at him.

"Jesus, Charlie." He thrust himself out of the chair, paced away, then returned to stand by the bed. "Turning down that blow job was the toughest thing I've ever done. I was crazy for you. So crazy, I couldn't take advantage of you."

She frowned. "Huh? I offered, and good God, what boy turns down a blow job? Yeah, sure, you were crazy for me."

"If I'd been *visible* to you," he said, some of his teen insecurity and frustration coming out in his voice, "you'd have realized you pretty much had a stalker."

Her eyes narrowed. "A stalker? That's creepy."

"Yeah. Sorry." He really had been a nerd. He sank down on the edge of the bed. "I didn't peek in your windows. Just followed you when you were in public, because I wanted to know you, wanted to feel close to you." How could he make her understand that he, wimpy

Lester, had been the only boy who *got* her. "Like, I knew you helped Mr. DiGiannantonio. He couldn't keep up the house and garden, and he hated the idea of going into a home."

She tossed her head, still gripping the dog. "He paid me."

"Yeah, right. That's why you did it."

Her face softened. "Okay, I liked Mr. D. He was nice to me, unlike the rest of this town." A pause. "When I left Whistler, I worried about him. Is he still alive?"

Finally, LJ dared to reach out. Not to hug her, because he guessed she'd reject the gesture. Instead, he leaned forward to stroke Romeo, letting his fingers brush hers. "He's in Glen Woods. A new seniors' home. It's a good place, and he's settled in okay. The old ladies love him."

A fond smile lit her face. "He's a sweetie. I never understood why his family so rarely visited. Where was he before Glen Woods? That dismal place he was always bitching about?"

"No, he was at home until a couple years ago. Then his arthritis got too bad."

Her brows raised. "But how did he manage?" Something in his face gave him away. "You?"

"Emily and I took over. He's a good old guy." He winked. " 'Course we just did it for the money."

She chuckled, and it seemed she'd finally relaxed. Her grip on Romeo eased, and a hand settled on the dog's back. LJ rested his own on top of it. "He'd love it if you visited."

A wistful expression crossed her face, then she shook her head. "I'm staying right here until the work's done and I can go back to Toronto."

Pieces started to fall into place. Her rejection of his dinner invitation, her refusal to shop for paint, the overflowing fridge and the bags of canned and packaged food. "Why?"

Her eyes narrowed and her jaw tightened. For a moment he thought she wouldn't answer, and when she did the words came out cold and clipped. "Whistler treated me like shit."

"I know." He squeezed her hand. "I'm sorry. But that was ten years ago."

She shook her head. "The memories suck. And I could run into people who knew me back then."

"They've changed and you've changed."

She pulled herself more upright, dislodging his hand and making Romeo shift position. "Yeah, right. You figure Joey's mom would give me a second chance?"

No. Ms. Anderson had a closed mind. Just like his own parents, who'd said Patty Shoemaker was crazy to leave her B&B to her troublemaker niece. Whistler might be a cosmopolitan community, but some people had narrow minds. "Others would. Show people who you really are rather than play the badass like you used to."

"Who I really am? A tattoo artist? That'd go over big." She tossed back her hair. "Why should I? I don't need the aggro. I'll be gone in a week."

LJ sensed she'd taken all she could handle. It wasn't the time to push. "How about I leave Romeo here tonight?"

She gazed up at him, biting her lip. Then she said, "Thank you. I'd be glad of the company."

"Don't see him complaining either." He smiled down at the two of them. "The guy's got it made. Sharing a bed with a pretty lady."

The smallest of smiles flickered on her lips.

He wished he had a clearer idea where things stood between him and Charlie. Could she get past seeing him as geeky Lester—damn, why had he told her he'd stalked her?—and get back to seeing him as the tool-belt guy she was attracted to?

* * *

The next morning, LJ arrived at the B&B early, hoping to have some alone time with Charlie, but Joey's truck was parked outside.

Romeo greeted him at the door, and in the kitchen he found Charlie and Joey at the table drinking coffee. She was in the purple top, her hair back in a ponytail, and had shadows under her eyes. Not knowing how to make things better, he offered a quiet "Morning" as he walked past her, hands full of doggie stuff, takeout coffee, and a breakfast burrito.

"Morning." Her gaze met his briefly, then quickly returned to some colored sketches lying on the table. Joey'd said eagles were wild, free, and strong, and she'd captured that in three quite different ways.

"You haven't lost your talent," he said, looking over her shoulder.

"Thanks." Again she glanced up, hazel eyes uncertain.

He'd settle for uncertain. It was better than distancing him with her tough-girl act.

After pouring food for Romeo, he sat down with his breakfast. Trying to keep things light, he said to Joey, "You're really getting a tattoo?"

"Yeah, but Charlie says we should work on the design, then I should carry it around for a while and, like, live with it."

"Good advice." LJ smiled at her, and her lips quivered in a slight smile, as if she was starting to relax.

Joey said to Charlie, "Hey, I got an idea. You ever done a snowboard?"

"A design for a board? No."

"I'm totally into boarding. If you painted the eagle on my board, it'd be sweet. Like, I'd fly. And I'd, you know, live with the design for a while."

"Hmm . . ." The sparkle in her eyes said she was intrigued. "Let's start by talking about the designs I did. Tell me what you like and don't like. Tell me about eagles, and why they have special meaning for you."

As Joey began to talk, LJ noticed Charlie's spiral-bound sketchpad lying half hidden by one of the drawings. He held it up and shot her a questioning glance.

She nodded.

He leafed through as she and Joey talked, turning pages with one hand and eating his burrito with the other, careful not to get crumbs or grease on the pad.

There was everything from sketches of him and his crew to bold abstracts to soft, swirly, flowery designs. Smiling appreciatively, he had the sense he was being watched and glanced up to find her gaze on him. When he mouthed, "Great," she gave him her first genuine smile of the morning.

The front door opened, and Romeo rushed out of the kitchen, then came back with Will, who greeted them and sat at the table. Quietly he studied the eagle drawings as Joey and Charlie resumed their conversation. Then, when LJ was done with the sketchpad, Will began to turn pages.

Joey and Charlie finished their talk, and LJ said, "Okay, folks, we need to get to work."

Will tapped the sketchpad. "Charlie, I'd love to show a few of these to my wife Sandy."

"Your wife?"

"She's a clothing designer. She works at a boutique in the Village, saving up money to go into business and launch her own line."

A grin flashed. "That's like my plan. To open my own tattoo parlor in Toronto."

Shit, thought LJ. She had serious career plans in Toronto. No wonder she was so eager to leave. Was there any hope for him?

"Sounds like you've got lots in common," Will told her. "Anyhow, your drawings remind me of her designs."

"Tell me which ones and I'll tear them out."

After she'd carefully tugged sketches free of the coil binding, Will said, "Thanks. I'll take good care of them."

Charlie rose. "I'm going back to my boring yellow paint. It really hurts, not doing murals."

"You should stay and run the place," Joey said. "You could put way sick stuff on the walls."

"Tempting, but I'll pass." Her dry tone said that staying was anything but tempting.

After getting Will and Joey working on kitchen cabinets, LJ followed Charlie to the second floor. She'd stripped down to the turquoise tank and was squatting on the drop cloth in the hall, pouring paint into the pan.

She glanced up, expression noncommittal. "Thanks for cleaning this stuff up yesterday. Sorry for my"—her chin came up—"little meltdown." Finished pouring, she rose, squaring her shoulders. "You should have told me who you were, right from the beginning."

Yeah, and have her think of him as a geek from moment one? Defensively, he said, "*I* recognized *you*."

"You knew I was coming."

"I'd have known you anyhow. Guy with a crush? Remember?"

She twisted her ponytail into a loose knot on top of her head and skewered it with a couple of stick-like things, then stared up at him. "Much as I hate thinking about that night, I have to know. Why did you reject me?"

Hadn't she heard him yesterday? "You were upset and just trying to be tough. To get back in control."

She grimaced. "Okay. But why would you care?"

Damn it, she sure had a low opinion of him. "Because I wasn't a dickhead like your date," he snapped, stepping closer. "I respected you."

"Respected me?" Her dark brows arched.

"Yeah."

Her exotic scent drifted toward him above the odor of

paint. It weakened him enough to admit the rest. "And I wanted more. I wanted you to want me."

Her face softened.

"It was hard, Charlie, turning you down. You have no idea how hard."

For a long moment, she said nothing. Did nothing. Then she took a step forward, so her hips brushed his. Jeans against jeans—instant arousal underneath his fly.

She wriggled her hips, and her eyes gleamed teasingly. "I'm getting an idea."

He could drop the subject of his teen geekdom, but he wanted her to know the rest. "I was the only guy who really saw you." He put his arms around her and rested his hands on the sweet swell of her butt. "The Charlie who rescued animals and helped an old man."

"That's"—her lips trembled. "Thank you for seeing that I wasn't all bad."

"I wanted you to see me, too. But you never did."

"I'm sorry."

They stood quietly for a few moments, bodies touching in the middle. He breathed her in, his heart raced, and he fought the urge to pull her tighter against his erection. It was about more than just sex.

Her clear hazel eyes met his. "I see you now, LJ." Her hips wriggled again, the pressure making him swell further. "And I feel you."

Oh yeah, that was what he'd wanted to hear. Gently, he traced the line of the dragon's snout across silky, warm skin. "I want you, Dragon Lady." As his teenage crush. As the tantalizing woman in his arms. And who knew, maybe even as his future. He touched her guardian dragon again, serving notice.

Her lips quirked. "And I want you, Tool-belt Guy."

"I'll let you play with my tool belt if you show me your mystery tattoo." The idea of another tattoo—maybe more than one?—hidden under her clothing drove him crazy.

A soft laugh. "Seems like a fair exchange."

Relief made him lightheaded, or maybe that was because all the blood had rushed to his groin. "You'll go out with me?"

She tensed. "No, I'll have sex with you. That's what this is about."

Not for him. She still didn't really see him, not as more than a guy with a good body who'd be fun for some casual sex. But it was a starting point. "Let's go to my place this evening. Get out of the construction zone." And get her on his turf.

She nodded, eyes bright, cheeks flushed.

He bent his head to kiss her.

She rose to meet him, and their lips touched, soft and tender. Despite the aching throb in his loins that urged him to do her right then and there, he caressed her mouth with his, letting his kiss tell her she was special.

Joey's voice broke the moment, calling from downstairs, "Hey, LJ, I need to know how big to cut this."

Charlie murmured, "Tell him big." Her hips thrust suggestively. "Big is good."

Chuckling, he stepped back. "Big," he promised. "And thorough. Satisfaction guaranteed, like I said."

"I'm beginning to believe you."

5

Later, after the men had gone and she'd made a quick dinner and fed Romeo, Charlie stripped and stepped into the shower.

As she stroked the teal-colored face cloth—a vivid, personal touch amid the bland décor—over her breasts, down her belly, and between her legs, her body hummed with anticipation. LJ was one sexy guy and he was going to be awesome in bed.

It had taken her years to get over the attempted rape. She stroked the tattoo on the back of her neck, blessing the day Ginger had picked her up, hitchhiking near Sylvan Lake, Alberta. The kindhearted woman had taken her home and fed her. A dozen years older than Charlie, she and her husband Jake had treated her like a little sister.

Thanks to them, she'd slowly begun to trust, and to heal. They'd taught her how to judge character, how to respect herself, and how to defend herself against men like Drew.

When they died and she left Sylvan Lake, she took their lessons with her. Eventually, she stopped holding on to her virginity and learned that her sexuality was a wonderful thing. One that she owned and controlled. Over the past years, she'd gone out with a number of guys, some as friends and some as lovers. One day, she hoped she'd find the kind of love her friends had shared. The kind she heard about now and then from tattoo clients. A love worth symbolizing in body art that would last her entire life.

She just didn't have a clue how to find it. Love was a big mystery. Infinitely desirable, but overwhelming, scary, and out of reach. Something she'd longed for as a kid, but never found. Not until Ginger and Jake gave her things she'd never known before: a real home, acceptance and love, a family. They'd been more her family than any blood relative ever had.

After the accident, she'd been alone again, so she'd hit the road. Inspired by the tattoo lessons Jake had given her, she found an apprenticeship with the artist who did the feather-flower tat from her design. Two or three years later, she wound up in Toronto, found work at The Barbed Rose, began to dream of opening her own business.

That was the future.

She stepped out of the shower and pulled off the shower cap. The present was LJ. The very sexy and intriguing LJ.

It was hard to get her head around the fact that he'd been the geeky Lester. And that Lester, like sweet old Mr. DiGiannantonio, had seen past her badass reputation. He'd *respected* her. No one in Whistler had respected her.

Of course, he'd also had a huge crush on her. It would have warped his judgment.

How did the adult Charlie measure up? Anxious and excited, she selected clothes from her limited wardrobe. Black leggings that hugged her hips and long legs. A coral cami—she liked layers and often avoided wearing a bra—and over it, a long, off-the-shoulder violet sweater.

Hair down and shiny, a touch of smoky makeup to accentuate her eyes and cheekbones, and she was ready.

"What do you think?" she asked Romeo, who watched from the foot of the bed.

He gave a yip and jumped off the bed, then scurried out of the room.

"Oh, thanks a lot. That really helps my confidence."

A moment later, she heard the front door open and LJ call, "Charlie?"

Aha. That's why the beagle had run off. "Coming!" She slipped into her boots and coat, grabbed her purse, and hurried downstairs, tingling with arousal and excitement.

LJ was in the entrance, hunkered down to pat Romeo, but stood when she walked over. He looked rugged and outdoorsy in jeans and a heavy winter jacket, with snowflakes melting in his black hair and on his shoulders.

She brushed her hand through his hair and flicked a scattering of melted drops to the floor. "It's snowing."

"Just started." He caught the lapels of her coat, angled his head, and bent to kiss her.

Mmm, his lips were cool at first, fresh like the outdoors, but they heated quickly as he explored her mouth with his lips and the tip of his tongue.

Sexy shivers rippled through her as her tongue met his, danced with it, and for long minutes they took each other's mouths greedily. She moaned as heat surged through her. Wanting nothing better than to strip off their clothes and go at it hot and hard, she fumbled for his coat buttons.

He broke the kiss and took a step back, throwing her off balance. "Hell, Charlie, this isn't how I want it to be."

"Feels good to me." Breathless from that stunning kiss, she burned with the need to feel his naked flesh all around her. Inside her.

"And it'll feel better." He tugged her toward the door. "Promise."

Grumbling good-naturedly, she followed as Romeo rushed past them into the snow. The chill air and soft kiss of snowflakes soothed her burning cheeks. LJ held the passenger door of the truck for her, then put Romeo in the back, where the dog curled up on a blanket.

LJ climbed in beside her and unbuttoned his coat. Rather than his usual tee and plaid flannel shirt, he wore a lightweight navy sweater that hugged his muscular torso. The man was so yummy. And so was the erection that bulged under his fly. She could hardly wait.

When he pulled out of the driveway, she was assaulted on all sides by Christmas. Lights twinkled around windows and twined through trees and bushes. Fringes of icicle lights hung from eaves, beside real icicles. Santas, reindeer, wise men, and snowmen littered front yards.

She hated Christmas, for all the things it was supposed to be and never had been. Decorated trees with gifts heaped beneath, bulging Christmas stockings, roast turkey and cranberry sauce, carolers on the doorstep. Family and friends sharing love, peace, and joy. *As if*. She huddled into her coat, even though the cab of the truck was warm.

One Christmas, her dad had stumbled into the sparsely decorated tree, knocked it down, and broken his wrist. She, at fourteen, had driven him to the emergency room because her mom was too drunk. The cops had caught her driving home from the hospital.

Another year, her mom had actually stayed semi-sober long enough to cook a turkey. She burned the potatoes, though, and Charlie's dad had yelled. The fight escalated, as fights did with the two of them, and her mom heaved the turkey across the kitchen at him.

Christmas, like every other day, had been a good day to escape the house.

She'd been sketching a mule deer in the snow the afternoon her parents set fire to the crappy basement apartment and lost their lives. The fire wasn't her fault. Ginger and Jake had finally made her believe that. Her parents had driven her out, time and again.

That had been the Christmas from hell. The dance and the almost-rape, her parents' death, Patty's clear distaste at having her niece forced upon her.

Since then, Charlie had avoided Christmas. It helped that Ginger and Jake hadn't observed it. They'd been spiritual, not religious, and celebrated solstice rituals that she'd enjoyed.

Charlie folded her arms over her chest and stared out the window. A gaudy reindeer-drawn sleigh twinkled atop a snow-clad roof.

"Charlie? You okay?"

That voice. Now that she knew LJ was Lester, she could hear a hint of the boy in the man's voice. He'd asked something similar that night when he drove her home, pulling her out of her miserable funk. She'd reminded herself that you're never vulnerable unless you let yourself be—and even then, you sure as hell don't have to let anyone else know.

"Sure." She uncrossed her arms and rested a hand on his thigh, warm and muscular under denim. Oh yeah, this reality was much better than her crappy memories. She imagined what he'd look like naked. Stronger, more masculine than any guy she'd been with. And his cock . . . She'd felt it against her belly. Impressive. Very impressive.

"Yeah, I'm just fine, LJ." Her fingers trailed up the inseam. "I've been looking forward to tonight."

"Me, too."

She made circles on his inner thigh, her fingers grazing higher each time, arousal quickening her blood as she drifted closer to the bulge at his groin. Hot, she used her free hand to unbutton her jacket, and squirmed against the needy pulse between her thighs.

Her fingers lodged between his legs, against the firm curve of his balls. Stroked.

He caught her hand and tugged it away. "Cut that out, or I'll drive off the road."

"Can't take it?" she purred.

"Got that right." He lifted her hand to his lips and nipped her index finger.

Arousal shot straight to her sex. "Are we almost there?"

"Another mile or two." He returned her hand to her lap.

It was as good a time as any to ask a question that had been on her mind. "You were a math science geek, right?"

He tensed, then shot her a glance. "Yeah."

"Some kind of boy genius? Yet now you're a contractor, not a brilliant scientist."

"I went to university, got as far as a master's in physics. Summers I worked for my uncle—he's the Banfield who started Banfield Renos—and realized I like this work better. It uses my body as well as my mind, and I like to build things."

"So, you work for your uncle?"

He shook his head. "Bought him out when he decided to retire early." He pulled into a driveway. "Here we are."

No decorations, she was glad to see. His home reminded her of a whimsical gingerbread house, with gables, shutters, balconies, scalloped eaves, even a little turret. Golden light gleamed from a couple of curtained windows. "It's charming." Her fingers itched to paint the trim in bright, fun colors.

They walked toward the front door, Romeo dashing ahead. "It's my aunt and uncle's. They designed and built it. They're in Florida, thinking about moving permanently, and I'm house-sitting."

He unlocked the front door and they went into a mudroom with ski equipment, a snowboard, and a collection of outdoor clothing.

As they took off their coats and boots, she asked, "What's in the turret?" She imagined a sanctuary where a person could curl up, shut out the world, paint, and dream.

"Me, right now. It was my aunt's reading room. I've loved it since I was a kid, so I've taken it over."

"I want to see it."

"Now? I thought we'd—"

"Now." She ran winter-chilled fingers over the front of his sweater, appreciating the fine, soft wool and the firm muscles beneath. Dipping under the hem, she brushed his bare six-pack, her cool skin rapidly warming. Anticipation trembled through her. It had been a few months since she'd had sex, and that guy'd been nowhere near as appealing. "Now."

"Want a drink?"

"I want *you*." In case her words weren't clear enough, she cupped his erection.

"Feeling's mutual." He dropped a quick kiss on her lips, then caught her hand.

As he guided her down a hallway, the dog padding behind, she saw warm light through an open doorway and smelled something fresh as a winter forest. In the hall, a blue runner ran down the hardwood floor and flower photographs decorated the walls. The decor wasn't her style, yet she felt a whisper of longing at the homey touches, so unlike the dump where she'd grown up.

They climbed a wooden staircase, up two flights, then LJ ushered her into a dark room and flicked a switch. Expecting light, she was surprised when a gas fire flared to life, illuminating the room with flickering golden flames.

She pivoted in a circle, taking in round walls and a high, pointed ceiling, a duvet-covered double bed, a dresser, two window seats, and bookcases full of scientific tomes and colorful sci-fi paperbacks. LJ was still a science geek.

The wooden furniture was simple and attractive, colorful rugs warmed the wooden floor, and several watercolor nature scenes were amateur but bright and cheery. The numerous windows would let in lots of natural light. It would make a perfect art studio. "I love it."

Romeo flopped contentedly in front of the fire. She'd have done the same if it wasn't for the very tempting man who watched her, leaning against the wall by the fire, hip-cocked and noticeably aroused. His black hair, jeans, and rugged masculinity somehow fit perfectly here.

"Me, too. Aunt Fran used to let me come up here and read or do homework."

"My aunt didn't want us at her home or the B&B. We weren't good enough."

"I bet she regretted it. That's why she left you the B&B."

"Maybe. Better late than never, I guess." She shrugged away the thought. "We're not here to talk about family. In fact . . ." She stepped closer until their fronts almost brushed. "Let's not talk at all. Show me what you've got, Tool-belt Guy."

"In exchange for that secret tattoo." He wove his fingers through her hair at the temples and held her head firmly as he bent to kiss her.

She surged into him, gripping his shoulders, and captured the kiss greedily. Since she'd first seen him, he'd turned her on, and now, being in his arms with a bed only a few feet away, passion and need fused in a fire that thickened her blood.

His lips were gentle and slow despite the erection that lodged firmly against her belly. A man with self-control.

Maybe she'd like him to lose control. She was hot for him, quivering with arousal, melting with need. He didn't need to seduce her; she was already there. She wanted him to be as hungry for her as she was for him. Once, he'd had a crush on her. She could make him lose control.

Sex, plain and simple. Sex, hot and hard. Sex that

wiped your mind clear of everything but the moment, the experience.

She deepened the kiss, taking his mouth with her tongue while she wriggled her hips to rub his erection in an erotic rhythm.

He groaned. "Shit, Charlie, I can't believe—" He didn't finish and she couldn't ask because his tongue dueled with hers and his hands grabbed her butt, squeezing, lifting, pulling her tight while he thrust against her almost desperately.

She moaned and wormed her hands between them, trying to pull off his sweater and undo his jeans all at once.

He broke away, gasping for breath, and hauled his sweater over his head.

She froze, breathless, too, and stared. Male perfection. Skin golden in the firelight, muscles strong and defined, a scattering of black hair, cocoa brown nipples. A perfect canvas for a tattoo, yet a great work of art—erotic art— just the way he was.

Her hands itched to touch him, itched so badly they fumbled with the button of his jeans.

He pushed her hands away and quickly undid his jeans and shoved them down, pulling his underwear and socks with them.

She sucked in a breath, taking him in. A lovely, hard cock, springing from a nest of black curls. Slim hips, lean, muscular legs. Her gaze drifted back. An amazingly lovely cock.

Everything inside her turned liquid with arousal.

Before she could touch him, he tugged her sweater up and pulled it over her head. Then he began to pull the tight, stretchy leggings down her hips.

His hands stilled, and she knew he'd glimpsed her tattoo. It wrapped around one hip and down the top of her thigh, extending halfway onto one buttock and partway onto her abdomen. Exotic, sensual flowers—rather like

Georgia O'Keefe paintings—bloomed amid twining vines. The blossoms were in shades of peach and apricot, of violet and indigo, and the vines were every green imaginable.

He peeled her leggings off slowly, his eyes wide. Men's reactions differed—from shock to disgust to arousal. LJ's looked like wonder. When she was down to a coral cami and a black thong, he stepped back and studied her. "Charlie, that's incredible." He ran a gentle finger over the petals that decorated her hip. "Beautiful. Sensual." Huskily, he added, "Sexy."

It was her symbol, her celebration, of owning her own sexuality. She would choose to whom she gave her body, and what she'd do in bed.

She chose LJ, and she wanted to do *everything* with him.

When he raised his eyes to her face, she saw the fiery glitter of sexual need. He took her by the shoulders and backed her toward the bed, then they tumbled onto the duvet, kissing hungrily. Hands and legs grasped, twined, then her camisole was off and her breasts smushed against the hard heat of his chest as he came down on top of her. Her hands dug into his butt, feeling firm muscles bunch and shift.

The head of his cock pressed insistently against the soaking wet crotch of her thong, rubbing her clit. She pulsed, she throbbed, she needed more. Whimpering, she squirmed against him. "God, yes, keep doing that."

Instead, he pulled away. "I want to be inside you."

She groaned with frustration, then yanked off her thong as he reached into the drawer of the bedside table.

In seconds he was sheathed and back between her legs. She lifted herself to him, body quivering. His cock brushed her damp, sensitive flesh, and she whimpered again. "Please."

He leaned forward, and his lips took hers. Panting with

need, she answered impatiently, yet his lips, his tongue were so sensual and skilled, they seduced her into dancing with them.

A second later she gasped as his cock probed her, blunt-headed and swollen. Big, hot, perfect. "Yes," she whispered against his lips.

"Oh, yeah," he murmured, black curls tousled on his forehead, eyes dark with passion. Then, in one long, smooth glide, he thrust in and filled her.

She gasped, moaned. Oh God, that felt so good.

He stopped, lodged deep inside her, the two of them locked together. Every muscle in her body trembled. Deep inside her, she pulsed around him, tiny ripples like shallow breaths.

"Charlie," he said. One word. A declaration.

She had no idea what he meant. All she knew was, it felt exquisite. The tension was almost unbearable, yet absolutely right.

Slowly, ever so slowly, he slid out inch by inch until he was almost gone, until she felt empty, craving his touch. Then he plunged back in, stroking her sensitive flesh with his rough heat, and she gasped at the shock, the pleasure.

Again and again he stroked, and the pleasure mounted until all she could do was moan and thrash her head on the pillow, craving that one thing to finally release her.

His hand came between their bodies, and the next time he thrust in, he caressed her clit and yes, that was it, exactly what she needed. She cried out as orgasm flooded her body in rich, pulsing waves of blissful release.

He plunged into her again, hard and jerky, groaning with his own climax.

Seconds, maybe minutes later, he collapsed on top of her. His chest heaved against hers as they both fought for breath. His head lay beside hers on the pillow, face turned toward her so his warm breath brushed her ear, her cheek, her neck.

Mmm, very nice.

"Wow," he murmured. "You can't imagine how many times I fantasized about that."

She smiled. "Having sex with a tattooed lady?"

"Uh-uh. With Charlie Coltrane."

"That's a lot of pressure to put on a girl. How did I measure up to the fantasies?" In fact, she did feel a bit insecure, but LJ was a considerate guy. He'd say the right thing. She could only hope he meant it.

Because this was good. She could do a lot of this before she headed back to Toronto.

"The reality's much better," LJ said. He had trouble believing he'd actually made love with Charlie.

Another guy might've been satisfied with living the fantasy just once. But his fantasy had never been only about sex.

He eased off her slim body to deal with the condom, then studied her as she stretched with a cat's grace. She was clean-lined, lovely, so sexy. The dragon, whose head she stroked, more like a habit than a conscious gesture, was fiery and passionate. The tattoo on her hip was sensual and utterly feminine. Naked but for her body art, black hair fanning out on the pale blue pillowcase, she was the most erotic thing he'd ever seen. "You're amazing."

"You say the sweetest things." Her grin hinted at private thoughts.

He wanted her again. Sex, yes, but much more. No other girl, no woman, had touched his heart the way Charlie had. He wanted to get to know the grown-up, to share himself with her, to find out what they might be to each other.

When he'd brought her to the house tonight, he'd had a plan. She'd circumvented it, wanting sex in the turret room. He slid out of bed and extended a hand to her. "Come downstairs."

"I like it here," she protested.

"I've laid a real fire." And he had a surprise, one he hoped she'd like.

"A real fire? That does sound nice." She put her hand in his and let him pull her out of bed.

They dressed and, leaving Romeo sleeping by the gas fire, went down the winding staircase. LJ took her to the kitchen and flicked on the lights. Touching her bare shoulder above the low neckline of her purple sweater, he said, "Drink? Snack?"

"A drink sounds good."

"Wine, beer, mixed drink? Or there's eggnog, fruit juice, and soda in the fridge."

She dipped into the fridge and came out with a tin of club soda and a bottle of lime juice. "I don't drink alcohol."

He got down two glasses, and ice from the freezer. "Because of your parents?" Everyone had known they were alcoholics.

She nodded.

While she made her drink, he poured himself an eggnog, skipping the splash of rum he'd normally add. Some guys thought eggnog was a girlie drink, but he liked Christmas treats.

"I don't mind if you have booze."

"I'm not much of a drinker." It was true; he could take it or leave it.

They went into the living room, where he'd left a lamp burning. The room smelled fresh and outdoorsy, thanks to the eight-foot Douglas fir that stood in a pail of water in a corner, surrounded by his aunt and uncle's tree stand, lights, and ornaments.

Charlie halted abruptly when she saw it. "A tree?"

"Picked it out this afternoon." Then he'd hauled all the trappings up from the basement. He touched a match to the fire he'd laid. "Thought we could put it up." It was one of his favorite activities.

When he turned from the fireplace, she was shaking her head. "I don't do Christmas."

"What? Why?"

"Because . . . Christmas sucks."

"Uh . . ." Then it dawned on him. Christmas was supposed to be a time of family and friends, of love and laughter. For her, growing up, it wouldn't have been.

But that was years ago. It was time she learned the season could be a joyous one. "It's just a tree, Charlie." He put on music, deciding not to push it by choosing carols. Instead he went with Diana Krall.

Charlie was still rooted to the same spot, so he opened up the tree stand. He hefted the heavy fir to place the trunk in the stand. "Can you hold this straight while I screw it in?"

"What would you have done if I wasn't here?" she muttered, approaching the tree warily.

"Struggled and cursed." In fact he'd have waited until his sister got home from university and invited her and some friends over. Now he hoped Charlie would get in the mood.

She moved closer and studied the tree skeptically.

"Careful of your sweater. Don't want to get pitch on it."

Cautiously, she buried her arms in the branches and gripped the trunk. Head averted so she didn't get poked in the eye by needles, she said, "It smells good."

Her begrudging tone made him grin. Quickly he did up the screws and stood back to look. "Great. Now, what do you think about the lights?"

She released the tree and stepped back. "Think about them?"

Hoping to engage her creativity, he said, "My aunt's gone through phases. We have big multicolored lights, small multicolored ones that twinkle on and off, white and gold lights, and clear twinkling lights. Which shall we use?"

She tilted her head, studying the tree. "Colored and twinkling. Little lights, scattered all through the branches."

Hiding a satisfied grin, he said, "Sounds good. I'll stand on a chair to do the top. You hand me the strings and tell me where to drape them."

An hour later, LJ said, "I'll turn off the lights."

Despite her aversion to Christmas, Charlie felt a thrill of anticipation. She hadn't had a tree in more than ten years, and when she'd been a kid it was a hit-and-miss thing. Some years there'd been a Charlie Brown tree, and she'd improvised decorations. Tonight, she'd enjoyed consulting over placement of ornaments, sharing touches and hugs.

LJ flicked the switch and she gazed at the tree, spellbound. Yeah, it was hokey, with tinsel and a collection of ornaments that included elegant glass ones, tacky souvenirs, craftsy decorations, and the clumsy products of kids in the family. Yet, there was magic in the green scented boughs, the bright sparkles of light that reflected off the strands of silvery tinsel, and the ill-matched but well-loved ornaments.

His arm came around her and she nestled into him,

thinking how wonderful he felt, as he said, "It's the best tree ever."

"I bet you say that every year," she teased.

"And every year it's true." He squeezed her waist. "But this year it's especially true."

He put a glass into her hand and automatically she lifted it and drank. Creamy richness filled her mouth. "You gave me the wrong drink."

"Sorry."

She took another sip. She avoided eggnog because of its association with Christmas and because most people laced it with booze. It was actually pretty good, with that hint of nutmeg.

"Did you celebrate Christmas when you were a kid?" he asked quietly.

"Sort of. Not really."

He didn't say anything, just kept that warm, supportive arm around her.

"One year, Mom bought a frozen turkey and thawed it, then she got so drunk Christmas Eve she never woke up to cook it." Though Charlie had friends, the only people she'd ever talked to about her childhood were Ginger and Jake, and then only after she'd known them for months.

But LJ had lived in Whistler. He already knew the worst rumors, and there was something freeing about being honest. "There were a lot of fights. One year Mom heaved the turkey at Dad, and another year the neighbors called the cops. And there was the year he fell over the tree and broke his wrist and I had to drive him to emergency."

He hugged her closer. "Shit, Charlie. I knew it was bad, just didn't know how bad."

She shrugged. "Yeah, well . . . My childhood sucked. Christmas was same old, same old." Worse, because for everyone else it was special. She rested her head against

LJ's shoulder, gazing at the tree rather than him. "Guess you know they burned the place down during the holidays. Since then, I try to ignore the whole thing. Don't need the bad memories."

He guided her to the couch, and they sat, his arm still around her. She curled her legs up and nestled into him, head on his shoulder. He smelled green and outdoorsy like the tree, with a spicy undernote of sweaty sex.

"After they died, you dropped out and left Whistler," he said.

"And vowed never to come back," she said ruefully.

"Your aunt wouldn't take you in?"

She snorted. "Yeah, but she hated the idea. She didn't want me. And the feeling was mutual." Screw Patty, the narrow-minded social climber.

"That's rough."

The last thing she'd expected when she came back to Whistler was that she'd be sharing memories. But LJ was easy to talk to. LJ was Lester, the kid who'd respected rather than judged her. She wished she'd opened her eyes and seen him, back then. Maybe she'd have had a friend.

"Mom and her sister were close, growing up. They were poor, and their dad was an alcoholic. They liked to party and hook up with what Mom called 'bad boys.' She got pregnant and married one. Not Patty. She found a respectable businessman, an older guy, and remade herself to fit into his world. Snotty bitch."

He dropped a kiss in her hair. "Patty didn't say much about you, but I bet she was sorry."

She shrugged. "Whatever." Then she admitted, "She called me this summer—I don't know how she got my number—and said I should come back. I said no and hung up."

"Maybe she wanted to apologize."

"She could've done that on the phone."

Charlie remembered that the lawyer had said he had some things for her. She'd told him to donate Patty's personal stuff to charity, but he'd said these were items Patty'd made him promise to hand over in person. Might there be a letter? An apology?

Did she feel like going into the Village to his office? Nah. All she wanted from her aunt was the inheritance.

As if he'd read her thoughts, LJ asked, "If you could have anything for Christmas, what would it be?"

"To open my own tattoo parlor in Toronto. I'm calling it Coltrane." She eased back in the curve of his arm so she could smile at him. "I've taken business courses." For her, the dropout who'd never been great at school, that had been a major achievement. Not one an academic genius like him would be able to relate to. "I've been saving, planning, but it would've taken another couple years to realize that dream. Now, I can do it as soon as the B&B sells."

Of course, long term, she had more dreams. To do other kinds of art; to have her paintings in an exhibit. To find the same kind of love her friends had shared.

"You deserve to get what you want, Charlie." LJ's face, lit by flickering firelight and multicolored twinkles, looked solemn.

"How about you? What do you want for Christmas?"

He gazed toward the tree as if pondering what he'd like to see wrapped up under it. "Guess I don't know yet."

He probably had most everything he wanted. "What do you do for Christmas? Go to your parents'?"

"Yeah. I go on Christmas Eve and sleep over. My sister will be home. It's family tradition to hang stockings by the fire and go to midnight Mass even though we're not religious. In the morning we open presents, and in the afternoon we get together with the rest of the family. We have a turkey dinner, watch some hokey Christmas movie. Nothing exciting, but it's nice."

No doubt the turkey always got cooked, and never heaved at anyone. "Sounds nice."

"If you're still here, you could come." Then a flicker of unease crossed his face.

Another memory surfaced. She shifted away from him. Oh no, Lester Jacoby would never have been her friend— nor would LJ. "Yeah, like your parents would invite me."

"Uh . . . what makes you say that?" His guilty expression told her he knew perfectly well.

"That day your sister thanked me for helping Romeo? She said she didn't care what her parents said, she and Romeo knew I was a good person." The girl's kind words had meant a lot.

He winced. "Sorry. My parents can be judgmental."

"I didn't give a damn what people thought."

"You do now." He met her gaze steadily.

"Do not." She thrust herself off the couch.

He stayed seated. "You stay in that B&B like it's a co-coon. You're scared to go out because someone might recognize you."

"Okay, fine. I *do* give a damn." She glared down at him. "It hurts. It always did. Then, I had no choice but to live in Whistler, so I toughed it out and pretended no one could get to me."

"You didn't even try to fit in. You dressed differently, blew off classes, let people think the worst of you rather than explain."

She jammed her fists on her hips. "Why the hell try to fit in when you know you'll never be accepted? Better to live life your own way, and tell them all to screw off."

He stood slowly, and she took a step back, her breath quickening with anger.

"Yeah, Charlie, I see that."

She searched his face warily. "Do you?"

"I envied your ballsy attitude. I didn't fit in either." There was pain in his voice. "I was the butt of jokes. I wished I'd had the guts to tell those kids to screw off. But I was a wimp."

Softening, she pointed out, "You weren't a wimp when it mattered."

"Any guy would've done the same when that dickhead came after you."

"No. Most would have thought I had it coming." She rested a hand on his chest and felt the quick thudding of his heart. "You defied your parents and brought your sister to thank me."

He raised a hand and enfolded hers. "Guess I had guts when it came to you."

Something about the way he said it, the softness in his eyes, made her feel all mushy inside. For a long moment, they just gazed at each other. A strange thought flitted into her mind. Could LJ be the special man she'd been longing for?

A log in the fireplace popped, reminding her where she was. Whistler, the place she hated. The small town with a long memory. As for LJ, he wouldn't invite her to his parents'. Probably, he wouldn't even tell them about her.

No, he'd never be her guy. In a week's time, she'd be gone, and this time she absolutely wasn't coming back.

She freed her hand from his and stepped away, rubbing her dragon's head. "That crush you had . . . That was a kid thing, right? I mean, I don't want you to think . . ." He had to know, as she did, they had no future.

He swallowed, and she saw the kid he'd been. Vulnerable, the way she'd been. "That we might care for each other?"

She shook her head. "You're great, but this is a fling. Just sex. You understand, right?"

He squared his shoulders. "I understand how you feel." He moved over to poke at the fire, then turned. "So, you want to go back? Or stay here?"

Stay with him in that turret room with the gas fire and the dog sleeping on the hearth? Oh no. The evening had been wonderful—and confusing and scary. She needed to be alone. "I'll go back, thanks."

She had too much pride to ask, but when he said, "Romeo'd probably like to go with you," she didn't point out that the dog wouldn't appreciate being roused to go out into the cold night. "I'd be glad of his company."

"Lucky beast."

7

Three days later, LJ had a quick shower after work, then drove to his parents' house, with Romeo in the backseat.

His folks had returned from their Mexican Riviera cruise. His sister, finished with law school exams, had picked them up in Vancouver that morning, and they'd all driven up to Whistler.

Of course he wanted to see them, but he missed Charlie. Yeah, he'd seen her off and on all day, but they were circumspect when Will and Joey were around. In the evenings at his place, they let loose.

Charlie insisted it was only—could only be—sex, and it was driving him crazy. Did she really share her body so generously with other lovers? Did she talk about the years she'd spent traveling around Canada, the string of loser jobs she'd had until she met her friends Ginger and Jake? Did she tell other guys how much those friends had meant to her? Did she talk about her dream of having an art exhibit?

Did she share memories from her childhood in Whistler?

He didn't think so. But maybe. With Charlie, he often regressed to the insecurity he thought he'd left behind with his teens. She totally fascinated him. And, though she definitely saw him in a sexual way and liked him as a person, she rejected the idea of caring for him. Whereas he couldn't stop himself from caring for her.

He'd seduced her with sex that made her scream in orgasm, romanced her with candlelight and love songs, shared the fun of decorating a Christmas tree, and still she went home each night to her solitary bed. He was running out of ideas.

Was there any hope that tonight she'd actually miss him?

When he opened the door of the family home, Romeo darted in, and the two of them were swallowed up in hugs. "Hey, you guys look great," he told his parents, both tanned and relaxed. "You, not so much," he said to Emily. "You okay?" Her face was pale and drawn, her blue eyes bloodshot.

Still, her grin was vibrant. "Just tired. It's been a tough haul, but I feel good about the exams. And it's Christmas, and there's snow on the ground just as there should be. Vancouver's so gray and green, it never feels like Christmas until I get home."

Soon they were all grouped around the kitchen table, with Dad at the head, Mom at the foot, and him and his sister across from each other. They were eating Emily's favorite winter meal: meat loaf, mashed potatoes, and a big tossed salad. His family serenaded him with the highs and lows of the cruise and law school.

"What have you been up to, Lester?" Mom asked. He'd given up trying to persuade her to call him LJ.

"Got going again on the reno project at the Mountain View."

Her gaze sharpened. "Charlotte Coltrane's back in town?"

"Charlie, yeah."

She sniffed. "Ridiculous, taking a boy's name. Though that was the least of her sins."

LJ's jaw clenched. He loved his parents, but sometimes they pissed him off. "Her only sin was being born to the wrong parents."

"Her parents weren't the ones painting graffiti or getting expelled," his mom said.

"She was only suspended." Three times. Before dropping out. "And her graffiti was *art*."

"Her graffiti was *illegal*," Dad snapped.

"I liked Charlie," Emily said. "She saved Romeo's life."

He shot her a grateful look just as their dad said sarcastically, "Well, that's certainly enough to judge a person on."

"It's more than you have," LJ accused his parents. "You didn't know her."

His sister leaned forward, likely trying to defuse the tension. "Is Charlie going to run the B&B?"

Mom snorted. "Not unless she's changed a lot."

He ignored her and answered Emily. "No, she plans to put the place on the market and move back to Toronto." Just saying it made his heart ache.

"That's too bad. What does she do there?"

"She's going to start her own business. She's, uh, an artist."

"Artist? What kind of artist?" his mom asked.

"All kinds." He was hedging, and Charlie'd hate that. "Mostly, a tattoo artist."

"Really?" Emily said excitedly, as his mother said, "Oh, dear God. Doesn't that just fit?"

"It's a respectable business, and she's talented." Long ago, he and Emily had learned there was little use arguing with their strict, old-fashioned parents. It was easiest to turn a blind eye to their prejudices and other outdated opinions. But he couldn't sit there and take it any longer.

He shoved his chair back from the table and stood. "For-get it. I don't need to defend Charlie to you."

"Lester!" his mom protested.

"I have to go. I told Mr. DiGiannantonio I'd go see him."

His father scowled. "Tonight, when we just got home?"

In fact, he'd left it vague with Mr. D, and had planned to spend the evening with his family. But he didn't want to spend another minute with his parents. "I'm busy these days, on a tight schedule with the renos. Charlie wants them done before Christmas." So she could run back to fucking Toronto.

Mad at the world, he strode to the front door. Emily caught up as he was putting on his boots. "Don't let them get to you, LJ."

"They're so fucking judgmental."

"They are what they are. You know it's easier to steer clear of the danger areas."

Her troubled expression made him ask, "You talking about Charlie, or something else?"

She glanced over her shoulder. "I'm dating a guy from the Songhees First Nation."

For their parents, there was no such thing as a good "Indian." "What're you going to do?"

"See how things go with him."

He sighed. "For basically decent people, our folks have a lot of prejudices."

She offered a small grin. "Amazing we turned out so good."

"We let them get away with it. Like, you not bringing this guy home for Christmas."

"I've only been dating him since September," she said defensively.

"If things get serious, you're going to have to deal with the parents."

She sighed. "I'll wait until then." Her face brightened.

"What about you and Charlie? You used to have a crush on her. Sounds like she's still cool. Is she married? Are you dating?"

"Uh . . ." Emily often did that, laying out so many questions he lost track. "She's cool, and a great artist. Not married. And, uh . . ." Dating? Charlie'd never admit to that. To keep things simple, he said, "I like her, but she hates Whistler and can't wait to leave."

Her mouth tightened. "No surprise, given how the town treated her. How people like Mom and Dad still view her." She touched his shoulder. "I'm sorry."

A few blocks away from his parents', LJ pulled the truck to the side of the road, opened his cell, and called the Mountain View. "Okay if I come over?"

"Sure," Charlie said, "but I thought you were at your parents'."

"I was. See you soon."

When he pulled up at the B&B, he gazed critically at the exterior. If Charlie wanted top dollar, she should wait until spring to sell, when the whole outside could be cleaned up.

He walked up the path and went in. He and his crew were currently working on the expanded dining room. Next, they'd move on to the reception area and lounge. The rooms had been opened up to better feature the free-standing stone fireplace that gave on to both rooms. Lots of work left to do, and he'd finally got Charlie to understand the project needed more than a week. Still, she was determined to leave before Christmas.

Discontent weighted his shoulders as he walked toward the kitchen, where she usually hung out. Her head was bent over a drawing, and she didn't notice him.

He glanced around. The kitchen had been expanded and modernized, but in a homey rather than institutional way. The lighting was bright and warm. Under it, the brown highlights in Charlie's dark hair gleamed. Her red sweater and a vase filled with colorful mixed blooms he'd brought over were cheery touches. On the table sat her open computer, a bunch of sketch papers, some of her drawing stuff, and a half-eaten piece of Sandy's Christmas cake.

Sensing his presence, she glanced up with a smile. "Hey."

"What are you working on?"

She pointed to a painting that was still damp. "The eagle for Joey's snowboard. What do you think?"

He stood behind her, resting a hand on her shoulder, and gazed down at the striking image in shades of blue and gray. Over the past days, as she and Joey talked, LJ'd been surprised to learn things about his apprentice. After two years of having Joey on his payroll, of chatting at lunch breaks and going for an occasional drink, he'd thought he knew all there was to know. Actually, he suspected Charlie's gentle but penetrating questions had helped the youth reach insights about himself.

"You do the same thing with your tattoo clients?" he asked. "Draw them out until you're sure they know what they want, and you understand it?"

She tilted a smile up to him. "Is that your way of saying you like the eagle?"

"Yeah. Joey's going to be the envy of all his friends. An original Coltrane snowboard."

An exclusive one, too. She'd told Joey not to bring his friends around. She was so damned determined not to become part of the community.

He glanced at the computer screen and saw clothing designs—blouses and short dresses. "Sandy's stuff?"

"Yes, she e-mailed them to me." Sandy, Will's wife, had come by after work a couple days ago, excited about the art Will had taken home.

"You going to work with her?"

"I think so." She tapped the computer screen. "Her designs are great. She's found some fabric she loves, but it's in solid colors and that's too boring." Excitement sparking her voice, she went on. "So I'd create art that'll work with her designs, then she'll get the fabric printed."

"Cool. You said you wanted to do art other than just tattoos. The two of you could go into business together."

She nodded enthusiastically. "We can work by e-mail."

Shit. Didn't she see she could build a career here? Tattoos, snowboards, and designer clothing. If only she didn't have such bad feelings for Whistler.

That reminded him of why he'd come. "I'm going to visit Mr. D. Gather up some of those drawings and come along. He'd love to see you." LJ was sure of that.

"You know how I feel about going out in Whistler."

"Resurrect the old badass Charlie who doesn't give a fuck what anyone thinks."

Her lips twitched. "You liked her, didn't you?"

"She was hot. But so're you. Come on, it's an old folks' home. We'll visit him, then we'll go."

She worried her bottom lip, clearly tempted.

"He's an old man. He doesn't get many visitors, and he hasn't got much time left in this world."

Another lip twitch. "You're shameless."

"Grab those drawings and put on your coat."

"Okay." Her face lit. "I'd love to see him."

Clutching her sketchbook and some loose drawings, Charlie followed LJ into Glen Woods, an attractive facility done in cedar with big windows. A middle-aged couple and an older woman sat on a floral-printed couch in the reception area, having a discussion that was clearly emotional.

She shivered, thinking about growing old with no family support. Mr. D was lucky to have LJ and his sister. As LJ strode toward the reception desk, she tucked her hand inside his arm. "You're a good man, Lester Jacoby."

He gave her a surprised smile, then put his hand over hers. "Thanks."

He'd grown up kind, competent, handsome, sexy—and pretty damned easy to care about. Too bad he didn't live in Toronto and have different parents.

"LJ," the receptionist greeted him. "Merry Christmas. Mr. DiGiannantonio will be glad to see you." She gave a pleasant smile to Charlie, who returned it.

How paranoid and self-centered she'd been, thinking all of Whistler would recognize and censure her. Maybe it was time to get over herself and be more open to the town. Musing, she walked down the hallway, LJ's hand warm atop hers.

"He's often in the lounge in the evening." LJ stopped in the doorway of a large room.

Inside, Christmas had exploded. A big tree laden with lights, garlands, and ornaments dominated one corner, one side table held a manger scene, and another had a Santa's workshop. Poinsettias, holly wreaths, boughs with pinecones, and Christmas cards littered other surfaces and hung from the walls.

It was gaudy, overdone, and actually kind of touching. Still, she had to comment, "Wouldn't want to be Jewish."

"They did Hanukkah, too. When the menorahs came down, the tree went up. They figure, the more celebrations the better."

"Keeps life interesting, I guess," she said approvingly.

She glanced around at the people: a half dozen seniors around a TV, a three-generational group taking up one corner, residents and guests playing games. "That's him, isn't it? Playing cards with those three women?"

"Yup. He's changed some."

"He has." Mr. D's white hair was almost gone, his large

frame had shrunk, and his shoulders were rounded. It was his smile she recognized.

LJ started across the room, his hand firm on hers. "Evening, ladies. Hey, Mr. D. I've brought a surprise."

Pale brown eyes behind horn-rims lit with pleasure. "LJ, my boy. And who's this?" He scrutinized her. "Can it be young Charlie Coltrane, all grown up?"

She stepped forward to take his hand. "Hi, Mr. D. It's good to see you."

He grabbed her hand in both of his and squeezed tight. "I must have been a good boy this year, because Santa brought me a gift I've been wishing for for years."

His unaffected pleasure warmed her heart.

The elderly women started cracking jokes about him being a good boy all right. He broke in. "Ladies, please excuse me. I'm going to take my friends up to my room." As he struggled to his feet, LJ put a hand under his arm to assist, then handed him a cane that had been resting against the table.

Charlie fell in with them as they walked slowly toward the door. So slowly, she heard one of the women say, "Charlie Coltrane. That name rings a bell. It'll come back to me."

She shuddered, then straightened her spine. What did old lady gossip matter to her?

With his arthritis, Mr. D moved so slowly it took forever to get to the elevator, then down the hall to his room, but he managed under his own steam. He ushered them into a small apartment with a bedroom, bath, and a sitting room with a TV, couch, and recliner. In an alcove sat a small fridge and a microwave.

He dropped into the recliner. "This requires a toast. LJ, get out the grappa."

LJ opened a cupboard and took out a bottle. "It's an Italian brandy," he told Charlie. "Very potent. There's also soft drinks, tea, or instant coffee."

She studied the contents of the fridge and took out a Sprite. "Thanks."

"Have a real drink," the elderly man urged. "It's a *digestif.*"

"And an acquired taste," LJ said wryly, handing her a tall glass, then pouring perhaps an ounce of liquor into each of two small glasses.

"Thanks, Mr. D, but I don't drink alcohol."

"Ah." He studied her for a moment, no doubt remembering her parents. "Wise girl. But it eases my arthritis and helps me sleep better than the doctor's fancy pills." He raised his glass. "*Salute.* To old friends, and seeing each other after all these years."

Touching her glass to his, she felt the burn of unaccustomed tears, and blinked quickly. Someone had missed her and was glad she was back. Someone other than LJ, who got her so confused. "Mr. D, you were always nice to me. It meant a lot."

"Ah, Charlie. You made it hard for people to be nice to you. You had such a chip on your shoulder, like you hated the world."

"I felt like the world hated me. Except for you. You gave me a chance."

"You helped me, that day I dropped my grocery bag. I knew you had a good heart."

Her parents and aunt hadn't thought so, nor the teachers or other students.

"Now, my girl, tell me what you've been doing these past ten years."

Sitting beside LJ on the couch, she gave an abbreviated—and lightly censored—summary, ending up with getting work at The Barbed Rose.

"A tattoo artist." Mr. D seemed more fascinated than repelled. "You must have tattoos?"

She showed him the one on her neck. "This one's for Ginger and Jake, the friends I told you about."

"*Magnifico*. If I wasn't all wrinkles, I'd get you to tattoo me."

"What would you get, Mr. D?"

"I'm an old romantic. My wife's name Rosa, and a heart and a rose."

She'd draw him a design anyhow, one that was soft and romantic.

"Charlie, show him some of your drawings," LJ urged.

"Yes, yes, let me see."

She showed him the swirly designs she'd drawn based on Sandy's clothing. Variations of Joey's eagle. LJ, Will, and Joey. A squirrel that frequented the tree outside her bedroom window. Romeo, dozing on the bed. The evening sun sliding behind snowy mountains.

The old man studied them, eyes bright with interest, making comments that showed his approval. "You should have an exhibit, Charlie." He gestured toward the pastel scenic on his wall. "That's an original. I paid good money. Your work is much better."

"Thanks. If you want one, I'd be glad for you to have it."

"Really? Yes, please. But I'll pay you. That's only right."

His acceptance of her, then and now, meant so much more than money. Gently, she took his hand. "No money between friends. Okay?"

His trembling fingers closed on hers. "Thank you, Charlie."

"Pick the one you like the best."

"I know the one. The flowery purple one."

She flipped pages. "This one?" It was a swirly abstract, vibrant yet with a gentle softness. She'd been thinking of spring violets.

"Yes, it reminds me of Rosa," he said.

Carefully, she removed it from her sketchbook. "I can't think of a better compliment." When she drew him the rose tattoo design, she'd use a complementary style.

"I can get it framed," LJ volunteered.

"I'd appreciate that," Mr. D said. "I don't want anything to harm it."

"Now," Charlie said, "what have you been up to since I last saw you?"

"Same old, same old." He waved a hand. "Finally got that wisteria on the trellis to bloom. Remember it?"

She smiled. "We pruned and sprayed and fed it, but it refused to bloom."

"I got many years' enjoyment from it before I had to sell the place and move here." He glanced at LJ. "Those last years were thanks to you and Emily."

He went on to talk about his house and garden, then his friends and activities at Glen Woods. LJ, who'd been nursing his drink, had just poured him a second grappa when a knock sounded on the open door and a female head appeared. "Hey, Mr. D, I hear you're receiving visitors— Oh!"

She stepped into the room, a pretty but tired-looking brunette in jeans and a puffy white winter jacket, holding a red poinsettia. "You're Charlie Coltrane, aren't you?"

Charlie recognized her from context alone. "Emily?" The cute adolescent had turned into an attractive young woman.

Emily grinned. "Wow, it's so good to see you again. LJ said you were back, but I never thought—" She laughed. "Exam brain."

Then her eyes widened and she looked almost panicked. "Oh, damn, I should have realized you might be here, too."

C harlie stared at LJ's sister. What was she talking about?

"I'm afraid—" Emily glanced over her shoulder, out the open door, and muttered, "Shit."

A moment later, an attractively dressed couple in their mid-fifties stepped into the room. Their tan would have told Charlie who they were, even if LJ hadn't echoed "Shit" under his breath.

She said a silent one herself, and straightened her shoulders.

His mother, who also carried a poinsettia, gave a social smile. "Mr. DiGiannantonio. When Emily said she wanted to visit you, we decided to come along to see my cousin, and pop in to wish you Merry Christmas." Her gaze flicked from Mr. D to Charlie.

Her husband was out-and-out staring at Charlie with a puzzled expression.

"How nice of you, Mr. and Mrs. Jacoby," Mr. D said. "Have you met my young friend, Charlie Coltrane?"

"No, we haven't," LJ's dad said shortly, and his mom chimed in with, "But we've heard all about Charlotte."

"Charlie," she corrected grimly.

The woman gazed down her nose. "I'm surprised you came back. I didn't think Whistler was *your kind of place*." Her inflection said Whistler was a decent place, and Charlie was anything but.

"Mom," LJ started, tone sharp, but Charlie cut him off. She'd always fought her own battles.

Rising to her feet, she said, "Believe me, it's not. Aside from a good friend or two"—she gave a solemn nod in Mr. D's direction—"it has nothing to offer."

She turned her back on LJ's parents and gathered up her drawings, glad they couldn't see the tremble in her fingers. To the elderly man, she said, "It's been lovely talking to you."

Expression grim, he said, "Thanks for coming, Charlie, and for the painting."

"My pleasure." She bent to kiss his cheek, then rose and stalked toward the door, nodding at Emily and ignoring the parents.

She almost ran to the elevator, heart racing so fast she could hardly breathe. She stepped inside, and the door began to close.

"Wait!" LJ jammed a shoulder into the closing gap and, laden with their winter coats, burst inside.

Swallowing against the lump of pain in her throat, she said sarcastically, "So much for that invitation to Christmas dinner."

His expression was stricken. "Screw them."

She wished she'd let him speak when he'd started to say something to his mom. Had he been going to defend her? Maybe even . . . claim her as his friend? He'd had a few seconds alone with them after she left, enough to gather up their coats. "What did you say to them?" Try as she might, she couldn't keep a tiny quaver from her voice.

"Nothing. They're jerks." He tried to take her arm.

She pulled away, stiffening her spine. She'd been right.

Even though they'd become friends as well as sex partners, it was purely temporary. She wrapped her arms around herself, one hand resting over her guardian dragon.

The elevator door opened and she hurried toward the front door, LJ striding beside her. He thrust her coat into her hands and she pulled it on as they went out into the cold.

In the truck, he turned on the engine to get the heater going. "I apologize for them."

She shook her head, staring out the window. "You're not responsible for them." Only for himself.

"No, but . . . It's not just about you. They're old-fashioned. People who are different are bad."

She glanced his way. Though his parents' bigotry was horrible, she felt a little better knowing it wasn't just her they hated.

"Emily and I learned it was easier not to argue, and just go our own way." He sighed. "But if we'd challenged them, they might have realized how judgmental they are."

Gee, you think? But she knew it wasn't easy. "It's hard to take on your parents."

He grimaced. "Yeah." A long pause, then he said, "Emily's dating a First Nations guy. She hasn't told them."

She shook her head. "Anything wrong with this guy except for being Indian?" Wryly, she added, "Like, has he graffitied the police station?"

"Not so's I've heard."

What would his sister do if the relationship got serious? At least LJ wouldn't have to worry about that, because theirs never would. Keeping her voice even, she said, "What happened tonight . . . it's only what I expected." From his parents, yes. And, really, what else would she have liked LJ to do? Fight with his parents over a temporary fling?

After a few moments of silence, he said tentatively, "Mr. D was sure glad to see you."

"Me, too." A smile hovered, remembering. "I'm going to do the rose and heart drawing. You'll take it to him?"

"You could take it yourself."

"I don't think so." Lovely as it had been to visit with her old friend, she felt battered and depressed.

LJ sighed. Then he touched her leg. "Charlie, will you come to my place?"

"I'm not really in the mood for sex."

"No sex then. We don't even have to talk."

He chose to take her silence for consent, and drove toward his place. Neither of them said a thing until they were inside, taking their coats off. Feeling chilled from the inside, not at all sure she wanted to be there, or how to behave, she hugged her arms around herself again.

"Want to relax in the hot tub?" he asked.

Hot tubs were a Whistler thing, and they'd yet to try his out. She imagined fresh, crisp air on her face and pulsing jets of hot water massaging muscles that ached from hours of painting. "Sure."

He led her into the kitchen. "How about making hot chocolate while I crank up the heat in the tub and get towels?"

A comfort drink. When she nodded, he took a tin of fancy Dutch hot chocolate mix and a bag of marshmallows from the cupboard, then left her alone in the kitchen.

She went to get milk from the fridge, and a ticket clipped to the door caught her attention.

A few minutes later, he returned. She looked up from stirring cocoa powder into steaming milk. "You're going to a sci-fi con?"

A guilty expression crossed his face. "Yeah. Pretty lame?"

It was, but sort of cute, too. He might be a science genius but he had a geeky hobby. "You're still the nerd at heart, aren't you?"

His throat muscles worked as he swallowed hard. "Yeah, I guess I am."

A grin twitched her mouth. "D'you wear a costume?"

"God, no." He took a breath, then went on like he was making a confession. "But I enjoy the conversations, and talking to authors and screenwriters. I've watched pretty much every TV show and movie that's come out. The world-building, the extrapolation from existing science, the insights about today's society, they all fascinate me."

She popped marshmallows onto the top of the chocolate. "I've done lots of sci-fi tats. And, by the way, you haven't lived until you've gone to a tattoo convention. Some sci-fi folks come too, and show off their ink."

Feeling more relaxed, like they were getting back to where they'd been before his parents showed up, she said, "Is the hot tub ready?"

"I'll whip off the cover." He peeled off his clothes and wrapped a towel around his hips.

"Mmm, nice uncovering," she teased. "Don't freeze off any important bits." She handed him the two hot mugs.

After he'd gone out, she stripped off her own clothing, wrapped herself in a towel, and pulled her hair up on top of her head, securing it with a clip.

She glanced out the window. LJ had removed the cover and was sitting in the tub, facing the door. The tub was set onto the patio off the kitchen, sheltered from neighbors' view, and open to the sky. A couple of patio lamps provided gentle light, and wisps of steam floated from the surface of the water.

Out she went, shivering, and dropped her towel beside his, in a small roofed space with benches and hooks. LJ let out a low whistle.

"Brrr, this is torture." She darted into the tub and submerged herself up to her shoulders. Heat slowly seeped into her as she settled against the rim of the tub across from him. "And this is bliss."

Jets propelled streams of hot water against back muscles that weren't used to such strenuous labor. The night was crystal clear, the sky black and full of stars. LJ's gaze gave her all the male appreciation a woman could want. He stretched a strongly muscled arm out of the water to take a mug of hot chocolate from beside the tub and handed it to her.

No woman could ask for a better sex partner. She'd focus on that, and try to forget the nastiness with his parents.

She sipped the creamy, rich chocolate, then deliberately ran her tongue around her lips.

Bliss and torture. Charlie had just used those words, and they described exactly how he felt being with her.

After tonight, he could hardly blame her for not wanting to stay in Whistler. And hell, if he really cared for her, he should be willing to move to Toronto. He suppressed a groan. He'd lived in Vancouver when he went to university, and cities gave him a headache.

And so did relationship shit. It was new to him, the intensity of feeling. The confusion and uncertainty.

In some ways, she made him feel great—like, when she could relate to the geeky part of him that loved sci-fi cons. Yet, when she insisted their relationship was just sex, she reawakened his old insecurity.

Maybe he shouldn't take it personally. There was so much going on with Charlie: her bad feelings about Whistler, her life and plans in Toronto, and, he figured, a fear of getting hurt. Everyone she'd been close to had rejected her except her friends Ginger and Jake, and she'd been devastated when they died.

That tattoo on the back of her neck wasn't just a memorial to them, he was sure. It was a celebration of true love, of two lives intertwined. It told him she craved that for herself. How could he get her to open her heart and see he might be the man to give it to her?

Then again, he didn't deserve her. He was still a coward. The boy who didn't stand up to his parents.

The sole of her foot brushed his calf, drawing him away from his thoughts. "What's wrong, LJ? You don't like my hot chocolate?"

He reached for his mug and tasted. "It's great. Thanks."

He noticed she was stretching and rolling her head, like she was working out kinks.

"Sore neck?"

"Sore neck, shoulders, back. I spend every minute either painting walls, ripping up carpet, or drawing."

"Come here, I'll rub your shoulders." Though he couldn't heal her emotional hurts, he could ease her physical pain. And tell her, through his hands, how much he cared.

She shifted to sit between his legs, her back to him. Gently he began to work the tight muscles of her neck and shoulders.

She groaned. "Nice."

And so was her slender neck, accented by a few tendrils of damp hair and her tattoo. So were her slim shoulders, the delicate line of her spine. He knew she had backbone to spare, but she let herself droop as his fingers alternately caressed and probed.

There was an intimacy to that as much as in lovemaking. It aroused him, a heat that filled him from the inside in a slow, nonurgent way.

He had no idea how long it was until she sighed, "Enough. If I get any more relaxed, I'll drown."

He chuckled and tugged her back against him so she

sprawled against his body as if he were an easy chair. Except, no chair came equipped with a rigid column of flesh. She wriggled her butt against his erection. "Someone's not so relaxed."

"Touching you turns me on. But we don't have to do anything about it." She was tired, stressed, and he was content to hold her.

She wriggled again. "What if I want to do something about it?"

"I wouldn't object."

"Do you have a condom?"

"Yeah." Of course he'd brought one out.

"I want to lie back and watch the stars, feel the cold air on my face and the hot water surrounding the rest of my body, and feel you moving inside me."

He sheathed himself, then stroked between her legs. Gently he separated her folds, then he eased his cock inside her. She gripped him like a hot, wet, silky glove. Her head fell back beside his and she tipped her face up to the sky. Soft hair brushed his cheek, and her exotic scent overrode the odor of chlorine.

Pumping his hips gently, he set up a slow rhythm and she let out a satisfied, "Mmm." Her hands rested on his thighs and his cupped her breasts, caressing her soft flesh, her hard nipples. So many sensations, hot and wet and slow, seductive and slippery, it was like making love in a dream.

He tilted his own head back against the rim of the tub, so he, too, could gaze up at the stars as steam rose around them.

"Beautiful night." Her voice drifted lazily, like another wisp of steam.

"Beautiful woman." He thrust into her again, harder, making the water surge and ensuring she felt him inside her core. "You're special, Charlie. You fascinated me when I was a boy, and you fascinate me now."

"You fascinate me, too, Tool-belt Guy." Her internal muscles gripped him, then released, and need quickened in his body.

Yet, hearing the word "fascinate" on her lips, he realized it was the wrong one. It wasn't intimate. It didn't imply true knowledge and caring, it was more like being spellbound. Bewitched and mesmerized.

He felt more for her than that, didn't he? But how could he analyze when stars gleamed softly above him, his nostrils were filled with her scent, and soft breasts filled his hands? When she was gripping his thighs hard enough to leave bruises and squeezing his cock as he slid back and forth inside her? When her hips were twisting restlessly, and she was giving little whimpers that told him she was close to orgasm?

His cock throbbed with need, and pressure built at the base of his spine. He slid his hand down her sleek belly, through wet curls, to find her clit, as swollen and sensitive as his own sex. Taking it between thumb and forefinger, he caressed and squeezed gently.

She pulsed around him, then her breath caught and her body clutched. A moment later, she cried out, spasming in release. He plunged hard, letting out a groan of pleasure as he pumped his climax deep inside her.

Water surged, and their orgasms spun out in slow motion under the starry sky, seeming to go on and on until finally the tremors slowed and stopped.

They lay together, joined, muscles relaxing, catching their breath. His arms circled her snugly under the soft fullness of her breasts. Hers rested atop, hugging him to her.

He squeezed gently. "Stay the night."

She tensed, then shifted off him.

The interlude of bliss was over. Sighing, he dealt with the condom as she went to sit across from him in the tub.

Her expression was defensive. "It's not a good idea. I should go now."

And maybe he needed time on his own. To figure out what he really felt for Charlie and whether he could ever be a strong enough man to deserve her.

"Okay." He shoved himself out of the tub, barely noticing the freezing air. "Let's get dressed, and I'll drive you."

LJ's parents and Emily were at the breakfast table when he strode through the house to the kitchen the next morning.

"Lester," his mom said, "I hope you've come to apologize."

"No." He squared his shoulders. "What you said to Charlie last night was unacceptable."

Three faces gaped up at him, his parents' shocked and his sister's lighting with the beginning of a smile.

He addressed his parents. "She's a good person. She always has been."

"The girl was trouble," Dad said.

"She had shitty parents. People judged her by them. No one tried to help her, not even her aunt. Yeah, she acted out, but she was a kid. A kid with too much pride to try to fit in and beg for acceptance. No one saw Charlie for who she really was. Only Mr. DiGiannantonio."

"A foolish old man," Mom said.

"A wonderful old man whose family neglected him. Charlie helped him. She cared about him when no one else did. You're so damned judgmental."

"Lester!"

"She saved Romeo's life, Mom," Emily put in, softly but firmly. "I'm with LJ." She rose abruptly. "You're wrong to judge people the way you do." She swallowed and glanced at LJ, then burst out with, "I'm dating a man from the Songhees First Nation. An Indian."

"Emily!" Both parents stared at her in utter shock.

"He's nice, he's smart," she said more calmly, "and maybe it'll get serious." She walked out of the room.

"And I'm dating Charlie." LJ was a little miffed his sister'd made her announcement first.

His parents exchanged glances that told him they'd been wondering. "Son, that's not a wise idea," his dad said. "You're being ruled by hormones."

He shook his head firmly. "It's a lot more than that." After a night's soul-searching, he knew he had truly fallen for Charlie.

His mom's eyes narrowed. "Don't bring that girl into this house."

No wonder he'd always been a wimp; it was what his parents had taught him to be. He shook his head. "Not until she's welcome. Mom, Dad, I love you, but I've kept quiet too long. You're narrow-minded and judgmental. It's wrong. If you don't change, you're going to lose me. Maybe Emily as well. Think about that."

"Lester!" his mother squawked.

He turned and walked out, feeling strong and confident. For the first time in his life.

The duvets, sheets, and towels Charlie had ordered on-line had arrived, and she took a set to the second floor, eager to try them in one of the guest rooms she'd finished painting. She was studying the results, pleased, when the phone rang.

Will yelled, "Charlie, it's for you."

"Thanks. I'll take it up in the suite."

She hurried upstairs. "Hello?"

"Ms. Coltrane, this is Jeff Mattingly."

Patty's lawyer and now hers. A man she'd never met. "Mr. Mattingly?"

"You haven't come by to pick up your aunt's things."

"Can't you send them to the B&B?"

"I undertook to put them into your hands myself."

She gave an exasperated sigh. "I honestly don't care about them. We weren't close."

"There's a letter."

Mouthing a silent *oh*, she sank down on the bed. Why did words have so much power?

Mr. D's kind ones, LJ's parents' scornful ones. LJ's

own. *Stay the night*. Each night, he asked. Each night it was harder to say no. There was so much between them, spoken and unspoken. Feelings that scared her.

"Ms. Coltrane? Are you still there?"

"All right. I'll come to your office." Chances were, she wouldn't see a soul she knew. Even if she did, it couldn't be worse than meeting LJ's parents—and she'd survived that.

Charlie tucked the manila envelope under her arm as she left the lawyer's office. She'd rip the seal later, alone.

She glanced around. For the first time since she'd arrived last week, she stood in the tourist center of Whistler, the Village Square. She'd always scorned that part of town, where everyone had money for expensive winter clothes and designer coffees.

It hadn't changed a great deal. Some different shops and restaurants, but the same aura of outdoorsy ritziness. And of course everything was decked out for Christmas. Windows glittered with snowflakes, tinsel, and ornaments. Wreaths and garlands hung from lampposts. Lights twinkled everywhere, wrapping around windows and eaves and twining through trees. Actually, it didn't look half bad. Thanks to LJ, her view of Christmas had softened.

The snowy street, like others in the core, was closed to traffic. Skiers and boarders strolled down the center of the road, and shoppers browsed along the raised sidewalks, staring into windows and reading menus. She liked how they were so casual and outdoorsy. In downtown Toronto, business attire predominated; in the dead of winter, people traveled underground. The weather was no colder than in Whistler, but the wind whistled down the city streets.

Okay, there were some things not to like about

Toronto, but lots to love as well. The city was cosmopolitan, with subcultures of all sorts. She'd found her niche. Found respect.

She set out down the Village Stroll. Earlier, she'd called Sandy, Will's wife, to say she had an appointment and might be late for their meeting at the Mountain View. Sandy'd told her to come to the boutique where she worked and they'd drive over together.

As Charlie passed a store selling winter clothing, two women emerged with stuffed shopping bags. The strains of "Joy to the World" drifted out with them and she hummed along.

She'd decorated a tree and no one had knocked it down. She'd made love in front of a crackling fire, beside that fragrant, sparkling tree. She'd drunk eggnog that was smooth and spicy, not spiked with hard liquor, and listened to a CD of a children's choir singing carols.

LJ had given her happy memories to replace the bitter ones.

What did he want from her? He dragged his heels on the renos, seduced her with a Christmas tree and a hot tub, and the way he looked at her . . . The warmth and hope in his eyes threatened to melt the ice around her heart.

Absently, she raised her hand, slipped it under the scarf wound around her neck, and stroked the tattoo at her nape. The feathers and flowers were each distinct and special, but so intertwined they could never be separated. Just as her friends had been. That was what she wanted. That big, mysterious thing called love. Could she possibly find it with LJ?

Ginger and Jake had been sensitive, patient, gentle. So, surprisingly, was LJ. A science geek, hot tool-belt guy who was sensitive. If it weren't for his parents—

A passerby jostled her, breaking her train of thought, and she paused to get her bearings.

"Oh!" she sighed. A huge tree rose in one of the village squares, majestic and glowing with lights. Beneath it, three young women wearing red Santa caps with white fur trim stood arm in arm, singing "Silent Night." A small crowd had gathered, listening reverently.

"Charlie? Charlie Coltrane?" An excited female voice drew her attention.

She saw a perky blonde in a pink and white toque, her pink jacket stretched over a pregnant belly. Charlie tensed. "Melody?" A cheerleader, the girl had dated the local basketball star. As best Charlie could recall, it was the first time they'd ever spoken.

"It *is* you!" she squealed. "I heard you were back."

"I bet you did," she said dryly.

Melody grinned. "Despite hosting the Olympics, we're still a small town. Wow, Charlie, you look so different."

Normal, she meant, in jeans and a winter jacket. Charlie had an urge to rip off her jacket and flaunt her dragon, to make some "screw you" quip like she'd have done in the old days. But she remembered what LJ and Mr. D had said, about how she'd never even tried to fit in. Politely, she said, "You look the same. Except for . . ." She gestured toward the baby bulge.

"Our second. I married Ken. No big surprise, eh? Love of my life, and all that." Melody was gushing as if they'd been close friends.

Charlie felt as if she'd gone down the rabbit hole. "I'm happy for you."

"How about you? I heard you live in Toronto? And you have your own tattoo place?"

"The gossip mill at work." One that expanded the tale with each telling.

A quick grin. "You always gave it good fodder."

"I suppose I did." But what she'd secretly longed for was the acceptance of girls like Melody, all pink, perky, and perfect.

"I still remember that mural of the teachers. The one you painted in the gym?" She giggled. "Now I'm a teacher. Grade ten. I often wonder how my kids would caricature me."

Charlie's lips twitched, imagining how she'd draw Melody.

"But then, they don't have half your talent."

Well, how about that? Melody thought she had talent. She softened the caricature she'd drawn in her head.

The other woman caught her arm. "So, LJ Jacoby's working for you. Can you believe him? Going from high school nerd to total hottie?"

"He's still the same guy inside." Open-minded, observant, sensitive. And too willing to knuckle under to his parents.

"Yeah?" Melody studied her curiously, then her pretty face sobered. "Being a teacher's made me see how tough high school can be. Especially for kids like you and LJ."

The other woman's perceptiveness surprised her. "It can."

Melody squeezed her arm. "I have to run, but if you're still here in the new year, we should grab coffee."

As she hurried away, Charlie stared after her. No doubt every word she'd spoken would be relayed via the gossip mill. Still, Melody had seemed more curious and accepting than judgmental. Seemed not everyone was as harsh as LJ's parents and Joey's mom.

Could she actually imagine living here rather than in Toronto?

Seated at the kitchen table after the guys and Sandy had gone, Charlie ripped open the law office envelope and spilled out the contents: a small jewelry case and a sealed envelope. She flipped open the case to see conventional, probably expensive, earrings and necklaces as well as a substantial engagement and wedding ring set, then shoved it all aside and opened the envelope. Out fell a letter handwritten on two sheets of heavy cream stationery.

Surprisingly, it was dated two days before her aunt's death.

Dear Charlotte,

Perhaps I should have persisted in trying to persuade you to come to Whistler so I could speak to you in person, but again I'm taking the coward's path. I know I did you a serious injury, and I'm sure you won't forgive me.

Charlie snorted. "You got that right."

Where to start? How to explain?

Once, your mother and I were best friends. We liked to party and drink, and we liked the wrong kind of boy. She got pregnant with you and married young, to a man much like our own father. It's a common cycle, the child of an alcoholic marrying one.

Charlie knew that. She knew, too, that her mother's own alcoholism had been almost inevitable in the circumstances.

When our dad died of cirrhosis and our mom remarried and moved away, I wanted a different kind of life. I got a secretarial job and won the attention of a successful businessman. Not an exciting man, but a good one, and a sober one. I entered a new world, and wanted desperately to belong.

As I became more respectable, your parents . . .

*deteriorated. Your mother asked me for money, and
at first I gave it to her, in secret. But it went to alcohol. I was facilitating, not helping.*

"Oh." Charlie hadn't known that, but a memory surfaced. She'd been five or six. Her mom had taken her to
the Mountain View. Patty'd hustled them into her office,
the women had argued, her mom had cried, then they'd
gone home and her mom had got plastered.

*And I was endangering my marriage. So, I cut
all ties. Yes, he and my new lifestyle were more important to me than my parents, my sister, and you.*

There it was, baldly stated. The truth Charlie had grown
up with.

*When your parents died, I let you down again. I
shirked my duty.*

Charlie shook her head. If there'd been no love, not
even affection, she'd been better off on her own. She hadn't
needed the message reinforced, day after day, that she
wasn't lovable.

*That was my sin, my shame, my secret guilt.
Since my husband passed, I've reflected on my
life and my mistakes. This past July, the doctors
told me I'm dying. It's cancer. Advanced metastatic
melanoma, to be precise.*

Cancer? But, no one had known she had cancer. The
doctor said she died of heart failure.

If it was true, Patty had called Charlie right after being
diagnosed. As LJ'd suggested, she had made her will out
of guilt. But why start substantial renos? To increase the

value of the inheritance? If so, why make Charlie live in the B&B until the work was completed? Confused, she turned back to the letter.

> *Now, my strength is failing. People will realize I'm ill. I don't want to inflict this on you, LJ, or anyone else. Besides, the pain is severe, and the medication no longer helps. It's time to end this.*
> *Forgive me for again taking the coward's path.*

She gaped at the wavery writing. *Oh my God.* Patty had committed suicide.

The doctor must have known, but he'd protected her reputation.

> *I am so sorry, Charlotte. I can never erase the wrongs I did to you, but I can try to make things right. I can give you the home I denied you ten years ago. Perhaps it will even bring you the love you were so long denied.*
> *I hope you are a better, braver woman than I, that you can come to terms with your own past, and that you'll live a happy, regret-free life.*
> *Your Aunt Patty*

Carefully, she set the letter down, surprised to find her eyes damp. Yes, her aunt deserved those feelings of guilt, but in the end she'd tried to do the right thing.

An apology, an attempt to right a wrong. Those were satisfying. It would have been hypocritical for Patty to pretend a love she'd never felt for Charlie.

But what did she mean about the Mountain View perhaps bringing her love?

Surely, not . . . LJ. Patty had contracted with him to do major renos, killed herself before they were done, and said that Charlie had to live in the B&B.

"Charlie?"

She jerked and pressed a hand to her throat, then turned to see him standing by the table in his jeans and jacket. "LJ. You scared me."

"You were so deep in thought you didn't hear me." He sat down beside her and pressed a kiss to her cheek.

She stared at him, still stunned by what Patty had written.

"What's wrong?"

"My aunt wrote me a letter."

He glanced down at the sheets in front of her. "Want to talk about it?"

"I . . . not now." As much as Patty might have wanted it, the Mountain View didn't feel homey to Charlie. The place where she felt warm and comfortable was LJ's house. "Can we go to your place? Cook dinner and sit by the fire?"

An hour and a half later, dinner was done and Charlie had told LJ about her aunt's cancer. Not her suicide, though. She'd allow her aunt the respectability that had mattered so much to her.

He shook his head in amazement. "I never suspected she had cancer. I feel terrible."

"And I feel bad for being rude on the phone. But LJ, she didn't want anyone to know. It was her choice to keep the secret."

"Are you okay? It must have been pretty emotional."

"It was. But some questions got answered, and I feel more at peace." She hadn't told LJ about Patty wanting to give her the home she'd denied her before, and hoping she might find love. That part still confused her.

He tugged her into his arms. "Peace is good."

Their lips met, and she sighed. This was what she needed. The warmth and peace LJ gave her. Tonight he'd been supportive, as always, but there'd been something slightly different about him. He seemed more confident, in a quiet way, and it made him even more appealing.

Was she falling in love with him? Could she let herself? Love had never worked out for her before. How could it, with a man who couldn't even tell his parents he was friends with her?

His lips trailed kisses down her neck, and she arched back to give him better access. The zipper of her top whispered down and his tongue traced the line of her dragon's head.

The dragon that protected her heart. He hadn't been doing such a good job.

Or maybe he had. Maybe he was letting her experience something new, the feeling of being cherished and supported, of sharing passion and tenderness, of caring and being cared for. Not love, not real love that lasted forever, but . . . a trial run.

LJ eased down the neck of her camisole to free her breast, then gently sucked her nipple into his mouth. Sensation pulsed through her, hot and heady. Arousal and caring, mixed together.

She eased away. "Upstairs, in the turret room." She wanted soft sheets and the ability to move freely, to twist and twine around each other.

Hand in hand they mounted the stairs, and piece by piece, without speaking, they undressed each other until they stood naked in front of the gas fire.

He was so strongly, perfectly male. Aroused, at ease with his nakedness.

He led her over to the bed and they lay side by side, moving together until arms and legs intertwined and their bodies pressed against each other from chest to thigh. His erection nudged her belly as they kissed in a slow, sensual dance.

"So good, Charlie," he murmured.

"Mmm-hmm." Achy arousal hardened her nipples and she rubbed them restlessly against him. Between her legs, another ache spread hot moisture as her body readied itself for what it most craved.

She slipped from his arms and wriggled down the bed, kissing the solid plane of his chest, teasing the hard nub of his nipple, making her way toward an irresistible goal.

Gently she grasped his shaft, smoothing her hand over the resilient skin, stroking up and down as he moaned with pleasure.

He rolled onto his back, giving her better access, and she flicked her long hair across his belly as she bent over him. Delicately, she touched the crown of his cock with her tongue, then laved it in a circular motion that made him jerk in the circle of her hand.

Once, tough-girl Charlie had offered Lester a blow job, trying to prove to both of them she wasn't vulnerable.

Now, as she sucked him into her mouth and swirled her tongue around him, as she slid her hand up and down his shaft, she didn't feel tough at all. With LJ, she couldn't be.

But she couldn't be vulnerable either. Couldn't give him the power to break her heart.

She took him deeper, concentrating on the physical sensation. Not allowing anything else. No thought, no emotion, just the moment. Sex, pure, simple, and wonderful.

Her mouth made slurping sounds as she worked him, and she hungrily inhaled the musky scent of his arousal. Heat coiled inside her and she shifted restlessly, thighs squeezing together, body aching with the need to have him fill her up.

He caught a handful of hair and tugged her away. "Together," he gasped. "I want us to come together."

Moments later, she was on top of him, riding him, arching so she could take him deep, and deeper still. Her hands gripped his hips, steadying herself, and she closed her eyes, concentrating on the sensations.

"Open your eyes," he demanded harshly. "Look at me."

Surprised, she did, and saw the heat in his blue-gray eyes, fierce yet tender. His hands caught hers, and he intertwined their fingers, using the strength of his arms to keep her balanced. Tension shifted from her arms to his and back again as she lifted up and down, freeing his cock almost all the way, slowly, so slowly, prolonging the anticipation, the moment when . . .

She sank down on him, taking him deeply as he pushed up inside her, filling her, brushing every sensitive, aroused cell.

She whimpered with pleasure, clenched internal muscles to grip him, then released him and began again. Each stroke took her higher, wound her tighter, built her need.

All the time, he held her gaze, that simple act even more intimate than what their bodies were doing. Intimate, confusing, yet wonderful. She could have closed her eyes, shut him out. But she didn't.

She leaned forward, changing the angle so his shaft brushed her clit as it slid out of her body. And rubbed against it when he thrust in.

"Oh, yes," she cried. "Yes, LJ."

They did it again, again, and pleasure spiraled, peaked, and finally broke in waves of pleasure as he plunged deep and hard in his own climax.

Lying with his arm around Charlie, LJ felt physically satiated, but it wasn't enough.

He squeezed her shoulder. "Don't sell the B&B, Charlie. Use it to finance your business. Set up your tattoo parlor in Whistler, work with Sandy on the clothing business, and do snowboard designs."

She eased back in his arms and studied him for a long moment, as if she was considering it. Then she sighed. "And have to deal with people like your parents? I don't need the grief."

"I've had my fill of it, too. This morning I told my parents I'd had it with them being so judgmental."

"LJ!"

"And I said I was dating you."

"You did?" Her eyes lit with wonder and, he'd swear, pleasure. Then her brows pulled together. "But we're not dating," she said quietly. "We're friends who are having sex."

"Oh yeah, I'm sure that'd make them happier." He was sick of Charlie's denials. She knew they were making love. "Go out with me. Then we'll be *dating*."

She sat up in bed, rubbing her forehead. "You know I don't belong here."

He could offer to go to Toronto, and he would if that was what it took. But Charlie'd never be a whole person if she didn't face up to Whistler. And to her feelings for him. "Don't refuse to see what we have together," he fired back, sitting up too, "just because you're scared."

"I'm not scared. I've built a good life for myself in Toronto. I have a career, friends. Respect."

"You could have that here."

"Respect?"

"Give people a chance. You've grown up. Show them who you really are, don't play the badass like you used to."

"I can't . . ." She frowned, then touched his shoulder. "Don't make things so complicated. Let's enjoy the sex and part friends."

Nerdy, insecure Lester would have given anything if Charlie'd even noticed him. Now she was screwing LJ hot and hard. But it wasn't enough. He deserved more, and so did she.

He'd tried being patient and sensitive, but that wasn't working. She'd been calling the shots, and now it was his turn.

That morning, he'd given his parents an ultimatum. He'd risked their relationship because the issue was important to him. And because Charlie was important. "I don't want to have sex with you anymore." He forced the words out.

"What?" She jerked her hand from his shoulder.

"I'm falling in love with you."

Her hazel eyes widened, gleaming golden. A smile curved her lips, then she straightened them and scowled. "You're realizing a teen fantasy."

"I'm long past that. It's the adult Charlie I care for. And you care for me, too." The old insecurity bit into him, but he pushed past it. "I won't have sex with you again until you admit we're making love."

She rubbed a hand across her dragon's head.

He grabbed her hand. "No, not that tattoo." He pulled her hand away and tugged it up to the back of her neck. "This one. The one that's about love. That's where we're heading, Charlie."

"I . . ." She looked so confused and troubled, he almost felt sorry for her.

But he wasn't going to quit. "There's a dance at the Fairmont, with the proceeds going to help needy families at Christmas. I want you to go as my date."

She'd started shaking her head when he said "dance" and now sputtered, "No, no, no. A Christmas dance? With all of Whistler there?" Her chin came up. "Oh, I get it, you're trying to prove something to your parents. Well, leave me out of it."

"The only point I'm trying to prove is that I care about you, and I'd be proud to be with you."

"You don't care what I want." She spat the words out

and swung out of bed. "You haven't listened to me from the day I arrived. Everything has to be your way."

He climbed out, too. "Uh-uh. You've been setting the rules from day one, and I've been knuckling under."

"Then we agree to disagree." Hurriedly, she pulled on her clothes. "I'm leaving."

The truck's heater hadn't kicked in yet, but Charlie didn't care. She was steaming. LJ clearly didn't give a damn about her.

After driving in silence for a few minutes, he said grimly, "You're a lot like your aunt."

"I am not! I'm nothing like her."

"Let me count the ways." He shoved a hand in front of her and actually stuck up one finger. "She was sociable but she always kept a little distance." He raised another finger, ignoring her glare. "Everything had to be on her terms." A third finger. "She cared too damn much about what other people thought."

She slumped back in the seat, arms wrapped tight around her body, refusing to respond. What had happened to the sensitive LJ she'd been getting to know and care about? He'd gone crazy, first saying he was falling for her—which he so obviously wasn't—then bullying and insulting her.

"Charlie, be yourself, be proud of who you are, and don't let other people hurt your feelings."

Like it was that easy? "In Toronto I don't have to take crap from people."

"You're running away again," he snapped. "If it was important enough to you, if *I* was important enough to you, you'd have the courage to deal with your past, with Whistler, and with all the reasons you're scared to fall in love."

Ooh! He'd said he was falling in love with her, but he didn't have a clue what love was. Ginger and Jake had always been gentle and caring, they hadn't beaten each other up with words. "You don't get it."

"It sucks to be you?" he taunted. "You're acting like a kid. Grow up and take responsibility for your actions." He jerked the truck to a stop in front of the Mountain View.

"It only sucks to be me when I'm here in Whistler. I can't wait to leave."

10

"Christmas is a good time to sell," the perky red-headed realtor told Charlie three days later, after a tour of the B&B. "People are enjoying Whistler at its best and thinking they'd like to move here. We'll price it to move and go for the quickest closing date we can get."

"Thanks." They'd signed the listing agreement at the kitchen table, and walked together to the door.

The last days had been nasty, as a clearly pissed-off LJ cracked the whip, and everyone worked their butts off, with none of the camaraderie they'd shared before.

He'd barely spoken to her, and that had hurt. Why couldn't he understand her feelings?

The realtor paused at the door. "You've done a lovely job with the renovations."

She nodded. Though the crew had rushed the job through, they'd paid attention to getting things done right. It would never feel like home, but she'd developed a certain affection for the Mountain View. And for Joey and Will.

And LJ. Or at least, the sweet LJ she'd known before he turned into a bully.

She called a taxi, then hurried upstairs to add the final items to her backpack. Gently, she folded the dress Sandy had given her. One of her own designs, it was a vivid scarlet and had a halter top and swirly skirt. Charlie had no idea where she'd wear such a dress, but it was a thing of beauty.

On the desk lay two drawings. The one for Mr. D, which she knew LJ would deliver, incorporated a heart, roses, and his wife's name. It was soft, feminine, romantic. She lifted the other, thinking maybe she should rip it up. But LJ could do that, if he wanted to.

It was the very first sketch she'd drawn of him: golden sawdust on strong cheekbones, blue-gray eyes steady and strong. She hadn't shown it to a soul. No need to keep it; that image of him was burned into her brain. And her heart.

Beside the drawings lay two envelopes. One held Patty's letter. She hadn't decided whether to take it or throw it out.

Christmas lights flicked on across the street. The woman crossed the living room, and the tree lit up. Soon her husband would be home and they'd share a meal, the way Charlie and LJ had done several times.

She unfolded the letter, and her gaze lingered on the last sentences.

> *I can never erase the wrongs I did to you, but I can try to make things right. I can give you the home I denied you ten years ago. Perhaps it will even bring you the love you were so long denied.*
> *I hope you are a better, braver woman than I, that you can come to terms with your own past, and that you'll live a happy, regret-free life.*

Well, soon things would be right, in that she'd have the money from the sale of the B&B. She could have had that without coming to Whistler. Why had Patty made her come here? Had it been her attempt to make Charlie come to terms with her past?

Had Charlie done that?

In some ways, yes. Even though LJ didn't seem to think so.

LJ . . . Had Patty really been trying to matchmake?

Maybe she, like Charlie, had been sucked in by LJ's masculine strength and apparent sensitivity. Perhaps she hadn't seen the bullying side of him.

Hmm . . . Charlie gazed out the window again, where the Christmas lights reminded her of the night LJ had persuaded her to decorate the tree. Even then, he'd had an agenda. But it wasn't so much bullying, as asking her to be strong and confront her demons.

What had he actually meant, that night when they'd fought? Had he been encouraging her to have enough self-esteem that she didn't care if not everyone liked her?

Wasn't that what she'd always hoped to be strong enough to do?

He'd said she was scared to fall in love, and it was true. Her heart had taken enough battering. It was so hard to believe a man might find her lovable. She touched her dragon. Her guardian had thrown up defense after defense, trying to protect her. Yet, now, her heart ached.

LJ had asked her to fight for them. He'd found the courage to take on his parents.

He'd said he was falling for her.

She'd never known LJ to lie.

She touched the tattoo on her neck. Jake had given Ginger a gentle, supportive love. Maybe he'd never had to challenge her or fight for their love.

When she'd designed their tattoo, she'd thought of the uniqueness of each of them, and of what made them special as a couple. When she'd designed other tattoos for lovers, she'd done the same.

Each couple was different. Of course they were, because each human being was unique.

She glanced down again at the letter and touched the words, *a happy, regret-free life*. Patty had lived with regrets until the day she died.

If Charlie went back to her safe little world, if she ran away from LJ, would she, too, always live with regret? The regret that she'd known a man who might love her, a man she might love back, and she'd thrown away all the glorious possibilities because she was scared?

On the desk lay the other envelope, this one much smaller. After LJ, Will, and Joey had left that morning, she'd found it on the kitchen table.

She opened it and shook out the ticket. He'd given her one final chance.

Downstairs, the doorbell rang. Her taxi had arrived.

Dressed in his best black suit, a crisp white dress shirt, and a striped silk tie, LJ entered the ballroom at the Fairmont. The chandeliers sparkled, banks of red and white poinsettias rimmed the room, and a tall tree stood in one corner, elegantly trimmed in gold and red.

An orchestra played at one end of the room and people in formal dress lined up at two bars. A couple of arches were hung with mistletoe, encouraging Christmas kisses.

Would she come?

For three days, they'd avoided each other. He'd ached for her, and he had no idea what she'd been thinking. Maybe he should have tried to talk to her again, but what more was there to say? All he could do was hope. It was Christmas, the season of love. Of miracles.

He went over to speak to his parents. Things with his folks were still strained, but both he and Emily were working on them. People could change. He firmly believed that.

His sister was here, too. Not with her boyfriend, who'd already made other plans, but with an old high school girlfriend. Emily came over and said, "Promise me a dance so I'm not a total wallflower."

"You and me both."

She glanced past him and her face lit up. "I take it back. Your dance card is full."

Heart racing, he turned.

Charlie. Stunning in a red flame of a dress. The first dress he'd ever seen her in. And heels that made her long legs seem endless.

The low V-neck revealed enough cleavage to make a man moan. The snout of her dragon breathed fire on her creamy breast, and its tail wrapped around her bare shoulder. She'd swept up her hair, baring her neck and the feather-flower tattoo.

Charlie, being herself. Not the in-your-face kid, but a grown woman who knew who she was and was proud of it.

He hurried to meet her, catching her hands in his. "You came."

"I want you. I want *us*, LJ. We're worth fighting for. I don't care about anyone else's opinion. Only yours." Her eyes shone with sincerity.

Yes. Finally. Perfectly. "Come here." Gently he tugged her toward one of the arches.

"LJ?"

He pointed up. "Mistletoe. Merry Christmas."

"Merry Christmas." She went into his arms, slender, warm, and lovely, and lifted her face to his.

He kissed her softly, thinking about that long-ago dance and her dickhead date. Tonight, she was a queen and he'd treat her with reverence.

Her arms circled his neck, her body fitting perfectly against his as she deepened the kiss and gave him a taste of her tongue.

His cock stirred, and he eased away, laughing. "You trying to shock people, Charlie Coltrane?"

"I was born to shock." Her eyes danced with humor.

He slid his hands down her back and let them rest at the base of her spine. "You're gorgeous. That's an amazing dress."

"Sandy gave it to me. And loaned me the shoes."

"I like you dressed up. But then, I like you in jeans. I like you in a towel. Most of all, I like you in nothing at all."

"Later. You invited me to a dance, and I want to dance."

He was proud of her. Proud that she didn't take the opportunity to rush home. "Me, too."

"Then I want to go home and make love with you." She gazed steadily into his eyes. "Because I do care, LJ. I'm sorry for the way I treated you. You're right, I was scared. Scared of rejection, scared of risking my heart."

"And you're not any longer?"

"Oh, yeah. But I'm tired of being a coward." She took a deep breath. "Speaking of which, we should say hello to your parents."

"Yes." In public, his mom and dad would avoid making a scene.

"Hey, are you two finished with that mistletoe?" a humorous male voice asked.

"Almost." LJ dipped his head to give Charlie another quick kiss, to fortify both of them.

Then, arms around each other, they headed across the ballroom. He felt tension in her body, saw the lift of her head when a couple nearby pointed and whispered. The gossip had started, but she held her head high.

Emily hurried over to join them. "Charlie, I'm so glad you came."

"Me too," she said. "I think."

His sister gave a knowing nod. "Are you going to confront the ogres?"

"That's the plan," she answered nervously.

"I'm coming too." She hooked her arm through Charlie's free one. "Three against two."

Linked together, they went over to where his parents stood, watching. No doubt they'd seen it all. Charlie's entrance. The kiss. Emily's gesture of support.

Their gazes darted all over Charlie, pausing on the dragon.

LJ faced them, shoulders squared. "Mom, Dad, let's do this again. I'd like you to meet my girlfriend, Charlie Coltrane."

There was a long pause, then his mother inclined her head slightly and said, "Charlotte."

Charlie freed herself from him and Emily and stepped forward. She held out her hand. "It's Charlie. I'm pleased to meet you, Ms. Jacoby."

His mother's mouth twitched, not with humor. "It's Mrs."

"Pleased to meet you, Mrs. Jacoby," Charlie said evenly, hand still extended.

After an excruciatingly long moment, his mother put out her hand and shook quickly. "The same." She paused, then grudgingly added, "Charlie."

Well, damn. He'd never managed to make his mom call him LJ.

"Mr. Jacoby?" Again, Charlie held out her hand.

"Charlie." His father shook it, then said, "That's an interesting tattoo."

"Thank you."

The dragon had done such a good job of protecting her heart. Now, it was LJ's turn.

In that moment, he knew he loved her. She was vulnerable, yet strong. Tender, yet passionate. She was the girl he'd had a mad crush on and the woman he'd fallen in love with.

"Charlie," he choked out and she turned with a look of surprise.

God knows what she saw on his face, because she nodded to his parents and said, "Have a good evening." Then she took his arm. "And now, you promised me a dance, LJ."

He squeezed her hand, and together they walked away, leaving Emily to deal with his parents.

When they were out of earshot, she said, "Are you okay? You know they may never approve of me."

"Or they'll get to know you, the way Mr. D and I did. In which case"—he stopped near the edge of the dance floor and took a deep breath—"they'll have to love you. The way I do."

Her eyes widened, then she gave a radiant smile. "You asked me once, if I could have anything for Christmas, what would I want."

"And you said, your tattoo parlor in Toronto."

"I've changed my mind. I want Christmas in Whistler, with you. And after that, spring, and summer, all with you. My dragon's released my heart into your care."

"I promise I'll look after it."

"I believe you. Now, how about you? I asked what you wanted, and you said you hadn't made up your mind."

"My impulse was to say 'you,' but I wasn't sure if that was just my old crush talking. And you were so determined to not get involved. But now, now I'm sure."

"And?"

"Of course I want you, but there's something more. I want a tattoo."

"What?" She gave a startled laugh. "A tattoo? Seriously? What kind of tattoo?"

"At the moment, I'm thinking of a big red heart with the name Charlie inside it."

She chuckled. "I'd never design something so conventional."

"Seriously, what I want is something like the one on your neck. Symbols for you and me, together."

Her eyes went misty. "I want one, too." Then mischief sparked. "We'll have fun working on the design. I'm thinking hammers to symbolize you, because you had to pound away at me until I realized the truth."

He chuckled. "Maybe we can work in some mistletoe."

"Sounds good to me."

He nodded firmly. "We'll find the exact right design. I want an original Coltrane."

She went into his arms and tugged him onto the dance floor. "LJ, you've *got* the original Coltrane."

Keep reading for a special preview of *Pelican Point*,
the first in Donna Kauffman's new series,
The Bachelors of Blueberry Cove.

Available this November from Kensington Books!

If she'd been hoping for some kind of sign about what her next step in life should be, she was pretty sure she'd been given several of them now. All bad.

"Can you unlock the door so I can open it from the outside?"

Wow. Deep voice. Very baritone. The kind that vibrated along the skin. And sexy. Just like his torso. And his thighs. Not to mention his . . . um, package. None of which she had any business thinking about. "Sure," she said, only it came out as a croak. She cleared her throat, or tried to, but the ball of emotions still wedged there made it impossible. So, she just nodded, helpless to stop the tears that were still leaking out and tracking down her cheeks, but beyond caring at this point, and fumbled with the little lock nub on the door, trying to pull it up. Grandpa Mac's truck predated automatic locks.

He stepped back and positioned himself at an angle, hand at his side, where she saw his gun was holstered. *Just in case I'm the crazy psycho and he's the one being stalked.* The thought caused a little splutter of choked laughter, which led to another, then another, only it wasn't funny. Her heart was pounding and it felt like her lungs were constricting, and she knew all the signs. Well, she'd learned them the hard way, ten months ago. Panic attack.

And for what? Because a cop was trying to help her change her damn tire? *Jesus, Alex, get a freaking grip.* Only she knew it just wasn't as easy or as simple as that. It had been a while since one had triggered, and she'd thought they were mercifully, finally behind her. *Yeah, well, think again.*

Then her door was carefully and slowly being opened from the outside, which was when she realized she'd kind of slumped against it, and didn't have time to adjust her weight. And that was how she ended up falling into the arms of Mr. Tall, Tight, and Baritone.

Her humiliation was now officially complete, she thought, somewhat woozily. She was having a hard time focusing. Must be the tears blurring her vision.

"Hey, it's okay. I've got you, I've got you," he said, voice steady, calm.

And seriously sexy as all hell. Honestly, he should have gone into radio. Or made a career out of singing those Barry White kind of sex songs.

"Can you stand?"

She would have nodded yes, but he turned her in his arms just then and their gazes collided for the first time. Her knees went distinctly wobbly. Because if his voice was all sexy sex songs, his eyes were . . . well, they were just plain sex. On a platter. With a big heaping side of *oh my*.

They were the color of hot, melted caramel, with alternating flecks of gold and burnished bronze radiating out from the dark center. Like . . . shattered topaz. And if that wasn't a generous enough gift from the gods, they were framed by thick, dark, ridiculously lush lashes. He was saved from being too pretty by the small scar that ran in a thin silver line from his hairline, across his temple, and cut a jagged line through the corner of one eyebrow. It looked old, pale, but it wasn't a clean slice and hadn't healed neatly.

His cheekbones were a shade too sharp, as was the angle of his jaw, and the strong slope of his very patrician nose. But then her gaze continued, and all of that, every bit of it, was balanced by his mouth. Which had clearly been a gift from the same god who'd designed those eyes. Full, sensual, even with the corners pulled too tightly, as they were now. She must have hit her head harder on the window than she thought, because she felt distinctly woozy again, and a little giddy. That had to be bad, right?

So was wanting to lift her head, just a little, so she could nip that bottom lip, see if it was as warm, as soft, as inviting as those eyes. Add in that sex voice and wow, she'd be putty in his arms. Actually, she kind of already was.

How convenient.

Her gaze drifted to his eyes, then back to his mouth.

He cleared his throat. His sexy, sexy throat. She wanted to bite that, too.

"Ma'am?"

"Alex," she breathed, not even trying to stand on her own two feet. "It's . . . Alex."

She felt his hold on her tighten momentarily. "Alex. Of course you are."

There was another pause and she thought perhaps a little sigh, though it didn't sound anything like the kind of sighs he was eliciting from her.

"Alex, have you been drinking?"

Mmm. She liked it when he said her name.

"Have you taken any medication?"

She shook her head, which made her vision swim a little and the twinkly lights come back. So she closed her eyes. And just focused on that voice. That calm, steady as rock, sexy, "sex god voice," she murmured. And then there was the feel of his arms. So strong, so supportive.

She could trust those arms. She could stay in those arms. The world was making a lot more sense as long as he held her. She felt safe. Cocooned. And at the same time, she felt alive, all of her dead parts coming burningly, achingly alive. And she wanted to trust that, too. To just . . . let go. Let herself feel without fear of only finding pain and all-consuming grief when she did.

She could let him be the strong one, the steady one. Not like it had been for the past year. When it was all on her. So much on her. But here . . . now . . . she could let go. Because he wouldn't.

Don't let go, she thought. She wouldn't be set adrift again. She wouldn't survive it. She'd drown this time for sure. Feeling suddenly panicky, she grabbed him. *I want to stay right here.* "Don't let me go." She dug fingers into his jacket, clinging, clinging . . . but feeling so distant, so far away, like she was falling. She gripped harder. "Don't let me go!"

"It's okay, I've got you. I've got you."

So steady. So strong. Then she felt . . . airborne. Weightless.

"Alex? Come on now. Alex!"

He sounded even sexier when he got all urgent like that.

"Stay with me. Open your eyes. Come on, stay with me. What are you on? What did you take? Alex!"

She smiled and let her cheek rest on his chest. Nice, hard, warm chest. Silly, sexy sex-god voice. Telling her to stay. She wasn't going anywhere. She liked it when he said her name. All demanding and commanding. She liked it a lot.

Don't miss these other value holiday titles,
available now from Kensington!

This Christmas . . .

YULE BE MINE
New York Times **Bestselling Author**
Lori Foster

"Lori Foster delivers everything you are looking for
in a romance."
—Jayne Ann Krentz

*Sparkling days, crackling fires, long steamy nights . . .
Christmas is all about making memories. In four delicious tales of seduction and romance,* New York Times
bestselling author Lori Foster brings you all the pleasures of the season—and then some . . .

Booker Dean knows exactly what he wants for Christmas:
his next-door neighbor, Frances Kennedy. And he's got a
gift planned for her that involves lots of delicious unwrapping.

Officer Parker Ross hates Christmas, while Lily Donaldson lives for it. But he's willing to be converted, especially when Lily is the one doing the persuading.

Sergeant Osbourne Decker suspects pet psychic Marci
Churchill is barking mad, but she's also a knockout. And
when she's accused of stealing a donkey from the local
nativity scene, he can't stop thinking about frisking her.

Furious at her cheating fiancé, Beth Monroe decides to
enjoy a payback tryst with his gorgeous best friend, and
finds that revenge is best served hot and sweet . . .

"Foster writes smart, sexy, engaging characters."
—Christine Feehan

**#1 *New York Times* Bestselling Author
Victoria Alexander**

HIS MISTRESS BY CHRISTMAS

*In this irresistibly festive novel from #1 New York Times
bestselling author Victoria Alexander, a beautiful,
self-sufficient woman has only one Christmas wish—to
be a mistress . . .*

For three years, Lady Veronica Smithson has been perfectly happy as a widow—and thoroughly independent.
Still, the right gentleman could provide the benefits of
marriage without the tedious restrictions. And in Sir Sebastian Hadley-Attwater, renowned explorer and rogue,
Veronica is sure she has found him.

Sebastian will come into his inheritance in a matter of
weeks—*if* his family deems him responsible enough.
There's no better way to prove his maturity than with a
home and a wife. But though the lovely Veronica will
share his bed, she steadfastly refuses to marry. However,
Sebastian has a plan.

An intimate sojourn at his new country house will surely
change Veronica's mind. For Sebastian never takes no for
an answer. And even in the midst of mischief-making relatives and unexpected complications, he intends to persuade his Christmas mistress that they belong
together—in this, and every season to come.

New York Times **Bestselling Author Jodi Thomas**
Linda Broday
Phyliss Miranda
DeWanna Pace

A TEXAS CHRISTMAS

*All she wants for the holidays is a man for
all seasons . . .*

*In the Texas Panhandle, the winters are long, the storms
fierce—and the Yuletide nights are sizzling.* New York
Times *bestselling author Jodi Thomas, along with Linda
Broday, Phyliss Miranda, and DeWanna Pace, bring you
one tempting holiday delight . . .*

On the eve before Christmas a blizzard arrived, trans-
forming a small Texas town into a night to remember.
Four ladies desperately in need of saving, four hard-ridin'
cowboys who aim to please. . . . When a lone farmer
strides to a pretty storeowner's rescue, their deepest
wishes just might come true. . . . A brave heiress can't believe a rugged angel is riding out of the night to save her
and her fellow train passengers—until she gets him under
the mistletoe. . . . A quiet loner wants to help a stranded
woman have a holiday to remember. . . . And a female sa-
loon owner tired of being scorned by respectable folk gets
some *very* naughty help from a handsome greenhorn . . .

"Readers couldn't ask for a finer quartet of heroes . . ."
—*Romantic Times* on *Give Me a Texas Ranger*

"Will warm your heart and bring a smile to your lips."
—Love Western Romances on *Give Me a Cowboy*

Books by Bestselling Author
Fern Michaels

More by Bestselling Author
Hannah Howell

Romantic Suspense from
Lisa Jackson

See How She Dies	0-8217-7605-3	$6.99US/$9.99CAN
Final Scream	0-8217-7712-2	$7.99US/$10.99CAN
Wishes	0-8217-6309-1	$5.99US/$7.99CAN
Whispers	0-8217-7603-7	$6.99US/$9.99CAN
Twice Kissed	0-8217-6038-6	$5.99US/$7.99CAN
Unspoken	0-8217-6402-0	$6.50US/$8.50CAN
If She Only Knew	0-8217-6708-9	$6.50US/$8.50CAN
Hot Blooded	0-8217-6841-7	$6.99US/$9.99CAN
Cold Blooded	0-8217-6934-0	$6.99US/$9.99CAN
The Night Before	0-8217-6936-7	$6.99US/$9.99CAN
The Morning After	0-8217-7295-3	$6.99US/$9.99CAN
Deep Freeze	0-8217-7296-1	$7.99US/$10.99CAN
Fatal Burn	0-8217-7577-4	$7.99US/$10.99CAN
Shiver	0-8217-7578-2	$7.99US/$10.99CAN
Most Likely to Die	0-8217-7576-6	$7.99US/$10.99CAN
Absolute Fear	0-8217-7936-2	$7.99US/$9.49CAN
Almost Dead	0-8217-7579-0	$7.99US/$10.99CAN
Lost Souls	0-8217-7938-9	$7.99US/$10.99CAN
Left to Die	1-4201-0276-1	$7.99US/$10.99CAN
Wicked Game	1-4201-0338-5	$7.99US/$9.99CAN
Malice	0-8217-7940-0	$7.99US/$9.49CAN

Available Wherever Books Are Sold!
Visit our website at **www.kensingtonbooks.com**

More from Bestselling Author
JANET DAILEY